Tempest Glory

Also by Russell Sullman

TEMPEST GLORY

RUSSELL SULLMAN

LUME BOOKS
A JOFFE BOOKS COMPANY

LUME BOOKS
A JOFFE BOOKS COMPANY

Lume Books, London

A Joffe Books Company

www.lumebooks.co.uk

First published in Great Britain in by Lume Books

We love to hear from our readers!
Please email any feedback you have to: feedback@joffebooks.com

Cover design by Imogen Buchanan

ISBN: 978-1-83901-565-6

For
Adam, Saphora, and of course,
April Munday

Prologue

An expanse of frosted blue stretching into eternity before him, a vast sheet upon which the scattered translucency of thin patchy cloud showed faint and pale, a clean and pure beauty across which a constellation of glittering specks leisurely progressed.

Each of the moving silver flecks scratched a tracery of razor thin lines of ice white, the tapestry of condensation marking the massed trails which boasted the impossible strength of the advancing enemy.

He felt fear slither coldly down his spine. *Oh, merciful God, so few of us against so many!*

Every time the enemy came, their glister grew ever greater.

Hesiod had recounted the story of Pandora's Box as warning, yet the Reich's leaders had paid no heed to the cautionary tale and had opened the bloody thing when they started all this madness.

Damn them, all of them, those criminals safe in their bunkers beneath Berlin, for they have damned us all with what has come and to all that which will surely follow in the coming months of defeat.

Memories of the feeling of smug superiority while escorting massed bomber fleets over Britain in the summer of 1940 and the hard enduring RAF defenders' fragmentary response, British fighters rising piecemeal in pathetically small numbers.

Time after time they came up, fearless but too few, and Dim Willi's disbelief at their intransigence, 'They're beaten! How many times do we have to shoot them down before they believe it?'

Dim Willi, that honest and forthright prodigious drinker of *Schnapps*, so proud of that stupid pointed moustache, lost in the white wastes of Russia more than two years ago.

And now it's our turn to face the fearful odds …

Eyes narrowing behind the tinted lenses of his flying goggles, *Oberst* 'Lucky' Max Winter sucked in a breath, his heart experiencing that familiar tumbling mix of fear and excitement once more as the adrenaline surged forcefully within him before battle.

And to face this formidable War Host it felt as if his two wingmen and he were alone racing into battle, horribly alone, yet he knew this was not so, for there were others rising to intercept the enemy, some already engaging with them in this pitiless arena, others returning to base or already dead.

If only they had had enough time to gain altitude and swoop down through the enemy fleet, the 'boom-and-zoom' tactic limiting the time it took to run the gauntlet and confounding the reacting gunners with their prodigious speed.

If only …

Behind them only their own mess of dirty smoke trails and empty sky while before them, as if from the naked blades and spearheads of a mighty War Host, the silver glint of The Horde.

A quick glance to his left showed that his wingmen were still with him, the battle formation of his three sleek jet fighters spread thinly in line abreast across a quarter of a mile, his wingmen tense shapes inside their shiny glazed cockpits, like insects fixed in amber, racing to a future unknown, into either another day's survival or eternal oblivion.

The fighter-bomber version of his aircraft was identified as *Stormvogel*, Storm Bird, but Max's Me262 was a fighter and had received the more graceful name of *Schwalbe*, which the Tommies would translate as Swallow.

Three Swallows against that advancing mass of heavily armed enemy metal.

There should have been another with them, four in all for his fighter *schwarm*, but poor Peterkin's port Jumo engine had cut out just after take-off and he'd had no other recourse but to keep his nose down, speed high and to turn carefully for home, praying all the while that there were no Tommy or Ami fighters nearby to kill him while he was so vulnerable.

Numbers often surpassed experience, and this was particularly true now, but with a hitching jet, the *Oberleutnant* could not have continued, the only option to return home to Rheine.

Yet all of them were painfully aware of the risk from enemy fighters which often prowled hungrily in the skies around Rheine, blurs in the haze, almost invisible as they skimmed the trees, hoping to intercept a slowing 262 on its landing approach with undercarriage extended and engines spooling down, the jet fighter vulnerable and defenceless.

There was no time to wonder if his young friend had returned safely, for above them a group of sleek shapes were turning towards them, the scintillation of light catching against diving fighters as they caught sight of the thick smoke trails beneath them from Max's little formation of Me262s.

Five, no, *six* flashing shapes, a group of American escort fighters frantically diving to keep the approaching jet fighters from their charges, their only chance a head-on attack at these speeds.

The plummeting sparkle of drop tanks detaching, an instant later a single drop tank as one of the enemy dropped later than the others, the second drop tank not detaching from its parent fighter, the USAAF Mustangs adopting a 'clean' configuration in readiness for combat.

Max keyed his microphone to order the attack, a single word, '*Horrido!*'

His men would know what to do, and he could sense them separating to open the distance from one another, to attack the lowest box of bombers to the middle and left of the approaching ranks of bombers, leaving the lowest box on the right flank for him.

The American fighters were coming down fast on him in a hard frontal attack in an attempt to make him break off his own attack, but he was confident in the knowledge that his Swallow was a target almost impossible to lead correctly in their gunsights and he turned her nose into them, remembering with a tight smile the illustration in the Luftwaffe fighter pilot's manual, and the hand-drawn picture of an attractive nude representing this manoeuvre, the memory helping as the tattoo of his heart calmed now that the enemy were entering the range of his guns.

Canopy defrost on? Cockpit heat turned down, his breathing loud and laboured, the pervasive stink of fear sharp, even if only in his mind.

Five endless, interminable years of war, and Spain before that, but always that sudden splash of fear in the final seconds before combat. What would the fools in Berlin think of their hero if they saw him now?

His *kameraden* were distant speckled green spearheads pulling thick shafts of dirty grey smoke as they separated and climbed at full speed for their chosen targets.

The pack of plunging enemy fighters were closing together, jockeying impatiently for position and eager to claim the rare honour of a Luftwaffe jet scalp, a tight cluster of dots rapidly gaining form as they tried to block him. The onrushing storm of their heavy 0.5 bullets carried on a twisting forest of smoke trails streaming towards him.

But the USAAF pilots were competing for position while also trying not to fly into one another, and the stream of bullets did not even come close to connecting with his speedy 262, dropping away below, but the closer they came the more likely one or more of them might get him.

Wanting to distract and clear a space to blow his way through the clustering enemy, Max laid his sights onto the enemy fighter formation, allowing for drop, and pressed down on the A-button with his thumb, pounding out a one-second burst of cannon from his upper two 30mm autocannon only.

He had meant to scare them and clear a path to the bombers, but through a mixture of luck and skill, at least one of the twenty-two explosive cannon shells fired caught the hung-up drop tank on the unfortunate enemy fighter head-on, igniting what remained of the fuel and vapour within it.

The enemy flight scattered wildly as one of their number flared in an eye-searing glare of light, the Mustang blown violently apart into an expanding cloud of shards of plastics, metals, Perspex and man, a dark-haired boy of nineteen from Stevensville in Montana, shredded and immolated in his beloved machine.

'*Abschuss!*' Max called out to inform his comrades he had scored a victory against the enemy; and then he was streaking through and beyond the P51s, buffeted by the expanding pressure wave of the obliterated Mustang, a single propeller blade scything past a blur barely seen; and then he was driving hard upwards through the surviving fighters' turmoil of tumbling slipstreams, praying his delicate Jumo engines did not suck up debris or stall, the remaining Mustangs now quicksilver streaks on either side then falling rapidly behind him, no time to feel the satisfaction of his success as the first of the bombers loomed ahead, rapidly closing the distance and a Me110 passing half a mile to starboard, a thin stream of white vapour marking its path downwards.

He eased her forward to streak through the bombers head-on, feeling the ice of fear vying with the burning madness of battle, his chest and stomach painfully tight.

The nearest bombers were identifiable now as Boeing B17s, the embroidery of thick white contrails unravelling behind them in the air.

Perspex turrets and silver wings glinting, innumerable guns flashing their hatred and now Max selected the lead machine of the box, thumb and finger closing over both the A and B firing buttons on the control stick, *now!*

This time all four of his autocannon hammered out a torrent of shells.

With a closure rate of around 1,000km/h, there was barely enough time to aim, fire and avoid ramming the targets.

A huge silver shape shuddering and expanding in his Revi gunsight, a vague impression of white flashes bursting and a cloud of smoke erupting from surfaces reflecting the sunlight, something ripped and spinning from the stabiliser and a burgeoning cloud of paint flakes from cannon battered metal, glittering and gyrating, and then he was past it, the huge tailfin passing inches below his port wingtip, easing his 262's nose onto the next bomber in line and his spurt of cannon shells missing it completely, feeling the solid punch of a bullet into his jet as she trembled and shivered in the turmoil of air pursuing the arrayed box formations of bomber squadrons.

No time to worry about damage as yet another bomber loomed, and then another, more above and to either side, endless silvered ranks of them, like swimming through a shoal of huge fish, index finger and thumb closing and the cannon ripping out again, feeling trapped racing inside a massive shoal of shining fish.

A single hit bursting open as the outermost port engine of a bomber bloomed livid with flame, the propeller churning and the Wright Cyclone motor gouting dirty blots of thick black smoke, the bomber disappearing like a flash of quicksilver beneath the sleek Jumo engine on his port wing.

Despite the undulating lashing net of heavy bullets from the fields of fire of the massed bombers which reached for him, his famous luck held, and only the turbulence of the enemy formation's slipstream plucked at his fighter as he finally emerged beyond and behind the last of the bombers.

A part of him marvelled that he had not collided with one of them in that congested air.

He gulped in mouthfuls of oxygen, his chest heaving and aching from the tension, knowing that more enemy fighters would be turning tightly after him, still others falling from above. Throttles forward to race through the bomber stream and even as he cleared the enemy formation, he stayed fast enough to make pursuit impossible, his heart pleading to run for home. *You got one, damaged more, it's enough ...*

But he needed to brave the terrifying gauntlet at least one more time ...

Ease her into a wide gentle turn lest one or both of his Jumos flameout, no sharp turns, easy, gently, but keep the speed high enough to evade the Ami fighters, turn back in a wide circling turn with eyes watching for escort fighters, wings cutting ruin into the field of contrails, eyes flickering anxiously for signs of any escort fighters nearby and the potential targets of damaged bombers.

There! A single bomber, fluttering streamers of bright flame and dark smoke pouring from one starboard engines, the battle to stay in formation and protected by her stable mates failing as she fell out of formation, the flowing trails of smoke like blood in the water attracting Max's searching eyes towards her, and he angled his fighter to the wounded B17.

Oberleutnant Peter Stark was waiting for him on the ground, still clad in his ridiculous 'lucky' scruffy orange-brown flying overalls, pulled down with its sleeves tied around his waist, his young face strained and streaked with grease, sweat and oil, but clearly delighted to see his unit commander's safe return.

For a moment Max saw not the veteran *Experte* with the Knight's Cross at his throat, but instead the anxious eyes of a young man relieved at the survival of one of the few remaining people left in the world he could consider to be family.

Max thanked God that despite his family's losses at home, in Africa, France and on the *Ostfront*, he himself did not just have his *kameraden* left to call kin.

Peter's smile was huge. 'Thank God!' Then, aware of the *Schwarzmanner* groundcrew already swarming over Max's jet, he straightened to attention smartly, clicking his heels. 'Herr *Oberst*. I hear you got one?'

Winter rubbed his mouth and indicated with a wave for the other to relax, hoping the boy wouldn't see the tremor in his hand. 'Two, Peterkin. Got a damaged B17, and put some holes in a few more, but I got a lucky hit on a Mustang, blew the poor bastard to hell.'

'How was it?'

'The same as always, we were too late and there were too many, the first pass was head-on, no time to gain height and swoop down.'

He reached out impulsively and grabbed the youngster's arm. 'We could have done with you there, but as usual, there were far too many.' He squeezed gently. 'I'm glad you got your bird down safely.' *Time to be leader,* and he put iron into his voice. 'I told you to use your parachute!'

Peter grinned, and Max noted the lines around his eyes, seemingly deeper each day. 'But you know, *Herr Oberst,* that the Amis machine-gun our boys when they parachute. Anyway, there were no Ami fighters around and my Schwalbe behaved herself, so easy. Piece of pie.'

They all called Stark 'Young Peterkin', and while the lad was still only in his early twenties, he had already packed a lifetime's worth of combat flying into just over two years. A stint on the Channel Front, then the interminable hell of the Eastern Front before returning to the defence of the Fatherland. Luck, skill, experience and combat success signified by the Knight's Cross at his neck.

Max barked out a laugh tight with tension and relief, certain that his face would crack if he smiled too wide. 'Piece of cake, you young *dummkopf.* The Tommies say piece of cake.' He let go of his wingman. 'Come on, let's find Tino and Ernst and have a cup of the General's coffee.'

Peter tried to hide his awe, but Winter knew the lad was still greatly impressed that his CO was an old friend and ex-wingman of the Luftwaffe legend, General Adolf Galland.

It was Galland, just before being relieved of command by Goering (following Gollob's trumped up charges), who had spoken with Hitler directly to have the Valkyrie conspiracy investigators called off and Winter appointed as CO of Testing Unit EKdo 156.

However, the 'testing' involved flying through hordes of high-performance enemy escort fighters to get at the less than helpless occupants of the bomber streams. Max's jets were faster than anything the enemy had, yet their numbers were being whittled down inexorably, and of his original cadre of thirty pilots, only ten now remained.

Because the 262 was at its most vulnerable when taking off and coming in to land, slow and helpless, the experience of landing was certainly no less terrifying than flying through a bomber stream in which the airspace was choked by streams of bullets.

Sheer speed increased the odds, but one had to be lucky as well as capable. They might be the elite of the *Jagdwaffe*, but they were not invincible.

Wiping away the grease and sweat from his face and nodding his thanks to the crew chief (whose oily, patched and crumpled black overalls were a testament to experience), Max led his young friend in search of the other two pilots of their schwarm, a soundless prayer on his lips they had returned safely or at least diverted to another field.

Chapter 1

April Munday picked up one of Molly's spiced biscuits, eyed it dubiously for a moment, and then put it back down on the plate.

Rose sensed his wife's outrage at the slight and felt a shout of laughter bubble in his throat, but sensibly swallowed the urge. Molly was the most extraordinary woman he had ever known, smart, elegant and sophisticated, and he still found it hard to believe that this beauty had chosen him over better men than he.

With guilty satisfaction Rose exulted in the knowledge that dearest Moll always put too much spice in the mix. It was somehow perversely comforting to know that this exceptional woman, the winner of not only the George Cross and the MBE for Gallantry, but his heart as well, was not completely perfect.

The medals were certainly well earned, but his heart was far less than she deserved.

Smiling gently at his wife, Rose picked up one of Molly's biscuits, his tongue girding its loins as he bit off a piece, the spice exploding across the inside of his mouth; he tried not to cough, instead forcing a smile onto his face as he pushed it down. 'Mmm, delicious, my love.'

Molly returned his smile as the spice burned its way down his throat, the beautiful warmth on her lips more than worth the heat stoked tingle on his tongue before the flames writhed down to his stomach.

'Of course, Nigel, my cousin, commands a Spitfire squadron.' April detached a raisin from Molly's biscuit and scrutinised it.

He felt his jaw clench, the smile plastered on. *Yes, I know, you've only mentioned it a thousand bloody times already …*

'I believe that the Spitfire is the best we have.' She sniffed the raisin. 'Don't you agree, Mr Rose?'

No, I bloody don't. Give me a Tiffie over a Spit any day. A Tiffie can give it but can surely take it too. 'I'm afraid I couldn't say, ma'am,' he answered diplomatically.

Go on, then, admit it. 'I've never actually flown one.'

The young woman looked startled, and then her face brightened. 'Oh dear, I'm sorry, what a shame.' She cheerfully popped the raisin into her mouth and smiled pityingly. 'I'm sure it's nothing to do with you. I hope you aren't too dreadfully disappointed, Squadron Leader?' She smiled prettily. 'And do call me April, won't you?'

'No, ma'am, sorry, April. But I've been lucky enough to fly some other grand kites.' Molly was smiling at him sympathetically, one hand lightly resting on the diminishing bump that was the legacy of their newborn daughter, Amelia, safe at home with Molly's old *ayah*, Noreen.

'Well, someone has to do it, don't they? Not everybody gets a go, do they?' She smiled condescendingly. It didn't help that she was very attractive, trim and petite in her green WVS uniform.

Rose sighed. *The girls are throwing a little goodbye party for me*, she says, *come and meet some of them*, she says, *it'll be a laugh …*

April Munday, bless her, was Molly's replacement as WVS area coordinator; the birth of their second child demanded a departure for Moll from performing war-service for a second time.

Whether in WAAF powder blue or the green of the WVS, Rose thought Molly was gorgeous. Even better in the buff, though, of course, he thought wistfully.

April was still twittering, and he dragged himself back to the conversation. 'D'you fly Blenheims, Mr Rose?'

Rose felt like screaming. *Blenheims? BLENHEIMS? For Christ's sake!*

'Harry's just back from fighting in France. He was in command of a Typhoon squadron.' Molly's calm voice was warm with pride, and he smiled back at her. 'He was at Caen and Falaise.'

'Caen and Falaise?' April's voice softened, and frank respect blossomed in her eyes. 'Oh, I see. My goodness! I'm told it was quite the ordeal?' She offered him the plate of baked lentil fingers, and he took one gingerly. The damned thing looked revolting, but Molly had assured him it was both nutritious and delicious.

'Jerry fought hard.' Memories of a dark carpet of German dead rotting in the hot sun on the roads to and around Falaise, dense curtains of flak so thick that it seemed impossible not to be hit, burning Typhoons falling from the sky, boys gone before he had managed to welcome them to Excalibur.

Memories of empty seats at mealtimes, sortie after sortie, from Normandy to the charnel house of Falaise, packing the few pitiful belongings of the lost in tents empty of all but their ghosts, the little that was left of his precious brave.

Boys, so many of them, dying a man's death far too soon. Faded memories of so many faces, a legacy of unrequited promise and unbelievable bravery.

'And I lost some very fine lads there. The very best.' He felt his voice catch and he fell silent, knowing that if he said more the penned emotion would be unleashed. He could not bear the thought that his beloved Molly would witness the shame and weakness of his tears.

What words were there to do justice to the incredible heroes he had flown alongside? How could he explain to April, this well-meaning young woman, how desperately hard they had fought and how testing it had truly been to body and spirit?

How could he find the words to describe those quite exceptional young men who continued to follow him into the danger without hesitation, their numbers whittled down by flak, fighters and fatigue?

And those who survived, their spirits drained beyond emotion and hope, automatons awaiting their turn to die.

A door banged shut somewhere, and Rose closed his eyes, grateful he hadn't so much as twitched in response.

And how could he explain the awful noise? The unholy cacophony that was the accompaniment to each low-level attack? The rumbling ripple of flak explosions, some deafening or faint according to proximity, a flow of dissonance wrenching discordantly over the sweet bellow of Sugar's Sabre engine, the whistle and whine of shells and shrapnel, and the merry tinkle and jingle of fragments against the canopy of her wings and fuselage, enough to make one want to cry out and which caught one's breath.

The awful din of hatred which the screams, invective, cries and static in his earphones could not drown out or lessen. Flying through the concussive slap of rippling flak bursts and the turmoil of air currents low down, fighting to hold her steady as the cushion of air beneath her strove to lift her into Jerry's sights.

Or that instant of terror when hot metal punched like a fist into her and one wondered if she would actually fly apart or not recover at the bottom of her dive as hands pulled desperately at the stick with the terrified exclamation stillborn on one's lips.

How could he explain to her any of *that*?

He knew that if he tried, his voice would surely break and the women of Molly's, sorry, April's WVS would witness the ungratifying sight of a man lauded by the papers as heroic 'Typhoon Rose' bawl his eyes out.

Rose had cried many times when alone, where no one would witness his humiliation and feebleness, yet the hurt remained raw, and he felt the weight of fresh tears gathering heavily behind his eyes.

He would not shame Molly by crying in this crowd of well-meaning women. Men don't cry, do they?

Tennyson had inscribed the feats of the Light Brigade in Crimea into glorious history, words commemorating an incredible act of dogged courage, but nothing of the painful reality of the plight afterwards of those lucky enough to have survived, or the lives of their wounded post-glory.

This, at least, was rectified almost four decades later in Kipling's reproachful *The Last of the Light Brigade*.

Rose, however, was not so thankful for Kipling's words, for he had been made to memorise the tracts by his headmaster as a penalty for some long-forgotten infringement.

In contrast with the light cavalrymen at Balaclava, the men of Excalibur Squadron, his companions and heroes, had charged into the most formidable and deadly of defences not once, but so many times he had lost count.

They had experienced the Valley of Death repeatedly, again and again, and paid the dues in lives, blood and pain.

What words were there which could do justice to those superlative souls he had commanded?

Death or Glory, indeed.

There had been much death in Normandy, far too much, and precious little glory, even though Rose had himself received a bar to his DSO for Excalibur's role in the Battle for France, yet he would have exchanged all the glory in the world for those precious brothers-in-arms he had lost.

'Squadron Leader?' April sensed his reticence and emotion, saw his tongue brush dry lips and a shadow falling across his eyes, and she pushed the tray of Potato Rarebit towards him. 'Do try these, too, Squadron Leader. They're really quite yummy. You'll like them, I'm sure.'

Rose blinked to clear away his melancholia, looking distrustfully at the unevenly browned grey-white splodges, slapped haphazardly onto thick slices of bread before being grilled. The monstrous abominations looked like something 'Shiny' Dewar would have rustled up eagerly at Excalibur's advance landing ground cookhouse in Normandy. Shiny had been nothing if not creative.

Euch! 'Erm, no, I won't, but thank you.' Molly returned his baleful glare with a gentle smile and a slow wink. *No help there then ...*

The new WVS area coordinator laughed lightly, her eyes dancing, the sound dainty as she pushed the tray closer. 'Oh, but you must try one, Mr Rose, you simply must. I insist!'

Well, the bloody things smelled alright, he thought grudgingly. With his fork Rose slid one dubiously onto his plate and nodded his thanks.

He half hoped the damned thing would slide off his plate, onto the floor and straight out through the door, but no such luck.

Nevertheless, he could begin to feel himself warming to the young woman.

And the murmur of that treacherous little voice in his mind, *of course, Harry, it helps that she's really rather pretty …*

April smiled disarmingly at him, and he returned it as she leaned forward and laid a hand on his forearm.

As Molly's eyes sparked fire, April patted his hand and asked conspiratorially, 'If you like, Harry—*oh*! May I call you Harry? Yes?'

He nodded amicably and she clapped her hands. 'Lovely! Shall I ask Nigel if he could arrange for you to have a ride in one of his Spitfires, Harry?'

Daffie had dug up the little coriander patch again, provoking their *ayah's* demented shrieks and dire threats of bloody revenge, and the poor creature (Daffie, that is) was now slinking in the rosebushes at the end of the garden while Noreen screeched her fury.

'I think I rather liked it when you were a Pilot Officer, you were a much sweeter young man then, Mr Rose,' said Molly.

Rose nodded, deepening his voice, eyebrows beetling. 'I'm a rather more dangerous man now, Mrs Rose, so you better give me a hug, or else.' The effect was ruined a little as saliva went down the wrong way, and he choked.

Molly smiled. 'Or else?'

'Or, er …' He floundered.

She settled against him, warm and fragrant, her hair soft against his cheek. 'Well, come on then. Spit it out, will you? What will you do?'

'Er …' Rose's mind had gone blank and he was unable to summon an outrageous claim. 'Well, I might go red and cry a little bit.'

'Just a bit?' She smiled her beautiful smile. 'Dear me, I must be losing my touch! Speaking of which, I thought you looked rather maudlin when we were at the flicks last night.'

'I was. I was feeling awfully upset that you like that bloody man so much. Brought tears to my eyes.'

She turned to look at him in surprise. 'Which bloody man? You know you're the only one for me.'

Rose snorted in derision. 'Hm, so you say, madam, but I'm not silly, y'know. I saw the way you were looking at him. I could see the way your eyes were shining at the thought of getting your hands on his poor tender body.'

'Oh, Harry! Honestly! You're so silly! Whose tender body, for goodness sake?' Molly replied in exasperation.

'Oh, don't pretend you don't know, you saucy but wilful creature,' he continued, shifting away slightly to show his disapproval but still keeping her safely within his embrace. She felt rather nice resting against him, warm and soft and fragrant. *Lovely, ta very much.* 'Laurence Olivier, that's who.'

'Harry! He was only narrating the story. He wasn't even on the screen!' She laughed. '*The way I was looking at him*? Really! You *are* a daft sausage!' She giggled and snuggled closer to him, one elbow digging into his ribcage, and warm soft buttocks settling softly and deliciously over his groin, pushing against him very delightfully. *Hmm, do carry on, Ma'am ...*

'Don't know why he's so popular. He's not much good, a bit wooden, if you ask me. And I really can't think why you like him,' grumbled Rose, adding sourly, 'I mean, honestly, Moll, he looks nothing like me.'

She smiled at Rose's jealousy for the legendary Shakespearean actor, and leaned forward to kiss him softly. 'Never mind, *mon cher*.

He is married, you know. Vivien would likely object strenuously if he even looked my way. Doesn't look like I'll have a chance to give him a kiss or step out with him, so I suppose I'll just have to settle for you after all, sorry and all that.'

He pulled a few strands of her hair with his tongue to his mouth, rolling them gently between his lips and mumbling through them. 'Oh goodness me! You mean years of nagging lie ahead?'

Please God, he thought. Shared decades of peace with Molly seemed like an impossible dream, but one worth daring to hope for as the Allied armies pushed on to the very borders of Germany.

'Of course,' Molly replied, and her heart murmured a silent prayer. *Oh please, dear God, give me the good fortune of a long and fruitful future with Harry*. 'Though I have to say you always seem a trifle deaf when I'm talking to you. You seemed alright when that girl was talking,' she added accusingly.

Rose feigned ignorance. *God! Will I never hear the end of that?* 'Girl? What girl are you talking about, my precious love?'

'Don't give me that dumb, innocent look, you cheeky brute. You know exactly who I'm talking about. The petite pretty one, April Munday, remember her? Had her hands all over you? Couldn't keep your eyes off her chest?'

'What? Who? Petite pretty one? Can't remember a girl like that, April Munday you say? Hands all over me?' *For goodness sake, I wasn't leering at her chest!* 'Hmm, not sure I know who you mean, but of course you know I only have eyes for you, my little rowdy flower.'

Rose raised his chin and announced virtuously, 'You're the only one for me, Moll. *Toujours et pour toujours*. Always and forever.'

A memory of a spent and sleepy Charlie, a shock of fair hair, sprawled flushed and naked amongst rumpled sheets with a satisfied smile on her face, guiltily dismissed. *It wasn't me, m'lord.*

Molly poked him playfully in the side with a sharp fingernail. 'Let her hold your hand, though, didn't you?'

'It would've been rude to snatch my hand away, my dearest love.' He nodded virtuously. April's touch had been warm and gentle, her fingertips soft. 'And I'm only a bit deaf because of Sugar's Sabre. Can't hear properly for ages after a flight.'

Molly cocked an eyebrow disbelievingly. 'Really? It seems to worsen only when I open my mouth?'

'Nonsense, beloved,' Rose wheedled. 'I hang on to each and every delicious word your delectable mouth utters.'

Molly laughed. 'What a lot of absurd jibber-jabber! A stream of endless nonsense, yet, quite strangely, I find that I love you nonetheless.'

He hugged her close, revelling in the sensation of her body curled intimately against his. 'A blessing for which I give thanks, Moll.'

Chapter 2

Sitting in his shirt sleeves at 83 Group's Forward HQ in the Dummelhuis Hotel at Eindhoven, Air Vice Marshal Harry Broadhurst rubbed his stomach to ease the burn of reflux.

I've lost so many! he thought despairingly. Too many.

He pushed 83 Group's Typhoon pilot casualty list away, as if it might help reduce the pain in his chest. *Arnhem was a disaster, but at least we're still advancing.*

His eyes stole back to the list. *But at what cost to my boys?*

A squadron commander at the beginning of the war, Broadhurst was involved in much of the fighting during the BEF's retreat in France and the ensuing Battle of Britain, flying into combat even when appointed a Group Captain, being wounded and winning himself a DSO and bar, DFC and bar for his fighting prowess.

Even as a senior officer, Broadhurst led from the front, exposing himself to the same dangers as his men had to face, and he was respected and loved in equal measure by them.

He was reaching for his cup when there was the sound of raised voices outside and suddenly the door slammed open with a bang; he looked up with irritation.

An RAF officer with four stripes on his sleeves stood in the doorway, gold-braided cap askew and the AOC's smooth aide peering nervously over his shoulder.

'I'm terribly sorry, sir. I told him you were busy!' squeaked the aide anxiously.

'That's quite alright, Arthur. Fetch another teacup for us? I always get a bit thirsty after administering a rocket to an officer who really ought to know better!' Broadhurst rumbled, his eyebrows lowering intimidatingly.

'Right away, sir.' The aide pushed the officer deferentially but hurriedly into the room and quickly closed the door behind him.

The AOC leaned forward on his elbows, and the desk creaked menacingly. 'I was rather expecting you when I heard that a Tempest with a Group Captain's pennant was in the circuit. Well, Group Captain? To what do I owe the displeasure?'

Group Captain (Acting) Daniel Smith, DSO and two bars, DFC and bar, DFM and bar, CdeG, RAF (but better known to one and all both in and out of the RAF as 'Granny'), grinned disarmingly, unrepentant and unfazed by Broadhurst's forbidding expression. 'Pardon the interruption, sir. I heard there was a Wing Leader's position going?' Granny saluted and bowed, trying not to wince. 'Thought I'd offer myself to you.'

'Hmm,' grunted Broadhurst sourly. 'What an unappealing prospect. Such propositions might work with the ladies, Granny, but it doesn't do a thing for me.' He sniffed. 'You were an obstreperous blighter when you were my fitter back in '36, straight out of Halton and knew it all. I have to say that nothing seems to have changed in the years between.' 83 Group's AOC sniffed again. 'Considerate of you to offer, old man, but the thing is I've already appointed 63 Wing's Commander.'

Granny wilted perceptibly and hobbled closer to stand before the desk. 'I must protest, sir. You need someone older and more experienced in command, and Squadron Leader Rose has only just returned recently from France.' Granny's backside was aching after the flight across the Channel, and he yearned to rub it.

'And a damned fine job he did there too. As did you, I might add, though I'd never say it to your face. Don't want to give you a big head, Granny, do we?' Broadhurst shook his head imperceptibly. 'As to the fourth ring on your sleeve, well I never!'

Broadhurst picked up his pen, put it down again, feeling his eyes being drawn back to those bloody awful casualty lists. 'As for Rose, different story, of course. He richly deserves the promotion, earned it, even if it's only an acting rank. I think you'll find Rose is eminently suited.' He looked across the room to the large map of northern Europe pinned to the wall. 'With 150 and 122 Wings now in Holland and with 44 just recently converted onto Tempests, 63 need a Wing Leader with a leader's experience of the current fighting.'

He leaned backwards. 'I needed a veteran, Granny, someone with bags of experience. After five years of this bloody war there're precious few of them still alive to choose from. You'd have done nicely, of course, but with a gammy leg and Hun ironmongery in your backside I can't use you. You're far more use to me as a Station Commander. Show 'em how it's done, eh?'

'With respect, sir, Flash Rose has been hard at it for too long. He's done enough. He's got a pair of tiny brats. They need their father, and he deserves a rest. Let me do it. I can do it, let me.'

Broadhurst picked up the teapot. 'He's had a rest these last few months. Y'know, Granny, I almost put him onto the same Blighty flight as you the day you were shot down and wounded, but I didn't. Couldn't afford to, even though he looked as if he had had just about enough. I needed him there on the front line. But it was the right choice in the end. He and his lads did magnificently, as well you know. Now I need someone to look after a Wing that's been cobbled together, a squadron of Aussies and another of Free French. Political nonsense, of course, but Rose will manage, I'm sure.'

'Leave him be, sir? Let him sit out the Final Act? He's earned the chance.'

'My, my, you're not quite yourself, old man. You're being uncommonly polite, almost servile. You've not cursed nor bawled at me once so far.' He grinned impishly at his ex-fitter. 'Not like you at all. Dear me. Feeling peaky, old chap?' The AOC tipped tepid tea into Granny's cup and sighed. 'We all of us have to pull our weight, Granny, I've decided, and that's that. He'd not thank you for asking.'

'Well then, he's a silly sod to have said yes.' *I shan't beg.* 'His little brats should grow up with a father. He's earned a long rest, but he's got this daft idea that he must share the dangers, not send others to face it alone, despite all he's already done. Doesn't know when to stop, to think about himself.'

'Sounds rather like a silly sod I know,' his AOC replied affectionately, pointedly staring at him.

Granny leaned against the desk, trying not to grimace as pain lanced through his knee and into his hip.

Broadhurst noticed his twitch. 'For goodness sake, Granny! Stop jawing and take a pew before you fall down!' He shook his head impatiently. 'And you think you can fly and fight Jerry like that?'

Granny sat, easing himself carefully (and gratefully) onto the chair and trying not to show his relief. *Just my luck to get shrapnel in the arse.*

There was a knock on the door and the hapless aide scurried in with a tray bearing an empty cup, an open jar of potted meat and a plate of buttered toast. Setting it down on one edge of the table, he fled as Broadhurst shooed him away and barked, 'More tea!'

As the door clicked closed, Granny eagerly reached for the plate and generously slathered a slice of toast with the paste, before topping it with a second slice.

His AOC fixed him with a baleful eye. 'Oh, help yourself, Granny, do.'

Granny had the good grace to look self-conscious, but still he reached for another toast even as he bit into his makeshift sandwich.

Broadhurst darkly watched Granny digging into *his* lunch for a moment, before reaching out to rescue the last forlorn piece of toast.

As he did so his eyes drifted to the scars on his hands, legacy of a Bf 109's cannon shell which had exploded alongside the cockpit of his Spitfire back in June 1941. The damned things still felt itchy. 'I've heard tell that he's not the only one.'

'Only one, sir?' Granny was already reaching for the sadly depleted jar of meat paste.

Broadhurst sat back comfortably and gave him an old-fashioned look. 'I've heard tell he's not the only one of my senior officers with a baby.'

Reaching for the teacup, Granny froze, his lips slick with butter. '*What?* Erm, I mean … I beg your pardon, sir?'

Smugly, 'Oh yes, a little dickie bird let slip that the senior WAAF at Havelock Barr has had some joyous news? Something about an impending stork's visit in the near future to some fractious and obstreperous Acting Group Captain? Good thing she's married to that particular bad egg, otherwise I reckon he'd have scarpered, the damnable rascal.' Broadie smiled coolly. 'Don't suppose she'd thank me much for sending you off to war with a peppered arse, d'you? Might be a tad upset for offering yourself, eh?'

'Err …' Discomfited, Granny could only stare. *Good God! How on earth had the old bugger found out?*

His AOC looked inordinately pleased with himself. 'I imagine you're wondering how the old bugger found out, eh?'

Further disconcerted, Granny shook his head and held up his sandwich in denial; a blob of dislodged potted meat tumbling into the 'In' tray. 'Oh no, sir, never, no, not at all.'

Broadhurst snorted. 'You're a deuced fine fighter pilot and Wing Leader, Granny, but a bloody awful liar.'

The AOC's lips quivered momentarily, and he held out his hand. 'I believe congratulations are in order twice, old man? Heard Belle got a very well-earned MBE, too. She must've earned it, having to work with a grouchy bugger like you, the poor girl. Deserves a bloody VC for putting up with you, if you ask me, 'though I dare say you aren't going to.'

They shook hands, the AOC adding gruffly, 'Anyway. Happy news is always welcome.'

Granny recalled Belle's face, shining with complete happiness when she had told him the news, such that his own eyes had filled with tears, and an incredible bloom of joy had ballooned in his chest. *At least I understand why Flash always walks around with that stupid smile on his daft face …*

A sniff from the great man. 'Don't suppose you've told your good lady you're here, Granny, eh? Would you like me to give her a call?' Broadhurst asked solicitously. 'Tell her you got here safe and sound? Offered yourself for another fighting command?'

He reached for the telephone, a smug expression on his face, and picked up the receiver. 'I imagine she's on duty?' Drumming the fingers of his other hand, he waited expectantly.

Bollocks, thought Granny, *Belle will give my poor arse a good kicking, dented or not, if she learns of this, the old sod's got me by the balls.*

The AOC's tone was kindly, concerned even. 'Got you by the short and curlies, have I, old chap?' He beamed amiably.

Gawd help us! It's true, Broadie can read minds! 'Prob'ly best not to call, sir.' Granny rubbed his face tiredly. 'Why him, sir?'

The AOC glowered. 'What d'you mean, you cheeky basket? Why not him? Johnnie Johnson's doing wonders with his Spitfire Wing, Harries and Bunny are being rested, Will Scarlet's missing and Bee Beamont's a POW. And to cap it all, Desmond's broken his leg riding a horse, although he's recovered well, and he was lucky enough to have Farmer Dring to look after things for him. A bloody horse if you please! I'm told the horse was a Jerry one, which explains a lot! God give me strength!' He shook his head sorrowfully. 'And with a bucketful of Jerry scrap iron sprayed into your backside, you silly clot, you can't even sit straight. Despite the balls-up at Arnhem, Jerry's reeling, and I need experienced leaders to keep the pressure on. And moreover, there's nobody else.'

He didn't let his eyes settle on the casualty list.

'Besides, Rose has proven himself umpteen times, not least with that dawn raid in September, showed initiative and leadership, and not for the first time. He's good, and capable Wing Leaders don't grow on trees. And he's quite diplomatic too, not like some.' He cast an accusatory look at Granny. 'Which will help a lot with that composite wing of Aussies and Frenchmen he's taking over. Australia House wants to have a ready-trained RAAF squadron with highly experienced Tempest pilots available for the big push against Japan, so we're going to give them Rose's new chaps when the fighting's done in Europe. And De Gaulle's adamant that some of his lads who were on Typhoons in Normandy should have the chance to carry on the fight in Tempests.'

Broadhurst glared darkly at the thin smear of dried meat paste left in the jar. 'You've done your bit more than twice over, Granny. Blitzkrieg, Battle of Britain, North Africa, Malta, the Channel Front, Ramrods and the Invasion, Normandy, Falaise and the Battle for France. The list goes on! You've done more than enough. Too much maybe. You've earned your rest.'

The AOC peered menacingly at him from beneath his eyebrows. 'Just be grateful I'm not having you court-martialled for wasting my time now, impregnating one of my excellent senior WAAFs with your onerous seed, or even for poaching my blasted lunch! Now get out of my office and go home.' He paused. 'Oh, and pass on my congratulations to your charming wife, would you, Group Captain? There's a good chap.'

Chapter 3

The Dutch coast spread before him, a ragged line in washed-out grey and an even paler green, the flat plain of land further beyond bleaching into the hazed and faded horizon, Great Yarmouth's battered but reassuringly familiar seafront a wistful memory left far behind them now.

A silent prayer on his lips, *keep the ones I love at home safe, Merciful Lord.*

Below, the tipping sea was rent and flustered even further by the wakes of many ships, their ragged smoke a guide to the priceless docks ahead.

The Rhine-Maas Delta slipped past some distance away to port, cluttered along both sides by the yards and docks of Rotterdam, the thick forest of masts, derricks and cranes beneath the grubby faux-clouds of their barrage balloons denoting the mass of shipping choking the harbour area; the already hazy air was stained thick and dirty with smoke, its odour seeping into the cockpit, catching in his throat despite the well-fitting oxygen mask strapped to his face.

He allowed himself a stolen glance as he passed over the polders and dikes. The area flattened four years earlier in the 'Rotterdam Blitz' of 1940 and later partially rebuilt remained indistinguishable from the rest of the city through the grimy veil of effluence.

His restless eyes picked out a pair of Typhoons skimming low and fast across the sea northwards like seabirds, while a mile or so to starboard an Avro Anson rocked its wings in greeting as it passed, and he could imagine the feeling of relief that would be filling the packed cabin, the blessed respite for at least a few days whether off on leave or having completed (and survived) a tour of punishing operations.

Would the Anson's cabin be rocked by the shouts and laughter of tension eased, or contain only the silent relief and gratitude of having survived the maelstrom?

The Tiffies were distant shapes over the water now, shadowed wraiths in the sea haze, and he found his eyes sliding back to the port wing.

It still seemed strange that the black and white invasion stripes were no longer there, ordered to be removed in September, just those on the undersides of the wings and fuselage remaining to assist in identification to Allied AA.

S-Sugar rocked in the uneasy air as if to remind him of the airfield's nearness, the tidal wetlands of Biesbosch now falling behind and the patchy clouds high above him as he soothed her and eased the nose down to begin their approach.

Sugar was his third fighter of that name. The first two had been Hawker Typhoons, marvellous kites which were reliable and resilient fighters, and which brought him safely through two long and arduous tours, first as a Flight Commander and then as the CO of Excalibur.

This third Sugar was a Hawker Tempest, a progressive development in the design of the remarkable 'Tiffie', with greatly improved handling and capability. Faster than Bf109s and FW190s in level flight and in the dive, it could also out-turn the 109 and the 190 (just). Over 20,000 feet the picture was not quite the same, but operationally most sorties would be at lower levels.

At first glance it would have been easy to confuse the two aircraft, but on closer inspection the differences would be obvious, the shapely lines of the Tempest almost a combination of the rugged Typhoon with the splendid Spitfire (but don't tell that to April Munday, for goodness sake!).

With larger tail-surface, a fin extending into the rudder, and far thinner, semi-elliptical wings came improved stability, speed and manoeuvrability. And like his previous two, this latest Sugar flew beautifully and just *felt* right.

Even better, this one carried the triangular pennant of an RAF Wing Commander and the letters HR-S on the fuselage, RAF Wing Leaders being able to embellish their fighters with their own initials.

Wing Commander Harry Rose! *Ruddy bananas!*

It was still hard to comprehend. A lot had happened since the day an inexperienced young Pilot Officer Harry Rose arrived at RAF Foxton back in 1940.

Still here, but as ever that insipid whisper in his mind, *but for how much longer?*

Already the airfield was drawing closer, and he fancied that he could see it through the stained and leaden air as he brought his Tempest lower, the glint of an aircraft taking off flashing like a distant beacon for an instant.

But with the large Luftwaffe airbase of Rheine-Hopsten less than ten minutes away by Hawker Tempest, and with a veteran's distrust of low-clouded skies, he was wary, muscles tense, eyes and neck turning, gloved thumb unconsciously stroking the gun-button's safety cover, half expecting to see a gaggle of bandits emerging from those treacherous clouds at any moment.

He peered at her worn photo, a creased and tattered faithful companion on hundreds of sorties since the summer of 1940, his thoughts returning to their parting, his feeble assurances and burning heart and her efforts to hide what she felt with a slipping smile, the tip of her nose and cheeks pink with disguised sorrow, and those beautiful dark eyes haunted and heavy with emotion.

Knowing that it might be for the last time.

Oh Moll. A wave of intense longing washed over him and he pushed it away angrily, eyes still searching the airspace for lurking and sudden danger. It would not do to think of such things, for the slightest lapse could bring the end.

Uncaring of his musings and emotion, the heaped sands of the dunes at *De Loonse en Drunense* slipped quietly behind beneath his starboard wing.

Nijmegen was to the north-east and Eindhoven to the south-west. Both were gains in the most recent advances, trophies of a partially successful Operation Market Garden, even though the ultimate goal to seize Arnhem and the Rhine had failed.

While the burgeoning terror in Blighty caused by the V2 attacks had been curbed as launch sites were overrun, the 1st Airborne Division suffered appalling losses, despite a ferocious tenacity that would become legend.

Harry Rose and Excalibur had not been a part of it.

Instead, he had been rested on extended leave with his family, leaving Excalibur Squadron with its new CO, the indefatigable Sid, ably assisted by his Senior Flight Commander, Jacko (*God help us!*), as they converted the squadron from Typhoons to Tempests.

Once the conversion was complete, Excalibur would join the UK's defences against attacks by V1 Buzzbombs, once more becoming a part of Fighter Command.

Rose smiled fondly, glad that his dear friends would be relatively safer flying from the British Mainland, the Allied advances pushing more and more V1 launching sites further east and out of range of British targets.

Having survived the fiery cauldron of ground-attack missions against walls of murderous flak in Normandy and then in the Battle for France, they had more than earned their respite. Having lost so many, Rose could not bear the thought that he might lose those precious few who had survived the fighting.

The runways of Volkel were a shining grey X ahead of them now, tiny amongst the snow-bleached fields, ice or water reflecting the dull light through the faint haze, the airfield very different from the PRU aerial photographs taken after RAF and USAAF raids of August and September.

Following the Allied raids, the airfield had been all but obliterated. But as they evacuated, the Luftwaffe's demolitions teams had blown up what little was left.

Rose glanced to the Tempest flying alongside in battle spread formation, a young Frenchman by the name of Luc Owen, fathered by a Welshman remaining in France after the Armistice. Owen had fought a long war, his chest bearing the DFC, DFM and a *palme*-encrusted *Croix de Guerre*, one cheek scarred by shrapnel at Dieppe and a broken nose following a crash in a Hurricane, Owen was now a Flight Commander in Rose's new Wing.

As Rose reached for the undercarriage lever, his restive veteran's eyes noticed a sudden pulse of light on the ground west of the airfield and a distant, tiny fireball blooming vivid yellow, a rash of smoke bursts from AA freckling the air, a glinting speck racing impossibly fast towards them.

At first, he was incredulous of the sheer speed of the approaching aircraft, but recalled the commander's intelligence briefing of a few days before on recent enemy fighter developments.

Crikey, Ada! It must be one of those bloody Jerry jets! He had heard plenty of stories about these wonder jets, but it was the first he had seen and his heart began to thump harder with excitement.

Rose keyed his microphone hurriedly, gabbling, 'Bluebell Leader to Bluebell Two, enemy jet ahead three miles, two o'clock low, going north! He's going too fast to turn away quickly from us, climb at full throttle and dive after him as he begins his turn eastwards. I'll try and slow him down for you.'

Already his stomach muscles and buttocks were clenching painfully, groin tightening rigid as stone as a thrill of fear raced up his back, as if in anticipation of the fiery punch of enemy cannon and machine guns which must surely be heading his way in seconds, and he gulped down a mouthful of oxygen jerkily, eyes wide in focus as he held the speck in his vision, desperately striving not to lose it in the gloom.

Instantly all the apprehension and doubts were expunged as the veteran's experience took over, knowledge and hard-learned skill guiding Sugar carefully but urgently into an interception at maximum range and at closing speeds that would allow for only the very minimum of firing windows before the Jerry was beyond range.

God, it's going to be close. I've got to make this count ...

The sleek Tempest flying on his wing had already broken away hard, soaring upwards and exhaust smoke streaming back in thick grey lines, his companion's voice confident and tight. 'Understood, Bluebell Leader.'

Rose flicked up the safety cover and switched on the reflector gun sight, its rosy glow reassuringly steady as he pulled Sugar's nose to port, one gloved hand squeezing the little pink bear in his pocket and the pebble, as if to reassure himself as he licked dry lips.

Dear God, that Jerry fighter was *fast*! There was no way he could get in place to deliver a front quarter attack with the speed it was doing as it noticed them and began to curve gently away north-eastwards, the dancing speck in Rose's windscreen resolving into a now-dull grey splinter borne on twin brown smoke trails, an arrow-head already passing into his eleven o'clock position and beginning to climb away.

Rose had meant to 'cross the T' but the damned thing was swifter than he had judged and now he jockeyed tensely for a stern shot from the retreating enemy's port quarter as the distance between them began to increase rapidly.

An emerald-green shape blurred by speed with a pointed and unglazed nose, two engines on swept back wings, and a sleek shark-like fuselage complete with triangular fin-like tail plane.

And, dear God above, strangest of all even though he had seen pictures and knew the thing was a Jerry jet, it still came as a surprise that there were no bloody propellers! The damned thing was a Messerschmitt jet, a whatchamacallit, a 262! Even though he knew by its speed what it was, actually seeing one was something else entirely.

Four 20 mm cannon, but its deadly nose was already long turned away from Sugar, the Jerry pilot racing away for home …

Mirror? Clear.

Eyes narrowing in concentration and holding his breath, rapidly calculating deflection and drop, Rose led with his gunsight and unleashed a prolonged burst of cannon fire, 'hose-piping' an inter-minably long four seconds worth of explosive 20 mm rounds, the recoil slowing Sugar; Rose bit his lip, feeling the vibration trembling through her wallowing airframe and into his arms and legs and up his spine as he fought to hold the aim steady as Sugar's Hispano pumped out a hundred and fifty shells, correcting for deflection, still aiming just ahead of it, carefully leading that tiny turning shape with what he hoped was just the right amount of deflection at this horribly long range as Jerry fled for safety, the acrid stink of cordite still as bitter and choking as its memory.

A quick glance up into the oppressive skies, nothing lurking in the piled clouds to bounce him, just Evans' Tempest high above, a dark cruciform now catching the light as Evans half-rolled off his climb, coming back down in a hard, sharp dive to pick up enough speed to catch the fleeing enemy.

Experience, luck and recoil created a slightly divergent deadly torrent of rushing metal, a spreading fan of high explosive ordnance which arced across and caught the fleeing jet at long range, just a few rounds and just for a moment.

In that instant Rose saw the rapid *flash-flash* pinpoint sparkle from at least two hits on the distant shape, and he wondered if he had truly seen the enemy jet twitch beneath the impacts.

He grunted with satisfaction as a single gout of dirty black smoke billowed and beaded one of the twin trails, but the fighter continued away.

Rose released the firing button, and the cannon mercifully stopped. Initially on operations, when the Tempest had been fitted with wings thinner than those of the Tiffie, the smaller, modified cannon would continue to fire until running dry.

Mirror? Clear.

Evans' Tempest was racing after it, using the dive to go even faster, a hawk swooping down into the kill.

Damn it! The bloody Jerry was going like the ruddy clappers! Soon the enemy fighter was fading into the haze, the orange dots of its engines all that was now visible. Tense with anger, Rose cursed.

Just as it seemed the enemy fighter would escape, one of the haze-faded glowing dots flickered and died. Evans' *whoop!* of joy resounding in Rose's headphones as the two other aircraft disappeared into the murk. Rose pushed the throttle forward, his mouth bone dry.

Mirror? Clear.

A sudden smear of light, shockingly bright in the grey light, dying and disappearing in a smudge of black smoke.

Jerry? Or, God forbid, young Evans?

'Got him!' said Evans, crowing over the R/T, ebullient and victorious.

'Well done, Bluebell Two, bloody well done and congratulations! It's not every day you get to kill a Jerry jet!'

Rose's skittish focus was on more specks in his mirror, but not Jerry, a tight pair of Hawker Tempests, too late, Volkel's immediate readiness kites?

Too late, lads, too far behind to have caught the German, yet chasing gamely nonetheless…

As Evans' fighter reappeared through the haze ahead, curving around in a wide turn to settle back into position on his wing, the section of Tempests swept past a quarter of a mile off his wing, the pilots looking their way and waggling their wings in salute.

'You winged him, Bluebell Leader, his port engine was smoking, and he'd slowed enough for me to catch up and give him a burst!' The man's voice was loud and excited. Then, sombrely, 'He blew up. Don't think he got out. Too low.' Then, more gleefully, '*Sacre bleu!* Half a kill before even joining Volkel!'

Rose felt his racing heart subside and he took a breath. 'No, not half, it's all yours, Bluebell Two. You were quick off the mark. He'd have got away if it weren't for you. Good response and a good kill.'

Not *quite* true. With one engine u/s and with his Tempest at full throttle and pushed through 'the gate', Rose could have caught him to deliver a coup de grace. 'Your kill, I fancy.'

I fancy! He cringed at his own words. *Dear God, I sound like the Scarlet Pimpernel!*

'Thank you, sir. You are generous.' The Frenchman was grateful, knowing that Rose could have claimed a half share in the kill, a half share of the glory.

Few Allied pilots could boast a jet in their scores, and Evans had just joined their exalted ranks.

Visible ahead of them on the snowy ground a smoking, sooty circular stain, countless tiny embers scattered and burning in and around it. No parachute.

There but for the grace …

His hands had begun to tremble now. What would Harry Broadhurst, his Group Commander think if he were to see his newest Wing Leader now? The great Harry Rose, *Typhoon Rose*, throat tight and shaking?

But, as he cast his eyes back to the lowering clouds, Rose was heartened to discover that after so long flying non-operationally, he had not lost his nerve after all, as he had so often worried.

But then, it had all happened so fast, and with time, might the gnawing anticipation and fear return?

'Good man. He won't be bombing any of our vehicle parks again.'

Even as he voiced it, Rose wondered who would mourn the German they had just killed, before recalling the earlier glare of the exploding enemy bombs. Before his demise, how many Allied soldiers had the enemy pilot killed? Who had he caused to be left bereft and alone and heartbroken?

With that grim thought his eyes skated for a second to her picture, hands automatically guiding them back on course for the airfield, with Volkel's Tempests acting as escort above and behind them.

Those same hands which had assisted in the death of a German airman just moments ago had held Molly only hours before, revelling in her soft embrace, the sweetness of her scent exchanged for the bitter stench of rubber, hot metal, oil, cordite and death.

From the peace of domestic bliss to the fires of war in so short a time. *Once more unto the breach…*

His return to operations inaugurated with spilled enemy blood, Harry Rose was back in the war.

Chapter 4

Volkel Airfield was initially set up two miles east-north-east of its namesake village in eastern Holland by a unit of the Reich Labour Workforce and local Dutch workers three months after Holland capitulated in 1940, to be used as an advance landing ground for Luftwaffe night fighters.

A year later, two of the three grass runways were paved, the existing large hangar and smaller buildings being joined in an expansion programme for more than forty covered aircraft shelters distributed amongst three dispersal zones.

Large underground fuel dumps were sited at the northern and western boundaries, the ordnance storage dump carefully hidden at the southern edge in the Oosterheide Woods.

Artful camouflage and landscape masking merged the Luftwaffe airfield beautifully into the surrounding countryside, while fourteen flak towers were scattered around to discourage potential attackers. However, these were not enough to daunt the five RAF and USAAF raids in 1944 which encouraged the final evacuation of aircraft in August.

With the approaching Allied advance, German forces withdrew, demolishing the surviving airfield infrastructure with explosives as they went, and soon thereafter, Volkel Fliegerhorst became ALG B80, RAF Volkel as its new owners took over.

As the green flare arced up brightly in welcome from a battered-looking watch tower, Rose lowered Sugar's undercarriage and lined up her nose with the runway stretching from west to east.

The RAF photo-reconnaissance pictures he had been shown at the Air Ministry revealed a demolished airfield, looking completely unusable, heavily pitted and almost completely obscured beneath a messy rash of bomb craters.

But now, despite being coated with a thin icing of snow, he could see that much of the damage had been repaired, the myriad darker tracks of vehicles, aircraft and people making the white ground a historical tapestry of the airfield's movements.

Yet Volkel looked no more welcoming than it had in the photo. The desolate and icy scene made him feel almost nostalgic for the dirt, sweat and dust of B2 Bezenville.

Volkel's main hangar was a blackened skeletal remnant, and the buildings a disparate hotchpotch of the repaired and the ruined; some of those which were once rubble gutted ruins had been roughly restored since, with more single-storey sheds and shabby caravans near the boundaries, and in the Western Dispersals were the twisted wreckage of gliders and their twin engine towing C-47s, undamaged Tempests parked in cleared spaces amongst the wreckage.

A pair of snowploughs were parked to one side, and scattered around like dandelion seeds were collections of tents and untidy piles of what Rose assumed (and hoped) were empty fuel cans, a smaller clumping of tents close to the junction of the runways the airfield's Air Traffic Control.

Each of the encampments amongst the puddles and mud featured its own complement of neat lines of fighters, the groups representing the individual squadrons and wings based there. While the runway itself had been repaired, most of the other craters had been filled in with rubble, with the perimeter track and taxiways narrowed in places by more craters.

Most of the unfilled or roughly filled-in holes were filled with water and lightly dusted with ice and snow, a hazard for the unwary or injured pilot.

More ominously, he saw that there were what looked like graves dug on patches of ground at a variety of points on the airfield perimeter, while on the road at the southern edge were the remains of smashed transport and armoured vehicles, torn and twisted and rusted a rough and sullen reddish-brown, a line of four Churchill tanks churning slowly past the wreckage along the rutted and uneven road, thick grey exhaust smoke swirling in the cold air.

Nonetheless, despite the inhospitable sight and the plume of smoke rising in the distance from where the 262 had dropped its load, Rose felt a thrill of nervous excitement and anxiety, for one of those gatherings of tents and aircraft comprised No. 348 (Free French) and 465 squadrons (Australia), the units which made up his new command, No. 63 Wing, RAF!

Despite the unnerving sheen on the brick-paved runway, there was no ice and Rose's landing was smooth.

He was directed along a taxiway to the perimeter track on the way to an encampment near the north-east boundary of the airfield, an airman guided him into position alongside a line of Tempests.

As Sugar's enormous propeller creaked to a stop, Rose checked once again that the gun-button safety was secure (*twist it again and the ruddy thing's going to break! Leave it alone!*), pocketed Molly's picture, unstrapped, and then disconnected his R/T lead and oxygen tube, before nodding to the airman outside and pulling back the canopy.

He gasped involuntarily as the bitter wind swirled into the cockpit, splashing against him like ice water, pressing sweat-dampened clothes against his weary muscles and shocking him after the warmth of the cockpit. Nevertheless he was grateful to ease his backside from the uncomfortable pleats of the folded dinghy.

The airman leaned forwards. 'Wing Commander Rose? Pleased to meet you, I'm sure, sir. Corporal Bell, sir, but most everyone calls me Jelly. Welcome to Holland, sir.' He smiled, almost shyly, his words eager. 'I hear you caught our recent visitor?'

'Yes.' Rose's voice was reedy with tiredness and dried by the oxygen of his mask, the tenor harsh, and he swallowed to wet his throat and soften his tone.

Covetously eyeing the impressive rows of Rose's victories on Sugar's side, Bell tentatively asked, 'Shall I add another swastika to your score, sir?'

Rose wiped his dried lips, already numbing in the cold, eyes on Evans' Tempest as it eased into position alongside, the *Croix de Lorraine* painted proud on its cowling.

Interestingly, a number of the nearby Tempests bearing the Cross of Lorraine also bore a painted red banner on their sides.

'Mr Evans bagged it.' He smiled, 'Next time, eh?'

Stepping onto the wing with the help of the disappointed Bell, Rose caught sight of a jeep speeding along the runway and was surprised to see a sledge with a single occupant being pulled along behind it.

Suddenly, as it reached the X that was the junction of the two crossed runways, the jeep braked hard and slid through a half circle.

The sledge continued on, the jeep's semi-twirl whirling it into a tight arcing pirouette upwards, and the occupant flew off it to hurtle head first into one of the filled-in craters. He could almost feel the crunch of the unknown man's bones in his own.

Rose winced in sympathy, and Bell chortled next to him. 'That Mr Powell! He'll do himself an injury one day if he ain't careful. Them Kiwis is a high-spirited bunch, right enough.' Then, eyeing Rose anxiously, he said, 'Um, beg yer pardon, sir, but you ain't a Kiwi, erm, New Zealander?'

God, it was cold. 'No, Corporal.'

The man's face brightened with relief.

From the crater a figure emerged, clambering slowly and painfully over the rubble with the assistance of the jeep's driver. Brushing himself off, the man shakily got back onto the sled, and the jeep screeched off again.

Tsk, tsk, the silly sod. That smash didn't knock any sense into his head. Thank God he's not one of mine. His feet wouldn't touch the ground.

Rose shook his head, but he knew that some found relief from the stress of operations in such insanely dangerous pursuits.

Balanced cautiously on the wing, he noticed two officers emerge from the dispersals hut, but he reached out to touch the fuselage behind the canopy, *thank you.*

Earlier in the week, Rose had met with another Harry in London, his AOC, AVM Broadhurst.

'The thing is, Rose,' rumbled the great man to him, 'you're doing a grand job on the staff, but I need a Wing Leader in Holland. I've a small composite Wing formed at Volkel, and they lost their Wing Leader to flak yesterday, the poor devil only took over last week. You'll be in command of two squadrons of Tempests, but your pilots are Free French and RAAF, attached to the RAF.'

Broadhurst shifted some papers around aimlessly. 'Don't ask. I need someone who knows what's what to take command.'

Rose felt the tremor in his leg, and he gripped his knee to still it.

Clasping his treacherous limb tightly, Rose thought of Molly and of his little ones, unimaginable miracles of life in the bloodiest of wars, and he felt that familiar feeling of loss and uneasiness again.

But to his ears his voice was quiet, calm and measured. 'Of course, sir.'

He didn't want to go, but what else could he say? How could he refuse? Harry Broadhurst had pulled Granny's 44 Wing (minus an already wounded Granny) from the front line after Falaise, its survivors from the Battle for France faded and dazed after many months of fighting before, during and after the Invasion.

They had been allowed to lick their wounds when other squadrons had continued the fight in their absence. Where Rose had returned to the ones he loved, others had taken Excalibur's place in the line as the advance continued into Belgium.

How, then, could he say no? His men would remain in Blighty in defence against the madman's terror weapons, and he was glad for he could not bear the thought that after surviving so much, he might yet lose more of them.

He had lost far too many of his precious men already in those continued forays, day after day, into the Valley of Death. His men would be safe, even though V1 hunting was still a hazardous task, but his own obligation was not yet done.

How could he face the man in the mirror or dearest Molly, unless he did his duty to be worthy of them both? Molly at least deserved a man worthy of her.

Strangely, amidst the growing turmoil of sentiment and trepidation in his mind, he found that the prospect of a battle command again elicited an unexpected feeling of anticipation and excitement, too. *I must be raving mad …*

Broadhurst nodded, and his eyes bored into Rose's. 'Good man. You're a war-substantive Squadron Leader at present, aren't you, Rose?'

Rose nodded. 'Yes, sir. Substantively, I'm still a Flight Lieutenant.'

'You'll be confirmed as substantive Squadron Leader, effective from today, and I'm appointing you Wing Commander, war-substantive. You've more than earned it, Rose.' The AOC's face cracked into his irrepressible grin. 'Congratulations, old chap!'

All of which meant Rose's permanent RAF rank (not just during wartime) was now that of Squadron Leader, and with his promotion to 'War Substantive' rank, he would be a Wing Commander for the remaining duration of the war!

Cripes!

Stunned, Rose didn't know whether to laugh or cry, and instead settled on humble gratitude. 'Thank you, sir.'

'Don't forget to put up your new rank stripes though, Rose.' Broadhurst stood and held out his hand. 'Good luck, Wing Commander.'

Wing Commander Rose!

Cripes, ruddy, bloody bananas!

Chapter 5

'So, that's him. Doesn't look like a fire-eater to me. The papers made him seem ten feet tall. Bit shorter than I expected.'

'*Oui*. But many of the greatest men in history were not tall, mon ami. You remember the greatest general of them all, Bonaparte?' Gabby smirked at his taller companion.

Sheep snorted but said nothing.

'The great Typhoon Rose. *Beaucoup de medailles*, hmm? A press-on type, perhaps, *cochon*?' His voice was grim. 'I am sick of the *putain de* glory-seekers.'

'How should I know, you silly sod? Can't tell by looking, can you?' Sheep grinned at him. 'Thought you looked a decent sort. Know better now, don't I? Just shows how wrong a fella can be.'

'*Imbecile*,' grunted the Frenchman.

'Crikey Ada! And for Christ's sake, Gabby, stop calling me *cochon*! Don't you know how to speak your own bloody language? How many times do I need to tell you? Sheep is *mouton* in Frenchie, y'know, not bloody *cochon*. Don't mess about, 'else the new Wingco's going to start calling me "Piggy".'

His friend nodded agreeably, smiling mischievously. '*Oui, cochon*.'

Sheep shook his head in resignation. 'Strewth! God give me strength.' He chewed a fingernail absentmindedly. 'At least he's VR, not a regular. Coupla blokes I know say he's a pretty good sort and a damn fine pilot.'

They straightened respectfully as the young Wing Commander jumped confidently down from the wing of his aircraft, smiling. 'Gentlemen! How d'you do? I'm Harry Rose, here for me?' *Thank God I didn't fall!*

Seems friendly enough, thought Sheep grudgingly, and saluted, *for what we are about to receive ...* 'Wing Commander Rose, sir, welcome to Volkel and 63 Wing.' He indicated the officer beside him. 'This is Hugo 'Gabby' Gabriel, 348 Squadron, Free French Air Force, and I'm Jake 'Sheep' Kelly, 465 Squadron, RAAF.' His accent proved the truth of the 'Australia' flash on the shoulders of his battledress, though it was softer than Rose had expected.

'Good to meet you both, gentlemen.'

Gabby nodded formally as he took Rose's hand. *'Mon plaisir,* sir.'

The Frenchman was slim and dark, the Australian leaner and much taller, a thick moustache forming a light brown fringe canopy over the even teeth of his grin. He took an instant liking to them both.

'The Adjutant, Squadron Leader Potter, should be along shortly, sir. It's a bit chilly, he prefers the warmth. Shall we get ourselves somewhere warmer with a nice mug of something hot? Jelly Bell will get your kit sent on to your quarters, and the Adj will take you to see Group Captain Jameson presently.'

Sheep waved vaguely to a battered-looking caravan some distance away, parked next to the empty shell of a gutted hangar bearing the legend *'Rauchen Verboten'* just beyond the Tempest dispersals area, rubble and twisted knots of metal everywhere. Rose would later learn this was Volkel's Intelligence Section and the 122 Wing Leader's office.

Patrick Jameson, CO of Volkel and 122 Wing, was not responsible for 63 Wing, but would provide support because of the independent remit given Rose by Broadhurst.

A highly decorated regular officer, Jameson had flown his depleted flight of Hurricanes onto HMS Glorious after the ill-fated Norwegian campaign in early 1940, only to lose them when the carrier was sunk in the bitterly cold North Sea by the German battleships *Scharnhorst* and *Gniesenau.*

Slinging his parachute pack over one shoulder, Rose followed Sheep as he led the way back to the hut, and thought of his first Flight Commander, Flight Lieutenant 'Dingo' Denis.

Dingo, bless him, had survived both the Blitzkreig and then the Battle of Britain, before being posted east to command a squadron of Spitfires in the struggle against an expanding Japanese Empire, surviving the devastating air raids on Darwin. Now a Group Captain, DSO and Bar, DFC and bar, Dingo was on the staff at the Royal Military College in Duntroon.

The tough Australian had added the ribbon of a George Medal to his ribbons in recognition for the rescue of the crew of a crashed bomber at his station the previous year, receiving singed eyebrows, and more painfully, a protracted ear bashing from his wife Dolly Denis for taking stupid risks.

Invalided out of the WAAF after being wounded at the same time as Molly at RAF Foxton during that fateful Luftwaffe raid at the height of the Battle of Britain, Dolly had recently given birth to their third child, a daughter they named Molly, and she had told Dingo in no uncertain terms what she thought of his heroics.

Approaching the dispersals area, Rose ran an eye appreciatively over the recently built building.

The main dispersals hut for No. 63 Wing was built primarily out of layered wooden planks, and the main room included a large brick hearth. It was a welcome sanctuary from the freezing temperatures outside, and the fireplace was a marked improvement on the pot-bellied cast iron stoves found in British military establishments.

Even when at full blast with the iron glowing cherry-red from the heat, the stoves made little impression on the biting cold of a British winter. It seemed that the teams of Dutch labourers and Allied airfield construction personnel knew their business, for the large ready room was pleasantly cosy, logs burning in the hearth with a number of sofas and chairs in a multitude of styles and decrepitude scattered around.

At one end of the dispersals hut, a second room served as a briefing room for the pilots, and would serve as an occasional Wing Leader's office. His main office was in another dilapidated caravan parked nearby.

A third, smaller room set to one side was the storage area for their flying kit, kerosene heaters keeping the parachutes dry, while a large black kettle was perched atop a metal frame, another kerosene heater heating it from beneath.

Despite the noxious fug of kerosene, old tobacco smoke and unwashed bodies, Rose felt instantly at home.

That evening, Rose addressed the officers and senior NCOs of his Wing nervously, and he found that he strongly needed a pee. He'd known the men of Excalibur for some time before assuming command (and lost many of them while in command), but this time the faces before him were those of strangers.

He spoke to them just before dinner, noting the tiredness amongst the press of faces on those who had been flying earlier that day. There should have been a young Sergeant Pilot named Granger amongst them, but the boy had not returned from a free ranging recce, and nothing had been heard from him since. Rose had spoken with Granger's Flight Commander, Gus Curran, a stocky young Flight Lieutenant from a rural community in New South Wales.

'He was there one minute, sir, next I know he's gone. No flak, no cry for help. Just gone.' His face was a mixture of bewilderment, anger and shame. 'He was just a kid.'

Dear God. I've lost one already, and I never even met him. And that dreaded but necessary duty for a boy entrusted to him but one he had never met. *I must write to his people, give thanks for their sacrifice …*

Rose did not insult or bore them with a long-winded droning speech of inspiration and encouragement after they had already had a long and wearing day of operations, for these men were all experienced, and most were veterans of a long and brutal war. They were here because they wanted to be, all volunteers.

Instead he recognised and praised their service, asked them to continue to do so under his command, the pretence of easy confidence and his incisive voice hiding the nervousness; he thanked them and promised to them his best at all times and vowed to be receptive, and reminded them that his door was open for whatever advice, support or help they needed, day or night.

He promised that he would give to them all that he had, and feared they would find him inadequate, and to his own ears his words sounded leaden and uninspiring.

As he gazed at the hard and strong faces of the strangers who were now his men, he saw much to inspire and encourage him, saw how the long years of war had changed the nature of those who flew against the enemy.

When he first joined Excalibur, squadron life had been light-hearted, everyone acting the fool, it all being a bit of a hoot. But it had all been transformed by the rigours and reality and utter brutality of years of war.

Gone were the days of the professional (and sometimes faintly disparaging) regulars and the easy-going but brave amateurs of the Royal Air Force Volunteer Reserve. Killing had become a science, and those who had not died in the first cruel years of war taught the warriors of today with the harsh-gleaned skills, imbuing in them all a professionalism that had been unavailable to Rose and his peers in that long ago summer of 1940.

These confident Australians and Frenchmen were arranged respect-fully in a semicircle before him and would have varied histories and backgrounds similar to his precious Excalibur Squadron men, including those who had fallen under his command.

All different, all unique.

One such was a young Frenchman, an olive-skinned and dark-haired Flight Lieutenant with haunted and intense eyes. He was a veteran; that much was obvious from the ribbons of the DFC, a much-adorned and faded *Croix de Guerre, Médaille Militaire, Médaille de la Résistance* and the '39-43 Star. The darkness in the eyes and the decorations were impressive, but Rose had fought alongside others with similar credentials.

What marked this Frenchman as different was a scruffy ragdoll tucked into the front of his tunic, its glittering button eyes more disconcerting than the Frenchman's.

The other was one of Sheep's boys. Despite wearing an RAF tunic adorned with Flying Officer stripes and 'Australia' flashes, the ribbons of a DFC, MM and bar, '39-'43 Star, Africa Star and one other unrecognisable ribbon, he also had on a dark grey turtleneck jumper, stone-grey woollen breeches, and jackboots.

Rose frowned as the youngster grinned uncomfortably under his scrutiny. 'What's this you're wearing?' he asked.

The boy looked down at himself. 'Sir? It's German uniform. And sir? I'm Micky Lynch.'

'I know it's a German uniform, Lynch,' Rose replied heavily, trying to keep a straight face, 'but why on earth are you wearing it? Are you a Jerry spy?'

The grin on the open and pleasant face grew uncertain. 'Uh ... no?'

'Are you asking me, Lynch?' Rose said with asperity.

'No! No, sir, I'm no Jerry spy! I'm saying no.' The grin had slipped.

Rose's tone was neutral. 'Then would you care to explain to me your outfit?'

The grin was gone now, and Lynch looked down at himself again. 'See, if I end up behind the lines, I can pretend to be a Jerry. It'll help me to escape and get back to the squadron!'

'Sir!' growled Sheep.

'Sir!' Micky added hurriedly.

There was something very likeable about Lynch, and while liking the youth's enthusiasm, Rose didn't think much of the idea. 'D'you speak German, Lynch?'

'No, sir.'

'And if you're stopped and questioned, you might be captured and Jerry might shoot you as a spy! And what if you land amongst our lot?' Rose hardened his voice. 'They may take one look at your uniform and put a bullet between your eyes. Change into proper uniform, er, Lynch, will you?' This was a laugh, for his men were dressed in a cosmopolitan variety of clothes including a mixture of RAF blue, darker RAAF blue, Free French Air Force blue, khaki battledress and civvies. One of the silly sods even had a battered bowler hat on his head.

Sheep guffawed. 'My bloody oath! And if the Poles catch you, Micky, you'll end up losing your balls, you soppy mongrel!' He cuffed Lynch playfully. 'How many times do I have to tell you? Now go and get into proper uniform, you galah, or else I'll shoot you my bloody self!'

Rose had been firm. From now on, excepting operational circumstance, they would be in number one uniforms at evening mess unless they were on duty.

No civvies, no battledress, and *absolutely* no Axis uniforms.

So many new faces, new friends to make, and new lives he was responsible for and earn respect from. How strange to look upon the faces of the living and yet see the faces of his honoured dead.

His glamorous 'Chorus Line' Quartet: Thomas, Andrews, Montalmond and Trent, the gentle Alexander Leslie from Trinidad and fatherly Pops Graham, Alan Winters with the baffling bellow of 'Drop your bloomers, the Navy's here!' every time he came through the door; and so many others, the novices and the veterans and those in between, lost in the long bitter years before and the months after the liberation of France.

They had been his men, his family and his responsibility, exceptional individuals who had flown with him and who had not survived when he and the lucky remaining few had. He felt their silent presence as he addressed the men before him.

The memories were so very painful yet unforgettable. How could one forget such men? When Sheep had first spoken to him, there had been a moment's dislocation for Rose, the accent awakening the painful memory of losing 'Fanny' Adams over Eglise Saint-Martin, and *that* reminded him of losing Whip, Excalibur's C-Flight Commander. But in losing Whip he had gained Daffy, whose love and warmth helped lift him through the desperate madness on the road to Falaise and the liberation.

When would the time come when little things would not awaken memories that were so painful, painful enough to take his breath away? He prayed for that time when he might forget, but a big part of him never wanted to forget them at all, ever. His friends had given their lives, and the pain of remembrance was the very least they deserved.

Granny took Rose aside the day after their return from B2 Bezenville; he had seen the unshed tears and the empty guilt in Rose's haunted face.

'The pain will never go away, Flash, me old frilly bloomers. You should know, we've both lost too many already.' His dearest friend had looked into the far distance and Rose had wondered what he saw, who he remembered.

'It's like a knife to begin with. Harsh and cold and sharp, cutting deep. But the sharpness of the edge will dull with time. It will diminish, but it will never go completely. Given time, you'll learn to live with it.'

His voice had been quiet but fierce, eyes wet. 'Those who survive will keep the memory of those lads alive and will be their testament and tribute. The ones who live must ensure we never forget the ones who don't.'

Sheep had the same tall, rangy stature as Dingo, lean and hard, but was fair instead of dark, and his accent softer. The lines on his face were fewer, and tempered by a ready smile and a bristling moustache.

'So, tell me, why do they call you "Sheep"?' Rose felt drained, and he took a sip from his hot, sweet tea, almost grimacing at its temperature.

Wouldn't do for the lads to know their new Wing Leader was a lightweight.

Sheep smiled. 'Someone put a tall tale around on my first squadron that I was a sheep farmer in Oz before this little lot, rounding up sheep every night, thousands of acres and millions of sheep, you know the kind of thing, so Sheep I've been since.'

Gabby nodded. 'Just so.'

Rose smiled. 'And? Is it true? Do you have some enormous livestock farm in the, er, the Outback?'

'Not likely!' Sheep snorted in derision. 'Come from a little town on the coast called Sydney. You might have heard of it?' He grinned cheerfully. 'Never been near a sheep in my life, 'cept of course when Mum would make mutton stew or a nice roast.'

He sat back easily. 'Tell a lie, though. There was that time when I was twelve, Dad took us to a farm when we were kids, said it would be educational. I was too small to shear a sheep, not like now, bloody things were bigger than me, so they put me with the Rousers to collect the shorn coats and sweep up after. Toughest bloody thing I've ever done.'

The tall Australian smiled fondly at the memories. 'Those Rousers were hard bastards with soft hearts. Used to make me drink hot black sweet tea to make me sweat, as if I needed it! But they would save me half a bottle of beer at lunch, and always had a packet of Minties or FanTales in the arvo for me.'

He saw Rose's mystification. 'Sweets, sir.'

Rose nodded. 'Ah.'

Sheep drained his mug. 'But, by God, it was a hard job! Wouldn't do it again. Came back smelling of dust, dirt and shit, wool fibres up my nose, between the cheeks of my arse, itching like crazy, and covered with scratches from the spiky burrs caught in the fleece.'

Sheep shook his head at the memory. 'No, sir. Gabs might tell you I was some daft uncouth bogan, but when Fritzy pranced his way into Poland, I was teaching science and maths at a very nice posh school in Somerset.'

Gabby tittered and Sheep gave him a bruising look. 'The headmaster tried to get me roped in with some hush-hush scientific types, but the thought of sitting the war out behind a desk with three square meals a day and a soft bed made me want to heave. So I volunteered for pilot training.'

He shook his head ruefully. 'Silly bastard, eh? Should've known better. Could've been having a bloody good root every night. Strewth!'

'Of course,' Rose said agreeably, wondering with mystification if a good root was what he thought it was.

'I'd love to give a nice Aussie kiss right about now,' Sheep grumbled wistfully, eyes faraway, holding out his mug to the orderly for refilling.

Gabby pursed his lips and winked. Rose, not wanting to ask but wanting to know, asked 'An Aussie kiss?'

'Y'know, mate!' Sheep grinned salaciously. 'A French kiss, but down under!'

Rose, who had enjoyed giving Molly many such kisses, could only smile fixedly and say, 'Oh.'

Sheep sighed. 'Instead, I get to share my evenings with my old cobber here, isn't that so, Gabs?'

Gabby's head bobbed. 'Just so, *cochon*. You are greatly blessed, indeed.'

For centuries, generations of Holland's priesthood had trained and prayed at the ancient seminary in Uden, but more recently it had also been the home of the airfield's Luftwaffe Flak regiment.

With the departure of German forces, the RAF officers of B80, RAF airfield Volkel, took over residence in the seminary, the faded scent of cologne in its corridors a lingering legacy of the Luftwaffe's Flak men.

To it the RAF had now added the fragrance of damp clothing, unwashed bodies, tobacco smoke, booze, bacon and beans.

The uppermost floor remained the preserve of the original occupants, the monks silently slipping like wraiths down the stairs on their way to worship at Uden's many churches.

As was usual in all hierarchies, Other Ranks were billeted separately from the officers, their home the nearby schoolhouse.

Rose was allocated his own room on the first floor, befitting his exalted position of a Wing Leader; it had a small high window looking down into the enclosed courtyard, a thin wooden bunk as his bed, a threadbare and thin mattress and RAF blankets, and a couple of splintered bullet holes in the wooden floor—evidence of the high spirits of some of the pilots of 486 Squadron, RNZAF.

Left behind by the last occupant, a half-empty packet of Churchman's cigarettes, a badly darned sock and a well-thumbed copy of *No Orchids for Mrs Blandish* had been left by Rose on the battered armchair at the end of the corridor.

While such lewd novels were popular amongst his peers (Granny regularly replacing each copy which Belle threw away), Rose wasn't having it sitting alongside the selection of books Molly had given him.

The ancient dark wood of the room would have made the room appear smaller and more enclosed if lit by candle, but the Wing's senior engineering officer had jury-rigged the monastery with lighting, and a naked bulb glowed bright in a makeshift fitting against the wall.

His new batman, a friendly and garrulous Tynesider named Sparrow, had already unpacked his kit, but left his personal effects neatly to one side for Rose to arrange.

On the small shelf beside the bunk, Rose now organised the books which Molly had chosen for him, a spray of flowers from their garden and most important of all, the picture frames of his family.

Her gentle smile soothed his eyes, but his heart remained wanting, his spirit feeling lonely and alone, and he sighed. Without the sound of Daffy's barking and children's voices, the place seemed inordinately cold and unwelcoming.

There was a rather nice pinup of a nude girl on one wall which he was tempted to leave, for she had a friendly smile (nothing to do with her pert breasts and nicely rounded bottom, of course—perish the thought!), but the only smile he truly yearned to look upon was the one on his wife's face in the framed photograph.

The monastery had none of the bright, open spaces like the lawn or the tended garden at home, none of the intimacy of Molly's orchard which he had become so used to over the last few months of blissful leave, and it lacked the warmth and comfort which filled his family's home.

But for now, this small, dark room smelling of tobacco, incense, timeworn wood and an era of worship was Harry Rose's home.

Chapter 6

'Time for a nervous wee.' Sheep grinned cheerfully as he stopped beside the tail of his Tempest, and, unzipping his trousers, he began to urinate copiously against her tail wheel, steam rising from the ground frost.

Daft beggar, thought Rose as he turned away, his lips cold and dry despite the compo tea which had burned them just moments before. *This wind is like ice, and your poor old todger's likely to freeze and fall off in these conditions.*

But he smiled to himself and kept mum, walking on to Sugar, admiring the dark and powerful outline of her, looming huge and heavy against the pale background of ice and snow.

They all had the little foibles they felt brought them luck, the habits that perhaps might increase the chance of salvation that much greater than those pilots who jousted death without superstition, though there were precious few of the latter.

Jelly Bell was almost an extension of Rose's fighter, a huddled figure on Sugar's port wing, his pinched face half obscured by the woolly balaclava and West Ham FC football scarf wrapped around his neck, his stocky shape bulky in a thick greatcoat.

Having conducted the ever-essential walk-around of Sugar, Rose passed up his parachute pack and maps, and accepted a helping hand onto her wing, making full use of the toe and finger-traps, anxious lest the crews and pilots witness the undignified sight of their new Wing Commander slipping unceremoniously off his fighter and onto his arse.

'The kite OK, Jelly?' With the prospect of action, the heaviness in his chest and the fluttering sensation between the pit of his stomach and above his bladder seemed to ease a little.

Jelly was cheerful despite the cold. 'Everything's pukka, sir, tip-top and Bristol fashion. She's a sweetheart.'

The Met officer had earlier assured Rose that despite the dirty grey cloud hanging unbroken above and hiding the pale sky from the ground, there would be no sign of snow until late afternoon, and Ops had not warned of any special operations in their sortie area.

The harness for his pack and seat comfortably tightened and, with his R/T leads and oxygen tube connected, Rose nodded to Bell, and the canopy was slid smoothly over him, sealing him inside her as he locked it into place. In the stillness, he reverently removed her picture from his pocket, and allowed himself to feel her smile.

With a reassuring smile, a thumbs up and a last flourish of his cloth on the Perspex, Bell jumped down. Starting Sugar's Sabre would splatter the canopy with oil, and it would likely need to be done again.

Today, Sheep would lead a flight of his Tempests on a free ranging flight, seeking targets from western Germany's rail and road network. Rose would be flying as Sheep's wingman, Hobart Red Two, and he checked the little bear and the pebble were in place (for the thousandth time) before setting Molly's picture securely into its usual place.

It was the first time he would fly with 63 Wing, and please God, not the last.

Lord, my God, protect me with your mercy until such time I return to those I love.

Please.

After an earlier discussion with their Wing Commander, Sheep and Gabby suggested an early morning low-level sortie eastwards to Coesfeld for an attack on the rail and road transport junction there. Any railway or road traffic targets of opportunity would be welcome, and the network arrangement there was not suited as a flak trap.

Since May, Allied fighter bombers had shattered the rail networks throughout occupied Europe and Germany. In addition to their efforts, USAAF fighters escorting bombing missions when released from their duties were permitted to range far and wide, with the *Deutsche Reichsbahn* railways losing locomotives and rolling stock at a rate it had been unable to replace, on some days losing more than forty trains. The loss of trained crews, the damage to the infrastructure and the clear up of damage made it a nightmare moving men and war materiel by rail.

With the paucity of trains, Allied fighter-bombers would need to be careful not to be drawn into a flak trap. A motionless train sitting in a rail siding beneath swelling clouds of steam would be an irresistible target, the unwary sucked into the spider's web until it was too late.

To penetrate any further into Germany would bring them nearer to the heavy concentrations of flak closer to the Rhine, which might be tempting fate a little too much for their new Wing Commander on his first sortie with the Wing.

Gabby and Sheep were pleased and relieved when Rose confirmed that he agreed there would be only one pass in all attacks. More than one pass over a well-defended target with a surfeit of flak guns could court misfortune, as bolder but less sensible pilots had found to their cost.

Sheep and Gabby would initiate their new CO's war against the homeland of the enemy gently.

Afterwards, they would cast an eye over the small fighter airfield at Coesfeld, fifteen miles inside Germany and around four miles south-west of the town of Coesfeld, and then on the way back sweep past near the major Luftwaffe airfield of Rheine in the hopes of catching enemy aircraft in the circuit, vulnerable as they circled, landed or took off.

Gabby would conduct a second flight into Germany thirty miles north of them, to attack river traffic on the Ems and the railway line at Lingen, close enough nearby should their support be required.

The eight Tempests flew just beneath the cloud at twelve hundred feet above the flat Dutch fields as far as Winterswijk, after which Sheep dropped the flight down into the thin haze at low level, between fifty and a hundred feet and on into Germany, keeping an eye open for electricity pylons and hidden flak batteries. Typically, pylons in both Holland and Germany rose to around a hundred feet and would be a hazard at zero feet.

At such low level and in a battle spread of fighters in line abreast, the enemy would have little time to bring their guns to bear before the Tempests had flashed past and disappeared into the haze.

However, Sheep reminded them at the pre-flight briefing to look out for concealed flak batteries, and that with surviving enemy flak units grouped inside Germany, the flak density would likely be far greater than anything Rose had experienced already.

After experiencing the thick enemy AA first-hand in the boiling cauldron of Normandy and onwards, Rose felt the fret of worry at the thought of flying through such fire again.

Rose found that he was leaning forward against the straps, peering through the windscreen, seeing imagined batteries in the shadows beneath trees even as he searched for enemy fighters and fought to avoid the undulating landscape, although the chance of Jerry bouncing them in such poor conditions of haze and low cloud would be very low.

Breakfast had been thin slices of a rather dense brown bread scraped thinly with butter, oily discs of fried powdered egg, and chunks of something tasteless he assumed (and hoped) was cheese.

Rose had just managed a slice of the bread, and now felt it pressing painfully against his breastbone; he swallowed hard to push the dry lump down, feeling the rising glimmer of acid, painfully warm in his chest.

They were fortunate, experiencing only very light, desultory flak as they skirted north of Oeding on the border, the flak bursts coming nowhere near the fighters. But at such low level as this, he felt his nerve endings tingling, and he reached out to touch her photograph for reassurance. In truth, many of the gunners were not keen to attract the attention of the fighters and held fire.

Ghostly hamlets and cottages disappearing as rapidly as they appeared, the veil of cloud above seeming to gradually lower, merging with the gathering haze, and with the reducing visibility Rose felt the unease of every fighter pilot as their awareness of the surroundings was diminished.

He felt the hair on his neck rise, and the prickle of unease edge through him, eyes stealing to the mirror. Nothing.

In these sorts of murky conditions, it would be difficult for the enemy to pick them up visually, for line of sight of ground-based defence would be restricted by the uneven terrain, but equally there was the risk they might blunder past Coesfeld altogether and carry on flying east. Good navigation was the key to success.

Scanning the gloom, he began to feel he were in a dream, for they were over Germany, but there was no response to their presence, the distance obscured and the ground changing below. It was almost as if they were being purposefully ignored, that they didn't matter.

Where the hell were all the massed battalions of flak Sheep had assured him inhabited this miserable, mist-shrouded and frozen land of the enemy?

Then that little murmur in the back of his head, almost heard and reproachful: *don't look a gift horse...*

Another road, like so many others they had already overflown, but unlike those earlier, this one had four Opel Blitz trucks speeding north. Rose pressed down hard on the firing button and his cannon hammered out a glowing stream of flaming shells, livid as careering coals in the gloom, but the trucks were already further down the road, Sugar's explosive rounds completely off target and wasted, hurtling away uselessly.

Sheep's cannon shells ripped away to tear through the road, then cut off almost immediately as he identified the racing vehicles, and Rose breathed a sigh of relief. He had fired instinctively, even as his eyes registered the large red crosses set in the white circles on their sides and tops.

Merciful God! They had almost destroyed a small convoy of *Wehrmacht* ambulances!

Already the vehicles were lost in the blanketed grey landscape behind them, like fleeting souls, and he was grateful, for those in the back of the ambulances now were no longer combatants but helpless survivors.

Lucky survivors. *And lucky me, for not having the deaths of the injured and helpless on my conscience…*

And then Sheep eased his Tempest away to port and Rose turned quickly with him as the parallel lines of a railway track appeared shining in the dullness, the outlines of buildings showing beyond. He was sweating and his eyes felt raw with the effort to search.

'Coesfeld.' A single word of confirmation from Sheep, and then, unbelievably, 'Train! Twelve o'clock ahead!'

Ahead, a dirty blot of smoke in the windscreen, a black and choking plume low but spreading as if to obscure the ancient buildings of Coesfeld and its station, blurred and indistinct and streaking past on either side of the racing Tempests as they flashed through the town like quicksilver, half-seen as Rose fell back a hundred yards and a little to one side of Sheep's Tempest, eyes picking out the green curve of carriages and their locomotive, the train pulling slowly out of the forked rails onto the track leading north-eastwards.

The first flak began to stream up from the town, but there was too little (*just takes one to kill you, don't get complacent!*) and too high, the gunner a teenage Berliner hurriedly trained and peering uncertainly through the smoke and gloom of the day, but close enough to make Rose cringe and curl forwards on his seat and pushed Sugar lower, seeking the dubious safety of low level and wary of the high trees, branches reaching out as if to catch Sugar, cautious of telegraph poles and wires.

Ragged grey streamers of smoke trailed back from Sheep's wings, flashes of impacts prickling in the train's dissipating plume clouds.

Even as he felt Sugar tremble beneath the expanding compression waves of the nearing bursts of flak, his eyes picked out the detail on the dark green carriages with their pearl grey roofs, the steam engine at its head an angular dark shape, green and black.

As Sheep's cannon flared bright again, Rose pressed the gun button, holding it down this time as his shells joined Sheep's to tear through the carriages, doors being ripped open as desperate figures dressed in field grey and blue uniforms tumbled out haphazardly, many without weapons and helmets, some rolling or running, others falling and lying still and passing beneath his wings.

But there were more than enough of the scrambling crowd dressed in shabby suits and dresses, but he felt no burn of shame or guilt, for much terror and misery had been perpetrated in the name of these people in countless countries and communities, and they were all of them part of the enemy war effort.

Neither was there a sense of satisfaction, just the burning desire to hurt the enemy and survive, and he kept firing. To get this bloody thing over.

The train was curving slowly along the track, and his torrent of shells tore into soil and gravel and flesh, and onwards, to sparkle fleetingly across the last carriage, a flatbed.

A quad-mounted *Flakvierling* 2cm Flak 38 autocannon had been mounted onto the flatbed and the combined fire from Sheep's and Rose's cannon had torn it viciously apart, the four splayed barrels now pointing battered and askew, and the fate of its hapless gunners revealed by the shining smears of scarlet on the cannon-battered metal of the flatbed's platform.

His turn was a touch tighter than he had intended, and Sugar's 20 mm shells sprayed across to one side of the train onto the crowd of fleeing soldiers and civilians, tearing bloody ruin into unprotected flesh.

Bitter smoke from the locomotive and acrid cordite harsh on his tongue and burning in his lungs, heart thumping fit to burst in sympathy with Sugar's cannon, teeth clenched hard together and muscles aching under his mask.

Caught up as he was with directing his fire onto the fleeing troops and seeing Sheep's cannon fire was slashing great holes and rents through the carriages, Rose's approach was further to starboard so as not to hit the Australian's Tempest than he would have liked, and now he found that he would have to ease her a little to port again to rake the enemy locomotive as Sheep zoomed clear.

But to do so would be to increase the chances of being caught at low level in the turmoil of the funnel smoke and Sheep's slipstream or, even worse, misjudging as he banked and colliding with the embankment.

Streams of smoke and steam were pouring torrentially from the shattered locomotive in greater amounts, and fearful the damned thing might explode at any moment, Rose now pulled Sugar into an even harder turn to starboard, fear and exhilaration fluttering through his heart, half expecting a thunderous detonation and for a mighty hand of concussive force to grasp and fling Sugar into the ground below, the pale blobs of some of the soldiers' upturned faces mirroring his own fear and also mindful that a single rifle bullet could bring him down.

During 2TAF's drive down to Falaise in the late summer, Rose once witnessed a Typhoon from another Wing fly over the locomotive it had been attacking the moment the latter exploded. One minute the other Typhoon was flying through the cloud of steam hanging over the railway engine, the next both had ceased to exist as an expanding bubble of flame enclosed them in raging fire and death.

Now he turned his Tempest away from the wrecked train, towards the high ground and the distant Benedictine Abbey at Gerleve, four miles east of Coesfeld, the Tempests' rallying point after strafing the rail line, jinking as he did so, a single glittering line of bright tracer flashing before him, chasing after but missing Sheep's fighter, the shells streaking dangerously close ahead and below.

Stick hard back to leapfrog the writhing lash of fiery enemy metal, then further back as before him Sheep climbed high above an electricity pylon, the chasing tracer spattering and exploding against the pylon in a shower of sparks and knocking it flat, cables pulling and dragging at the next ones in line.

Sugar was skittish in his hands as he took her higher, Rose gasping and straining in fear as more pylons began to fold over beneath them, the collapse of one drawing at the others and smoke billowing heavily from the smashed train behind; Rose felt horribly exposed as the beautiful landscape opened panoramically below him, praying there was no flak sited at or near the Abbey, the imposing Benedictine building elegant in pale brown brick and light grey tiled roof nestling comfortably amidst the trees of the sloping incline.

Expelling the monks years earlier, the Nazis had taken the Abbey as their own, replacing the place of worship with a military hospital, and so there was no flak (*thank God!*), only the defiant hostility of those brave few wounded soldiers and Wehrmacht medical personnel who had not fled for cover but instead stood or sat and stared as the Tempests wheeled above.

In the distance near the town was a flare of light and a glowing golden fireball as the locomotive exploded, the blastwave reaching outwards.

Eight pairs of eyes in the cockpits anxiously scanned the heavens for prowling enemy fighters, the flight re-forming before setting course south-west for a sweep past Coesfeld airfield, dropping back down to zero feet and spreading wide apart, Rose feeling the relief as he counted none lost, his fingers slipping across the creased photograph before settling the oxygen mask more comfortably against his sweaty face.

But in his mind, that little voice: don't count your chickens, *you're not home yet …*

Eight Tempests, their dark deadly shapes emerging from the haze at low level, burst out over the boundary, and Rose saw the boxy airfield buildings, a large hanger and scattered aircraft while before him, a parked fighter.

He lined up Sugar's nose and fired a one-second burst, deadly dark and white blooms of fire and smoke already blotting the air above as the defences awoke to the danger and opened fire.

Even as his cannon shells ploughed towards and through the fighter, Sheep blurted an oath over the R/T in his headphones. 'Crikey-bollocks! We're at Coesfeld's dummy! Keep your head down, for Christ's sake, and get out of it sharpish!'

As with too many Luftwaffe airfields, a second fake airfield was constructed close nearby to confuse and draw attackers from the real thing, surrounding the dummy with flak positions. Despite knowing the area well, at low-level it was easy to drift off-course and end up attacking the wrong place.

The dummy airfield at Coesfeld-Velen was only three kilometres from the real airfield of Coesfeld, and with the cloud lowering, diminished visibility, shifting winds and the first snowflakes falling in the gathering haze, the conditions conspired against the Tempests.

However, as the barrage of flak opened up, the blooming layer of shell bursts were so close above Rose that it felt as if he were beneath a forest of flash-bulbs, brown smoke billowing and hiding the dirty clouds above, the ripple of bangs crashing against the thunder of her Sabre.

As a flak trap and with no real warplanes or vehicles to worry about, the flak barrels could be pushed lower, leaving the men in the Tempests little if any leeway as they blasted across the dummy airfield.

The stick shuddering and jumping as he fought to hold her steady, with the shockwaves from the flak above pressing her down against the opposing buoyant cushion of ground effect which was pushing up against her, throttles forward, eyes searching for the boundary, a prayer on his lips, wanting desperately to look at her picture, to check the bear and the pebble were with him even though he knew they were, stomach muscles rigid and buttocks wet with sweat.

He pushed Sugar as low as he dared, and he ducked down as an AA shell burst close and he felt her slide to starboard, *Bang!* A touch on rudder, hold her, and then a second, *BANG!* An even closer pulse of concussive pressure, the shock wave forcefully sliding Sugar sideways and down, and she yawed to port and he quickly applied right rudder to correct as his insides lurched.

The enemy guns were flashing their message of hate at them from across the far boundary, and the men in RAF blue crouched low in their cockpits as shot and shell and shrapnel surged in a bowel-wrenching wave towards them, sanctuary beyond the guns as they raced into the ravening enemy fire.

God! I'm so low! The ground was terrifyingly close, and as if in confirmation, just for a bladder-loosening instant, the blades of her propeller, just half an inch or so of the gleaming disc of her spinning blade tips, caught the grass below, gouging out a furrow of fresh earth and shredded grass, the Tempest jerking and enveloped momentarily in a smeared cloud of brown.

He pulled back instinctively as the tips of her propeller kissed soil to gain clearance; his heart jerked to his throat in fear, mouth fearfully dry, and feeling the crust of undigested crust of bread move up to press against his breastbone again.

Had it been concrete hard standing or tarmac it might have been curtains for him, but the softer soil was far more forgiving.

Initially mistaking the loose dirt and the propeller's growl as a hit on Sugar, the momentary loss of light as earth plumed over Sugar in a swell of faux smoke, Rose heard himself whimper and thought he was finished, that he was dying.

Then, realising he wasn't and grateful for it, he pushed down on the surging spike of terror and anxiously scanned the controls, but knew immediately from the way Sugar felt and sounded that despite the momentary contact all was well with her.

His bowels had pitched with his heart in the evanescent loss of light, and now his eyes sought the dummy airfield's boundary, *how far?* Estimating how much more he must endure, throat too sticky to swallow, he felt the light spatter and fleck of dust and dirt against her just for a fleeting moment before Sugar was through the cloud, and he was grateful that the big air intake had been outside the expanding halo of ballooning dirt and dust and she'd not ingested any.

If stones and soil had been funnelled in and wrecked Sugar's Sabre, so low and at this speed he would have augered in, feeling nothing and knowing only an instant of shock before the eternity of darkness as she would have dug a final resting place for them both in this German field so far from home.

Panic tugged at him as tracer flickered horribly close above the canopy, *I've got to get out of here!*

Rose pushed her Sabre into full +24 boost; the extra boost provided by the 150 Octane in Sugar's tanks pushed him back hard into his seat and he half-closed his eyes as a driving gush of sparks and flame poured from Sugar's exhaust stacks, making it appear as if she were aflame.

The sudden disappearance of Rose's Tempest within an all-encompassing and flowing dirty brown-black cloud and the sudden torrent of fiery sparks must have deceived the enemy gunners, believing that Sugar was mortally damaged and that they must have shot him down.

With the gunners believing Rose was done, the severity of the flak seemed to diminish almost to nothing as gun barrels were trained after the other Tempests and far fewer shells were blasted towards Sugar.

He pushed her hard for the boundary, jinking hard with his heart in his mouth, a flaring banner of light as one of his men was hit, a gout of painfully white flame and the wounded Tempest was a burning torch ploughing into the ground, the harsh glare of the explosion horribly bright amongst the glittering flak, gouts of brown earth thrown into the air and cascading over the nearest gunners.

Sheep's cry, thin with strain. 'They got Sparky! The bastards!'

His only thought was for deliverance, knowing that he had already lost one of his number but, desperate to survive, Rose fired a long burst of cannon fire to distract the enemy as the boundary drew close, seeing his explosive cannon shells hack into the contours of the ersatz airfield facilities before him, hoping that his shells did damage and sobbing into his mask without realising he was doing so as the glittering, glowing Nazi hatred criss-crossed the air with a web of destruction.

And then the pretence of the 'buildings' had blurred past, a mock flak tower sliding beside Sugar's starboard wingtip with the real guns falling behind and receding fast, the sky open before and above him as she spurred beyond the devastating burning lattice of shell bursts, only the occasional line of glowing tracer now arcing short behind.

Nothing in his mirror and no bandits above!

Hunched forward, eyes on the ground ahead and the enemy sky above, his body tight with fear and tension, Rose cried out aloud as the surviving Tempests burst out from the Killing Ground and back out over onto the open fields. '*Oh, thank God!*'

Blurred ground and just the twisting, racing shapes slipping across the undulations of his companions as they fled the spider's parlour, one of their number reduced to glowing embers and ash behind them.

Shaken to the core by the close call and sitting in a holed Tempest shuddering from the damage of a torn wingtip, Sheep decided against rounding off the trip with a visit to Rheine-Hopsten to check for lone aircraft in the circuit as originally planned, desperately keen instead to get his new Wing Commander back to Volkel, and himself around a mug of tea and a sandwich or two.

They had been lucky. Had there been the number of flak cannon at the dummy which would have been found over a major airfield like Rheine, it could have been far worse. Doing the same thing at Rheine would have guaranteed the loss of at least half their number.

As Volkel appeared ahead of them through the haze and falling snow, Rose glanced at her picture, feeling the emptiness caused by her absence and the distance between them, spirit low despite the miracle of survival in the face of the dummy's flak trap.

His first trip as a Wing Leader had been a close call, survival and death separated by a hair's breadth of good fortune, but somehow Rose's luck had held once more.

Merciful God, thank you.

Sheep was mortified, his oil-smeared and greasy face still ashen from the hair-raising experience at the dummy airfield, and his words came out in a rush of apology and recrimination. 'I'm sorry, sir, took a wrong turn, must've misjudged the headwind. Didn't mean to take you over Coesfeld's dummy. I thought you were a goner when your kite disappeared inside all that smoke and dust.'

The normally ebullient Australian Squadron Leader was uncomfortable and uncharacteristically crestfallen.

Rose wearily cuffed away sweat with his sleeve. 'It happens, Sheep, we were just pushed adrift by the winds, it happens. It's just one of those things.' He was grateful for having survived, but his relief was soured by the bitter loss of a young man he had barely known but who had been one of his own. The misery in Sheep's eyes visibly showed his pain.

Just one of those things.

Another dreaded letter to write to broken souls, another letter to justify somehow the ending of dreams and happiness. 'Sheep, tell me about young Stewart? I need to write to his people.'

Sheep nodded soberly. 'Of course, sir. He was a good lad.'

They all are, chum, but we only truly realise their value when we lose them.

Feeling utterly drained, Rose stuck his hands into his pockets so the others could not see them shaking as they walked back to the dispersals hut for debrief.

Behind them, Jelly surveyed Sugar's dirt and smoke-stained fuse-lage, shook his head, and called out quietly to his friend, already reloading the Tempest's ammunition trays. 'Blimey, Fred, I think we've got a real fire-eater here!'

Chapter 7

My darling Moll,

It's been just a day since I left home, but oh, how much I miss you and my cheeky wee puddings already! Give them both a big kiss and a hug from me, will you?

And that bloody awful hound! How is the daft old thing? Still slobbering over everything, I'll bet! Please thank Noreen for her lovely tomato chutney and the salt/spice mix, does wonders with an oily powdered egg omelette! The others are envious of me, but daren't ask their snooty WingCo to share!

I shan't ask anyone to kiss you for me though, my wonderful love, because that's my job alone, and how lucky I am for that! I'm not sharing!!!

I've got a smashing bunch of lads, and will tell you more when I can, but I've also discovered that my French is not half as good as I fancied!

We had the most atrocious breakfast today, never seen the like, had yellow chunks of something which tasted of nothing. Thought it was cheese, but the Lord alone knows what it really was! And the burned soya link sausages—urk!

Made me feel quite misty for one of 'Shiny' Dewar's incredible creations! Can you imagine? Ruddy heck! But at least Shiny tried to make his grub look edible! I think even dearest Daffie might have turned her nose up at what I had!

Shouldn't joke about it, though. We're lucky to have it. The locals have had a bit of a rough time under Jerry, and you can see it in their faces. The poor devils look quite brutalised, gaunt and half-starved. They call it 'Hongerwinter', and it's been a brutal famine for the poor things. They were even eating Sugar beets and Tulip bulbs, just to survive.

Jerry has so much to answer for.

There's a little girl we see, eight or nine years old, I think, sitting on a shabby bed in her front garden, always smiling and waving at us, bless her. Makes me realise how lucky we are that Jerry never got across the water. The boys make sure she gets plenty of sweets and chocolates—her teeth must be dreadful!

God, Moll, how I miss you! How I need one of your 'Extra Special Hugs'! I really need to touch you and draw in your scent (even if my little Millie has just been sick down your back!).

I love you. I love you more than I can say.

Darling, it's been a hectic day, and I'm quite worn out, so I'll be off to bed shortly. I've got a narrow wooden bed about three feet wide in a dark little room.

I've been spoiled rotten by sharing that lovely big, soft mattress with you these last wonderful weeks. I feel so very far from you now.

Darling Moll, thank you for blessing my life with yours, and for being my wife. I reckon I'm the most fortunate man alive!

My eyelids are dropping now, my precious, darling love, so I'll bid you adieu for now.

I'm going to rush to my bed to lay my head down, so that I can close my eyes and dream of you.

Je veux tellement être avec toi, mon amour.

Harry,

x-x-x-x

(A kiss for each of my babies, but two just for you!)

Chapter 8

Gabby and Sheep were waiting for him the next morning at breakfast.

Weather conditions had worsened overnight, the Met officer promising more low cloud and flurries of snow, so flying had been cancelled. It would give Rose an opportunity to wander about his Wing and get to know his people.

Standing self-consciously with his two squadron commanders were Micky Lynch (properly dressed this time) and the intense young Frenchman with the staring ragdoll.

Gabby half-bowed respectfully, and Rose tried not to look amused. *At least he isn't kissing me on both cheeks.* 'Sir, we have each allocated you a regular wingman for when you fly. This is Francois Marais and Amélie.'

Rose inclined his head as the youngster also responded with a half-bow, pointing first to the doll and then himself. 'Amélie, *enchante monsieur. Et je suis* Marais.'

By unusual happenstance, Molly had chosen to name their newborn daughter Amelia, and now he wondered who it was that named the ragdoll.

'*Un honneur, Colonel.*' The boy's voice was soft, but (as expected) Amélie said nothing, her button eyes regarding him emotionlessly.

Oh God, does the lad even speak English?

As if reading his Wing Commander's mind, Marais diffidently continued, 'I also answer to Frankie, sir. Amélie is pleased also to make your acquaintance.'

Il parle Anglais! Thank God for that! He nodded to the doll, feeling daft. 'A pleasure, Amélie. Frankie it shall be.'

Gabby indicated Lynch. 'And of course you know Herr Leutnant Micky Lynch, *l'imposteur allemand.*'

Rose nodded sternly. 'Micky. Good to see you properly dressed.'

Micky smiled bashfully and Rose thought he might even curtsy. 'Sir.'

'I'm afraid there'll be no flying today, lads. Hopefully it will give me an opportunity to find my way around and get to know the men.'

He thought of the dummy airfield again, a young man lost for no gain whatsoever.

'Gentlemen? I'm not sure what you've been told to do before, but there'll be no attacks on flak traps. No gain, no point.'

They said nothing but looked relieved. He had not dismissed his two new wingmen so that they, too, heard, and would be sure to tell the others via the grapevine that the new Wing Leader was not going to throw them away on senseless attacks.

The smell of fatty bacon frying and burned toast was overwhelming the seminary's background scent of tobacco, sweat and cologne, yet despite this Rose felt his stomach grumble. 'In the meantime, join me for breakfast?'

The bad weather limited operations for a further three days, and it was only later on in the day on 11 December that Rose flew his next sortie, this time a strong patrol comprising two flights of eight

Tempests at eight thousand feet, and another flight led by Sheep as high cover at twelve thousand.

They were circling ten miles from Rheine, hoping to intercept jets taking off to attack the day's USAAF raid on Wilhelmshaven.

Here in the sunshine, two thousand feet above the heaped cloud layer, Rose felt the contentment of a fighter pilot with altitude and good visibility. Having spent much of the past year and a half on ground-attack sorties, it was a pleasure to return to the freedom of clean open air.

Group now dictated that 2TAF's Tempest squadrons (while still to remain available for ground-attack missions) would now be used primarily to help maintain Allied dominance in the air. They would fly clean, unencumbered by bomb racks or rocket rails.

In the bright cold sky, with an unbroken cover of cloud below and an early afternoon sun lowering in the sky, they flew in a loose formation of two finger-fours and bobbing in altitude to confound the radar-guided heavy flak which might be below, with Gabby and Rose each leading a flight of eight.

The expanse of heaped and towering sun-limned cloud surfaces reminded Rose of the fluffy eiderdown blanket on their bed at home, and *that* reminded him of Molly lying on it, delicious curves edged in gold in the early morning light; but before they distracted him further, he banished the memories to enjoy at a more opportune time.

When he was back in his narrow wooden cot at the seminary tonight (*please God*), he would allow himself the indulgence to think of her, but now was not the time or the place for such diversions.

Much darker grey clouds were stacking higher to the east, promising yet more snow for later in the day, and in the far distance, beyond their cloudscape, the faint smudge that were dispersing banks of heavy black smoke, spreading eastwards with the wind, the legacy of German cities burning after reaping the whirlwind.

Rose found himself endlessly glancing towards the sun, the whispers of anxiety gnawing softly at his mind. Control's far-seeing radar would warn him of danger, yet he could still feel the crawling unease prickle at his skin and the flutter in his chest.

In the remoteness beyond, up between the high, tumbling cumulus peaks, myriad faint white lines scraped eastwards, pale across the cobalt sky, what seemed like hundreds of USAAF bombers heading into Germany. And even more numerous, the thinner streaks of their long-range escorts at higher altitude. Beneath the carpet of cloud, the Nazi airbases would be hives of activity as fighters were readied and launched.

German radar would have already warned Rheine that there were enemy fighters nearby, so it was likely that they would also launch a defensive screen of piston-engine driven fighters to keep the Tempests occupied before the jets were sent after the bombers.

It was certain more were in the air already as fighter sweeps to clear the airspace protectively for the jets in their vulnerable take-off and climbs.

Like many Wing Leaders, Rose had incorporated his initials into his callsign, and just as Douglas Bader had chosen 'Dogsbody' earlier in the war, so Harry Rose was 'Hotspur'.

But now, with a Free French squadron in his Wing, Rose wondered what the young Frenchmen under his command thought of it.

The fact that they flew with the long scarlet banner of St Denis, the *Oriflamme*, painted onto their kites (in addition to the Cross of Lorraine) which warned of taking no prisoners, but also suggested that they had not quite forgotten about the Hundred Years' War, and

Rose hoped they would not resent him for the hundreds of French dead and wounded at Mers-el-Kébir, or the French civilians killed before and after D-Day. At least during Operation Torch, the Allied invasion of French North Africa, the Vichy French opposing the landings were Axis forces and the enemy.

And of course Molly had been less than happy with his choice, for Sir Henry Percy of Northumberland had died while fighting against the Crown at the Battle of Shrewsbury (killed by the future King Henry V, if Moll's beloved Shakespeare were to be believed).

Perhaps I ought to have chosen Molly's suggestion after all? He whispered the unfamiliar word into his mask, *Hamster*. She'd laughed and hugged him when Rose (cross with himself for not knowing) had asked her what a hamster was. He had hoped it was something noble and grand, like a griffin or a dragon perhaps, but it turned out to be a tiny animal with golden fur, rather akin to a rat without a tail.

A *rat*, for goodness sake!

Feeling slightly miffed, the innocent amusement on her lovely face pricking irrationally at his ego, Rose peevishly rejected the suggestion out of hand.

So Hotspur he remained. (Granny had not been particularly helpful, first suggesting 'Harem', then proposing 'Hairyarse', 'Hitler', 'Himmler' and 'Hermann', all of which received a very crude and direct response not usually given to acting Group Captains by acting Wing Commanders.)

Here and now, though, he wondered if he had made a mistake. His French boys were a touch more mercurial than his easy-going Aussies, but nonetheless, they were a good bunch of lads who got along and worked very well together.

Rose keyed his microphone, eyes restlessly scanning the perfidious blue grandeur, slowing his breath to try and ease his beating heart, lips dry from anxiety and pure oxygen, licked once with an even drier tongue. 'Hotspur leader to Kenway, airborne with eighteen Tempests, what's the form?'

Kenway was 83 Group's operations control centre.

'Kenway to Hotspur Leader, many low-level contacts over Rheine. Stand by.'

A moment's flutter of his heart and an anxious tightening of his stomach muscles, and then the apprehension was replaced by the overwhelming exhilaration of the coming combat, a yearning glance at her picture, cupping the pocket containing the little bear and pebble in his palm for a moment for reassurance.

Lord God, keep me lucky …

Sure enough, a scant thirty seconds after Kenway's response, enemy fighters began to emerge distantly from the uneven cloud layer, tiny metal slivers glittering like needles as they sliced through, one, two, six, more, until there were around eleven or twelve of the tiny shapes.

'Hotspur Leader to Marengo, turning to starboard.'

Flashes of light as the ragged formation of enemy fighters banked towards Rose's sixteen Tempests, each flight of eight in line abreast, with Gabby's Marengo flight in line abreast now falling back to a mile astern of Rose's Hotspur Flight.

With their own fighters in the area and soon to be indistinguishable from the RAF fighters above cloud when battle was joined, the defences would hold fire so the risk from Rheine's flak was lessened for the moment.

The enemy were a tight group of black dots against the lighter white and grey, their formation opening and spreading out now, racing fast from a lower altitude towards them, engines at full throttle pulling dark exhaust trails behind them.

Sheep: 'Hobart Lead to Hotspur Leader, more bandits climbing out of cloud ahead of you and below, need a hand?' Rose scowled as a second group of enemy fighters sliced through cloud behind the first.

Damn it!

'Maintain position, Hobart. Your chums won't be long.' Voice calm despite the adrenaline spiking through him, a quick glance all around, still half expecting more of the enemy to bubble out of cloud to one side or behind the Tempests.

Sheep's concern and disappointment was obvious, but Rose was right, with their diversionary fighters engaging the Tempests, the jets would not be too far behind as they launched to intercept the USAAF bombers.

The plan was for Rose, Gabby and their sixteen Tempests to distract and engage with the covering enemy fighters while Sheep and his flight overhead would swoop down onto the Messerschmitt 262s as they took off for the bombers, slow and vulnerable as the jet engines spooled up in the first part of their sortie.

Safety to 'off' and gunsight switched on, a tiny adjustment so it was not too bright. A quick scan of the instruments, mirror, and another sweeping glance across the immediate sky.

'Kenway to Hotspur Leader, two bandit formations active over Rheine.' Rose didn't bother responding, grateful that the sun was behind them and muttering a silent prayer that no bandits were hiding in it, for Sheep and Kenway would have warned him if there were any lurking in the light.

While head-on passes with high closing speeds were terrifying, a small target profile and varying approach angles were not ideal for calculating drop and deflection to the enemy and also minimised the window in which to take aim when compared with an attack from astern of the enemy.

The collision of Rose's Hurricane with a Bf109 back in 1940 remained a disturbing memory, but in reality the chance of colliding with an approaching enemy aircraft was unlikely. Knowing this did not ease his apprehension, and he hunched in anticipation of the coming pass.

The enemy aircraft in the first group were dangerously close now, growing shapes visible as the snub-nosed Focke-Wulf 190As spread apart in matching line abreast to counter the open battle formation of the widely distanced Free French fighters of Rose's Hotspur Flight.

No more time …

Radial engines looming, sun lustred spinning propeller discs and swirling propeller hubs, vivid lines of tracer and cannon fire already reaching out towards them, silvery shafts and smoke trails twirling and spiralling, and Rose cringed behind the apparent protection of Sugar's powerful Sabre engine, thumb smashing down hard onto the gun button.

A booming clap of sound above the thunder of Sugar's engine and a blur of shadow over her as the bandit seared past, Sugar buffeted roughly in the enemy slipstream and slowed by recoil, and he fought to hold her steady as she careered her way through the thrashing turmoil of air.

A moment of exhilaration in his survival, Frankie (and Amélie) still on his wing, black smoke trailing behind them and he feared they had been hit but realised immediately that the smoke was from a 190 as it went the other way.

'*I have it! Il est mort!*' A cry of triumph over the R/T. Frankie must have got one!

You jammy blighter!

Gabby's Marengo Flight following behind would pile into that first lot of Jerry and protect the Hotspurs from the 190s reversing after them.

'Hotspur Flight, stay with me.' His voice sounded reedy and high in the earphones, breathless as he gasped in more oxygen, knowing that after passing through Rose's formation, the first wave of 190s would be in disarray, meaning to turn after Hotspur Flight but unable to as Marengo Flight's approach meant to do so would be disaster for Jerry.

'*Oui,* Hotspur Leader.' Curtly, as Gabby engaged the enemy.

He did not look back, knowing that Gabby's eight Tempests were creating further disarray as his Frenchmen turned hard after the first wave of bandits, Rose knowing his tail was safe for a moment or so, confidently facing the second wave.

In his mirror the first group of 190s were turning desperately, the enemy formation exploding outwards, dirty streaks of exhaust smoke curving in wild patterns behind them, and Gabby's men would be in amongst them, but the second group of enemy fighters, a mixed gaggle of the longer-nosed 190Ds and more of the snubby 190As, twelve or fifteen of them, *God help us,* were already closing with Hotspur Flight.

In the cloud over Rheine he glimpsed multiple straight lines of dirty smoke heading northwards, the faraway air torn through by Jumo engines, and a gleeful shout over the R/T. 'Hobart Flight attacking! Hobart Red section go after the leading four, Blue with me, second group! Safeties off, hit the drongos hard!'

Mirror, clear, eyes sweeping behind, around and ahead, beneath the tails of the Tempests on either side, the first wave of 190s no threat, their formation broken and their pilots fighting for their lives against his Free French boys.

No time to check on Sheep's faraway evolving fight for he had his own to face.

A second gaggle of bandits arrayed in line abreast like the first before them were closing alarmingly fast, one 190D directly before him, and Rose resisted the shrieking urge to cower again; his eyes focussed into the reflector gunsight, thumb pushing down hard again on the gun button, firmly holding onto the control column and trying to ignore the reaching streaks of enemy hardware lancing and curling towards him, forcing himself upright against the instinct to duck as once more Sugar's cannon hammered out a lethal tattoo.

Incredibly, unbelievably, three piercing flashes strobing bright and harsh on the rapidly closing bandit, *flash-flash-flash,* two explosive stars erupting at the root of one wing and another on the cowling, a sudden puff of smoke and a burst of flame, the long nose pulling up and the 190D crabbing sideways slightly, dirty blots burgeoning around the onrushing humped shape and snatched carelessly away by the slipstream, another flash of flame and the smear of smoke, the bandit looming enormously in the windscreen for a heart-stopping instant as another of Sugar's shells exploded against the 190's port horizontal stabiliser, ripping it off completely.

With cordite and terror thickly coating a throat bereft of all moisture, Rose jerked himself backwards, unable to even cry out, the enemy fighter filling Sugar's windscreen and beginning to roll upwards and to starboard, the swastika on its tail huge and slewing so close to the canopy that he thought it must surely catch the Perspex and then onwards to rip off Sugar's vertical stabiliser.

Something *spanged!* off Sugar's cowling, the sharp sound and bump making his heart lurch. The discordant grumble of the enemy's BMW powerplant a burst of sound heard momentarily over the steady thunder of Sugar's Sabre, the enemy blotting out the light for an instant; the fear of collision ripped bloody claws down the back of his spine.

But there was no neck-wrenching impact, no moment of disbelieving comprehension, no out-of-control final tumble in the final confused seconds of life to an indifferent ground, no gale of howling air whipping blood across broken glass.

Instead, Sugar continued to fly onwards, ploughing powerfully through the tumultuous air of the enemy's wake as if nothing had happened.

Nerves screaming and heart clamouring madly from the near miss, Rose sucked in a lungful of pure oxygen and hauled Sugar around hard, the harness cutting painfully into his shoulders, hoping that Marengo Flight had broken up the first gaggle of 190s, although Gabby's eight would now have the second set of 190s on them.

Ahead, a single 190A, turning hard and rolling inverted as it caught sight of the approaching Tempests, dived down into cloud. In the far distance another fighter, flashing as light caught its side, too far away to tell if it a friendly or not. As ever, one second the sky was filled with wheeling fighters and in the blink of an eye the packed sky had emptied.

'Hotspur leader to Marengo and Hobart'—a rasping croak from a throat dry as dust, swallow and cough it out—'we've done what we came to do, give Jerry a last crack then break for home.'

Frankie (and Amélie) were still nearby and in close to Sugar as Rose pulled Sugar around. Already the dirty grey of cloud was close enough to touch.

Thank God for cloud!

Mirror, clear.

Eyes around, no one behind, no sign of Red section, one Tempest disappearing into the cloud below, chasing a Hun or out of control?

Above, a pair of Tempests were chasing a single FW190D, twisting and turning and boxed in, distant flickers of light where others fought hard some distance away, veiled amongst the grey, heavy peaks, a confusion of shouts and cries over the R/T, two ragged trails of dirty smoke disappearing into the cloud but no sign whether they had been his or theirs.

Of the one he had winged in the head-on pass, there was no sign, but half a mile away and at the same height a single snub-nosed 190A turning away, its wings waggling uncertainly, a simple innocent, just asking to be attacked.

Rose had seen this picture before and he craned his neck around to check above and behind, eyes picking out four more bandits curling around the peaks of stacked cloud, closely followed by yet another pair, turning a mile and a half behind; already they were at his eight o'clock.

Frankie had seen the trap too, the boy's voice urgent yet measured. 'Hotspur Leader from Two, six bandits, *monsieur,* eight o'clock!'

The poor little innocent singleton flying all alone in front was the tethered goat to draw them in, the six 190s closing in a mile behind the Tempests, the wily hunters stalking their prey, and no other friendlies to lend a hand nearby.

Sod this for a game of soldiers.

'Hotspur Leader to Two, time to go down.'

'*Oui,* Leader.'

Not liking the odds, Rose pushed down her nose and bent forward the throttle, checking to see that trusty Frankie was still with him, knowing that they would out-dive the stalking 190As easily.

With six of them hunting Rose and Frankie, the odds were piled against their two Tempests, for at this altitude the turning circles of the RAF and Luftwaffe aircraft were reasonably similar, but the Tempests had a speed advantage over the enemy of around 50mph and were faster in the dive.

The pursuers were too far behind as the two Tempests plunged earthwards through the cloud, and Rose breathed a sigh of relief that they had managed to both draw off the covering force of 190s to allow Sheep to bounce the jets, and in so doing, given the 190s a bloody nose.

He could at least claim a damaged, perhaps a probable, and it appeared that Frankie had scored a confirmed victory.

Hopefully the boy's camera would have recorded it.

Let's just see if there's any action beneath cloud …

Chapter 9

They emerged from cloud at just under five thousand feet, the light in this overcast world of low bellied cloud was leaden after the brightness above, and Rose was grateful that they were not near enough to enemy light flak for it to have a go at them.

He had feared that they might have wandered into the defensive flak perimeter around Rheine, but fortune was on their side, and they were closer to nearby Emsdetten than Rheine.

The Luftwaffe airfield was some distance north-east of them, faint in the haze, its three concrete runways, each almost a mile long, forming a dark triangle in the greying snow-covered landscape, its two smaller grassy satellite airfields flat areas amongst the trees beyond Rheine's boundary, connected to the main airfield by just visible taxiways.

On the ground, three crashed aircraft were burning, oily black smoke billowing into the air from their pyres, burned spatters and embers on the dirty grey-white ground, a parachute low down close to the ground, and he was heartened to see it was Luftwaffe yellow, not the bright white fabric of RAF parachutes, feeling gratification in this confirmation that at least one of the enemy had been downed.

In the distance eastwards, something was falling and burning wickedly, a flaming torch well alight and snaking slowly downwards out of cloud, a spiral banner of thick black marking its uncontrolled descent.

Frankie's voice, crackling urgently in his earphones. 'Hotspur Two to Leader, four bandits, one o'clock, heading away, two thousand feet below!'

Rose's eyes slashed down to port; automatically pulling back on the stick to bring Sugar out of her dive, turning after the new enemy.

Four FW190As, unevenly spaced together in a wavering finger-four formation, the fighters too widely spaced, three silver shapes speckled a delicate pale blue and the fourth incongruous in a heavily worn uniform dark green livery, the short ugly snouts of the little fighters pointing towards Rheine.

Bloody hell! A quick glance around, but the space around them was clear, his mirror (*thank God!*) empty.

The six hunters above, if they were still chasing after Rose's Tempests, had not yet emerged from the clouds. By lucky happenstance, the Tempests had emerged from cloud in a perfect attacking position behind and above this new enemy quartet.

A few seconds earlier and they would have appeared ahead of the bandits and before the enemy guns. Luck makes the difference.

The silly sods are flying as if they are at an air display! All absorbed on staying in formation instead of watching their tails and each other.

And then it dawned on him. These four weren't veterans, that much was obvious, the uneven formation betraying their greenness. This was a Luftwaffe training flight which had inadvertently found itself in the midst of a knife fight between Rheine's covering fighters and 63's Tempests.

With so many of the enemy pilots continuing to fly until they were wounded or killed, Germany's Fighter arm was filling its emptying ranks with bomber pilots or inexperienced new boys. And now some idiot on the ground had left them up there rather than recalling them to safety when Rose's Tempests had first appeared.

Yet how else can the uninitiated find the experience needed to survive but in battle?

Whatever qualms he might have felt years before about killing these inexpert German boys was quashed by the sure knowledge that they must not be allowed the chance to become experienced veterans.

Mystifyingly, they had not been warned of enemy air activity by Rheine, an unforgiveable mistake, which would cost them dearly.

Rose had seen enough of his own new boys torn from the sky by an unfeeling enemy, smooth-faced boys killed within hours of having flown in from Blighty, and had himself been lucky enough to survive the first few uncertain sorties to gain the skills and experience required to improve one's chances of survival.

There could be no mercy nor remorse, no hesitation when the prize of victory they fought for was so valuable.

This was no game, and the enemy fought without remorse or humanity.

His instincts screamed, *go home!* But his mirror was empty and they were perfectly placed to smash down onto the little group of 190s, an opportunity too good to miss, and Rose eased Sugar after the bandits, staying high, just below the cloud, eyes alternating between the surroundings and his mirror, mindful that any moment the bandits from above might slide through the cloud and they would have to run, and as they got closer to Rheine, they got ever closer to the flak of the airfield's deadly flak corridor.

The silly buggers must be asleep!

'One burst, Hotspur Two, you take the port element wingman, I'll take the starboard one, then get down to zero feet and head for home at full throttle, OK?'

'*Oui,* received, Hotspur Leader, *bonne chance!*'

Instantly, Frankie tipped over and away, lunging into a tighter banking turn towards the 190 on the far left of the formation, and Rose cast his eyes once more into the mirror, heart thumping.

God help us, but how impatient and eager the youngster sounded! No tremors there, just eagerness for the hunt.

But still there was nothing behind or above and, reassured, Rose pushed Sugar into a steep dive after the enemy, edging slightly to starboard for a three-quarter astern shot from the bandit's five o'clock, feeling the rush and the clawing anxiety that these unfortunate amateurs might yet see him before it was too late, although if they fought as poorly as they kept a lookout, he was in little danger from them.

And still he feared the emergence of wraith-like shapes slipping through the clouds, swarming into his mirror, but there was still only empty sky behind as Sugar carved down after her victim.

Rose felt his shoulders tightening in anticipation of imagined cannon shells punching through Sugar, the prickling of imminent danger, and he knew they were almost out of time.

The dark green airframe of his target was beginning to lag behind its silver companions, its shape drawing closer before him, the swept-back canopy creating the fuselage's hunched shape, and he throttled back and pulled back into a gentle dive, so he would not overshoot until the distance between them was less than three hundred yards, the Luftwaffe pilot still looking at his element leader, unaware of the danger, a large yellow number 5 bright on its side.

Sighting carefully and leading the bandit by a pinch above and half a fuselage length ahead for deflection in his gunsight, chaffing at the tightness of his mask against his sweating cheeks and the clamminess of his shirt, the thrill of a perfect bounce …

He felt the urgency grip him but took a deep breath and eased back on the throttle further before pressing down firmly on the gun button.

Sugar's four 20 mm Hispano cannon thumped out a ruinous fusillade of explosive shells, and his estimated deflection, born from years of experience and against a target flying straight and level was faultless, correcting as she slowed from the recoil, the spraying fan of hot metal peppering the space occupied by the bandit.

Firing a rapid series of bursts, gradually closing the distance between them to one hundred and fifty yards.

The cannon shells ripped across the short space between them to splash and ripple explosively along the enemy fighter from the cowling just in front of the cockpit back to the rudder, the clean lines of the trim little fighter ravaged beneath a sparkling curtain of white flashes and hazed by flakes of fragmented paint and metal, the sheer force of the broadside of cannon shells pushing the enemy fighter physically to port, one wingtip rising as if imploring for mercy where there would be none.

The image of the hapless 190 was imprinted in his mind as he eased Sugar into a gentle bank to port, pushing the stick further forward, the 190's canopy shattering into whirling crystalline powder amongst the blooming smear of metal shreds and paint flakes and smoke, snatched away by the slipstream, torn fragments and panels blown or ripped off as Sugar's merciless cannon fire ravaged devastation across it, a sudden sheet of searing fire, flaring like a giant flashbulb and expanding to contain the German fighter completely, until it was a flaming torch curving earthwards.

That crawling sensation again, fear gnawing, stronger now and tightening in the back of his neck as the hairs on it rose.

Mirror? Clear.

Bloody Hell! Four bandits seen through oil and smoke-tainted Perspex, half a mile or less ahead and heading towards Rheine, ghostly shapes sliding out like shadows from the cloud above, while a quarter of a mile behind *them*, a trailing pair of 190s, pale blue undersides streaked and stained by dirt, oil and gun smoke.

The pursuing hunters still stalking their prey, but already too late.

God willing …

He felt an insane urge to pull her nose around and up to starboard, to lunge at full throttle to blast red-hot high explosive destruction into one of the hunters, but it would be utter madness to do so, for he would be caught up in the middle of all the others. If he did as his instincts cried out, he *might* get away, but it was just as likely he would be trapped by the others.

Time to get out of it …

'Run, Hotspur Two! Go! Get out! *Quickly now!*'

And he was already rolling Sugar to port and downwards, full throttle, and greedily sucking oxygen into his lungs, gasping it down against his tightly rebelling throat as the pressure of the dive pushed him back, neck and chest aching with his stomach muscles tensed and buttocks painfully tight, the shattered 190 he had smashed a guttering bright ball of flame twisting untidily earthwards and away, trailing an uneven trail of oily black smoke, shedding incandescent cinders and burning fragments as it went down.

The leader of the formation they had just hammered finally awoke to the danger, and now he climbed away trailing thick exhaust smoke at full throttle.

Beyond him the leader of the second element was also climbing, and he too was trailing smoke, but the hot dirty flow was streaming back from a battered engine cowling streaming flame, and it seemed Frankie must have given it a quick burst which had connected for the German pilot was pushing back his teardrop canopy as the flow of smoke thickened, while further below his wingman's 190 was spinning slowly downwards, minus its entire tail assembly.

God! Looked like Frankie had given both of 'his' bandits in the second element a thrashing!

The trailing pair of the hunters' formation of six had noticed them and were themselves banking hard around, reversing terrifyingly tight as they caught sight of the battle behind, the four ahead of them matching them almost instantly, but they were banking to starboard; the Tempests were diving away to port, increasing the separation between them.

And he was turning, banking harder to port, pushing forward the throttle as the surge of triumph was swamped by the urgent need to flee, the sure knowledge that danger was creeping up on him, that if he remained any longer he would not return.

Superstitious nonsense, to be sure, but a sensible man dare not tempt fate.

Frankie's Tempest, G-Gilbert, was a slowing shadow against the cold grey-white backcloth below, levelling out low and turning gently, waiting to reform with his leader and ready to support him from pursuit if required.

Forming up, the two Tempests blasted back into Holland at full throttle, sweat trickling down their bodies, throats sore and parched from pure oxygen, cordite and tension, tired eyes sweeping repeatedly from mirror to sky and back again, grateful survivors of the deadly German skies.

He daren't ease his focus on the potential dangers around them, eyes remaining busy, and comforted by the soft bumps formed by the bear and pebble in his pocket, he placed his fingertips on her picture, feeling her nearness in his mind, grateful for his survival.

Lord my God, thank you for our salvation.

All but one of Sheep's men had already landed when Rose and Frankie entered Volkel's circuit, the missing man a young NCO named Rogers, from Cairns in Queensland.

Rogers had chosen to strafe Rheine with boyish enthusiasm, but the outermost ring of flak had cooled his ardour by blowing a sizeable hole in one wing. He would return twenty minutes later, thanking his lucky stars to have survived the flak, swarming fighters and the perilous trip back, only to be savaged far worse by his irate squadron commander.

Gabby's flight was landing as Rose taxied into dispersals, and Jelly was all smiles as Rose held up one finger and winked, throat so dry he could only croak, 'A 190, near Rheine.' He remembered the 190 he had damaged in the second head-on wave. 'One damaged, too. Thanks to you and the lads, Jelly.'

Sheep was standing beside Sugar's wing as Rose jumped down, muscles aching and greasy with sweat, shoulders, spine and backside aching, desperately craving a cup of tea and a good long hot soak, followed by a short kip.

God, I'm exhausted, must be getting old …

Nonetheless, Rose fixed a smile onto his face. 'How'd it go, chum?'

Sheep was cheerful, their interception of the Me262s a resounding success. 'It was a bonzer do, sir!' he gloated. 'Two confirmed, two probable and two damaged! Moggy Cato and I damaged another but the drongo scarpered into cloud with his starboard motor and one wing burning, and we sent a fourth spinning earthwards, upside down and out of control with its engines flamed out it, didn't see the pilots get out of any of them.' His moustache hung, limp with sweat and smeared with oil, but his smile was huge. 'Two were up to speed, bastard fast, outpaced us completely, and two more scarpered by diving back into cloud, but not before we'd dented the bastards with a few rounds.'

'Crikey! Well done!' Two jet kills confirmed, two likely destroyed, perhaps more of them damaged, and the jet formation shattered. That would please the Brass no end.

Sheep turned as Frankie trotted up. 'Hey, Frankie, Amélie looks positively breezy, did the Wingco bring you luck?'

'It was the perfect bounce, *monsieur*! Four Boches asleep at three thousand feet over Rheine!' Frankie crowed, his voice thin and the usual frown gone, his dark eyes animated and wide; even Amélie's button eyes seemed to glisten with good humour.

Rose clapped him on the shoulder. 'Frankie got two 190s, maybe three.'

The boy looked at Rose, Amélie's blank stare seeming almost reproachful. 'Amélie and I. Amélie and I fight together, *mon Colonel*.'

Oops. Rose cleared his throat. 'Of course, I'm sorry, Frankie and Amélie, *pardon*.'

Sheep was impressed. 'Three Jerries? Fair dinkum? You beauty! Fancy joining 465 squadron, cock?'

'He is mine, *cochon*, cast your covetous eyes away.' Gabby's tone was light, but Rose saw the darkness in his eyes. Frankie had noticed it too, and now the smile fled from his face, and he tucked Amélie inside his flying jacket, crossing his arms to clutch the doll tighter.

'*Qui?*'

Gabby seemed to deflate before him. 'Giles. Head-on. He collided with a 190.'

Sheep's smile was gone. 'Giles? Gobby Giles? Jesus.' Rose saw Gabby's pain now mirrored in Sheep's eyes.

The tall Australian saw the question in Rose's eyes. 'Flying Officer Giles Herceux, fine bloke.' His moustache twitched but there was no warmth in it. 'Where one word would do instead of ten, Gobby'd say fuck all. Cheated like a starved bastard at cards and had a little Wren back in Harwich, sweet on him she was, a really nice kid.' He shook his head. 'This'll kill her, poor girl.'

Frankie nodded and spoke quietly to the doll. '*Elle a été appelée Mabel, non?*'

'Mabel. Yeah.' Sheep shook his head. 'Christ, poor Gobby.'

Poor Gobby, indeed, but poor Mabel, too. Rose's voice was soft, trying vainly to recall a face and failing, *dear God.* 'I'm sorry, boys.'

Gabby said nothing, but Rose gripped his shoulder gently, sharing it best he could, feeling like an interloper in his own Wing, despising himself for not having had the chance to know his lost boy, feeling once more that familiar ache.

I didn't even know him, can't remember his face, but he was one of mine and I just lost him. A brave man and a missing son. The third member of the Wing I've lost.

Herceux was a stranger to him, but he felt the bitterness of the loss nonetheless through the blunt sorrow of his men, reawakening the memory of his own quiet friend from Excalibur Squadron. Willy Wight, dear old Quiet Willy, shot down and killed in the attack on the airfield at Beaumont-le-Roger just after the invasion.

It could have been any of us. It could have been me.

Once again, that perfidious whisper, *and it yet might …*

Sheep's face was tight, his voice bleak despite their success. 'Fuck me.'

Rose put an arm carefully around Gabby's shoulders, feeling the stiffness of his friend's body and the restrained emotion. 'Tell me about Giles over a drink? We can remember him together.'

Gabby sighed and Sheep nodded, the lines of his face hard. 'We will, mate.' He reached out and grasped Rose's wrist gratefully, his words fierce. 'I'm glad you're here to share it with us, cobber.'

Another letter to write, more tears to shed.

Just one of those things.

Chapter 10

Despite the poor light in the dispersals hut, Sheep was peering intensely into a small handheld mirror, fingernails gently combing through his moustache.

'If you look too long, *cochon*, the Evil One will appear and stick a pointed fingernail in your eye.' Gabby's voice was indifferent and his eyes were closed, an unlit cigarette hanging from his mouth as he slumped on the battered settee.

'If you were seeing what I was seeing, cobber, you wouldn't be able to look away either.' Sheep arched an eyebrow coquettishly at himself. 'See, my dearest ma told me I was gorgeous when I was two, and things ain't changed since, thank the Lord.'

Gabby opened an eye for a moment to stare at him with disdain. 'I don't need a mirror to see the detestable sight that enchants you so greatly, *mon brave*.' The young Frenchman brushed at his spotless trousers and put back his head against the stained cushion again. 'My eyes have the calamity to regard your *visage révoltant* every day. It is an unkindness upon them. Why is it do you suppose that I have them closed now?'

Sheep tucked the mirror away carefully. 'Fair dinkum, then, you miserable old so-and-so. I'll tell you why I'm checking. I look every day just to make sure that I don't look like you.' He mock-shuddered, pulled a face and winked at Rose. 'Can you imagine how bloody awful that would be? Bloody catastrophic.' He shuddered again.

'You should pray to the Almighty to look like me, *mon niais brave.*' Gabby's voice was scornful. 'At least then you would only be stupid and dull.'

'Now then, chaps.' Rose tried not to smile, lapsing tactfully into silence, and maintaining an air of ambivalent nonchalance.

'You've heard of Dorian Gray, sir?' Ignoring Gabby's words, Sheep looked at Rose quizzically. 'The Picture of Dorian Gray? Dear ol' wild Oscar's tale?'

Where was this going? 'Mm? What of it, old chap?' Rose put down Molly's beloved dog-eared copy of Gummere's 1910 version of the Old English classic, Beowulf, one finger keeping his place.

While heavy going, Rose enjoyed reading it immensely, for he understood what it meant to be enchanted (although his enchantment was with an extraordinary and lovely human woman, not a shape-changing monster like poor Beowulf).

He could still just distinguish the faint fragrance of her perfume where some drops must have spilled, and he would trace her scrawled *Miss Molly Digby, Roedean School, 1932* with his fingertip. Nowadays, the school belonged to the Admiralty and was known as HMS Vernon.

Sheep pointed at Gabby accusingly. 'I have to spend a fair whack of my time with Gabby, got no choice, have I? Wouldn't if I didn't have to, of course, and I'm worried that I might end up looking more like him! I have to keep checking that I don't. I mean, can you imagine?' He rolled his eyes dramatically and touched his face, then flapped a hand at Gabby's. 'Going from this to something like that? Blimey! Be a ruddy catastrophe! Poor bugger's got a face like a dropped pie.'

Gabby sat up in outrage. '*Stupide! Imbécile!* In Wilde's story the painting absorbs the sin and the anti-hero is refreshed! The portrait and the anti-hero do not end the story looking the same! *Crétin! Quel salaud!* Any more of this *foutaise* and there will be shouting!'

Sheep shifted in position and winked at Rose. 'Alright, alright! Keep your ruddy hair on, will you? Crikey bananas, Gabs, you're being a mite sensitive, mate.' He winked again, 'Though if I looked like you, God forbid, I'd probably be a bit sensitive too!'

The tall Australian fixed Rose with a gloomy look. 'Don't know what you're grinning about, sir. Imagine looking like this sorry bugger, Christ! Couldn't be uglier if he tried, the poor basket! Face like a ripe old fart trapped in a bottle, eh, Gabs?' Sheep shuddered theatrically then patted Gabby's hand kindly.

Gabby growled quietly and, wisely, Rose maintained his diplomatic silence, trying hard to keep an expression of neutral solemnity on his face as Sheep continued plaintively, 'I have nightmares that I'll wake up one morning and when I look in the mirror, it'll be Gabby looking back at me! All pinched and dried out like a prune, shrivelled up and simpering back at me like some ugly drongo.'

The Australian gave a mock shudder. 'Wouldn't have a Buckley's with the Sheilas! No ruddy chance! They'd either drop down dead at the sight, faint or run for the bloody hills sharpish screaming bloody blue murder! I'd have to take Holy Orders and become a monk! Gabs, you ain't the ant's pants, and the most you're likely to get even if you have a good wash is a right rusty hen, so you'd best get used to living in a monastery.' He nodded sagely, offered kindly, 'Tight pants'll help, if you ask me.'

The tall Australian leaned over and patted his friend's arm again. 'At least you've never been with a woman, eh, cobber? Can't miss what you ain't had, eh? *Désolé mon pote, pas de baise.* You were born ugly, but at least you don't know any better, eh?' Sheep fondled his moustache languidly, preening. 'I wasn't and I can't, sorry and all that, but there it is.'

Gabby snorted in disapproving exasperation. '*Merde, cochon,* but you are the fool *extraordinaire.* For a man with a countenance like the *derrière* of the toad, you are *stupide* to think as you do.'

Sheep grinned cheerfully at his disgruntled friend. 'Sour grapes, cobber, sour grapes.'

Chapter 11

He still felt the rage burning him inside as he looked down at the airfield below, surprised that despite having seen so much death over these many years of war, he had not become immune to its awfulness.

Ten of his men (*ten!*) dead, including four of the new replacements. Two of them on their first operation. Boys just about able to wipe their own arses trained to fly high-performance fighting machines and thrown unready into the cockpits of 190s. Three others had been intruder and bomber pilots, re-mustering from a spent force into fighters to replace the terrible erosion of the Luftwaffe's fighter force.

Winter had no cause to protest or rail at fate, for he was responsible for the death of enough of the enemy's inexperienced boys himself. This was the true reality of war, little room for humanity as boys died a man's death on both sides, no mercy when the choices were victory or defeat.

Only one of his men, a veteran *Oberfeldwebel* from Schonau, had escaped the destruction of his jet, but with two broken legs and concussion, he would not be flying again for some time, if ever.

Conceivably, the NCO was the lucky one, for he had survived and this business would be over long before his injuries were healed, and he would live. He'd fought a hard war, and earned the chance to survive.

And he had lost not just his precious and irreplaceable pilots, but so many of their vital fighting machines too, four 262s, and seven 190s.

With his own jet down for much-needed maintenance and an engine change, Winter was flying 'Black 5', an FW190A (not one of the longer-nosed Fw190D 'Dora-9' fighters which were a powerful development of the superlative FW190A) which had once, gloriously, wrested air superiority from RAF Fighter Command until the very timely introduction of the *verdammt* Hawker Typhoon.

The last of the jets were taxiing along now from their reinforced refuges in the forest towards the longest of Rheine's runways, the writhing plumes of steam as the Jumo's blistering exhausts scorched the icy wet ground creating a rising bank of faux-fog rolling restlessly across the field and into the air, showing their progress and marking them out on the flat expanse as obvious targets from a distance.

Winter explored the overcast for enemy fighters, guts twisting with worry for his exposed and vulnerable men on the ground, a solitary belch uneasily filling his mouth with the bitter taste of his ersatz coffee and cigarette lunch.

But luck was on their side, and the sky remained clear of Allied fighters as the first pair of jets took off and began the long climb to interception.

Once the 262s were safely away, his mixed bag of sixteen FW109As and FW190Ds would set course for the enemy formation currently bombing Hamburg, intercepting the bombers on their homeward leg. Despite Goering's edict that head-on attacks were forbidden, he would launch their attack in that manner, but from above and in sections of four fighters.

With the closing speeds so fast, his 190s would be ephemeral targets for the nose and upper turret gunners, and fleeing at full throttle would make them too fast for the rear and side gunners to aim at.

But he knew that a veritable cloud of escorts would be flying ahead of the bomber formations, and, in reality, pounding through the shielding Mustangs and Thunderbolts to successfully strike at their larger brethren would be a near impossibility.

In addition to which, when the bombers now saw the German fighters massing ahead ready to attack, the USAAF formation would turn away to port or starboard by around thirty degrees, so that only the most experienced of their attackers might hit them as the angles of approach changed.

Until late 1943 the bombers had been protected only by short range Spitfires, and Luftwaffe interception at the coast would waste the RAF fighter's fuel and cause them to head for home early, but with the advent of first the P47 and later the outstanding P51, the situation had evolved unfavourably against the Luftwaffe.

Winter's restless eyes watched the outer lower cordon patrol schwarm of 190As circling protectively to the north of Rheine, covering the vulnerable arrowhead of 262s as they gently accelerated upwards.

The high cover patrol flying above cloud to warn of Allied fighters would remain where they were.

With their faster brethren safely on their way, Winter drew his 190s together around him and pushed up into a hard battle climb in a defensive close formation, for the enemy fighters were never far from the bombers.

On the far distant horizon of rolling rough grey cloud, the ever-present blotch of Hamburg's smoke was growing thicker into the filmy older stain of yesterday's fires, stretching vast in the sky, winds daubing at its upper edges and pushing them messily eastwards; the spreading blemish signifying the Allie's strength, the fresh fires of Hamburg started before the older ones had even burned out.

The sixteen FW190s from JG35's 3 and 9. Staffel formed a tight knot at twenty thousand feet, the ground below only very occasionally visible through breaks in the cloud, and the sky ahead of them sparkled with the fearsome sight of the approaching cliff face of bombers, box after box of them stacked between sixteen and eighteen thousand feet.

Closer still but higher up, massed shoals of *Ami* fighters shining like specks of quicksilver between twenty-four and twenty-two thousand.

For an instant, more and more often these days, Winter was reminded of the summer battles of 1940, the British countryside green and beautiful below, its RAF defenders often attacking in derisible packets of three or six aircraft, the laughably Forlorn Hopes of incredibly brave men attacking in the face of overwhelming enemy numbers, brave men whose fate was to become additional victory bars on his Emil's rudder scoreboard.

And now it's *our* turn to face the impossible odds, he thought grimly.

Already the lumbering wall of *viermots*, a veritable wall of steel, was beginning to veer to their starboard, each box of bombers turning in perfect unison, and he cursed angrily. His men were still too far, and as the bombers turned away, he would be forced to turn after them such that their approach would bring them into a front quarter attack progressing into a side attack, with the number of defensive guns they would be facing increased. Not as bad as a stern approach, but not a great deal better.

And to make matters even worse, one of the fighter formations was coming down, a line of fighters, rolling down hard to catch them.

But too late, for in judging the distance to the bombers, Winter reckoned that his men would be starting their attack before being intercepted, and the USAAF fighters would have to pull back to avoid entering the bomber formation's lethal envelope of defensive fire.

He pulled his 190's nose upwards, and her poor straining BMW seemed to scream all the louder as he dragged her higher, turning towards the approaching fighters, having expected the 190s to dive now corrected for their unexpected bunt upwards, but Winter had no intention of engaging them if he could deliver at least one attack on the bombers, and converted his turn to port into a roll downwards, knowing his boys would follow without being told.

'*Hummeln*, split and spread, sting well, *kamerad. Puake-Puaka! Attack-Attack!*' Terse, clipped words for his men, and the sixteen diving fighters separated smoothly into two sections of eight loosely spaced aircraft in line abreast as they acknowledged, '*Victor-Victor!*', the feared 'company front' attack, its paucity of numbers perhaps making it not so fearful, spreading wide apart as the bombers beneath appeared once more in their windscreens.

Each of the sections would fall on different 'boxes' of the leading rank of bombers, lunging at them from an angle of fifty degrees from above, making it much harder for the gunners as they tried to aim and calculate deflection while having their guns angled upwards at high barrel elevation.

Fortunately, only three machine guns, in the nose and top turrets, would be firing forwards on each of the bombers (rather than the 6-8 MGs they would face in a stern attack).

Unfortunately, the waves of bombers directly behind would also be firing at them, and his 190s would be racing into a flailing whirlwind of death, although the closer they got to their targets the less the enemy would fire for fear of hitting the bombers leading the formation.

Winter muttered a final prayer, hoping the youngster acting as his wingman today had taken to heart his last-minute tips before take-off.

The boy's face had been pinched and pale, another skinny, half-starved youth from the German heartlands. 'Get close enough, Horst, then aim at least one to two lengths ahead of your target before firing. Remember, don't fire too soon, and for goodness sake don't pull away, just begin to bring the nose up enough at about 250 metres to avoid flying into your target! Stay on my wing, but if you lose me, just keep on going after until you're out of range of their gunners, understood? Then break for home. Don't try a stern attack until the next mission, just one pass at them today, OK?'

The lad's teeth were chattering, whether from the cold or with fear Winter could not tell. But he tried to make light. 'Victor-Victor, sir,' he said, using the fighter pilot's radio term for 'received and understood'.

Winter showed his teeth in a smile, but there was no humour in it, for he had already lost too many boys like this one. 'Good lad. Try and find a *Herausschuss*, a separated or damaged *viermot* after the initial attack, but if the Indians come, don't try and out-dive them, unless cloud is near. It might have worked for your instructors in the past, but the *Amis* can out-dive us easily now. Just remember that Thunderbolts can outmanoeuvre a 190A, and the Mustangs are far faster than we are.'

'Indians' was the German flyer's slang for enemy fighters.

The boy's eyes were like saucers, but better the youngster was scared than cocky. 'It will be chaos up there, so if you lose me, don't worry, the bastards will be low on fuel by then. If you get caught up in a crowd of them, just keep turning, diving and climbing randomly like a madman until they have to break off and go home. And if it's close enough, use the cloud to hide in until they piss off. I need live pilots to defend the Fatherland. Don't be a dead hero!'

Winter had smiled reassuringly at the terrified youngster, but knew it was most likely this first operation would be the boy's last. 'Keep in mind what I said, Horst, alright? Just keep jumping around. It's not that easy to slap a flea on a dancing pig's arse!'

Here and now, Max dismissed his concerns for the untried youth flying alongside, instead quickly checking for the pursuing fighters (Mustangs?) noting with satisfaction that they were wheeling away as the 190s closed with the bombers, and that his own men had spread out into attack formation as he planned.

No more time to think as he lined up Black 5 with his intended target, a ponderous B24 Liberator bomber, the leading aircraft in the lead element of the squadron combat box of twelve aircraft, likely the unit's squadron or Wing Commander. The B17 Flying Fortress was a more formidable foe in terms of defensive armament and sturdier in the strength of fuselage than the B24 Liberators, but a large formation of the latter was intimidating enough nonetheless.

Stinky Werner from 9. Staffel had fought against Patton's French advances in the early autumn, and liked to recount ad nauseum shooting down a low flying Liberator one evening just before dusk over Saumar. As he'd opened fire, fluid momentarily streamed back, before suddenly igniting and burning its way back to the bomber which then exploded in a huge ball of flame that lit the surrounding countryside with a brilliant flash of flame, burning fuel cascading down, tossing Werner's Bf109 like a dry leaf and scorching the paintwork from his aircraft.

Somehow Werner recovered control of his Gustav to learn at debriefing that fuel was being flown in to Patton's men, and it was one of these refuelling aircraft he had destroyed.

Without bombs, the bombers returning home were unlikely to explode, but even then it could happen if he hit their fuel tanks, and so Winter, remembering Werner's experience, still tensed as he chose a target from the glittering mass.

The mass of aircraft ahead suddenly sparkled with a flickering constellation of muzzle flash from hundreds of machine guns, and suddenly a swarm of glowing tracer was rising lazily toward them, a luminous cloud of deadly fireflies growing so thick that it seemed impossible to pass through it and live.

Beside him his wingman Horst, seeing the forest of tracer rising reacted instinctually, pressing the triggers and opening fire while they were still hopelessly out of range, but Winter was unflinching and focussed completely on 'his' Liberator.

Drei, zwei, ein ... los!

Black 5's MG131 machine guns and MK108 cannon spat out even as he felt the crunch of hits on his own aircraft, as if someone were battering at her armoured airframe with a hammer, shuddering from both recoil and impacts, but his luck held and she continued onwards.

The silver Liberator in the upper corner of his Revi gunsight flashed and puffs of short-lived smoke mushroomed and billowed as his own 30 mm shells bit savagely into her, hits sparkling backwards from the mid-upper turret to the rear turret, blowing flesh, plastics and metal to shreds and ripping large chunks of metal from her airframe, a banner of flame flickering to suddenly pulse bright and sweep back from the junction of that heavy fuselage and those ridiculously narrow wings, the bomber expanding dangerously before him.

At least one of Black 5's cannonshells had smashed into the bomber's fuselage to rip flesh and metal fragments out through the starboard waist gunner's position, the shattered Plexiglas glistening outwards in a curling fountain of scarlet from the shredded gunner, his fragments painting one oval vertical stabiliser with streaks of bright red.

And then he was easing back, expertly pulling her up and over, just enough to streak past over the bomber he had hit, the bombers of the low-low element suddenly appearing to one side but he was going too fast to turn and rake them with gunfire, nose down and content to dive away as their bullets pursued him, so fast that the gunners would be unlikely to be able to bring their guns to track him as he scorched past them, the taste of stale coffee, Scho-ka-kola chocolate and cordite bitter in his mouth.

His rottenflieger Horst, absorbed in battering his own Liberator, realised too late that he had little room to pull up and over his target, and as he desperately hauled back, his 190's starboard wingtip clipped the upper edge of one of the battered enemy's twin-tails, and his fighter was thrown into a vicious flat spin, the B24's vertical stabiliser whirling away like a huge frisbee.

The shearing impact knocked the young German unconscious, mercifully sparing him as his fighter's starboard wing was ripped off at the root, the whirling trail of fuel released from the tanks beneath him igniting and turning the 190 into a ball of fire which smashed into another Liberator following behind and below, crushing the nose of the aircraft disastrously and instantly killing the pilots and Bombardier, fire and flaming debris jetting along inside the big bomber to kill the remainder of the crew, the wings peeling back and detaching from the stricken B24 as it fell, its compatriots jostling one another as they strived to avoid the deadly shotgun blast of flaming fragments which blasted through the formation.

Miraculously none of the other bombers were brought down by burning debris or collision as they crowded one another in the packed sky, but in his one and only operational mission, Horst had destroyed two bombers; the three crew members of the first Liberator managing to escape by parachute were the only survivors.

The stream of aircraft comprised hundreds of bombers, extending back over the clouds by some distance, and rather than escape below, Winter pulled back into the stream where defensive fire would be lightest and the targets thickest, a bomber coming so impossibly close he saw the pale blobs of its shocked pilots' faces; somehow missing it, he hammered out another hastily aimed stream of bullets and explosive shells at the bomber in the high level group in the box behind, but it too was a rushed burst and it seared past to one side of his intended target, and he had wasted precious ammunition, but no matter, for the sky ahead was laden with more targets, blurred into streaks of silver by speed.

It was more perilous than he remembered, like running into oncoming traffic on an autobahn, and Winter certainly had no death wish. Death by collision or by machine-gun bullet? If he had to choose he knew which he preferred, and he heaved back on the stick, threading Black 5 out of the bomber stream and into cleaner air.

Black 5 soared upwards until she was more than a thousand metres above the massed Liberators, out of range of their machine guns and already a pair of Mustangs were turning and diving from above, dangerously close and no sign of his *rottenfleiger*, but he pushed her down again, selecting another target, seeing the glowing cloud of tracer rising and draw closer, and the P51s turned away.

Young Peterkin had once (only just) made it back to Rheine, and been pulled from the wreckage of his 190 at the end of the runway, shaking like a leaf but smiling in his luck of having survived once more. In a halting voice Peter described the defensive fire as 'seething', and truly the description was apt, already the bullets were like a heavy storm reaching for him, those few which found him clattering against Black 5 like the rattle of hailstones or pebbles, making the 190 twitch and Winter fret and sweat.

Some others came awfully close, but not quite close enough, their whip-crack gale of sound wavering, the shredding of the air audible over his strained BMW as the dense curtains of bullets raced close past him, ebbing and flowing according to their nearness.

Multiple trails of smoke were sprawling away from the huge formation as their damaged elements fought to keep up with their compatriots, or fell away out of formation. In the distance something exploded, a dirty rosette of fire and silver petals falling, too large to have been a fighter, while something else large was in a flat spin downwards, the dots that were men falling slowly out of its embrace.

He saw a 190 tumbling, no flame nor smoke, but a dead hand at its controls guiding it into an uncontrolled tumble earthwards, another no more than a ball of flame going straight down.

As with all the very best fighter pilots, his gunsight was almost superfluous, a hunter's long experience and instinct guiding his eye, and now he dropped down onto the bombers like a hawk falling onto its prey.

Winter felt a powerful exhilaration despite the oncoming torrents of glowing destruction, a feeling of false invincibility even as he tracked a Liberator on the starboard edge of the formation, punching down on the gun buttons and seeing the smoking rounds curve towards it, their almost instantaneous eruption *bang-bang-bang-bang!* against the port wing of the B24, a sheet of dazzlingly white flame suddenly flowing back as fuel spilled out of its punctured wing, burning fuel cascading out in burning whorls, hauling on the stick back to clear the bomber ...

It passed beneath him, and he knew it and the men which crewed it had no chance, pulling back again to repeat the manoeuvre, calling out his victory, '*Abschuss!*'

Similar cries sounded in his ears, but the earphones also carried to him the dreadful last calls of those who were injured, or dying.

A flicker of light caught his eye and he saw a burning parachute falling, the canopy collapsed as fire consumed fibre, its wearer helpless as he fell in a long descent to death. German or American, he wondered, then grimaced at the foolishness of the thought, for it made no difference for the unfortunate beneath it.

He felt the strain in his arms and the greying of his vision as he tired, swallowed the bitterness in his throat and took a deep breath, suddenly aware that a flight of six cumbersome fighters were closing with him, P47 Thunderbolts!

God! The *Amis* were already too close! To dive again would allow the enemy to pepper his arse with 0.5 mm bullets; he could not normally outmanoeuvre them in a 190A, but in this battle-worn fighter, already wallowing at this altitude, it was nigh on impossible.

I should have taken one of the Dora-9s, he thought despairingly, but he knew that if he had the choice to make again, he would still have chosen to fly what his men were flying, even if it was this clapped-out FW190A.

His father, a survivor and highly decorated hero of both the first war and this one, had taught his sons that a leader must share the same dangers as his men to be worthy of them. He practised what he preached, and had been captured in Normandy with the remnants of his regiment, staying with his men even though he could have escaped. Max was not the only one with luck in the family.

Joachim, too, had lived by the code, had been loved by his men, and disappeared alongside them in a brutal and inhuman frozen maelstrom called Stalingrad. There had been no luck for the round-faced youngster with the shy smile and kind heart, and the memories of his lost little brother still twisted like burning coals in his heart.

And now Winter was going to pay the same price in this willing but tired old warhorse.

Tracers zipped past him in a glowing line and he pulled her up into a steeply climbing turn, the speed falling off rapidly and, as Black 5 slipped sideways, he pushed her nose down, the 190 falling into a spiralling dive almost straight down; he counted to five before kicking rudder and ending the spiral, pulling back hard, and her engine was screaming as she began to climb upwards again, the pressure on his chest harsh and his vision darkening as he threw her into a tight turn to starboard, fingers feeling as if they might break, his clothes saturated in cold sweat, the harness digging painfully into his shoulders as he was dragged to one side of the cockpit by the force of the turn.

Straining his neck, he looked back and his heart sank to see that three of the enemy had stayed with him and again a stream of tracer reached out for him, but his turn was just tight enough that it curved uselessly away below.

Another full revolution of the turn, however, and he would be finished as the enemy throttled back and tightened the turn into their ascendancy.

Got ... to ... get ... away ...

Stick to one side all the way back, kick hard right rudder, and Black 5 reared up into a vertical corkscrew, reeling upwards just as the tail-end of a burst of 0.5 bullets blew a hole in his starboard wing, and she lurched, her speed falling off and slowing into a stall even as another burst of machine-gun fire splashed across her fuselage and wings; a sudden and shocking explosion of Plexiglas as his canopy shattered and he felt the mighty blow as metal punched hard against the armour plate at his back and he gasped in shock despite himself, a tempestuous storm of freezing air slapping and thrashing at him as he fought with the controls.

His map, pushed down the side of the cockpit, unfurled in the whirlwind and plastered itself against his face and chest and he just about managed to take one hand off the control column, holding on for dear life with the other, hastily tearing the damned thing off to be torn away by the ravening slipstream, before grasping the column with both hands again, as the shrieking gale buffeted him.

Winter allowed the 190 to slip sideways through her decaying turn, until her nose was pointing straight down, feeling her shudder as more bullets bore into her, the fighter's centre of gravity seeming to shift towards her tail and the damage in the wing and fuselage setting up an unpleasant trembling vibration in her airframe.

He felt the sudden change in her engine's note, but he still had some control and he wrestled with the control column, exerting all he had, fighting against her urge to lift, while simultaneously straining to keep her tail from going through the vertical and beyond as she was inclined to do; his face was a rictus mask of effort as he tried to gain the sanctuary of cloud. Close, but not close enough.

A red light was flickering dolefully on the console, blurring in his eyes by the vibration, the indicator warning him that he had less than ten minutes of fuel left, and he pulled the nose up a little, a little more, the heaviness of her tail flattening her trajectory, feeling the resistance and the quivering in her and he knew the faithful little fighter was doomed.

The shadowed field of furrowed heavy cloud was much closer now, but the shuddering in her battered airframe was worsening.

He had very little time, likely only seconds before Black 5 broke apart, with the chances of escaping a tumbling fighter minimal, but with hands made clumsy by the slipstream's pummelling, he reached down for the harness and, releasing it, eyes warily on the sharp edges of what remained of the canopy, he braced himself to climb out.

Without warning, the ravening slipstream swirled around him and he felt himself lift and was plucked from the cockpit, wrenching at his neck before the oxygen mask was snatched from his face and radio leads were violently severed from the aircraft, his goggles torn off in the tumultuous air and his left boot heel glancing against Black 5's vertical stabiliser, sending a spear of excruciating pain streaking from his foot up to his hip and tearing off his boot.

Falling through the air, the blast of air sealing his nostrils and stinging his eyes, he squinted anxiously around him, one hand on the parachute canopy release.

It was a common occurrence for the USAAF fighters to shoot at Luftwaffe pilots as they hung suspended and helpless, and he fought the urge to curl into a protective ball.

Shooting a pilot beneath his parachute might not be chivalric, but it made tactical sense. A downed Luftwaffe pilot shot down over friendly territory could climb back into a fighter later the very same day to try and kill more of their bomber boys.

A dead German fighter pilot could not.

After seeing bomber after bomber fall and hundreds of their fellow countrymen die, the *Ami* fighter boys would show little mercy to someone who might kill more of their compatriots the following day.

And with shame Max knew that men of the Luftwaffe themselves were also responsible for the deaths of those hanging helpless beneath their parachutes. It was something he had never done, could never do.

But his pursuers were gone, being low on fuel they were content in having shot Black 5 down, and he cupped his hands over his mouth and nose the better to breathe.

The cloud rushed to meet him, plunging him suddenly into an icily clammy limbo.

Unseen below, what was left of Black 5 impacted a turnip field and blew apart, the BMW engine pushed deep. Already his drubbing heart was slowing now the danger was past, but breathing in this thrust of air was taxing.

Hoping there were no more enemy fighters below, and with a muttered prayer to the Almighty, Winter held his breath, quickly checking his parachute harness straps were tight, recalling how poor Johann had almost emasculated himself over Cuxhaven when loose leg straps had stopped his freefall with violent abruptness via his groin. Johann still walked with a limp and swore that each of his balls had its own sack.

Swallowing in apprehension and feeling his testicles crowd back tightly, Winter closed his eyes and pulled the large door-handle shaped ripcord release D-ring, *whooshing* out in relief and giving silent thanks to Gettwert of Berlin when the parachute streamed out smoothly and snapped open unseen above his head, jerking him into a more controlled descent; his stomach lurched as his body was wrenched by the sudden deceleration, but his testicles remained whole and uncrushed.

It was the second time he had used the thing, the first time over Russia, and the experience was no more pleasant than the first, and he fought down the rising gorge and sudden sense of vertigo.

His leg had been numbed by the glancing blow with Black 5, but now his tingling toes began to burn from the cold, and feeling the icy air whistle between them through his frayed sock, he realised he had lost his boot, and he wiggled his toes in an attempt to ease the pain and check they were undamaged.

They stung sharply and pain lanced up into his hip, but not as badly as they would have if he had broken them. Reassured, Max wiped his streaming eyes with his stained sleeve, the leather of his jacket pungent with sweat, smoke and cordite, grimacing as his leg began to throb, the moisture seeming to billow through his clothing and leaving him cold and wet.

He re-emerged from the moist opacity of the cloud back into clear air and was surprised and gratified to see to his left the great brooding expanse of the Oldenburg Forest, a stretch of snow-coated trees extending away into the distance, while to his right the distinctive shape of Bremen at the fork of the Weser and the Werdersee.

The tiny shape of the Am Wall smock windmill was just visible through the pollution and thick columns of smoke, the unique blades still miraculously untouched despite the months of relentless bombing; the twin towers of Bremen's St Peter's Cathedral on the north side amongst the blackened ruins of the city, while

Bremerhaven far to the north was shrouded and invisible in the smoke and haze.

The USAAF fighters must have pursued him some distance south-east of the bomber stream, but it could not be better, as his streaming eyes found the Focke-Wulf Flugzeugbau AG factory industry airfield of Bremen-Neuenlanderfeld, south-west of Bremen.

Aware of his vulnerability and feeling helpless, Max searched the sky, apprehensive of any USAAF fighters which might be lurking, but there was nothing.

The Focke-Wulf factory was a huge complex, once comprising the twelve enormous buildings of the construction plant itself in the north-east corner of the airfield, almost sixty brick structures, five large hangars and four paved runways each around a kilometre in length, but much of it was now like the city itself, just wide tracts of rubble, craters and blackened ruins.

But there were at least two fighters just visible, parked alongside the end of one of the runways. Hopefully there might be a 190D down there with his name on it ...

The still-smoking smoke generators dotted around the field meant to obscure the visibility had not protected the site, but the smoke-filled air made Max's eyes water further and his nose began to run; he sneezed and broke wind simultaneously, causing a sharp bolt of pain to race down his leg.

Despite the pain, and the desolation of the city below, he felt fortunate. What a stroke of good fortune! He had visited the Focke-Wulf factory site on a number of occasions, to give morale-boosting speeches to the workers, had attended a lunch held in honour of a number of *Experten* (including himself), and once even picked up a shiny new Dora-9 to fly back to Rheine.

Much of the manufacturing plant's machinery and personnel had been sent eastwards because of the regular bombing raids, but as far as he knew the facility was still operational, albeit at a greatly reduced capacity.

With a bit of luck, he might be able to wander in and perhaps appropriate another Dora-9 to fly back home in!

That would make their eyes stand out! The *Herr Oberst* leaves Rheine in a battle-worn 190A, shoots down one (maybe two) *viermots*, and returns triumphantly in a brand new 190D-9!

Now, that would be a tale and a half to tell!

His toes were numbing again with the cold, although the pain still continued to throb up his leg, and that reminded him of his lost boot.

To fly home in a lovely new aeroplane, he would need to borrow a new pair of flying boots. Contemplating his sweat-saturated clothes, oil-stained jacket and tattered sock, he realised he was not looking his best. *I'm not cutting a particularly dashing figure here …*

The flying boots had been a very comfortable worn-in RAF 1939 Pattern issue, a pair he had purloined years earlier from an abandoned RAF landing ground in North Africa during the great advances of 1941.

They had been a pleasure to wear and to have lost one was a true loss, although thankfully he had another pair in his quarters at Rheine.

His Knight's Cross with Oak Leaves, Swords and Diamonds was back at Rheine, but his face was well known throughout Germany, and while he might look rather bedraggled at the moment, his reputation would be enough. He did not even entertain the possibility that his injury might stop him from flying for some time.

Better by far to have lost my boot and poor Black 5, he thought ruefully, *than to have lost my life.*

Lucky Max.

Still lucky. Still alive.

For now.

Chapter 12

Following the destruction of Rotterdam in 1940, Antwerp became the largest channel port of Europe, and was earmarked by the Allies as an important logistics stepping stone for the advance into Germany.

Because of this strategic importance, Antwerp and its surrounding area was subject to a tenacious defence by the occupying forces, resulting in the Battle of the Scheldt.

The war-weary First Canadian Army under Guy Simonds (including attached British and Polish units) found itself going into action once again, first capturing Zeebrugge and then clearing the southern shore of the Scheldt estuary including the town of Breskens.

Understrength and suffering from battle exhaustion from the unrelenting advance begun at Normandy, the valiant Canadians, an all-volunteer force, had been in constant action for months against heavily layered defences in depth, with little respite between battles and no leave home.

The island of Walcheren, a veritable fortress, was taken after further bitter fighting involving the Canadians (yet again), Highlanders of the 52nd Infantry Division and members of the British 4th Commando Brigade.

With the Allies close to the city, the Belgian resistance seized the port facilities before they could be destroyed by the Germans, leaving the port operational when the city was liberated by the British 11th Armoured Division. Before use, however, the approaches to the port had first to be cleared of mines, and the first vessels were able to dock in late November.

With the liberation of Antwerp, occupied Belgium was at last free.

The stars to the east were faint, bleached points of light as dawn drew closer in the darkness of a clear night sky. Volkel lay beneath a thin sliver of moon that lit nothing, just as the eastern horizon became barely discernible in the first faintly glowing flush of predawn light, confirming what the Met officer had already glumly promised that the weather would only draw colder, the frost each morning thicker and the fingers of Rose's dutiful but suffering ground crews stiffer and more painful.

Rose yawned, the icy air burning down into his throat to sear his lungs, making his teeth ache. His nose was watering, and he hoped he wasn't coming down with a cold. Conversely, the cold air was soothing where he had cut himself twice while shaving.

He also felt sick and unhappy, but just before an op that was par for the course. Only when he was in the air with his attention focussed on his men and the sky would the anxiety dull and diminish.

Another dawn imminent, another fresh beginning he could not share with Molly and the little ones, another day's creation which found him lonely and alone, isolated and detached in the midst of his men.

Another day which might be his last.

Around him the sharp crack of Coffman starter cartridges and the deep boom of Sabre engines being run up in readiness for the coming sortie east and the coughing and sneezing of men frozen rigid from working through the night in unbelievably atrocious temperatures.

Chiefy, a huge bear of a man from Aberystwyth with leathery hands like shovels and a gentle, lilting voice that he could roughen to sandpaper at will, was made even more massive by the bulky layers he wore.

When in his office, Chiefy smoked an appallingly smelly dark shag in a stubby little pipe, and so Rose's dealings with the senior NCO were often in the open air.

Cuffing and wheezing through a reddened and streaming nose, his senior groundcrew NCO eyed the shaving cuts on his Wing Commander's face with bright eyes animated in the pinched circle of white skin revealed by his balaclava, and confirmed that in addition to Rose's aircraft, there would be twenty serviceable Tempests for the raid.

Rose nodded his thanks; twenty-four would have been better, but a strike by twenty-one aircraft would be enough.

As the burly NCO walked away, one of the fitters trotted up to him. 'Chiefy!' he called excitedly, 'I've found the leak in E-Eskimo's fuel system!'

Chiefy seemed less than impressed. 'Well? What the fuck do you want?' He bellowed like an enraged bull, 'Give you a medal or a chest to pin it on?' He trumpeted a sneeze. 'Don't stand there giving me cow eyes, go and sort it out, lad!' Bemused, the youngster scuttled off.

Chiefy turned and beamed at Rose. 'A few kind words always help, sir! As does a hefty kick up the arse! Time to go and gee-up the lazy beggars!'

Rose smiled as the normally soft-voiced Chiefy walked off into the darkness, shrieking raucously at his hard-working men, loud enough to awaken the residents of the Eagle's Nest in distant Berchtesgaden.

Yet despite his ranting and cursing, his bite was far milder than his bark and he was appreciated and respected by his 'erks' in turn.

Working in the bitter cold, the mixture of mind-numbing fatigue and frostbite was becoming a worsening problem for the ground crews as temperatures dropped, and one of his engine fitters had already lost a part of one finger as a result of frostbite caused by evaporating fuel.

With Chiefy's advice and agreement, Rose had shortened by a fifth the length of time the 'erks' worked in the open air or under tarpaulin during a shift, while arranging for a medium-sized structure to be built by the hard-working local Dutch workmen near dispersals as a shelter in which his men could gain temporary respite from the cold.

Furthermore, Rose had seen USAAF groundcrews at Eighth Air Force bases using five-gallon containers filled with 100-Octane and lit by a match to keep themselves warm during the British winters. The thought of filling a storage tin with that much fuel and sticking a match in it gave both Rose and Chiefy the screaming twitch.

Initially trying the concept out using the much smaller metal boxes in which the Coffman starter cartridges were provided (after all, hadn't the British Army repurposed the oil, water and petrol cans, better known as 'flimsies', into the stoves soldiers now knew as 'Benghazi burners?'), Rose and Chiefy found that the damned things would spring a leak as the box warmed or the poorly soldered seams split.

After accidentally burning down a storage tent during test-trials (and scorching a batch of tins of bully beef immediately recorded as 'destroyed' by the Stores Officer and distributed amongst the grateful Dutch workmen), Rose and Chiefy concluded that two half-filled Jerricans evenly spaced would suffice very nicely after all to make the ground crew's shelter a cosy retreat.

As an unexpected bonus, buckets of water suspended over the Jerricans also provided the essentials for a nice hot mug of fresh compo tea for the men.

Notwithstanding the hardships, Volkel's groundcrews tirelessly continued their relentless work, day and night, to keep the fighters serviceable, while also finding time to do what they could for the civilians who had suffered so cruelly under the Nazis.

The previous day an 'erk' from 122 Wing had been 'Santa' to the local Dutch children from the town. Leading Aircraftsman Fred Fazan from London was convincing in his new role, stepping down onto the brick runway from his 'new' sleigh, a Tempest of 122 Wing, his eyes bright and voice kind behind the characteristic bushy white beard.

122 had been collecting money and sweets for weeks, while in their precious free time, the weary groundcrews scrounged wood and metal from the wreckage of Volkel's buildings to make toys for the little ones.

The excited youngsters flocked around the young Londoner, their gaunt and pale faces bright and transformed with pleasure and wonder. The children, both boys and girls, wearing threadbare clothes and battered wooden clogs were without coats despite the cold.

There would be food and a little concert afterwards in a school hall near the seminary. The New Zealanders of 122 would start with 'The Fighting Kiwi' and finish with 'I'll be seeing you.' Rose's Aussies would sing 'Waltzing Matilda', while Gabby's boys had chosen 'Chant des Partisans' as their contribution.

Watching the children's shy pleasure in their Christmas miracle, Rose remembered his own precious little ones and their wonderful mother, and felt the wet glow of emotion in his eyes and a hitch in his throat.

Dear Lord, thank you for protecting my precious ones from the awful hardship of occupation. Most of these youngsters here have known nothing but this their entire lives.

Once Rose and his men discovered 122 Wing's plans, there had been a whip round and the collection of treats at Volkel to make this Christmas one of note for the children's memories in later years, and Rose murmured another prayer of thanks for his good fortune in serving alongside such exceptional men as these.

That evening, the voices from a choir comprising ground crew from 122 Wing floated hauntingly across the icy expanse of Volkel, their voices conducted into harmony by the Wing's Padre, Squadron Leader Morgan. Men listening sighed, put down pens or tools and thought longingly of the ones they loved, and wept.

Rose standing alone beside the Ops caravan and listening was one of those with cheeks wet from tears, the feeling of melancholy and loneliness overwhelming and heightened by the cold darkness and the ethereal voices raised sweetly in song.

Group had received intelligence the previous day that two or three Staffels of Bf109s, around thirty or more fighters, had arrived at Essen-Mulheim from the southern front to join in the Defence of the Reich.

The Nazi fighters would be based closer to the bomber routes and able to get quickly into the air and in position for a second and perhaps even third intercept after refuelling and rearming.

Volkel's OC, Group Captain Jameson, asked Rose if he would pay the Germans an early morning call as the 109 pilots readied for their first day of operations.

The attack would be of Wing strength, a single high-speed pass at zero feet with Gabby's squadron, while Sheep and the rest of his squadron would be above in the support and flak suppression role.

With any luck they would catch the enemy fighter Geschwader on the ground and exposed.

An icy breeze gusted and slashed across Volkel, whipping restlessly at his clothes, showering Rose with a spray of powdery flakes of snow from the roof of the dispersals hut, and he shivered, the phrase *'someone walked over my grave'* running unbidden through his mind, and he shivered again, harder.

Which of us will survive today? And, God forbid, which will have their grave dug for them in Germany by their shattered, falling Tempest?

The usual sensation of sickness and apprehension before flying. *And might it be me today?*

He closed his eyes for a moment, the cold biting into his cheeks and his lonely thoughts turning to home, idly wondering if Molly were asleep or feeding their little girl.

The lines around her mouth and the tiredness in her beautiful eyes, always so full of love and concern, the signs which told him the story of her unvoiced fears for him.

He yearned for the sound of her voice, the cheeky impertinence when she teased him, the warmth in her eyes when she looked at him.

Oh, how I miss you, Moll.

Rose sighed, his fingers straying back over the pocket containing the worn photograph, and he wiped his streaming eyes, *this flipping wind …*

He needed to get inside and brief his lads but was loath to enter the smelly, smoky room. There was the clang of metal nearby, and a muttered curse from an unseen erk, a bobbing torch searching for the dropped tool. Further away a Sabre crack-banged into throaty life, the revs rising and falling as it was tested amidst clouds of blue smoke and a fluster of sparks.

Dearest Lord my God, be with us this day …

His hand slipped further to cradle the little bear and the smooth pebble, irritated by his early morning melancholia, but unable to shake off his feeling of dark apprehension.

Daffie's loving gentleness would have dispelled his mood, but she was not here, better off where she was, safe with those he loved at home.

He turned as the faded buzz of conversation from within grew louder, the hut door creaking open behind him, Sheep squinting into the implacable darkness, a palm-shaded torch pointing at the ground. 'You out there, sir?'

Time to go.

Chapter 13

Another Tempest was made serviceable at the last minute by Chiefy's frozen stalwarts as his Wing ran up their engines to taxi out.

Already strapped in, Rose clapped his hands in tribute from the cockpit to the senior NCO, giving him a thumbs up.

Mindful of his watching men, Chiefy half raised a hand stiffly, a slight twitch in acknowledgement, before casting a jaundiced eye on his group of exhausted erks, as if daring them to so much as smile; but, dead-tired and half-frozen after a night working under tarpaulins in the bitter open air, they were finding it hard enough just to keep their eyelids from drooping.

Twenty-two Tempests from a possible twenty-four, and in these horrible conditions.

Bloody amazing.

When we return, thought Rose gratefully as Frankie taxied alongside into position, *I'll stand Chiefy and his amazing lads a crate of beer.*

And that ever-present contrary spark in the back of his mind, *but only if …*

There was a mist shrouding the borders of north-western Germany, a dull orange ball bisecting the horizon presaging dawn for the Tempests at ten thousand feet, the moon a frail wraith almost touching the ground behind, beneath them a wrinkled sheet of black broken by the sullen red glows marking the burning of distant cities, smudged columns and clouds of smoke underlit by raging fires, thinning and spreading into the heavens, the Harz mountains a rugged and brooding shadowed outline to starboard.

Rose had been uneasy about the threat posed by the experienced warriors of Germany's night fighter arm, but his high-performance Tempests were not ponderous four engine bombers, and those enemy crews which had survived were chronically fatigued beyond exhaustion after yet another night of fighting overwhelming numbers over their own homeland.

When flying night defence operations in Beaufighters over Britain during 1941, Rose and his friends were released just before dawn when no more raids were expected. The skies above Britain in the first flush of early morning light was not the place to be for a lone Luftwaffe raider.

Nor were the skies above Germany at dawn the place to be for Luftwaffe night fighters intended to intercept bumbling bombers or Mosquitos, for an Allied intruder or the ever-roving groups of nimble Allied fighters would welcome such a prize.

Furthermore, the murk from burning cities and the Tempests' shifting altitude made a firing solution for the radar-controlled flak nigh on impossible, particularly the morning after another battering from the 'heavies' of the Allied Air Forces when the exhausted and battered gunners would be quite happy to remain anonymous.

Essen-Mullheim was built as a civilian airfield in the 1920s, six kilometres from Essen and eighteen from Duisburg, a circular landing ground which had since been extended to the south-west in 1940 to accommodate the four long runways needed for wartime use.

With the hazardous nature of flying low over the rugged terrain of the Rhine at night, Rose and his squadron commanders had decided that 63 Wing would approach at high altitude from the west before dropping down and making the final approach from the darker western skies, with their targets backlit by the first gleaming of the new day's sun.

There would be only a single pass across the field and they would flee eastwards at full throttle into the climbing sun over Bredeney.

No flak and the stick forward as his heart battered against his chest, feeling Sugar dive and his parachute uncomfortable and buttocks shifting for comfort, trying to control the tightness in him and failing, eyes flicking momentarily from the mirror to her picture and a bright memory of her laughter and her hair shining in the light.

But this was no time to think about anything but this instant, here and now, over Germany …

Despite the discomfort of his oxygen mask sticking to the cuts on his face and the insipid stink of dying cities just discernible, he felt the exhalation sear through him.

Prop to fine pitch, safety off and thumb ready on the button. His skin was wet with cold sweat despite the heat of the cockpit, the soft red glow of Sugar's instruments casting faint shadows on his face and across the cockpit.

Beneath them the early rays of the morning sun were picking out the dazzling winding curves of the River Ruhr below, thick columns of smoke rising miles ahead where Essen was burning and Duisburg now sliding to port, a vague and melancholic shadowed sprawl of craters, ruined streets and battered spires, the scattered glow of fires burning amongst the tumbled ruins as the survivors tried to get warm as daylight crept closer, the flak silent.

There! A glance at his map to confirm the kink in the silvered reflections of the River Ruhr, and Mulheim ahead to port was their reference point, an uneven patch of destruction following Bomber Command's solitary major raid eighteen months earlier, a single chimney to mark the wrecked Freidrich Wilhelm iron and steel works where once four stood.

Rose's eyes sought out where Mulheim-Essen runways should be, searching through the haze and fug of dirty air, but the field itself was built on high ground.

Select M ratio, radiator shutter in the up position and stick forward, watch the throttle, and as he led them down he kept an eye on the altimeter, ready to level out at no less than a thousand feet to avoid plastering himself and his young Frenchmen across the rocky, irregular terrain, while also getting a better look at the airfield for targets.

As they dropped like stones, the emerging sun before them edged back to just beneath the horizon and they re-entered the twilight world of predawn, the lemon-yellow of the horizon darkening once more to a pink-violet glow, but not before he glimpsed the keyhole shaped airfield ahead, directly ahead and to starboard of ruined Mulheim, shadowed smudges scattered around and to the sides of the runways, where he imagined there were gatherings of aircraft being prepared for the daylight raids of the USAAF.

Rose had worried that his timing might be off and the sun would be rising brightly in their eyes to confound their attack, but his luck remained good and the Wing arrived just before the hot orb would cut above the airfield's horizon and hopefully the rising smoke of burning Essen would dim its brilliance as they fled into it.

Thank God.

A glance to either side to check the other Tempests were in an uneven line abreast formation, spaced apart and diving together, another glance into the mirror to show empty darkness behind them, and one at her tattered photograph, perhaps his last (*I love you so very much, Moll*) and knowing Sheep's men, high above, would have passed above already, out of the range of the light flak, yet too nimble and speedy for the heavier 88s.

And the AA batteries would welcome no attention, for there was still no flak as the gunners nervously watched the Australians wheeling above. The pebble-like rattle of the radar-controlled stuff in their headphones but nothing, incredibly, hurled aloft. As usual at the briefing they had learned of the areas of flak concentration, but of Mulheim-Essen's defences there was little information, although Rose knew that the industrial heartland itself would be thick with flak.

He could feel with his heightened senses Sugar beginning to slip, a little trim to counteract the onset of yaw to port …

The river was passing below them, the land and the southern main road suddenly flashing beneath, gentle pressure back on the stick as the land began to rise up, ease her further, for the airfield itself was just over 430 ft above sea level and he tilted her upwards.

His already tensed stomach and groin tightened further and the tingle of anticipation lanced through him as the ground rose up before smoothing beneath their rushing wings, Mulheim-Essen's perimeter fence rushing at them from the shadows as he eased Sugar down, gentle rudder and ailerons to keep her weaving.

The crackle of Sheep's voice in his headphones, relaying to them clearly but quickly. 'Gun emplacements, eight of them on the northern perimeter, looks like the light stuff. Heavy flak probably in the adjoining town. Fighters fuelling on either side of the main runway, 'bout midway, concentration of more kites on the eastern edge, two flak towers beyond.' And then, softer, '*Chookas!*'

No acknowledgement for the vital information expected, and none given. A tight smile for his friend's good wishes, the Aussie theatre performer's equivalent of 'break a leg'. Sheep and his men would make a single diving dummy attack from above to draw off the guns from Gabby's men, giving them precious seconds while the muzzles were turned away upwards.

One dummy attack was enough, for the risk of collision with Rose's low-level attackers as they clawed away upwards after their strafing pass would be very real.

He was slick with sweat, the sound of his laboured breathing loud and almost drowned out by the thunder of Sugar's Sabre; he lifted then dropped her over the fence, pushing down against the first upswell of air which threatened to push them up into the flak which was sure to erupt, now shielded from the flak by their closeness to the ground and the longest of the runways stretching ahead, two other shorter runways crossing it to make a huge asterisk.

His eyes registered in an instant the hollow skeletal shells of the hangars and the mounded rubble of broken buildings, the ground torn by a heavy rash of craters and the staring emptiness of the pre-war terminal building at the far north-western border.

A battered-looking Junkers 52 in patchy grey and green paint was parked close to the perimeter fence and a Tatra fuel bowser drawn alongside, but they had already passed by and there was no opportunity to fire at it. The three black-clad groundcrew could only stare, transfixed in open-mouthed terror and deafened witless as the line of sleek Tempests thundered past over their heads by what must have seemed like only inches, the men infinitely lucky not to have been blown to bloody rags.

The sparkle of flak and a rash of white bursts of 20 mm as the defenders opened up on Sheep's diving Tempests, even as the Australians were pulling up safely out of range from the feint.

Another quick check across the instruments and he was satisfied: *concentrate, breathe, and slow your heart, damn you!*

At last, a solitary line of tracer glittered silently into the sky, flicking out tentatively from somewhere to the left, a necklace of sparkling orange destruction, but it was too high, the gunner fearful of hitting personnel and materiel on the ground, and it arced away uselessly above and behind.

Ahead from the eastern end of the runway, sunlight shone on the shining edges of a single spinning disc (a fighter?), as an aircraft crawled slowly along one taxiway, but he could not align his guns on it for it was too far off to port.

Suddenly an intense flash and the taxiing aircraft was transformed into a swelling smear of fire and smoke as Frankie or the other Tempest to port beyond his wingman found the full fuel tanks with 20 mm.

Gabby, voice terse, tight with tension and excitement: '*Avions ennemis à gauche! Viens avec moi, enfants! Taïaut!*' But Rose had no time to look as the Frenchman led the other flight to port towards the enemy aircraft he had seen, for there were more cruciform shapes lined up ahead of Rose's flight, long shadows from the new light of day picking them out, and his thumb tensed with instinctive readiness as they loomed ever closer in his windscreen.

Sure enough there were six of them, a line of trim single-engine fighters facing east, facing away, and men swarming away desperately as Rose and his Free French fighter pilots closed the distance to bear down on them, a bowser lumbering ponderously away as the tired Gefreiter (dreaming just moments before of his bed) behind the wheel floored the accelerator and screamed desperate encouragement at his vehicle, the fuel line stretching taut to a partially fuelled fighter.

From another the driver leaped down from the cab, his arms and legs pumping, a turning face blanched by fear.

The parked enemy fighters were neat little Bf109s, their slim, deadly little waspish shapes clothed in drab blue-grey, and the one at the southernmost end of the line was in his sights; worries and anxiety now forgotten and the concussion from the first bursts of light flak pushing from above corrected for and ignored, Rose jamming down on the firing button, tensed muscle and tendon in tight hands fighting and adjusting for the ground effect pushing him upwards towards the tracer and flak; a little more throttle, but not too much, just enough to hold her velocity steady against the sharp recoil as Sugar's guns violently ripped out fiery anger, and the 109 was trapped in his gunsight.

At this speed the target would be in his cross hairs for a mere instant and he corrected to try and keep the enemy in his gun sight for as long as possible to maximise the damage inflicted by his guns.

Explosive cannon shells tearing out of Sugar's cannon quartet on smoking, twisting trails, a long two-second steady burst of fire, Rose leading the target as he had done so many times before and spreading destruction across a length of 100 feet as it tore jagged furrows into the tarmac then climbed onto the enemy fighter, a cloud of pulverised concrete dust and paint flakes obscuring the doomed 109 as he kept Sugar's nose (and cannon) centred on the target.

Painfully mindful of the increasing closeness of the ground

beneath, he adjusted her angle, smouldering metal and fragments spinning from out of the burgeoning cloud, vivid flashes of flame, a small explosion, another, and it canted over onto one side, then collapsed as one then both main wheels were ripped off, the fuselage crumpling beneath the explosive hammer-blows and the Daimler-Benz blown apart, but they were far too close and he hauled her up, almost too late, Sugar zooming high like a startled bird over the obliterated Messerschmitt; cringing and feeling naked by his increased exposure, he was grateful the wreck beneath did not explode as Sugar passed over it.

Like fiery whips, flaring tracer was flailing away at them from all sides now, but almost all of it was higher up for fear of hitting friendly groundcrews and parked vehicles and aircraft, but Rose saw one burst of tracer racing low across the grass which ripped right across in front of Sugar's nose to smash an Opel truck into a rolling mess of torn, burning metal and rubber. Rose smiled grimly, the enemy gunner would think twice about firing low next time ...

It felt as if they were in the midst of a cloud of vivid orange fireflies, fireflies which could rip Sugar apart into a thousand unrecognisable pieces and kill or maim him. And everywhere the lethal rash of white smoke from bursts of light flak.

Sugar and his muscles shuddering in the turmoil of shrieking, tortured air, his heart jerking with the kick and bang of another hit.

Need to get lower ...

Under normal circumstances, Rose would have tasked each flight to fly closer to the perimeter where men and machines usually were, to make the gunners think twice about firing into their own, but Mulheim-Essen had been a pre-war civil airfield and the original unusually circular arrangement of the main airfield's boundary made it difficult to fly straight and exit cleanly through a corner, while flying across the centre increased exposure and the risks from flak.

Even as Rose hurriedly eased the Tempest's nose back down again, the fleeing bowser seemed to expand impossibly in size for an instant before bursting apart, an eye-searing blurry blob of intense golden-yellow flame to starboard, an intense light bulb flash that cast everything into momentary shadow, the burning wreckage hurling out smoking, glowing fragments and the bowser's remnants bouncing away, wickedly sharp fragments of twisted shrapnel tearing the life from the second bowser's driver as he fled on foot, a red-hot shard of metal blistering comet-like across Sugar's path trailing sparks, another scything like a tracer round terrifyingly close above her canopy bubble (and Rose's head), while the rumble of the explosion was a low, angry *ba-BOOM!*

The harsh concussive slap of the exploding fuel bowser's shock wave slammed against her but he fought against it, and his heart jerked inside him as she lurched sickeningly to starboard, and he corrected her with a touch of rudder as a flak shell burst above, pummelling at her, and he was pushing Sugar down again, as close to the oil-stained tarmac as he dared, loosing off a few rounds of cannon fire as another old Junkers trimotor workhorse slid through his sights, but too late to hit it and the rounds went hurtling off uselessly into unknown oblivion.

The Tempest to starboard surged forward eagerly, sliding carelessly to port as it did so, skidding across in front of Sugar at full throttle as it bore down on another parked aircraft, gun smoke streaming back from its wings and over Sugar, spun into curling whorls by her spinner, and Rose pulled his thumb from the gun button just as he had been about to press it, terror in his chest for he had almost shot the silly bastard down. 'Hotspur Four, slip starboard.'

'*D'accord, leader.*' Words gasped out through a breathless mingling of exhilaration and fright.

Ironically, the abandoned second bowser had escaped their cannon fire and remained untouched, its fleeing driver killed in the explosion of the first one. His heart lurched again as he felt metal fragments punch into Sugar, the smack of the bowser's explosion against her fuselage, the *thump-thump-thump* of closer flak bursts.

Sucking in a chestful of oxygen and cordite, trying not to choke and cough, and blinking away sweat from stinging, straining eyes. Eyes in the mirror, no bandits, just rising smoke and emptiness, Sugar's Sabre screaming defiant thunder, the confusion of cries and yells in his headphones.

Her canopy was streaked with oil and smoke, and he peered through the grime to the tumult of explosions, hazy drifts of smoke and lines of tracer for more targets, heart pumping painfully.

He knew that the airfield gunners often set up interlocking fields of fire but, whereas the men of the USAAF began their attack runs from higher up to maximise target opportunities and bullets on target, the RAF usually flew far lower to evade the fire as most gunners feared hitting their own.

Dearest Lord my God, let there be no flak curtains at our height, see us through this chaotic furore safely …

Again several thumps striking hard against her, crisp and hard, *crunch-crunch-crunch!* Felt through his feet and backside rather more than heard, but she continued smoothly as if nothing had happened, *good old Sugar!* His eyes strained ahead as he hunched forward, smoke and oil streaking across the windscreen, the harsh bitterness of gun smoke and fear tearing at his windpipe.

Trees stretched in a dark irregular blur to either side of the airfield, above them a patchy layer of rippling white puffs of light flak, a lethal crop but no sign of the flak towers or hidden fighters, flashes of light and glowing lines of tracer in the shadowed north-eastern corner of Mulheim-Essen, and then a larger flash, a short-lived but bright light flickering hard and dying to port, and the anguished cry, anonymous, breathless and high-pitched, '*Oh, Mon Dieu! Mon Dieu! Petit Jacques est mort!*' The brief flash signifying the sudden and violent death of another young man under his command.

Gabby cried out, '*Gardez votre avion bas, faites attention aux flak!*'

A recollection of Granny's sad and drunken words one evening following one particularly bad day for 44 Wing in Normandy, 'They glow hard and bright, these boys they send us, but dear Lord! Their light burns out so quickly.' His voice had been bitter with loss. 'Damn this fucking awful war!'

Boys who fight and die as men. Heroes all.

No time to reminisce over poor Little Jacques or to mourn him, a stream of glowing shells coming straight for them from the raised carpet of forest at the eastern perimeter (high, from one of the flak towers?), more winged shapes and a jumbled impression of twin engines and tails catching the glow of the newborn sun on the horizon.

A brief touch of the button and more shells poured out from Sugar to cut through the gathering grey haze of gun smoke from gunfire and flak, another billowing cloud enveloping the shapes as his shells smashed amongst them, an aeroplane with twin rudders and spiky antennae bristling from its nose, the Dornier (or perhaps a Me110 night fighter? Impossible to tell at this speed), rocked by the flickering of bright white flashes of high explosive 20 mm slashing catastrophically across it to tear through its wings and fuselage, half hidden by the expanding swell of paint flakes, fragments and blotted smoke, an Opel truck beyond it caught by the fan of Sugar's shells and ripped to pieces, what little remained battered into junk and rolling onto its side by Sugar's devastating broadside.

All the while close above them the deadly tangle of glowing tracer and the rich rash of black and white flowers of bursting smoke, a false ceiling of fire and destruction.

The eastern boundary looming, a dark and snow-frosted wall of trees straight ahead, the blunted *crump-crump-crump* and the *zip-zip-zip* and *crack! crack!* of tracer and flak, the high-pitched mosquito whine of debris and hot shell fragments flicking past Sugar dangerously close, his breathing rough and irregular with the chatter of his men in his earphones, the crashing thump of her cannon pounding out explosive shells, the defiant dominance of Sugar's Sabre, strong, steady and reassuring, her armoured cockpit his battlements. A coarse and ragged cacophony of blood and flame as the thought of clearing the treeline and being naked to the rising flak nagged at him.

Ahead of him pale lemon light seeped into the grey of the dawn, gleaming against the fuselage of the Tempest which had powered past earlier, now swaying as it received hits but continuing to hurtle onwards seemingly unaffected, a trail of grey smoke, quickly thinning and trailing away into nothing.

Concentrate on the shadows ahead. Might there yet be more aircraft hidden beneath the ice-covered canopy ahead? Surely trees are the best hiding place from the air … ?

With the dawn rising and the impenetrable darkness of the shadows on and beneath the brooding trees beyond the perimeter taxiway, Rose could not tell. Something exploded lividly behind them, the wave of pressure blast expanding outwards and he felt Sugar sliding, her tail lifting and he gasped involuntarily, the acrid rending deep within his throat, pulling back on the stick and weaving an erratic path, something *thunking* into her.

He had caught up with the others now and dropped her nose a touch to bear on the jumbled shadows, firing a long two-second burst; ease stick back and forth, allow for deflection, gentle irregular pressure on the rudder bar, *port-starboard-port-starboard* to create an expanding fan of explosive shells sweeping out onto the ground and into the shaded depths, some rounds ricocheting high into the sky, fireflies flashing emptily in the forested blackness. He cursed at the wasted shells, but was belatedly rewarded with the eruption of a boiling yellow-bright explosion, rising upwards and spawning further secondary explosions, bright burgeoning flowers wreathed in billowing black smoke.

Where the bloody hell is that bastard flak tower?

Venomous red and yellow flecks of fire sparkled within the thick crop of white bursts daubing the pale sky, but no sign of the poisonous twinkling of muzzle flash from the distant flak towers in the east, the sun a bright ball rising beyond the trees.

And the memory of a hard-earned warning, *Beware the Hun in the sun ...*

Might the flak tower be concealed within the light of the rising sun?

Immediately he pulled back and, with a little touch of pressure on the rudder, he fired off another two-second burst into the brilliant golden orb ahead, and wondered if any of his men were watching and wondering, *The old man's lost his marbles ...*

Nothing to show for his efforts but under the foliage a carpet of fire was now raging where there once had been the indistinct blotted emptiness of shadows; flames and thick black oily smoke rising and surging through the branches, smaller secondary explosions flaring hard beneath them, and the twirling smoke trails of exploding ammunition streaking outwards in all directions.

Rose hunched down and curled forwards, so that his eyes were level with the console harness biting into his shoulders, his shirt sodden and the sweat an irritant trickling down between his tensed shoulder blades, his buttocks and groin tightening to stone in expectation of rending hot metal pieces despite the armour beneath him.

Please God, let nothing explode beneath me, and save me from the raging fires below. Easing back the stick slightly, he watched for the others to allow a slight bank further to starboard to avoid passing directly above the conflagration beneath the steaming, smoking canopy, the trees like a cliff face rushing towards him, taking her just above the treetops, low, low as he dared above their clawing branches as they reached to take Sugar down, her propeller disc scything through the tallest tips, pushing her lower against the cushion of air to minimise his outline against the sky as the enemy gunners emptied their magazines after the racing Tempests.

The cloud of thick smoke climbed high up before him like a great black wall, blocking out the light of the sun, and a tiny part of his primal consciousness, fearful of the heavy darkness, screamed for him to turn away but he held her steady and Sugar plunged into it. Yet it was a smoke screen against the enemy gunners, blocking their view of the RAF attackers.

And then they were through the black drift, Sugar's canopy dirtied by oil and smoke, his restless, aching eyes searching for his men in the brightening firmament (*surely it must be too early for roving enemy fighter patrols?*), fearing what he might see or rather those who were missing from their number, a pair of distant fleeting shapes to starboard skimming the treetops, loyal Frankie trailing close behind (*thank God!*) but capturing his attention a wooden tower rising just above the trees almost straight ahead.

The gun platform of the flak tower was shredded and the flak gun itself was gone, the crew blown away beneath Sugar's fusillade of a few seconds earlier, fragmented wood and what looked like a bleeding haunch of meat hanging from one splintered, red-washed pillar, all that remained of the crew of the flak tower, blown apart by his last burst into the sun.

It was only a glimpse of that flayed remnant of a man, seen almost too fast to even register, for his attention was now focussed behind his fleeing fighters but the air behind was stained by flowing smoke, his relentlessly searching eyes catching sight of a ragged swirl of white blossoms chasing after their tails as the other flak tower inexpertly sprayed tracer after them.

No time to explain, the flame-spitting tower too close to turn into, stick back into his stomach and rudder over as Sugar soared upwards for precious altitude, throttle back but not too much as her speed bled off, watching for collision with other Tempests as they fled. He pulled one wing over and hauled her into a turn to line up on the enemy even as he levelled her wings and pushed her nose forwards again, gasping with the effort, his straps pulling back against him and the mask sliding painfully across the cuts on his face, squashing down against the gun button and smashing out two one-second bursts; a torrent of explosive cannon shells whipped into the trees before five or six slammed hard against the flak platform (*built from wood not concrete, just like the first, thank God!*).

The enemy gunners had eyes only for the Tempests bolting away and climbing hard to starboard as Sugar's shells exploded on their way through the tower, and his target disappeared inside an expanding cloud of fragmented tree and splintered wood, metal, and the shreds of its crew.

And he was hauling back at full throttle, surely now out of range of the airfield defences, the sky filling his windscreen, the spreading pall masking the ruined airfield and its numerous dead and the plume of white snowflakes behind which Sugar's slipstream raised from the branches she had skimmed so closely behind and now beneath in his mirror, a few bursts of smeared black from the heavy flak as they rocketed skywards, but ineffective against their speed.

As Rose and his Free French fighters levelled out alongside Sheep's squadron there was that familiar ache again, for amongst the stained formation two spaces were empty, Jacques plus one other, and he allowed himself a guilty peek at her picture as he pressed a palm momentarily against the side of the cockpit in thanks to his mount.

They got two more of mine, *but not me, Moll.*

And he was ashamed for his salvation and of the feeling of relief which filled him.

Watching the Intelligence Officer move amongst his men, Rose felt that familiar slump of melancholia with the anti-climax which comes after an operation. It had been successful, fourteen aircraft confirmed destroyed, including eleven of the newly arrived Bf109 fighters.

They had been damned lucky in the attack. Used to almost daily attacks by USAAF fighters, the gunners had been unfamiliar with the RAF tactics of attacks low down on the deck. Hitting both flak towers had been a spot of luck for them, and the thick smoke from the myriad guns and the explosions and fires from whatever had been hidden beneath the perimeter trees had masked their escape upwards from much of the flak.

Gabby was talking gently with Jacque's best friend, the youngster's eyes red and vacant with shock, Sheep's arm around his shoulders.

Just one of those things.

In the end, miraculously, it had been only Jacques they had lost, Rose's memory of a thin face, a tight mop of curly black hair and scarred hands, sitting amongst Rose's Frenchmen, quiet and watchful, occasionally bringing out his flute to play them a cheerful tune (or five).

Gabby had spoken with admiration of the man's experiences in escaping from Nazi-occupied France in 1941, and of his eagerness to strike back.

And now he was gone; all that knowledge, all that experience, another who laughed, loved and cried like them all, gone in a single bright flash of light. Ironically, his had been the Tempest which had been made serviceable just as they had been about to depart.

Did I kill Little Jacques by asking for Chiefy for a maximum effort in getting kites serviceable?

Like so many others he had known over the years, so many lost in these interminably long years of war, faces fading in time, the numbers of his honoured dead ever increasing.

And he was tired. So very tired.

Tired of the emptiness, the pain and the loss. Tired of the dreaded letter he must write.

Tired of the acid burning in his chest after each op, and the whispers of dread burning at the edges of his mind.

His fingers crept up to his pocket, the edges of her photo sharp beneath the fabric.

Weary of his continued separation from her, of his loneliness even in the midst of his excited men. He thought he would cry and closed his eyes so that his men would not witness his weakness and shame.

Dear Lord God, how much more must we endure?

When will this thing *end*?

Chapter 14

Rose sighed and read aloud, '*Ywis and nought at wene, The gode ben al oway.*' He looked at his friends and shook his head.

What a load of old nonsense! How on earth did Moll expect him to understand this gibberish? How did she even understand it?

God help us all, but did anyone actually understand it? Or did they pretend they did just so they could look clever?

'Ah.' Gabby nodded wisely. '*Sir Tristrem*. Hmm. The beautiful tale of love, *non?*'

Sheep looked up from his *G8 and His Battle Aces* pulp magazine, his expression thoughtful and he spoke softly. "*It is a certainty, the good are all no more*". Touching, eh? Enchanting words.'

'*Oui.* Captivating and glorious. Middle English is much clearer than the babble English language spoken today, *n'est-ce pas?*' Gabby looked pointedly at Sheep before glancing apologetically at his Wing Leader. '*Oh. Uh ... pardon,* sir. I meant only of course the *merde* that falls easily from this big ignorant pig's lips.'

'Oh, no, not at all.' Rose tried not to show his astonishment, *Lord merciful God!* Sheep and Gabby actually understood this impenetrable gobbledegook?

As if to make amends, Gabby stared scornfully at the big Australian. 'At least when you speak, sir, I comprehend. When this *gros cochon* jabbers the brainless *ordures,* it is incomprehensible grunting to me. Sometimes I wonder if he has learned to break wind with his mouth.'

Sheep rudely stuck two fingers up at the Frenchman (overlooking how reviled the English longbow archers had been by the French), but Gabby had not forgotten and he smiled grimly. 'Ah, *oui*! The archer's fingers! You remember what happened to the apprehended bowmen, *non*?'

Archers captured by the French during the Hundred Years War first had suffered the fate of having their fingers cut off, before being tortured horribly, and Rose suppressed a grimace at the sheer awfulness of their torment. It must have been a very brave and strong man who chose to be an English archer at that time.

Seeing Rose's expression and fearing he had spoken out of turn, Gabby was mortified. '*Oh! Pardon*, sir!'

Sheep grinned at Gabby's chagrin and leaned towards Rose conspiratorially. 'Sir? I need to warn you, it's a bit personal, but you must be told.' He glanced at Gabby. 'Gabby, I need to tell the boss. Don't be crook, OK? It's important.'

Gabby ignored him, looking down and apparently engrossed in the copy of *Esquire* he was holding.

Sheep's tone was solemn. 'See, Gabby's got this strange thing he does, and as his senior officer, you need to know.' Sheep pulled cautiously on his moustache, eyes anxious, adding urgently, 'You need to be warned!'

'Oh?' Intrigued, Rose closed the book he had been trying to read. It was the same story with Shakespeare's works, all of it incomprehensible gibberish.

He had always found Shakespeare heavy going, but Molly adored the Bard. He read it, re-read it, and read it again, but it remained impenetrable twaddle, the Lord only knew how she made head or tail of it.

But then, she was simply remarkable.

At least he made her laugh by screeching Hamlet's *'Get thee to a nunnery!'* when he was attempting to read the Prince of Denmark's tale one evening in front of the fire and she had smiled saucily, expertly undone his flies and lifted her dress waist high, elegant legs parting and bending to straddle him, his breath catching in wonder when he saw she wore nothing beneath, her lips gentle against his and the heady scent of her eagerness thrilling and captivating both his brain and 'very best bits' simultaneously.

And yet which of them was it now living in a monastery?

As Molly's delicious softness had settled warmly against his rather willing and very eager groin, she whispered reprovingly to him, 'You do know that the term nunnery was slang in Elizabethan England for a brothel, don't you, my naughty boy?'

He had known nothing of the kind but had been too busy greedily caressing the smooth tautness of her buttocks to care, electrified by her touch, his mouth bone dry and throat tight in excitement and anticipation of what was to come.

What a woman! There were not enough superlatives to adequately describe her.

Intelligent, sophisticated, elegant, beautiful and extraordinarily brave, as evidenced by Molly's excellent George Cross, and her MBE with silver oak leaves, awarded *'For Gallantry'*.

A woman and a warrior, the epitome of all those who had kept the darkness at bay after the fall of Europe.

And it's *me* she chose to share her life with, *me* she gave her heart to, and *me* who fathered our babies!

Savouring the knowledge and trying not to feel smug in his good fortune, Rose touched the pocket that held her precious photograph, his faithful companion on operations since 1940. His fingertips passed gently over its edges through the fabric, each fold and tear in it having the familiarity of an old friend, and he sighed with longing, wishing he could hear her voice and reach out to hold her hand.

How he had stolen the heart of a woman as remarkable as Molly was even more incomprehensible than Shakespeare's prose. It was an unfathomable reality, but one he was extremely grateful for each day.

The big Australian was still talking and Rose tried to look interested, reluctantly dragging his mind away from the lovely thoughts of his wife.

Oh Moll, how I miss you …

On the other side of the room Johnny Iremonger was chatting animatedly to his lads. Recent plans were for experienced Spitfire pilots to join Tempest Units as budding commanding officers, and Johnny was to be replaced as CO of 486 Squadron by the popular fair-haired 'Spike' Umbers from 3 Squadron.

Evan 'Rosie' Mackie, an RNZAF Mediterranean ace, would be joining 274 Squadron as a CO-in-waiting as well. Rose and Mackie had met once in 1943 at a 'bash' when the latter had been with the Tangmere fighter wing, and he was looking forward to seeing Mackie again.

Sheep's face was sombre as he stared at Rose. 'Are you listening, sir? Only, you looked a bit blank for a moment. But then, I find my mind goes a bit blank as soon as old Gabs opens his mouth and starts his flappin'. You with me now, sir? Yeah? Right-o, then. Well, Gabby's a bit French, right?'

Sheep nudged the young Frenchman playfully. 'You are, aren't you? Vooz et French, nest par? Yeah?'

Gabby continued to ignore him, but turned a page in his magazine with such force that Rose heard paper tear.

'See? Moody and magnifique. Painfully Gallic, even.' He nudged Gabby affably. '*Zut alors! Vive la Madame Guillotine! Escargots au beurre! Liberte, egalite, fraternite!*' He paused, then continued, '*Pomme de terre et la oignon, oui?*'

Gabby sniffed derisively, and snapped another page across.

Rose shook his head. *Dear God, what nonsense.* 'Well, come on then, Sheep, for the love of mike, spit it out, will you? I can already feel petrification setting in.'

Sheep's voice dropped to a theatrical whisper, and he leaned forward conspiratorially. 'Sir, you must never leave your Daks unaccompanied.' A shifty glance at Gabby. 'Promise me you won't, will you?'

Daks unaccompanied? 'Daks? I beg your pardon?'

'Uh, sorry sir. Daks is Aussie for trousers. Never leave your trousers unaccompanied. I forgot you're not an Aussie.' He smiled genially. 'Never mind, though, can't all be perfect, eh?'

Trousers unaccompanied? Baffled, Rose raised his eyebrows. 'What are you blethering about, old chap?'

'Your strides, sir, your trousers. The things on your legs, keeps 'em warm and covers yer knobbly knees. Stops spiders crawling up your arse. With me now? Well then ... Gabby has a habit, can't help himself, poor soul. See, if you're careless, and you leave your trousers lying around, he'll whip 'em on quick as you like, and before you can say "*Vive L'Empeurer*", he'll be prancing around like a good 'un, thrusting out the Can-Can and tooting the Whore's Whistle.' He nodded sincerely. 'Fair dinkum!'

He elbowed Gabby. 'You were on the stage at the *Folies Bergère*, weren't you, Gabs? Flapping your bare arse cheeks on the stage to an orchestra? Backside going like a pair of ruddy bellows, I hear?'

Sheep smiled warmly at the young Frenchman. 'You were the talk of Paree, I heard, Gabs, old cock. At least when folks could talk, that is, 'coz they say the booming crack of your bum cheeks slapping together drowned out all other conversation. The Lion of Verdun, Petain, went to one of his shows, sir. You know what a moralist the old bastard is? Well he tried to stop the show and came out as deaf as a post, poor cove.'

He shook his head sadly. 'Got too close, apparently, so the poor ol' Lion of Verdun got caught by the turbulence between Gabby's oscillating bum cheeks, got slapped back and forth between 'em like a tennis ball and then almost got sucked up Gabby's arse! He was so dazed by the slapping that he couldn't do anything to save himself. It was only Petain's aide-de-camp managed to grab hold of the old coot's ankles before he got drawn in, saved the Lion from a fate worse than death.'

He gave a mock shudder. 'Didn't break anything of course, just shock and bruises and a little bit sticky, apparently, the poor old sod. So much for that old refrain '*They shall not pass!*' The poor old bugger almost passed up Gabs's rear end!'

Sheep patted his friend kindly on the arm, and grinned evilly at Rose. 'I believe that the poor old dear lost his favourite Ceremonial Kepi, both shoulder tabs and his sash in the process. Not sure if Gabs has'—he coughed delicately—'erm, managed to recover them yet. I reckon Gabs kept it as a souvenir of his hero. Anyway, I reckon that's why Petain didn't have the heart to fight Jerry back in 1940, he couldn't, see? He was still in shock, still seeing stars and couldn't hear a bloody thing with Gabs's bum wax in his ears!'

He looked thoughtful. 'Y'know, if they'd had Gabs on the Maginot Line back in 1940, he could've blown away a Panzer army with his bum rippling out the Whore's Whistle. Or at least he might've blistered their paint and asphyxiated the crews with his festering farts.'

Gabby viciously turned another page and Rose fancied he could hear the grating squeak of molars grinding against one another.

The tall Australian smirked at Rose. 'Just imagine it, sir. Onion and garlic-tinged clouds of poison gas. What a toxic mixture! *Phew!* They didn't use him, though, because it goes against all the rules of war. Doesn't bear thinking about what might have been, though, does it?' He waved one hand vaguely in the air. 'Would've poisoned friend and foe alike! The Geneva Convention bods would've taken a very dim view of *that*!'

Gabby *tutted*, threw down his magazine at last and looked across at his friend acidly. '*Trou du cul!* Continue this childish noise, *cochon*, and there will be much shouting.'

'Fair dinkum. Josephine Baker might've been known for her singing and her dancing, tits, banana skirt and all,' the tall Australian continued, unfazed by Gabby's outburst, 'but good ol' Gabs was famous for his Amazing Clapping Arse.'

'The Whore's Whistle?' Rose was baffled.

'C'mon, sir. That Jerry dirge. Howl it out at all the Nasty Rallies under torchlight in Nuremberg, not that I'd know anything about that.' He waved an imaginary conductor's baton. 'Y'know, dee-dah-dah-dum, dum-dum?'

Rose pondered this mystery for a moment—*howl it out at all the Nazi Rallies?*

What on earth … ?

And then the penny dropped. 'Oh … you mean the Horst Wessel! Sheep, you daft bugger, it's called the Horst Wessel.'

Sheep beamed his mischievous lopsided grin again, reminding Rose of Daffie's daft, adorable grin. 'Coo, fancy that! Blow me down the stairs with a feather! And there I was all this time thinking it was called the Whore's Whistle!' That bristling moustache curled further up. 'That's something, learn something new every day, eh? *Set kelka shows,* eh, Gabs?'

'*Mon Dieu!*' Gabby bristled. '*Regardez*, sir, this big pig is an *idiot.*' The Frenchman grimaced in disgust, adding moodily, '*Mon cochon malodorant,* you speak tolerable French, even though with the shocking accent, yet you perhaps think I *comprendre* you better with the execrable grammar and pronunciation?'

Sheep winked at his friend and picked up his magazine again. 'Not your fault, cobber, you're French. Not everyone gets to come from down under.' He added, oddly and bafflingly, '*Je ne regrette rien,* eh? *Zut alors, suivez cet œuf!*'

Gabby gazed dolefully at Rose. '*San cervelle.* You see, sir? A gangling pig breaking the wind *putride* with it the wrong end. No wisdom, *absurdité*, just the empty, senseless noise and stinky bluster. *Pah!*'

Chapter 15

Twelve Tempests, a broad arrowhead formed by three sections of four, each quartet in ragged line abreast, flying just below a gloomy ceiling of patchy, broken cloud in the miserable grey light. So low that the lowest streamers of murky grey were torn into whirling shreds by racing propeller discs and hard edges and lost in their slipstreams, the German city of Goch close to the border a darker grey blotch blending against the pale dreary ground through the haze.

Ten miles to their north, twelve more Tempests decorated with the scarlet banner of the Oriflamme and the Cross of Lorraine, flying a parallel course. Each of the formations would provide mutual support for the other.

There were random flashes of light and bursts of black smoke chasing after them, for with their open formation and bobbing progress they were capricious targets, and would likely yield nothing in return to the gunners of the 88s, only the dull roar of their Sabres, the scratchy sound of their breathing and the frustrated rattle of the German radar in their earphones.

It was bitterly cold outside, although the Met officer had cheerfully assured him that the winter of 1940 and 1941 had been far colder before warning Rose of deteriorating conditions in the following days, of fog and rain and more snow.

With conditions likely to ground them, Rose decided they would sortie into Germany while it was still possible.

Get a few licks in, so to speak.

The Luftwaffe infrequently engaged in combat now, and he was hoping that they might be able to draw them out. After five years of war, there were few fighters and far fewer veterans than ever before left in the enemy ranks, and each one lost reduced the Luftwaffe's deficient capabilities further.

The cloud seemed to suck up the light and the soft red glow of Sugar's instruments cast faint shadows into his cockpit.

Rose had chosen to lead the starboard section of four Australian Tempests—young Micky Lynch was his wingman to port, and the two fighters of his second element out to starboard were Don Jardine from Pallamallawa and Doug Fletcher from Agnes Banks, both men hailing originally from New South Wales.

The formation flew close beneath the patchy cloud to protect them from the threat of a bounce, although now Rose agonised that either friendly or enemy fighters might unknowingly slice through the irregular grey ceiling without warning to scatter his men, or worse, collide with them. It was an unlikely worry, but he fretted nonetheless.

Eyes roving to a patch in the cloud, anxiously seeking bandits, his anxiety was unfounded and the brighter sky above empty.

In his earphones the genial crackle of Sheep's voice. 'Hobart to Kenway, twelve airborne. Anything doing?'

'Kenway to Hobart, standby.'

Just the gentle crackle to break the silence, interminable seconds that seemed like hours, then, 'Kenway to Hobart, bandits active west of Cologne, please investigate.'

'Hobart to Kenway, height and number?'

'Kenway to Hobart, low level, below angels four. Number unknown, possibly ten or more.'

'Hobart to Kenway, Ta, mate.' A pause and then, solicitously, 'Hotspur One, fancy taking over a mob of rousies?'

Every time he flew with the Australians, Sheep was ever courteous, but Rose was happy to let his friend stay at the head of his squadron and he replied in the same vein. 'Hotspur One to Hobart Leader, your squadron, chum.'

When flying with the Wing, Rose led from the front, but when his squadrons were operating independently, Rose flew as a guest, as Section Leader or even as a wingman, letting his deputies lead their own units. He would not usurp his friends' position, for they were skilled leaders in their own right and knew their men better than he.

Eyes unfocussed and never still, never centring on a single point, searching for hidden distant motion, another deep inhalation of oxygen to improve his visual acuity and to steady him, feeling the prickle of discomfort in his lungs, conscious of the heavy lurch of his heart.

Mirror, front, starboard, behind and beneath his men's tails, to port, scan the instruments, all clear and back again to the mirror, then repeating it again.

And again.

And again …

Low-level bandits, perhaps heading westwards? A fighter bomber raiding sortie or fighters collecting into one of their massed formations of thirty or forty plus before trying to intercept the incoming USAAF bomber formations?

The idea of a 'Big Wing' seemed to work better for Goering than it had for the RAF in 1940. Probably because the Germans had more warning as the formations gathered and coalesced and the knowledge that the USAAF bomber stream always branched off from the same overwater approach route.

It was much more than the hard-pressed little RAF band of brothers had had in 1940.

His tummy burbled angrily.

Lunch for Rose had been a solitary digestive biscuit dunked into a lukewarm cup of milk, his stomach rebelling as Rose watched the men of his Wing heartily tucking into platefuls of fried bully beef stuck between thick slices of toast, the atrocious greasy slab of meat and bread washed down willing throats with copious amounts of steaming compo tea.

Digestives (and malted milk biscuits, too, he had discovered) had been a blessing for Rose in the cause of digestion.

It was said that the bicarbonate in the digestive was an effective antacid, and certainly Rose had found warm milk and a digestive or two sufficient to settle the discomfort and burn in his chest before a sortie, while with malted milk biscuits the milk powder was both gentle and nourishing on his stomach.

Sheep and Gabby and a few of their pilots had driven down to the 2TAF HQ Stores in Eindhoven and thoughtfully pilfered a large number of tins of McVitie's digestives and Elke's malted milk biscuits for their Wing Leader from the AOC's personal stock, enough to last Rose well into the spring.

Fortunately for his band of miscreants, there had been no missives in the past week calling for two light-fingered Tempest squadron COs to appear before the AOC for an almighty 'rocket', so it appeared (fingers and toes crossed) that the cheeky buggers might have got away with it, and Rose was grateful for their thoughtfulness.

He was disturbed from his reverie by the crackle in his headphones.

'Hobart Leader from Hobart Red Four, thirty plus bandits at ten o'clock, two thousand feet below.'

Cripes! Deep breaths, safety off and gunsight on, all clear?

Sheep's reply was immediate. 'Roger, Red Four, I've got 'em. Three miles and closing, turning to port.' Then, 'Come and join the party, Gabs, thirty plus 109s.'

And the laconic response. *'Je serai bientôt là, mon ami …'*

Rose could now see that the enemy formation consisted of Messerschmitt Bf109s, a mixture of 109Fs and 109Gs, their striped camouflage and colours gaudy like a shoal of fish against the drab grey canvas of the ground as they passed below the turning Tempests in a loose formation.

The RAF fighters were in an ideal position to initiate a textbook bounce, and Sheep wasted no time. 'Hobart Blue and Hobart Red, follow me. Hotspur Section, cover us against those who climb up above us.'

Jerry's so busy concentrating on staying in formation that they hadn't even noticed the Tempests, or had perhaps even misidentified them as 190s, the dozy bastards …

Rose licked dry lips and swallowed as the other two sections pushed down into a dive towards the enemy's rear, eyes stealing to his mirror again. 'Roger, Hobart Leader.'

To his Section, 'Wingmen back into covering position, Hotspur Three, wide to port.'

But the bandit leader was no inexperienced fool, and even as Sheep's eight Tempests raced down, small bombs detached and fell away from beneath the wings of the 109s and thick lines of black smoke poured from their exhausts as they broke apart to port and starboard to their original line of flight in a practised manner, their noses sweeping tight to turn in towards the attack from above, contrails streaming from their wingtips.

These ones weren't going to scarper for home.

Damn it!

Still out of range, Sheep's two sections now split apart into four pairs, the distance between each pair opening and the wingmen sliding back to cover their leaders from behind, the eight Tempests looking horribly outnumbered as they streaked after the bandits. At least 109s couldn't turn inside a Tempest, but with so many of them to face …

'Hotspur Leader, come on down!' Sheep's voice was strained as he and his men fought hard to gain a position of advantage.

But as he opened his mouth to give the order, everything changed.

'Hotspur Leader, break starboard! Break! BREAK!'

Micky's desperate scream was still piercing his eardrums as instinct and lightning-sharp reflexes took over, muscles tightening and working to fling Sugar into a hard turn to starboard, pressing hard on the rudder pedal and stick over into his thigh, fingers painfully tight around the circular grip as he gasped and panted, the forces pushing him backwards and crushing, straining eyes reeling to the mirror, conscious of the gathering greyness at the edges of his vision.

A cold stab of fear tearing at his innards and raising goose bumps at the image reflected, a sleek 109, its dark silhouette twinkling bright as the enemy pilot opened fire.

Christ! Where did he come from?

But the sudden turn took him out of its trajectory, and he was already out of the line of fire, the bullets and shells from its guns blistering past him harmlessly to port (*dearest God, thank you*).

Still turning, feeling his chest burn and the ache in his lungs and twisting neck as he tried to look back over his shoulder, knowing that the Jerry fighter could not close on him in the turn, Micky's high-pitched voice was loud in his earphones. 'He's fucked off, leader, I ruffled his tail feathers with a burst of 20 mm!'

God bless you, Micky! 'Good work, Two, I owe you a beer!' he rasped thinly, feeling Sugar's tremors through the control stick (or was that in his hands?) as he brought her out of the turn, eyes looking for fresh danger.

That had been bloody close!

A good wingman was an invaluable asset. Staying back in the 'wings' and not on the main stage, so to speak, they kept their leader safe while the latter could concentrate on the art of killing.

In their position they had to keep station on their leader, often through violent manoeuvres, as well as keep one eye on the sky and the other to ensure that both his leader's tail and his own were safe, eyes constantly straining through the sky and holding position.

A difficult supporting role with little glory but plenty of work.

Young Brat Morton, Granny's excellent wingman in Excalibur Squadron (and Rose's too, back in 1940), had once told Rose that it took him a little time once back on the ground for his eyes to refocus and to stop sliding around from point to point. Hearing this, Granny had charitably told Brat to 'stop being such a silly arse, you tart'.

As a junior officer, Rose had done the same, but the RAF piecemeal formations fighting in the face of overwhelming numbers during 1940 often led to desperate unequal duels in which one was often struggling alone, while night fighting later in 1941 was a solitary profession by its very nature.

And on his return to Excalibur in 1942 after flying a desk at the

Air Ministry, he had been appointed as Flight Commander with his own wingman.

With this most recent life-saving warning, Rose was immensely grateful that he had the experienced Micky and Frankie sharing the role of his wingman. Sheep and Gabby had chosen well.

Ahead of them, another pair of 109s emerged suddenly from the cloud, slanting down towards the desperately uneven fight below, noses down as if catching the scent of their prey, slim and deadly, clad in mottled silver and blue, dark against the cloud.

A quick glance in his mirror and ease out of the turn to point Sugar after this newly emerged pair, the leader already too far away, but the lagging enemy No. 2 close enough to catch.

They're caught up in the hunt and haven't seen us yet …

'Hotspur Two?'

'Clear, leader, no worries.'

He eased Sugar after them, *come on, come on,* descending and curving around wide to close the range after the enemy wingman, knowing that Micky would protect him from more bandits, and conscious of the twisting shapes of the battling fighters below and the cacophony of warning shouts and cries in his earphones, a mile away three 109s in line abreast jockeying for position behind a solitary Tempest as it dived away from them at full throttle, another Tempest turning stealthily after the enemy trio, while to starboard a ball of fire dropped beneath a dirty shroud of spreading oily smoke.

Estimating deflection he skilfully led the target in a starboard quarter attack approach, curving into a three-quarter astern attack with the distance closing fast, feeling the fire of urgency in his chest with Sugar arrowing around after the bandit and from three hundred yards in the 109 wingman's five o'clock he jammed down the gun button, the thunder and recoil powerful as a two-second burst of explosive metal blasted heavily across the intervening space between contrails of grey smoke, to sparkle and burst against the foreshortened shape like the bright white stabbing prickle of firecrackers; the 109 surrounded by a fleeting dark smear of smoke and debris which immediately plumed behind into her slipstream, the bright smudge of a small fire at the root of one wing and then going out, as a line of white (glycol?) flowed back in a thin streamer from beneath her engine cowling.

Got you!

With his glycol coolant tanks holed and leaking, the 109's Daimler-Benz 605A engine would seize up within a matter of minutes.

The bandit pulled up sharply, a thoughtless manoeuvre by its pilot, presenting Rose with a larger target profile, and Sugar's next two-second burst was a storm of metal battering across and into the 109 from stem to stern and from wingtip to wingtip, the lengthening stab of fire a twisting streamer.

One moment the little enemy fighter was struggling, shuddering, smoking and flaring beneath the merciless fury of Sugar's exploding cannon shells, and the next there was a flash and a huge sheet of flame as the German pilot and his aircraft were swallowed up by an expanding bubble of searing yellow-white fire, the 109 exploding violently as the storm of 20 mm tore through her fuel tanks, the ferocity of the explosion tearing her apart and blasting out blazing fragments, smoke streaking in all directions with the shockwave of the detonation.

As he hauled Sugar upwards and away with straining arms, Rose felt the wave of concussive pressure from his enemy's death grab at Sugar, heaving and battering at her, but he managed to hold her, just retaining control. A large chunk of what looked like a piece of spinning tailplane bearing its hateful swastika flashed past, close enough to make him cringe but not close enough to damage Sugar.

Eyes swept around, nothing in the mirror, the cloud unbroken by the emergence of more bandits. He thought of the shredding violence of the explosion, his clothes damp with sweat and fear, and drew in a mouthful of oxygen through stiff, dry lips. 'Hotspur Two? Micky?'

'Clear behind, leader. Congrats, good job.' Clipped, efficient, a professional, no sign of edginess in the chirpy, easy-going boy who had welcomed his arrival at Volkel in a Nazi General's trousers and boots.

Good lad.

Eyes slipping from cloud to cloud, a gentle see-sawing of the rudder to clear the blind spot beneath and behind, the reassuring and pugnacious shape of Micky's Tempest a quarter of a mile behind. No sign of the Tempest which moments earlier was being pursued by the trio of bandits, none of *their* pursuer.

In the distance, a thin black line of smoke slanting downwards denoted the death of another fighter, and in the middle distance the jumbled murmuration of Tempests and 109s thickening the sky, a mess of aircraft in which two of their number suddenly collided shockingly, creating a thick smear of fire from one, while the other just fell away, spinning out of control and out of the fight.

In his headphones the whoops, warnings and colourful expletives of his fighting Aussies were now joined by the quickfire Gallic invective of his Frenchmen.

Gabby's boys had arrived and it would be a fairer fight now.

Down below, oily smoke was billowing angrily up from a frosted field, *ours or theirs?* The line from Brooke coming unbidden, *'a corner of some foreign field'* ... and he shivered, restless eyes skimming the sky for threats and seeking targets in the far-flung gyrating mass of high-performance aircraft.

'Hotspur Two to Leader, three bandits at zero feet, three o'clock, heading east.'

Bless that boy's sharp eyes!

There. Darting shapes, so low that they seemed to skate across the fields, rising and falling lazily above the undulating ground, little shapes with blunt snouts and long triangular canopies in an arrowhead formation, heading away from the fight.

FW190s! *Cripes!* Where on earth had they come from?

More importantly, were there more of them?

Rose took a quick glance at his mirror, throttle and stick forward, knowing Micky was in position and matching him as their fighters raced after the fleeing enemy, the fear which bruised his soul gone for the moment and only the overpowering lust of the hunt, sensing her impatience as Sugar twisted after the fleeing enemy trinity of fighters, the land and clouds tilting and sliding, the power of her Sabre sweet beneath his fingers.

The ground was a vague blur seen through the raindrop-sullied and stained Perspex, the gathering specks of rain smearing the windscreen and distorting the tiny cruciform outlines of the bandits as they skirted thickets and copses, their shapes wavering and dancing in the sparse but deepening haze as more rain began to fall and visibility worsened, occasionally disappearing against the drabness of the landscape.

An autobahn flashed past, pale and straight in the dowdy landscape beneath their shadows, the boxy shapes of its traffic unidentifiable, military and civil vehicles jumbled together and indistinguishable.

In the distance were the faint, ghostly fingers of the smashed chimneys of some unknown factory, pointing reprovingly into the darkly closing sky. More flashes of flak bursting and dying in the stiffening rain.

Flying into the swelling gloom with ever increasing rain and the ceiling of clouds lowering threateningly, Rose realised that although they were gaining ground on the 190s with their superior speed, he would lose sight of them in the gloom before they were close enough to fire on them, and he cursed the weather.

With the risk of high ground seen only at the last moment, it would be madness to continue the hunt under these conditions.

His neck was tingling with foreboding. 'Two, we're onto a hiding for nothing with this game, we're going to lose Jerry in the rain. I'm taking us back to the main fight.'

'Received, Hotspur Leader.'

A single line of tracer, a thin lash of yellow cutting faint through the gloom from somewhere to starboard, but the gunner was nowhere close and it curved upwards too low, while further back and behind the brief bright sparkle of deadly flak, too far behind to hurt them, dulled and half hidden within the obscuring curtains of rain.

Rose pulled Sugar up, heeling her into a turn to starboard, seeking better light and altitude.

'Bandits!' called the boy flying behind. 'Hotspur Leader, three 190s, heading west and climbing into your eight o'clock position, quarter of a mile behind you!'

Closing fast on the ragged formation chasing after his Wing Leader, Micky led the hindmost 190 in his sights and gave it a hurried burst of 20 mm, the cannon shells erupting briefly against the bandit's fuselage, the enemy entering a turn to starboard and into the stream of shells.

For a second the glistening 190 shimmered beneath the explosive flashes, a thin stream of smoke fluttering and twirling, the propeller wind milling unevenly and nose tipping downwards, but there was no time to see more as he guided his Sugar around after the remaining two 190s on his Wing Leader's tail, heart thumping madly as he checked quickly to his rear to make sure no one was chasing after *him*.

Ahead of the young Australian, Rose pushed the throttle further forward, panting as his throat tensed with dread, *Dear God, help me!* Desperately pulling Sugar higher, the pursuing bandits looking horribly close as he craned his neck around, hoping (and praying) he could outclimb the pursuing 190s for just long enough before they could catch up and jockey into range, knowing the bandits had the advantage in the climb, and hoping the power of Sugar's Sabre might just hold them at bay for a moment or two; he felt the icy sharpness of fear's claws tearing at his guts and scraping down along his spine, the hairs on his body bristling and the mask tight and sucking painfully at his face where he had cut himself shaving as he twisted his neck to see.

'Have they seen you, Micky?' Rose's chest was tight with tension, his words forced out.

A half mile behind Rose, the third mortally damaged 190 fallen away behind and forgotten, Micky eyed the remaining pair of little fighters trying to catch Rose, their mottled dark paint schemes gleaming and wet, glistening shapes racing after Rose.

'Don't think so, Leader. I fell back a bit when you turned back for the main fight.'

Micky thought his voice would break as the distance closed between Sugar and her hunters, felt it rise in pitch and, embarrassed, he called out, 'Standby to break, Leader. Break to port—NOW!'

Rose grunted as he kicked rudder hard over and the stick pulled back tight, even tighter into his stomach the moment Micky blared into his headphones, muscles straining and throat parched with fear,

Sugar straining and her wings almost vertical as Rose threw her into a vicious turn to the left, feeling his breath catch, neck straining and his stomach and buttocks clenching tight as dried leather while the forces pulled and pummelled him, his spine aching with the effort and the harness taut and cutting into him through his battledress, *careful ... watch your airspeed!*

Rose whooshed a mouthful of oxygen, face set in a straining grimace, a thin cry torn from his lips by the ferocity of her turn, dirt from his boots and fragments of his map-marking chalk ricocheting and floating through the cockpit.

Oxygen was burning like ice at the scars in his labouring lungs, tearing at his chest and fiery in his straining throat, greyness begin to crowd at the periphery of his vision, and he groaned.

God! Can't breathe ... easy, keep it tight but for goodness sake don't stall her, watch out for that tell-tale shudder ...

Were these fighters the very same bandits they had been pursuing into the rain earlier? Had the bastards seen the trailing Tempests turn away and thought to come around and attack them?

Behind Rose, the 190 leader pulled a hard left turn after Sugar, and Micky spat out an oath as the second 190, the wingman, suddenly aileron turned to starboard, characteristically hard and tight, smoke driving thicker from his exhausts and white trails of condensation streaming back from its wingtips as the enemy wingman caught sight of Micky's Tempest; the Focke-Wulf's wings and nose swiftly lifting and turning, her foreshortening shape flashing bullets and cannon shells to blister past his Tempest's wingtip in burning lines of molten fire, the bandit a dark shadow terrifyingly close as it tore past, still turning to get behind him, Micky knowing he had little time left before the enemy wingman would be lining him up in his sights.

He's turning after me and I don't have long, but I daren't leave the Wingco's arse hanging wide open, best make these next coupla seconds count ...

Micky lined up on the wickedly turning 190 leader, pulling hard in the turn and then harder still as if he could feel the other 190 curving around after him and grateful for the armour plating at his back, gauging the angles and deflection and feeling the sheer power of his fighter as he loosed off a two-second burst of 20 mm, followed quickly by another, and then a third.

Jerry'll be crawling right up my bloody arse, got to get out of it ...

Not waiting to see the results of his actions, Micky pushed down his Tempest's nose and slammed forward her throttle, eyes watching the returning curve of the enemy wingman's 190 in his mirror apprehensively, and he began to pray.

Micky's first burst caught the 190 leader's port wing even as he was lining his sights on Rose's Sugar, slashing the black cross painted on its wing and jamming the aileron up and twisting the 190 further to port, the worst position to be in as Micky's second burst arrived and the enemy fought to control his damaged and suddenly unruly fighter.

The arrival of Micky's second burst of explosive 20 mm ended the veteran Oberleutnant's struggle, battering bloody horror into the 190's cockpit, its BMW radial engine, out across its starboard wing and ripping it in half inboard of the large *Balkenkreuz*, and thrusting the ravaged bandit into an uncontrollable spin earthwards so that Micky's third burst sailed off into oblivion; a plume of powdery flakes of paint and fuel vapour marked its terminal fall, the empty, dead eyes in the bloodied head of its pilot not seeing the approaching ground, his days of victory and glory over.

Shocked by the loss of his leader and his inability to protect him, witness to his leader's final descent in the torn wreckage of what had once been a high-performance fighter, the 190 wingman was possessed by an overwhelming urge to pursue and destroy the Tempest which had appeared without warning from behind them and which had already accounted for Hans; he loosed off a hurried and reckless burst of fire in his fury, poorly aimed and falling short of Micky's Tempest, R-Rooster as it began to pull away as he thrust forward the throttle.

Just as it seemed that Micky must have escaped, a burning shape emerged suddenly from the clouds above, impossible to identify whether Tempest, Bf109 or FW190, just a burning mass of flames shedding glowing scraps and pulling a thick dirty streamer of oily black smoke unevenly behind it, the wreckage tumbling haphazardly directly across Rooster's nose.

Taking urgent avoiding action, Micky instantly pulled Rooster into a climbing turn to starboard.

The sudden, unexpected climbing bank deprived the young Australian of his speed advantage in diving away and allowed the pursuing bandit to cut inside Micky's turn and close with the floundering Rooster, now passing just above yet impossibly close to the falling torch, one wingtip scything a line through the ragged oily smoke.

Beneath them both, Rose had completed his turn and was pulling Sugar upwards after the two turning fighters, still seeing in his mind's eye the lines of glowing tracer which had passed so close beneath Sugar, then fallen away, knowing he was finished just before Micky shot the 190 leader off his tail, heart walloping wildly against his breast bone by the very nearness of death.

Micky had killed two out of the three bandits, but now he was being chased by the third.

Rose heaved back on her control column, a touch of rudder and aileron to line his sights up on the quicksilver shape of the 190 as it curved around in a tight climbing turn after his wingman, the enemy's guns striking out at Micky, the youngster jinking desperately and escaping that first burst, only just, slipping and rolling as the bandit cut inside his curve to close the distance between them. The boy had saved him twice today and now it was time to return the favour.

'Keep turning, Micky, I'm lining up on him,' grated Rose breathlessly, face set in a grimace, the forces slamming hard against his body and fighting his limbs, blinking against the sting of sweat in his eyes to clear them. Sugar had powerfully closed the distance, cutting into the 190's turn just as the bandit had done as Micky banked hard over.

'Roger, Leader.' His words were grunted through anxiety and exertion.

Allow for deflection but mind Micky's tail …

Almost … there! The sight pulled to half a length ahead of the 190's black-and-white spinner, thumb jerking down on the gun button and a torrent of cannon shells from above and dead astern of the bandit at just over three hundred yards, lancing across the distance to flash deadly bright strikes against the 190's port horizontal stabiliser, shredding it and blowing off the entire elevator in one twisted piece.

The enemy pilot's head jerked around in shock as his aircraft shuddered and shook beneath the ruinous impacts, seeing Rose's Tempest behind him as if for the first time (*you forgot about me, Fritz, didn't you?*), the brown leather helmet and goggles staring at him clearly through the bandit's canopy, shocked awareness calling him to use his superior roll rate to reverse out of the turning circle Micky was pulling.

The German pulled his fighter harder into one of the 190's

characteristic tight turns, too tight, far tighter than his fighter would allow, teetering on the edge of a stall as his airspeed bled off steeply, with Sugar's spray of cannon shells hungrily chasing after it; one-two-three explosive flashes speckling hard against the battered tail of the 190, the torrent of cannon shells streaming past or slamming into its rear, and the 190 wallowed and faltered, one wingtip dipping uncertainly as yet another series of flashes danced and burst along the rear of her fuselage.

With impacts catastrophically smashing into her airframe, the resulting force and damage disrupting her airflow and aerodynamics and bleeding off her speed further, the 190 reeled, slipping over the edge, and stalled, flicking over violently downwards into an uncontrollable spin.

Every enemy pilot killed meant one less for others to face, but as it gyrated earthwards like a battered sycamore leaf, shedding pieces of itself as it went, Rose found himself urging the enemy pilot to bail out but knowing it was impossible as the pressures pulled off one wing so the tumbling descent twisted chaotically, swinging the wreckage erratically within the spin.

The unbearable forces of the spin snapped the young *Feldwebel's* harness, twisting and throwing his body this way and that, bones breaking and consciousness lost quickly before his head smashed against the canopy to break his neck, thrusting him into death and sparing him further pain and torment.

Rose circled the vanquished 190 on its final journey, eyes searching to ensure more bandits would not creep up on him, but the only other aircraft left in the sky was R-Rooster as Micky rejoined him.

What was left of the last 190 finally slammed cataclysmically into the ground, a brief flash spreading into a smeared bloom of yellow-white flame in an expanding cloud of fire, smoke and fragmented pieces of man and machine.

Another explosion, billowing smoke was dragged away and thinned by the increasing wind.

Rose drew in a deep breath, the pure oxygen and cordite stinging in the tautness of his lungs as he pulled up towards the ever lowering, darker clouds, the light and visibility dipping as the shadowed curtains of rain and sleet drew closer. They had been victorious, successful despite the imbalance in numbers, yet he felt his emotion drain tiredly into an overwhelming feeling of relieved salvation.

Around them were no signs of the other Tempests of his Wing, nor of the Bf109s they had bounced, just the columns of thinning smoke from their trio of FW190s, the yellow-brown creased blot of a collapsed parachute, its gaudy colour on the pale ground to prove that at least one of their opponents had survived the short-lived but savage fight Micky and he had survived.

There but for the Grace of God … he thought with gratitude and relief, and then, *God help us, don't know how much more of this ruddy lark my poor old ticker can take* … In his mind's eye he saw again the ugly snout of the 190 in the mirror, and an icy wave washed over him, and he shivered in reaction despite himself.

He had been saved by Micky today, and been lucky, damned lucky to have come through the violent bout with the scalps of another Bf109 and three FW190s between them.

Micky brought me luck today, thank you, my Lord God, thank you! For the mercy of our redemption and the gift of our salvation.

Eyes turned from his enduring search of the skies to steal a glance at her photo, *and for the chance for these eyes to look upon my love again.*

With the fight apparently over and with weather conditions rapidly deteriorating, Rose decided there was no reason to remain. 'Time to go home, Micky.' He had had more than enough and was drained.

Now the danger had (seemingly) passed, he began to worry about who they might have lost. Would there be more letters to write to the grieving, so damned close to the end of European hostilities? *Please God, let my boys have survived the fight …*

'Right you are, Hotspur Leader. I'm right behind you, all clear,' Micky replied cheerfully. *O, the resilience of youth!*

'Micky? Thanks. I owe you a beer.'

'Or maybe three, Leader!' Chirpy and lively now, he'd recovered fast from the tension, the cheeky little brute, but aware of the threat still inherent in these hostile, brutal skies, Rooster was on station with Sugar, reliable and faithful, a dark shape reassuringly behind.

God bless you, Micky.

It was the 15 December 1944, and the piled cloud, driving rain and sleet promised that flying might be curtailed for the next day or so.

Rose was grateful. *A day or two on the ground will be most welcome.*

To the south, an army waited, hidden in the dense forests of the Ardennes beneath a thick canopy of snow. More than 400,000 heavily armed men waiting in the bitter cold for their commander, OB West, to give the order to go.

Gerd Von Runstedt had already reached the rank of full General before the war and was a seasoned and capable officer but cruel and uncompromising in war, as exemplified by his endorsement of the Reichenau Order in Russia, the autonomy given to the vicious monsters of the evil *Einsatzgruppen* and the Commando Order of 1942, to name but a few.

Recalled to arms by Hitler, he had been made a Field Marshal in 1940 (and appointed OB West for the first time).

Appointed as Commander then dismissed, his loyalty and experience had made him indispensable and led him back to overall command of German forces in the west for a second time, facing an enemy now standing at the very gates of his beloved homeland.

Victory while fighting the Allies in the west and the barbarian hordes of Russia to the east was an impossible dream—he knew that, for he was no fool—but if Germany could inflict enough damage to make the enemy to the west parley, might they not be able to join forces to defeat the implacably advancing communist steamroller?

It was a last throw of the dice, a desperate one, but one which might yet save Germany.

However, an old and tired man by now, Von Runstedt vacillated against the Tyrant of Berlin's eagerness and insistence, considering his troop numbers far below what they should be for the new offensive to succeed, and he asked once more for additional troops.

Impatient and irritated by the old Field Marshal's caution, and deciding that Von Runstedt had had his day, Hitler decided he would supervise the offensive himself, arriving on 10 December.

Hitler would bypass OB West, and issue the necessary orders directly to the senior commanders himself.

Knowing that the terrible weather would neutralise the superiority of Allied Air Power and that his men waiting in the Ardennes faced an enemy half their number at this weakly held point of the front line, Hitler believed that a blow here would force apart the British and American forces while also creating differences amongst the enemy.

Furthermore, there was but a short distance to the coast, the initial assault would enjoy forested concealment, and the advance would create an increased bulwark of defence for the German industrial heartland of the Ruhr.

Believing himself a genius and Germany's glorious saviour, *Der Fuhrer* gave the order.

The Battle of the Bulge had begun.

Chapter 16

The Ardennes is roughly the shape of an arrowhead resting between Liege and Bastogne in Belgium, and Germany's westernmost city of Aachen, with its tip pointing southwards.

It comprises the generally open but narrow northern Low Ardennes and the wider southern High Ardennes (with many ridges jutting from a high plain), the two separated by the slender length of the Famenne Depression and the Eifel range of mountains to their south.

The overall area was well provided for with roads meant for the rise in tourism in the 1930s, but they were winding and twisting, the sheer drops often half hidden by fog and more than terrifying in some parts.

The topography of the High Ardennes favoured the use of smaller, autonomous fighting units, due to the limitations of rocky terrain and a collage of dense forest, while hampering the urgent movements of larger formations of men, machines and materiel.

Located between the movement of weather systems, one eastwards and the other westwards, the region suffered extreme bad weather. Freezing winds amalgamated with heavy rain, sleet and snow to make conditions for those spending any time in the outdoors very miserable indeed.

The cause was a result of the eastwards drive of the Atlantic climate chafing up against the westwards flow of weather from the heart of frozen Russia, thereby creating starkly hostile conditions.

And so it was at the end of 1944, when it was considered most unlikely that such an area, a bottleneck to invading armies and be an exercise in madness for commanding Generals and Logistics Officers, could possibly be a point of danger.

Who would undertake such lunacy? Surely only a complete idiot would even think it.

This despite the successful and rapid advance of German armies through it before, once in the Battle of the Ardennes in 1914, and then again in 1940 during Blitzkrieg. The Germans had twice already cut sharply into Belgium through the Ardennes.

Why on earth would they attack through the Ardennes again?

As ever, the lessons of history were forgotten, and youthful lives would once again be the payment.

Accordingly, the line was left lightly defended.

Six Divisions of American troops, comprising a combination of inexperienced soldiers and weary veterans being 'rested' after taking part in much heavy fighting were manning the eighty-mile front under these highly unpleasant conditions.

And so it was for the massed troops of the Fifth and Sixth Panzer Armies, Army Group B and elements of the Seventh Army as they began their advance well before dawn on Saturday, 16 December 1944.

The weather at Volkel was atrocious.

Cloud was low, less than a thousand feet, patches of mist, fog and rain making visibility poor, less than two hundred yards in some places. It was what those in the RAF would term as 'Harry Clampers'.

Granny once told him, back in 1940 when they were both Pilot Officers (one highly experienced and the other greener than grass), that while 'Clampers' was obvious (i.e. being clamped in by weather), it was apparently common practice for the 'Harry' bit to be used decorously in place of a rude word.

Not quite sure if his leg was being pulled, Rose had thought the use of his first name in such a context was unfair and scowled, much to Granny's delight.

A grinning Dingo later reassured Rose that 'Harry' was prefixed only to indicate something was sizeable. For example, 'Harry Famished' meaning very hungry.

News of the German offensive was a very unwelcome and worrying way to start the day.

With flying unlikely, Rose decided to clear up some of his pending paperwork and to prepare for the counteroffensive, and where better to start than at breakfast?

Many of the pilots had already finished breakfast and were gathered in small groups, smoking and talking quietly about the shock of the unexpected German offensive which had overshadowed news of Glenn Miller's disappearance over the English Channel the day before; in the background, the decrepit gramophone was quietly playing 'Whispering Grass'.

Rose found his two squadron leaders eating in the refectory. Gabby was agitated, and Sheep was soothing him. 'Gabs, soon as the clag lifts, we can give the Yanks a hand. With the weather as it is, flying would be madness.'

'I understand, *mon brave*, but they need us *now*.' Knowing there was nothing that they could do, at least for the moment, Gabby sighed.

Sheep slobbered up the last of his egg and cast avaricious eyes on Gabby's plate.

Dear Lord, thought Rose queasily, *Sheep's guts must be made of cast iron!*

'Gabby, Sheep, morning, chaps, I was going to sort out a rota for a twenty-four-hour pass over the Christmas period but this damned enemy offensive has put the kybosh on that. Can I have a moment to pick your brains for a maximum effort flying schedule?'

'There is little of any use inside the big pig's head, monsieur,' said Gabby acidly, pushing aside a burned slice of bacon and picking morosely at the oily powdered egg concoction before him. 'Look at the toilet paper this fool reads.'

Sheep slurped a mouthful before putting down his mug of tea to look up in outrage. 'Toilet paper? This is art, cobber, and what's more, it's a warning.'

'Warning? *G-8 and the Battle Aces*? Pah! *Casse-toi!* The only warning I see is that we now serve with simple-minded fools promoted to Squadron Leader beyond their ability. Pardon, Wing Commander Rose, *monsieur*, I was mistaken. I must reconsider my earlier words. It is clear that there is nothing of use to man nor beast within the emptiness of this animal's skull.'

Sheep's eyes slipped to Rose's. 'It's a warning,' he repeated solemnly, his voice funereal, completely ignoring Gabby. 'A warning about what could be. See this? It's a story about ol' Johnny Hun using giant bats with poisonous breath and farts. The bloke who wrote it must have met Gabs, how else would he know about something like that?'

Gabby's eyebrows beetled, his expression darkening, and his voice became a thin scream that barely turned the heads of the few stragglers having a belated breakfast.

'*Va te faire foutre! Créature inutile*! You talk of toxic breath? The stinking pig that smokes an evil-smelling pipe packed with Mahorka cigarette tobacco? Is it the pan calls the pot black?'

'Strewth! It's the pot calling the kettle black, you daft plum,' sniffed the Australian airily. He waved the tatty magazine at his friend. 'You could learn something from this, chum.'

'Learn something? *Mon Dieu!*' Gabby's earlier agitation was gone, and now he rolled his eyes and scoffed derisively. 'They fly machines from the last war in that rag! *Quelle folie!* Against zombies! And the giant bats? *Giant bats? Merde,* what can I learn from such putrid piss?'

Sheep grinned. 'Crikey Ada! Easy there, chum! Talk about emotional!' He held open the magazine and displayed it to them. 'Look! Look at it! Poisonous bats, see? How would you fight 'em, sir? I reckon you could out-dive one, but at low level, hard turns, or maybe a climb in full boost?'

He had seen some strange sights during his time in the service, but Rose was certain he'd seen nothing like the creatures revealed on the pages, even when flying by night.

But on second thought … there had been that Czech lad on Excalibur in '43, always wore dark glasses during the day and was a real press-on type, but nowhere to be seen between sorties. Usually disappeared at night, too, and he had been unusually popular with the station's WAAFs.

Hmm. *I wonder …*

There was a clatter as one of the pressed into service 'waiters' dropped a stack of dishes amidst howls of derision. It was a far cry from the sophisticated environment of a pre-war RAF Officers' Mess—red carpets, real china crockery and elegant WAAF waitresses quietly gliding between tables. And with the scattered khaki uniforms they had been issued with to ensure that RAF blue was not mistaken for *Wehrmacht feldgrau* or the blue uniforms of the Luftwaffe (even though the order to wear khaki had long since been rescinded), the room looked more like an Army Mess Hall, albeit with some rather grand decoration.

But after eating in the drooping tented Messes of muddy Normandy, it wouldn't do to look a gift horse in the mouth.

Sheep's voice deepened further to an elegiac tone. 'There's more stuff in Heaven and Earth that's mysterious and chancy than you can dream of, Yorkie lad,' he said, misquoting the Bard solemnly.

Where have I heard something similar … ?

'Mysterious and dangerous, me old stickyarse, totty just laps it up, just can't get enough of it,' Granny had once confided to him. 'Why d'you think Belle's besotted with me? Can't help herself. Slave to her desires, she is!' He'd lifted his pint of bitter triumphantly.

Belle had made a face and added tartly, 'Slave to *his* desires, more like. The only thing that's mysterious is why on earth I stay with him, because his breath's certainly more than dangerous after an evening in the pub!' Then she had laughed happily as Granny wrapped his arms around her and hugged her close.

Rose smiled warmly at the memory.

In the far corner of the room, 122 Wing's Jameson nodded to Rose, folding his newspaper scrupulously as a plate was placed before him. Taking one look, Jameson's brow darkened and, shaking his head, he got to his feet and disappeared in the direction of the kitchens, taking care not to step on the broken crockery.

Oh Lor'. Jamie looked a bit unimpressed. Wonder what delights await me for breakfast?

Just then, as in answer to his question, his batman scurried to their table with Rose's breakfast, grinning cheerfully as he clattered cutlery onto the table. 'Here you go, Mr Rose, sir, nice spot o'grub! Warm you up nice, like, set you up for the day! It's brass monkey's weather out there!'

Stomach lurching painfully as he swallowed a mouthful of bile, Rose stared at the plate and sighed. On it was a large oily flat splodge of powdered scrambled egg, bacon seared to a dark crisp and a curled-up sausage that looked as if it had died in agony, but still he mustered a smile of gratitude for the man. 'Thank you, Sparrow. Some hot tea and toast, if there's any going, would be most welcome. A preserve, too, if there's any?'

'Yessir! Rightaway, sir!' Beaming like an idiot, the man scuttled away. The supply situation had improved immensely with the opening of Antwerp in late November, and with provisions reaching them more easily (including fresh bread from the mobile field bakeries), meals were generally much tastier, although much more exotic food would often find its way onto their plates.

With the Wehrmacht abandoning supply depots containing tens of thousands of ration packs in the face of the Allied advance, the men of 2TAF would occasionally experience some quite interesting meals. The most recent being from German iron rations which included pea soup from Erbswurst sausage and Hartkeks, hard bread crackers.

In addition, Rose had developed a taste for the ersatz high-energy bars, cheese and a delicious mix of powdered milk and coffee, all of which were to be found in the special *Fallschirmjäger* fighting meal packs.

The few 63 Wing pilots still at the other tables seemed to find the oily and charred offerings much more to their taste than their CO, tucking in with a great deal of noisily enthusiastic gusto.

His squadron commanders were still eyeing him expectantly, and Rose cleared his throat in embarrassment. 'Oh! Um, well, yes. Nice. Very nice.'

Gabby stared at him as if he had gone mad, but Sheep wanted more, grinning exultantly. 'See? Go on! See, Gabs? See? Go on, then, sir! Tell him! Tell this dopey galah what's what, will you?'

Good grief! Tell Gabby *what?* That the Wing might possibly get bounced by giant bats at twenty thousand feet breathing out poisonous fumes? By *zombies?* God help us all. What would Bader have done if he were here? Probably would have shouted loudly and kicked some backsides, hard.

Rose cleared his throat, adding weakly, 'The drawings are quite nice.'

Gabby *tsk-tsked* and tossed his fork onto Sheep's empty plate, a scornful smile at his lips. *'Ecoutez, cochon!* The pictures are pretty! *Alors!* He nimbly jumped to his feet and, leaning forward, patted Sheep gently on his head. 'Enjoy the pretty pictures, *mon ami*, for I have more important work to do preparing for a break in the weather than gazing upon your *putain* scribblings.'

The young Frenchman straightened his tunic and bowed respectfully to Rose. *'Veuillez m'excuser, Monsieur Commandant?'*

Rose smiled and nodded. 'Of course, Gabby. Let me know about the rota.'

'I shall discuss it with the Pig, sir.' Gabby glanced indifferently at his friend. *'Cochon.'*

Sheep rudely blew him a juicy raspberry in return, and then called,

'Gabs! Hey, Gabs! Can I have your tucker?' Already he was reaching for the blackened and burned strip of bacon sitting forlornly in Gabby's oily plate.

'*Embrasser mon cul, cochon!*' The words were thrown carelessly over Gabby's shoulder as he walked away.

Rose sighed. This was going to be a long day, but Sheep beamed at him, cheerfully unrepentant, jaws straining on the bacon. 'Doubt he'd turn into a beautiful princess, even if I did, sir!'

Embrasser mon cul. Kiss my arse, indeed.

The weather cleared briefly on the morning of the 17th, and 2TAF put up a maximum effort. With a belligerent Luftwaffe doing the same in support of their advance, the day promised a lot of action.

In a progressive series of sweeps, Allied fighters scoured the skies of north-western Germany to beat away any enemy attacks on Allied ground-attack aircraft.

At the hurried Wing briefing, with the *cra-ack-boom* of Sabres coughing into life outside and the roar of other fighters taking off reverberating like thunder across Volkel, Rose reminded his men in his packed briefing hut of the dangers of misidentification in the packed skies, and also warned that, with the fighting men of both sides so close together, all Allied armour and transport would be wearing an easily visible thick white stripe to identify them as 'friendlies' from the air.

The bitterly cold morning air was thick with the noxious odour of cigarette smoke and unwashed bodies as he finished his address with, 'The boys on the ground are hard-pressed, we've been knocked back and Jerry's made some big advances. Let's maximise sorties while the weather's clear, give the Joes on the ground support while we can.' The Met officer had already warned them that this was a transient improvement at best interspersed with plenty of bursts of rain.

In the air twenty miles south of Rheine and in the company of seven other Tempests while leading Gabby's second element, an alert Rose spotted a formation of around fifteen or twenty Bf109s sliding westwards around two thousand feet below.

Gabby began to set up their bounce, curving gently to port, when Gabby's number 2 cried out, 'Break, break! Bandits high, seven o'clock! Six 109s!'

Breaking down and to starboard, Rose glanced over his shoulder.

Damn it! 'Marengo Flight, evade but do not engage! Do not engage! They're Mustangs!'

He had been fearful that the P51s might not recognise the Tempests in the heat of their dive, but their leader immediately pulled up, the others tight with him except for one, a blur of quicksilver closing with Rose as he brought up Sugar's nose, and he cringed as the Mustang swept past at full throttle, buffeting Sugar and close enough to touch, the sight of a cheeky wave from inside the USAAF fighter's canopy momentary, before the USAAF fighter barrel rolled and shot upwards again like an arrow from a bow.

Lord! That had been close! I'd like to wring that cheeky sod's neck!

Gabby now, breathing hard into his mask, 'Marengo flight, 109s climbing fast into our six o'clock, a mile behind and below.'

So much for bouncing the bloody bandits! The enemy were chasing after Marengo now, a loose gaggle of bandits rising after them, the loose formation opening into groups to chase after Marengo's separated Tempest pairs.

Knowing they had the advantage in straight line speed, the Tempests increased throttle to create some distance, and again Rose saw a flash emerge from the thick cloud far above at his twelve o'clock. *God almighty! There're more above!*

And then, just as he was about to call out a warning of this new threat, Rose realised he was mistaken as the flash grew into a silver streak diving steeply; *it's that ruddy cowboy again!*

For fuck's sake! 'Clear off, Yank!' he shouted uselessly, then felt daft because the Mustang pilot couldn't hear him.

He watched the American fighter lest it fall upon his Tempests, but the lone Mustang knew who his enemy were and its nose tracked the pursuing 109s, unaccompanied and unafraid but ready to tweak a German tail or two.

If you were one of mine I'd teach you a thing or two about discipline, you cheeky little bugger …

Then the pluming glitter of shell cases and smoke streaming back from the USAAF fighter's wings as it opened fire with six .5 machine guns, and the loose formation of Luftwaffe aircraft twitched before scattering like flushed pheasants as one of their number suddenly exploded beneath the fusillade of characteristically USAAF pinkish-red tracer.

The sleek wasp-like 109 caught in the deluge was instantly transformed into an expanding ball of churning fire even as the Mustang eased the angle of its dive to chase after the 109 on the far right of the formation which had broken to its starboard and dived downwards, both passing beneath the Tempests and disappearing into the haze lower down, the Mustang closing the distance rapidly using the speed gained by its dive and firing short, sharp bursts.

But Rose was no longer watching the antics of the American pilot, his eyes following the other scattering bandits, attention focussed on a

109 to his starboard as it rolled over and went straight down, exhaust smoke thickening as it dived away at full power, *you'll do, Fritz …*

'Going down, Hotspur Two …' Stick over and back, hard right rudder, pushed back into his seat and his harness tight, and the world spun around as Sugar tipped over after the plummeting 109, the bandit shrinking and fading against the hazy landscape as he kept his eyes locked onto the little shape as it began to pull out.

'*Oui, Colonel,* I have your tail.' Frankie plunged after him, the boy's eyes, their speed and Sugar's armour plate combined as his shield, and Rose eased back on the stick, rolling to port and through a half-roll, before banking to starboard and edging upwards into a gentle curving climb, copying the enemy pilot's every move, pushing through the buffeting slipstream of the bandit.

Mirroring the enemy's move, Rose could feel the tightening of excitement, the fighting madness sharpening his reflexes and awareness.

He would have dearly liked to spare a glance at Molly's picture, but dared not look away, his limbs guiding Sugar to follow the speeding shape his eyes were focussed on.

Desperately, the enemy pilot threw his striped grey-black machine harder into a turn to starboard, ailerons catching at the air as Rose fired a one-second burst of 20 mm, the harder turn giving the terrified *Fahnrich* temporary respite as Sugar's cannon shells arced uselessly away from him.

He could not outrun nor out-turn Rose, nor could he climb in search of the safety of cloud. The only sanctuary lay in the misted haze that hung over the land below, but concerned that he might crash into uneven high ground seen too late in the limited visibility at zero feet, the German youngster pulled his straining 109 into the turn, disregarding the lesson drummed into him, *if you have a Tommi on your tail, drop down to low level and jink like crazy.*

With Frankie close behind, Rose pulled in after the 109, gaining on it and knowing that he had the enemy pilot dead to rights, for Sugar would out-turn him without effort, Jerry just did not know it yet.

Again as Rose let loose a ranging burst, the enemy pilot twisted his fighter into a sudden turn to port, and only three of Sugar's shells smashed into the 109, ripping away the starboard wingtip in a shower of fragments and savaging an aileron, the force of the impact making the bandit shudder. The burst would have fallen short had the German lad not turned into the trailing burst, the 109 passing through and catching the last of Sugar's explosive rounds.

Three rounds of 20 mm can be enough to send a target into the ground, but somehow the boy managed to keep his fighter in the air, the uneven lift making the 109's starboard wing drag, causing her to fly with one wing down. The frantic boy at her controls settling her back into level flight, despairing as the sleek Tempest slid in behind her; his 109 wallowing as he tried to balance his damaged fighter with a little slip.

It's like shooting fish in a barrel, thought Rose, finger poised.

But he couldn't fire, the deadly shape of the swaying 109 somehow seeming helpless, and despite the fighting madness he could not do it, watching the erratic see-sawing slip of its flight as the enemy pilot fought to counter the unequal drag.

It was not the first time he had found himself behind an unsuspecting target and shot it down without warning or qualm, but for some inexplicable reason he found he could not make himself press the gun button.

And then a premonition, sharp and clear in his mind—*a life for a life, kill this German boy today and you will not live to see the end of the war.*

But if I let him go, he'll survive to kill others; and just visible in the distance was the dark stain of brick and concrete that was the waiting sanctuary of Rheine.

'Hotspur Leader?' A question in Frankie's voice, wondering why Rose, the accomplished fighter pilot and combat leader, the publicly acclaimed 'Typhoon Rose' who had once taken on six bandits single handed over the Channel, was hesitating.

Each passing second brought them ever closer to Rheine, and Rose knew that compassion was a dangerous indulgence, for even as Rose hesitated, the enemy flyer's countrymen were ripping their way into Allied forces.

Without inflexible resolve, we might yet lose this bloody war. But I've never thought like this before, what's come over me?

Beneath the oxygen mask Rose licked dry lips, the cordite pungent to his tongue, his heart fluttering. 'Frankie.'

What's wrong with me? Merciful God, strengthen me against weakness, for those reliant upon our strength. His eyes dropped for a moment to her beautiful smile. *Thank God she's not here to see this. Moll would despise me for being irresolute and weak in battle.*

'*Oui, Hotspur,*' less formal and now familiar with his leader, still just the hint of a note of question in the boy's voice but no hesitancy on his part as G-Gilbert surged past eagerly, Rose closing his throttle and slipping aside to starboard, falling back to cover the young Frenchman even as the 109's canopy opened and the enemy pilot emerged.

But as soon as the enemy pilot released his grip on the control column, the 109 seemed to veer to one side, the port wing lifting and the 109 yawing, the German scrabbling for a handhold, reaching back down into his cockpit.

Rose's eyes were elsewhere. *Sky, behind and below, mirror, clear.*

Warily he surveyed the hazy firmament for danger, eyes sweeping surely but quickly from below to above and around again, never stopping but seeing all, feeling the swelling burn of loathing that he had wilted in the height of battle.

At three hundred yards from the 109, Frankie fired a long three-second burst of just over one hundred and thirty 20 mm explosive rounds at the floundering bandit.

Sky, behind and below, mirror, clear.

A rash of white flashes burst like thrown firecrackers thrown randomly across the fleeing shape, rippling and twinkling fitfully along the wings and fuselage of the bandit, the canopy and engine cowling torn apart, shedding a trail of fragments which mixed with a curl of thick smoke, the first bout of fire as the entire rear half of the aircraft was blown off and the battered starboard wing torn untidily in half; the 109 transformed in an instant to a flaming torch, the remains its unfortunate pilot just one of the burning, smoking lumps of debris as the shockwave from an exploding 20 mm shell flung his broken corpse away from the fighter.

Sky, behind and below, mirror, clear.

The burning, twisted hunk of wreckage arced downwards with gravity dragging at it, flaring fiercely as exploding fuel and ammunition tore it apart into rapidly dwindling pieces.

I should congratulate him, thought Rose, but felt ashamed.

Sky, behind and below, mirror, clear.

But there is no place for shame in battle, only for anger and madness and fear, for as the smoke of the 109's demise thinned, he saw danger as it came out of bellying cloud a mile to starboard, three shapes and a trailing fourth, stubby noses and the humped fuselage of FW190s.

A moment later another pair of fighters, followed closely by a second pair in line astern.

'Bandits at two o'clock, Hotspur Two, one mile.'

A chance to redeem my weakness and vacillation with that 109?

But there are more of them than we ought to be dicing with, far more. Eight versus two.

As if mocking his reticence, a memory of the newspaper cutting in Molly's scrapbook, screaming in huge letters *'Hero Air Ace takes on Nazi Squadron alone!'* The boys never let him forget *that* one.

But Frankie was keen, still leading them and exultant in the killing of the 109 and his voice imploring, 'One pass, Hotspur Leader?' Already Gilbert's nose was turning towards the enemy, pointing slightly ahead of the lead trio so that they would 'cross the T' towards the rear of the enemy formation at the conclusion of the approach.

Unless Jerry turned into them, and with the 190's ability to reverse fearsome, this could be bloody, for them both.

This is madness. 'OK, Hotspur Two, one pass and home. You remain leader.' He licked the bead of sweat from his lips, eyes straying to her smile. 'Don't hang about, understand? One pass and dive until we're clear.'

He took a moment to place his hand over the bulge in his pocket formed by the little bear and the smooth pebble, reassuring.

Merciful Lord protect us in the midst of our folly.

'*Mais oui,* Hotspur.' The young voice was tight, his shape hunched inside Gilbert's cockpit.

Rose felt the flutter of apprehension, but only for a moment because the fighting madness began to glow brighter within him.

Sky, behind and below, mirror, clear.

They raced into the interception, the distance between them disappearing all too soon, two dark shapes below the enemy horizon with

Frankie dropping them by a hundred feet, each second Rose expecting the enemy to turn into them, and fervently praying they would not.

Sky, behind and below, mirror, clear.

The enemy might have seen them at the end, but too late and they did not have time to respond as eight 20 mm cannon opened fire.

Firing from six hundred yards and blasting an explosive broadside into the enemy's flank, almost three hundred rounds of 20 mm smashed out at the enemy.

Frankie had judged the approach just right, hitting the enemy formation at its rear, no trailing German fighters to grind out bullets and cannon shells at the attacking Tempests, these Tail-end Charlie's concentrating on covering their formation's rear, not seeing the Tempests as they seared into range.

Rose, focussed on 'his' FW190, saw the white smudge of the pilot's face, saw Sugar's cannonshells slash off the 190's aerial and clip the spinning propeller, one black blade flung in a blur away from them as the clear spinning disc slowed and windmilled, another shell blowing a ragged hole clear through the rudder and then he was past.

'Full throttle, Two, 'til we're clear, don't hang about!' he choked out, feeling the cramp of fear in his stomach and shoulders relax into the elation of success and survival *(you're not out of the woods yet, you idiot!)*, the gloved fingers of his right hand touching her photograph for the shortest of moments.

God, how I miss you.

'*Oui, Colonel.*' Breathless, words thick with gladness.

Sky, behind and below, mirror, clear.

Rose opened the space between them, glanced back past Sugar's tail to see scattered fighters pointing in all directions, one falling away with a shattered propeller and the top of its rudder missing, another streaming thick black smoke and white glycol vapour, the teardrop canopy pushed back.

Sky, behind and below, mirror, clear.

His mouth was parched, but still he managed to grunt out a 'Well done, *mon brave*, keep the lead and take us home.' Though it sounded more like a criticism than a congratulation.

Frankie got one by the look of it, and mine's surely at least a probable. He'll want to share the earlier 109 I couldn't finish off, but I would have let it go. It belongs to him. He did well, and I'll tell him so.

I redeemed myself despite my earlier failing, he thought wearily, keeping station with the youngster and scanning the clouds as they made for home.

A moment's weakness I'll never allow again. Men, most of them little more than boys, are being killed right now on the snow and blood-laced ground, killed without mercy, and for a moment, I was unworthy of their sacrifice to hold back this new push.

I will show no mercy, he swore to himself, *dare not show it, until this tragedy is over. I've killed so many, and I must keep on doing it again and again until it's over.*

For the ones waiting for us, the ones I love, for all the lost, the endless murdered millions, and, merciful God forgive me, for myself.

Dearest Lord God, grant me your blessed salvation.

Save me so that I may know the peace that must surely come soon?

Merciful Lord, please let me live.

That afternoon, the terrible weather returned with a vengeance and the Allied air forces were grounded.

For the next few days there would be no flying, and released from the scourge of Allied air attack, the Axis forces were now essentially fighting a pure ground war, the surging German push achieving great success as the front line bulged ever westwards beneath the Nazi drive to Antwerp, the protuberance cutting through the US Forces to separate the British and Canadian armies.

Across the airfields of both sides, fighters lay ineffective beneath tarpaulin, their ground crews soaked and frozen as they struggled to maintain their charges, running up the engines many times every night, the sound of Coffman cartridges banging regularly across the wide expanse of the airfield like thunder.

Endless days and nights of low cloud, fog and rain, snowfall and greatly reduced visibility, impossibly severe conditions and freezing temperatures, superlative ground crews with ice-numbed bodies maintaining machines in a state of readiness under the worst of circumstances, although on the positive side it also meant that Jerry would be highly unlikely to sortie over the Allied Lines.

All the while, as their air forces remained impotently on the ground, Allied troops were fighting the weather and desperate actions in the face of the ferocious German assault.

At Volkel, despite the atrocious conditions, an alert pair of Tempests remained at constant readiness, with a third always as spare. They were placed between the questionable shelter afforded by the rubble of two of the large brick storage sheds on the western boundary, ground crews bent over beneath the protective sheets as they fed hot air via long collapsible tubes from the pre-warming van into the radiator intakes to warm up the Sabres to more than a hundred degrees to keep the oil from freezing.

On the 18th, rumours began to circulate that enemy commandos were operating behind Allied Lines, creating confusion and interfering with traffic movements. It was even claimed that the infamous

German commando, Otto Skorzeny himself, was engaged in these operations.

In the distrust, confusion and ensuing chaos, a US General ignorant of American Baseball was confined at gunpoint, while a US Army Captain wearing German boots was locked up for days, and a number of US units fired on one another, resulting in dead and wounded. With the risk posed by these commandos, sidearms were to be worn at all times, even when going to the bathroom.

On the 19th, a grouchy and soaked Rose returned to the seminary after spending another day in his freezing Ops caravan poring over maps of north-western Germany.

He went immediately in search of the Wing's senior engineer officer to ask him about airworthiness and have some food, but seeing the weariness and worry on the man's lined face while nursing a congealing meal and scrutinising a sheaf of papers, Rose just nodded a greeting instead, leaving the poor man alone at his table to wonder how on earth he and his exhausted and overworked erks were supposed to keep two squadrons of Tempests serviceable and airworthy in unspeakable conditions.

Understanding his debt to this man, Rose made his way to the kitchens, and instructed a waiter to replace the engineer's meal with a fresh one.

You're the ones who make it happen, chum, you and your lads.

The refectory was quiet, most of the men having eaten before turning in to catch up on their sleep, so he decided to see if any of his men were still awake, perhaps share a beer with them.

I should have collected a sandwich and a mug of tea for myself when I was in the kitchen. Could collect my chocolate ration, I suppose ...

Shifting his pistol's holster to one side, he thrust the gilt cigarette ration tin into his pocket (another for Granny's collection) and tore open the chocolate ration wrapper to break off a piece of Cadbury's.

Sucking a piece of the chocolate, Rose found Micky and Frankie talking quietly over a can of beer in a corner of the bar, just beside the stove. Amélie, as usual, was tucked comfortably into the front of Frankie's tunic, a silent observer, her shock of ginger 'hair' nestled comfortably beneath the young Frenchman's chin.

'So I creep up on him, jumped to my feet and shouted "*Hande hoch*, you Jerry bastard!", but the bugger jumps up and scarpers, his drawers flapping around his ankles, a torn strip of Jerry newspaper flapping from between the cheeks of his bare arse, and I've got my pistol in my hand and I let fly.' Micky shook his head sadly. 'I emptied my pistol at him, but no coconut.'

Frankie looked mystified. 'No coconut? You shoot to the coconut? Not to *le salaud Boche*?'

Micky scratched his head. 'No, Frankie. It's a saying. Remember what I said about sayings? When I said "no coconut", it means not hitting the target. Y'know? From a coconut shy?'

'*Merde!* A shy coconut? What is this you speak?' Frankie thought for a moment, and then his brow cleared. 'Ah, I see, you mean that you miss it, the coconut? The bullet is shy of it, the coconut? What of *le Boche?*'

Micky's voice was plaintive. 'Look, cobber, forget the ruddy coconut, will you? I was shooting at the bloody Jerry, not at a coconut.'

Frankie looked mystified, 'Not at coconut? Why then you say it?'

'Chrissakes!' Micky cried out in frustration. 'How many times do I have to tell you, Frankie? It's a bloody saying!'

Frankie sniffed, 'It is of no wisdom.' He put the beer can to Amélie's embroidered smile. '*Enfant, non? Fini? Bon!*' Lifting it to his own lips, he took a mouthful. 'You English have sayings are twiddle.'

'Twaddle,' Micky corrected, then he blinked and straightened from his slouch in outraged indignation. 'Hey! Whaddya mean, "*you English*"? I'm no ruddy Pom!'

Rose grinned secretly to himself. Micky would be mortified to know his Pommy Wing Leader was standing behind them, eavesdropping.

Frankie ignored him blandly. 'French sayings have sense.' He thought for a moment. '*Ecoutez*, Micky. *Ce n'est pas la mer à boire*. Is meaning, "It is not that you drink the sea." No twiddle of coconuts.'

Micky scoffed. 'It is not that you drink the sea? What the suffering bastard arseholes does that ruddy tripe mean?' Micky felt Amélie's glittering eyes upon him. 'Oh, pardon me, Amélie.' He chortled and doubled over. 'It is not that you drink the sea? Ha-ha!'

Frankie frowned at Micky's merriment. 'It is meaning something like "It is no difficult thing, it is not difficult, like drinking the sea". You see? Is poetry, *non*, Micky?'

'Is festering bollocks, Frankie.' An apologetic smile and a shrug. 'Uh, sorry, Amélie.'

Finally noticing Rose standing in the shadows behind them, the two youngsters, a little the worse for wear, unsteadily got to their feet despite Rose's gesture for them to remain seated. '*Colonel!*'

'Can I join you, lads?'

Rose pointed at Micky's chest. Beneath the young Aussie's 'wings' were his rather impressive row of five ribbons. Led by the DFC, it included the Military Medal with the tarnished rosette of a second award sewn onto it, the ribbons of the '39-'43 and Africa Stars, and another ribbon Rose had never seen before and could not identify. An unusual and very impressive display indeed.

'Tell me about your MMs, Micky. Been meaning to ask you about them. How on earth did you come by them?'

Like all of the bravest men Rose had ever met, his young wingman was bashful, hesitant to talk of the acts of gallantry which had earned him his awards. 'Bardia, sir, Western Desert. I was with 6th Division, 2nd AIF, then with 9th Division at Tobruk. It was a bit rough for all of us. Lots of brave lads, but not enough medals.'

The cheeky, daft, brave-as-a-lion lad who thought a German General's uniform trousers might help him evade capture now looked uncomfortable, eyes pleading that Rose ask no further. Too many memories, too many dead friends. Remembering only reawakened the dull ache of loss.

The guilt of surviving when others had not, the burden of remorse felt by the ones who still lived. A guilt which Rose that never left him.

Rose already knew Micky's story. Intrigued the first time he saw the youngster's unusual row of ribbons and the scars from shrapnel on his hands and neck, he had asked for the story from Sheep about the boy with the veteran's eyes who was to be his wingman.

Micky had been a private soldier during the Battle of Bardia in early January 1941 in which he received his first Military Medal. The first battle of the Western Desert campaign, it was also the first action to involve an Australian Army Division and be planned and enacted by Australians, and the first in which an Australian, Major-General Iven MacKay, was in command.

Micky had led the survivors of his platoon after the officers and NCOs were cut down on the first day when supporting the sappers breeching the western defences of the Italian Fortress.

Made into a Corporal by his Colonel, he took his shrunken group of men into two days of heavy no-quarters fighting amongst the low brick buildings, and survived to see the small coastal town fall in a great victory. But the Italians had fought with courage and ferocity, and the price of the victory for the gallant Australians was more than a hundred lives and over three hundred wounded.

Transferred to the 9th Division a month later, Micky was serving amongst them when they remained to defend Tobruk from the advancing Afrika Korps and deny Rommel the use of the port.

In a siege which lasted for more than seven months during 1941, the gallant defenders, comprising 9th Australian Division and British, Indian, Polish and Czech troops, resisted all attempts to dislodge them. This ragtag collection of exceptional soldiers from the Commonwealth resisted Germany's iron veterans, and named themselves the 'Rats of Tobruk'.

Micky's courage on more than one occasion in aggressive patrols through No-Man's land around the beleaguered port before the gradual withdrawal of the Australians had seen a second Military Medal award.

Having suffered the heat, swarming flies and choking sand of the North African ground war, Micky put in a transfer request to the air force. With the request supported by an effusive recommendation from 'Ming the Merciless', General Leslie Morshead himself, Micky had transferred to the RAAF, been commissioned and found himself flying Typhoons after flying training at RAAF Station Deniliquin, flying Wirraways close to home.

Despite the dangers and losses of training, he was able to mend in mind and body from the ordeals of North Africa.

Thereafter he was seconded to the RAF and served with distinction in the run up to the Invasion and the subsequent Battle for France, earning his DFC in August 1944, before his transfer to 63 Wing.

Respectful of Micky's reticence, Rose pushed no more, but curiosity of the final, unfamiliar ribbon won out and he asked about it.

In this there was no diffidence. The ribbon was that of the unofficial 'Rats of Tobruk' medal, initially fashioned and made in Tobruk from aluminium and copper, collected from the wreck of a Stuka dive-bomber and empty shell cases. Micky was inordinately proud of the award which marked him as one of the few who had resisted the best efforts of Rommel to take the valuable port facilities. It also explained the cartoon rat painted onto R-Rooster.

'Tell me about home?' Rose asked.

Micky smiled, took a sip from his can of beer. 'Home's a place called Griffith in the Riverina.'

Rose, who had never heard the name before, asked, 'The Riverina?' It certainly sounded rather exotic.

'The most beautiful place you could find anywhere on God's earth, sir. I was born in Melbourne. Things were pretty rough when I was a kid. Dad lost his job in the Depression, and so we were evicted from our house in the city. He had to take us to the unemployed camp at La Perouse in Sydney, where we stayed in a little tin shack with two other families and lived on soup and bread from the soup kitchen. Mum cried all night and Dad was always angry, used to shout about how it was a helluva way to treat an Anzac, but I was happy there. I guess when you're full grown you know what you've lost.'

'Dad finally got a job at a vineyard in Riverina, and we moved there. As I got older things got better and I got a job soon as I was old enough. Lots of farms, and lots of pests to ruin crops and herds.'

'Pests?'

'Yeah, uh, sir, I learned how to get rid of pests in crops.'

'So you became a pest controller?' Rose smiled. 'From pest controller to a Rat of Tobruk!'

'Yeah.' Micky chuckled and nodded, his eyes still focussed on the past. 'It was a good life. Lots of fresh air and banter. We mainly treated crops against fruit flies, grasshoppers and locusts, but sometimes with larger pests like rabbits, dingoes and joeys. And weeds, of course, prickly pear, lantana, St. John's Wort.' He grinned toothily. 'Learned a lot about poisons and chemicals.'

Poisons! Cripes! Better not get on the wrong side of this lad! 'Well, Micky, I'm glad you're here and not in Riverina.'

'Thanks for saying that, sir, but I'm not. It's a lot bloody warmer there!'

Rose sighed longingly, running his fingers around his shirt collar still cold and soggy from the rain. 'Warm, eh?'

'Warm as you like, sir, and loads of cold beer and lovely Sheilas!'

His hand went to the pocket containing her photograph. *Loads of lovely Sheilas, eh? Hmm, Moll would love that, I don't think!*

They laughed, and Rose savoured the intimacy with his men, then turned to Frankie. 'How about you, Frankie, er, you and Amélie?'

He could have bit his tongue, for the boy's smile disappeared and his eyes darkened, but his voice was even. 'Little to tell, *mon colonel.* We had a little farm in Brittany, a little family, *maman, papa, ma soeur et moi. Les Boches* come, family *fini*, and the farm is no more.' He stood suddenly, clasping Amélie tight to his chest, his sorrow contained. '*Mon colonel*, you must be tired and hungry. I bring you something. *Attendez ici, s'il vous plaît.*'

Before Rose could say another word, the young Frenchman had gone.

Seeing his CO's stricken expression, Micky sighed. 'Don't mind him, sir. He can't bring himself to speak about it. His folks were involved in the Resistance, and Fritz found out about it. One day they were there, the next they were gone, including the real Amélie, his kid sister. He went home a couple of months back, and the locals were looking after the farm for him, told him they'd carry on until he returned for good. He brought back that ruddy ragdoll with him, takes her everywhere. Gives me the willies, she does, keep expecting her to jump up and dance a jig or tell me to piss off.'

Micky pursed his lips thoughtfully. 'I think he went a little bit potty, but he's a good lad, and he just wants to get his own back on Jerry. This is his way of making up for not being there for his sis. He blames himself for not being there when she was taken, the daft galah.'

Rose closed his eyes in sorrow. 'God, Micky, I didn't know.'

He thought back to his time in Normandy, when Excalibur was flying from B2 Bezenville, just before Caen had finally fallen.

One of the local farmers supplying 44 Wing with fresh produce had invited them to his farm for an evening meal. Granny, Rose, and Will Scarlet found themselves driving slowly down a rutted track as the sun dipped and the violet and pink of early dusk faded gloriously into the darkening sky as it crowded in from the east, the incessant, endless sound of vehicles and artillery somehow absent and the only thing (once Granny switched off the engine of their jeep) was the muted twitter of birdsong and the soft buzz of bees.

Nervous of the risk from snipers or Nazi collaborators, they had armed themselves, but instead found a tranquil peace which seemed a world apart from the ceaseless trudge of war behind them, and the farmer's welcome had been warm.

As their host poured the wine and his wife brought out plates of a simple rabbit and vegetable stew, Rose gazed around the front room and marvelled at the simple life they led.

A subsistence farm like so many others in rural France, there was no machinery, no tractors, no technology of any kind which might make the man's life easier.

The darkness of the room made him feel as if he were in a cave, a fire burning fitfully in the grate despite the warmth of day, an old yoke hanging before the mantelpiece, the room redolent of burning wood, pipe smoke and fresh bread. On the mantelpiece itself were arrayed two delicate porcelain plates decorated with painted red roses, two or three pieces of cheaper pottery, and, incongruously, a rather scruffy-looking teddy bear sitting beside an unlit lantern.

Above it, just below the low-beamed ceiling and neatly hung on the bare stone wall were three picture frames, one of a parrot, the second one faded, showing their host and his wife on their wedding day, he a *poilu* proud and straight-backed in infantry blue with medals on his chest and she demure and slender in lacy white.

The last was of a young man in the uniform of a naval sub-lieutenant, standing self-consciously on what looked like the casing of *Rubis*, a Free French submarine Rose had visited early in 1944 for lunch when still at RAF Tealing in Scotland while flying for Charlie's Special Typhoon Experimental Night Unit.

The French sailors had been reserved but welcoming, the sub's dog Bacchus even more so, cocking a friendly leg against Rose's. The incredible four-course meal had more than made up for the uncomfortably wet sock and shoe; a young French Wren Third Officer known to all only as *Touche* acted as an interpreter, and it had been a very pleasant and memorable evening.

Charlie had thought to keep him safe by having him posted to Scotland, and he smiled as he recollected her concern for him, but in the end the Air Ministry decided he would be better employed back with Excalibur Squadron and returned him back to his command.

He had enjoyed being back with his men, but in the ensuing months had lost so many of them both before and after the Invasion that it had broken his heart and almost his soul.

The weather in Scotland used to be pretty cold, too, but there had not been the freezing thick fogs like winter in Holland, fog so extra cold it caused windows, windscreens and canopies alike to thicken with a layer of translucent ice within seconds.

He must have met the young man smiling in the photo, and Rose remembered a shock of dark hair and an easy, friendly smile as he marvelled at how small the world was to now be sitting in that same young man's childhood home.

Later, as rough-cut slices of bread, cheese and fresh honey were laid before them with a jug of warm milk, Rose relished the warmth and low conversation, gazing out through the small window into the night beyond, the inky blackness broken only by the false dawn of still-burning Caen's angry glow beyond.

After all the fighting and the hate and the pain, I could manage a life like this, warm and uncomplicated, shared with the precious ones I love. To be awoken by the chatter of the morning chorus and see Molly's waking smile, to kiss and caress and taste her in the paleness of the early light of dawn, to later tend the land and enjoy the glad chirrup of laughter from our children under bright blue skies, truly heaven on earth.

He thought of the young *poilu* in the faded photograph. *Was this the peace you craved after the incessant thunder of the guns, the wretched misery of the trenches and the endless lines of the horribly dead? To try and forget it all in the shared love and companionship of a kind and loving woman, the scents and sounds and beauty of nature, to feel absorbed in serenity and peace after the endless unrelenting clamour and terror of war?*

It was a lovely memory, one he treasured, but one which now dulled as Rose glimpsed Frankie returning, his sister's doll staring out from the front of his tunic again, a couple of sandwiches and a cup of something hot in his hands, and he felt a wave of sorrow and melancholy wash over him.

The young submariner's farm had survived the occupation unscathed, but Frankie's did not. How can a man recover from such a thing? For the temerity of resisting their country's violation, a family and home had been destroyed without care, as if inconsequential.

'The chef say he will bring it some soup presently, *mon Colonel*.' Rose felt the doll's black button eyes on him, as if she could read his thoughts.

Rose smiled his thanks to Frankie, taking the plate, the warmth of fresh bread and the sharp tang of pickles filling his nostrils, a lump of emotion lodged in his throat.

Just one family and home destroyed by the evil and insanity of a handful of men who had given free rein to others filled with evil inhumanity. Will we ever know how many such families and homes were destroyed when this insanity is finally done? How many such stories will remain untold and how much suffering unknown?

Oh please, my Lord God, my most merciful God, let me see the end of this, please give me the peace I crave so dearly, please give me the sunrises and sunsets with Molly that I yearn for so very much.

Please let me live. So that I may enjoy the blessing of my children and for the love of your blessed gift, my beloved Molly.

Let me see this through, and allow me to enjoy the peace.

As he bit into the cheese-and-pickle sandwich, listening to Micky tease Frankie again and see the young Frenchman's shy smile return, Rose felt like covering his face with his hands and weeping, for all that was lost, and all that could yet be lost before the end of the hate.

Chapter 17

The first six days were ones in which there was little aerial resistance, and on the 16th after a massive artillery barrage, the Germans advanced along a forty-mile front extending from Belgium in the north to France in the south, a counter offensive targeting Antwerp, Liege and Brussels, to split the Allied forces into two and choke the Allied supply line.

US 9th Air Force valiantly put up their fighter bombers, sortie after sortie, but with the poor weather, visibility and forest hiding many of their targets, the brave men in their Thunderbolts could do only limited damage to the enemy, despite their repeated valiant attempts to pierce the clag.

The next day, with weather clearing in the morning, US aircraft provided air support to the US 1st and 3rd Armies, 2TAF providing plenty of fighter cover. However, most of 2TAF's Typhoons had to abort their ground-attack missions due to low cloud and bad visibility.

US 8th Air Force and RAF Bomber Command struck deep into Germany to destroy transport hubs and roads, aiming to disrupt the enemy offensive's reinforcement and logistics chain. With railheads pushed back further into Germany, reinforcing combat units and supply convoys were forced to rely on the jammed roads and face endless delays.

With a number of US commanders caught by surprise and unable to reach their commands, Bernard Montgomery took control of all British and US units in the north while Bradley retained his 3rd Army in the south.

Between the 19th and the 22nd of December, more impossible conditions prevented tactical sorties by 2TAF and US 9th Air Force, while high, dense cloud made any strategic missions by Bomber Command and US 8th Air Force difficult.

The valiant and dogged resistance of Monty's US 1st Army against the 6th Panzer Army managed to limit the German advances to the north, but the 5th Panzer Army found greater success and managed to push the salient further forwards in the south.

A very well-publicised event for the Allies in the German southern push was their failure to take the encircled town of Bastogne, held by the rather pugnacious Brigadier-General Anthony McAuliffe who had arrived just in time to be encircled by the Germans. His US 101st Airborne Division together with components of 10th Armored and 82nd Airborne conducted a heroic and tenacious resistance before their later relief by General Patton's forces.

The gallant and unyielding defence of Bastogne in the south of the salient is often quoted as the key event that led to the eventual failure of the German offensive, but this might be so because there were many war correspondents present in Bastogne who were keen to describe it as such because they had been there, but while this encirclement did indeed create an obstacle to the enemy advance, the southern Nazi push flowed around Bastogne and continued.

While the magnificent defiance in the heart of the southern Axis advance disrupted the progress of man and machine and was a significant event which played an important part in the German failure, it was to the north that the Nazi units were contained and the advance blunted sooner.

With the loss of support from the north as the northerly advance was first controlled and then beaten back, the southern advance faltered and without 6th Panzer's support from the northern flank, the unsupported southern advance was stopped and in time pushed back.

Quite possibly the true pivotal event of the Battle of the Bulge was the inability of the 6th Panzer Army to take the Elsenborn Ridge in the north, wherein the Panzer's thrust was diminished and confined, the enemy's aim to spill out over the ridge and then spread north and westwards frustrated.

During a ferociously plucky and structured retreat, the US 2nd Infantry Division and the inexperienced 99th Infantry Division battered 6th Panzer away from taking the ridge, thereby forcing the Germans to advance on a substitute route south of Elsenborn Ridge where it would be met with and stopped just short of the Meuse by Monty's men (the US's 2nd Infantry Division, 30th Infantry Division, and units from 82nd Airborne).

One of many outstanding actions of the Battle of Elsenborn Ridge was at Lanzareth, involving a handful of inexperienced men from Intelligence and Reconnaissance Platoon, 394th Infantry Regiment, US 99th Infantry Division.

Commanded by twenty-year-old First Lieutenant Lyle Bouck, the eighteen-man platoon (and four Forward Artillery Observers) held off an entire Battalion of German troops, killing or wounding ninety-two of the enemy and delaying the advance of the enemy armour for the best part of a day. With the men finally captured after an incredible and stoic defence, they were led away as POWs to an equally difficult time in captivity.

Whereas the platoon's defence should have been remembered alongside Horatius's defence of the bridge, the Lanzareth action was to remain almost completely unknown and unrecognised for many decades, with Bouck himself considering his defence a failure for having had the temerity to be beaten by overwhelming numbers and a lack of support during their delaying action.

It would take almost forty years for the platoon to be recognised, with the belated award of a Presidential Unit Citation and decorations to every member of the unit.

The valiant Bouck himself would receive the Distinguished Service Cross, the Silver Star, the Bronze Star and three Purple Hearts for his gallantry.

I&R Platoon's war had lasted less than a day, yet they had played an instrumental part which would prove significant in the failure of the Nazi's final offensive. It was just one of the innumerable gallant actions (many of which will never be known or recognised) which would contribute to the final failure of the Germans in the Battle of the Bulge.

Until the 22nd, thick fog and low-lying cloud encased the entire area. 2TAF flew a handful of ground-attack missions on the 22nd, but without significant result in the dreary arena of veiled cloud and rain.

And then, late in the afternoon of 23 December, the weather began to improve, though still with dense, low-lying cloud, the thick carpet of fog clearing and visibility opening.

Rose joined Gabby's men in a fighter sweep north of Rheine, but they saw no action, just catching the frustrating sight of a Me262 flashing through cloud a couple of miles to their south, too far off to catch.

Sheep took his squadron further east and somehow found two half-tracks trundling along the road amongst the trees about three miles south of Krefeld through a small break in the sheet of cloud.

Seeing the Tempests, the infantry jumped out and scattered, running for their lives as the Australians reduced their transport into burning, twisted shells. The Aussies also saw the Luftwaffe from afar, a distant *schwarm* of four FW190s which turned as soon as they caught sight of Sheep's men, smartly disappearing into cloud to the east.

On Sunday 24 December, Christmas Eve 1944, Volkel was a hive of activity. The wind was still bitterly cold, but the sky miraculously clear at last.

Rose led a fighter sweep at 16,000 feet twenty miles north-west of Bonn in the morning with Sheep leading the second section of four Tempests, and Gabby thirty miles to the north, leading another eight Tempests to the area between Wuppertal, Dusseldorf and Cologne.

Hobart Flight would hook around Bonn in a wide curve to avoid the city's flak, before adopting their north-westerly leg. Rose was debating with himself about sending Sheep's section higher and a mile or so south, feeling the hair on his neck bristle and wary of a bounce from out of the sun.

The US 9th AF and 2TAF were already hammering at the Nazi advance in the Ardennes, and their fighter sweeps would also act as an outer layer of fighter cover. In the meantime the men of the 8th AF would be attacking enemy airfields further north and east deeper inside Germany.

With unrestricted views of clear skies, the men in the Tempests could see the thick, smog-covered sprawls of dirty grey industrialisation bleached by distance, the city edges leaking into the snow-covered land-scape below, the air over them foul with smoke and smog, spreading to create a dirty layer of haze.

How liberating to feel unbound from cloud, no longer restricted to a few thousand feet but to see eternity, to scan an unlimited horizon for the first sign of the enemy.

A squadron of Marauders were heading south-east to their five o'clock, the two ranks of fighter support five thousand feet higher. Seeing the Tempests below, a flight of six dropped down to inspect them, but the fighters turned away as Rose waggled his wings, the sun bright on the large RAF roundels on Sugar's wings.

No lone-wolf Yank today, he thought, remembering the lone Mustang which had savaged the formation of 109s on the 17th, and recalling the story told to him by a USAAF Major a few weeks earlier of an American boy from Missouri named 'The Kidd' Hofer.

A brilliant pilot but a lone wolf, Hofer had achieved around thirty or more aerial and strafing kills in the single year of combat before his death.

Rose thought again of the unknown Mustang pilot. *I hope you stay lucky and make it to the end, Yank. Bravery deserves luck.*

For once, it was he who saw them first. *Will miracles never cease?*

Initially, he thought it was just dirt on Sugar's canopy, a smear of tiny dots, like fine dust, but the dots were moving, appearing above the layer of haze in formation.

'Hotspur to Hobart Flight, twelve aircraft five miles at eleven o'clock! Hobart Leader, take your section up and come around at 'em from out of the sun.'

A surge of excitement and fear, *Jerry or friendlies?*

'Hobart Leader, received and understood, Hotspur.' Sheep's section pulled up and away, growing smaller and fading into the brilliance of the sun as Rose continued to scan the sky above, around and below; the Tempest with the picture of a rat painted on its side was just behind and to port, while to starboard his element of two, Hobart Red section, Flying Officers 'Wally' Wainwright and 'Bluey' Cooper (like all 'Blueys' in the military so called because of his red hair).

Feeling absurdly smug in having spotted the enemy first, Rose pulled back the stick and, to the right, a touch of rudder to gain height. A few more thousand feet of height wouldn't hurt, particularly if it brought them closer into the corona of the brilliance of the sun as the other aircraft drew nearer, range closing to three miles now.

'Hotspur Section, battle spread, safeties off.'

Micky: 'They're bandits, Hotspur Leader, mixture of 190s and 109s.'

Glistening shapes clearer now, some blue-grey and others green, slicing through the air two thousand feet below, their canopies glinting.

Flick the switch for the gunsight, twist the knob from 'safe' to 'fire', the enemy now at their ten o'clock and below on a reciprocal course and still not aware of them. *Too busy staying in formation? Perhaps they think there are only four of us and so we won't attack …*

Recent Luftwaffe doctrine seemed to place large formations in a wheeling and turning arrangement, which made no sense to Rose and often led the enemy paying too much time to formation keeping while trying to avoid hitting their chums.

No time to waste, they'll see us at any moment.

'Hotspur to Hobart Leader, any company?' He felt the comforting shape of the little teddy bear and the pebble in his pocket.

'None, Hotspur, all clear.'

'Where are you?'

'Two thousand above you, a mile back.'

'Join us, will you? We'll separate the brutes and you smack 'em.'

'Right-o, Hotspur.' He could hear the eagerness in Sheep's tense voice, felt his own rising.

A glance at Molly's picture, another at the instruments and a hurried prayer, *Lord God please keep us safe this day ...*

'Hotspur, attacking.' Stick forward and left, kick left rudder and she yawed and rolled to port, nose dipping and turning and the horizon tilting and rising, the sun sliding up and away and the bandits still just pootling along as if they hadn't a care in the world as eight Tempests fell on them from the heavens.

The descending turn brought them into a slanting approach which turned into a three quarter one as the distance shortened, his eyes on one of the leading four FW190s, Sugar's nose leading it for deflection. Already the formation was coming apart as the bandits finally began to scatter, but too slowly.

Sheep, tersely, 'Hobart Flight, attacking.'

And Rose was in range, easing off the throttle, his thumb stabbing down a three-second burst as his target was jettisoning bombs and a centreline auxiliary tank. Released of its burden, the 190 began to lift and he cursed for his burst of 20 mm skimmed just below it, but some of his rounds must have clipped the tank for it exploded while still close to the enemy aircraft.

There was the searing flash of the explosion, a sullen *THUMP!* more felt than heard, and the 'scribble' grey camouflaged fighter was silhouetted for an instant against the sudden glaring flash of light, the shock of the concussive slap pitching it further upwards, nose tilting down and blowing fragments off it, just as the internal tanks were set alight.

He felt the shockwave and saw the expanding spherical wave of condensation from the blast wave speed outwards, and through which Sugar now juddered for a moment as Rose held her nose down against the wave, while in front the 190's wings folded up and backwards with bright flame sheeting along the fuselage, the broken airframe of the bandit rearing up and rolling to the left as Rose's ensuing bursts of fire finally caught it, pounding what was left into yet more pieces.

In his peripheral vision he glimpsed the 190 next in line shuddering beneath the impact of Micky's cannon shells; a sudden burst of flame and the bandit was swamped in blazing petrol, one wingtip coming up as it fell away trailing a thick plume of oily black smoke.

Rose choked on the stink of burned oil and cordite, feeling the urge to hunker down in the cockpit, eyes forward but neck twisting to search for sudden danger.

We've scattered Jerry, push Sugar down and open up the throttle, dive through them fast and hard to increase the separation while Sheep gets in amongst the bastards from above.

'Micky?' He made a face at the high-pitched shakiness of it. *Damn it*, he sounded as if he were about to burst into tears!

'Here, Leader.' Excited and breathless, victorious.

'I saw yours go down. Good shooting.'

As ever, he had been holding his breath and now he sucked in a deep draught of pure oxygen, feeling its cold burn against healing scars; he grimaced in discomfort and twisted his neck to look back.

A frozen tableau of widely separated bandits, the dirty smears of their victims now spinning earthwards, another 109 falling, streaming ragged smoke and flame, the sound of Bluey's victory yell deafening, more Tempests amongst Jerry as Sheep's flight tore into them, a 109 which must have been at the back of the formation with its nose pointing towards them but too far behind and unaware of the Tempest dropping into place behind it, faithful Micky close and falling back from line abreast to cover Sugar's tail, eyes taking in the air above, around and below, no threats yet, thank God.

Full throttle to gain some safe distance, no sign of his second element, and he hoped they were alright as he judged he had enough separation from the bandits and heaved Sugar around into a wide sweeping turn; he heard the first yells of triumph and warning, Sheep calmly telling his men to keep an eye open for more, heard the curses as the bandits, their wits at last about them, twisted away and tried to escape.

The bastards had been carrying bombs, an interdiction raid to support their men on the ground, *but not anymore.* He scanned his instruments for any tell-tale signs of damage, but all was as it should be and he smiled at her picture. *Still here, my love.*

The fight had now broken up into scattered dogfights between individuals and pairs spreading over a larger area as some tried to escape those who chased after them, the sky seeming so much emptier than it had before when he had looked back, at his seven o'clock an out of control Bf109 in a flat spin disappearing below, another heading north-east sharpish (*don't fancy a stern chase while braving the flak belts of the big cities*) and a Tempest a mile away, shrunken by distance and hotly pursuing another 109 into the dirty layer of haze eastwards towards Bonn.

Be careful, chum, all alone and heading into Germany, risky. Not the wisest thing to do, but then in the heat of the moment, one easily got distracted.

'Hotspur Leader to lone Hobart Tempest west of Bonn, break off pursuit immediately and rejoin, repeat, rejoin.'

There was no reply, and for a moment he thought of giving chase, but by then the solitary Tempest had faded into the haze and searching for it would be unwise within close reach of Bonn's flak batteries, and so he eased Sugar around to the north-west.

Three or four smoke trails and a thinning smudge (*from my 190?*) marred the once clear sky, the yellow of a distant parachute far below, no more sign of Jerry, suddenly almost peaceful after the harrowing violence of a moment ago.

'Hotspur Two to Leader, one aircraft, nine o'clock, range two miles and a thousand feet below.'

I didn't even see it, so much for keeping a good look out. 'I see it, Two, follow me down.' His voice was brusque with irritation at himself, not fair on Micky, and he reproached himself.

Better soften your tone, you miserable old so-and-so …

'Thanks, Two, I missed him.'

The aircraft turned out to be a smoke-stained P47 Thunderbolt, a D variant with a distinctive 'bubble-top' canopy, although a large chunk of it had been blasted away, and shrapnel strikes had ripped large holes into both wings while the starboard aileron (what little was left of it) and rudder were both frayed.

They closed carefully with the damaged aircraft, her port side displaying on the nose the legend 'Ornery Olive' in cheerful yellow letters, accompanied by a life-size painting of a blonde wearing a wide smile and cowboy boots but absolutely nothing else, clutching a large hammer in with both hands. Arrayed beside the nude was an impressive scoreboard of bombs, swastikas, trucks and tanks painted in white against the green camouflage.

While Micky's painted Tobruk Rat was an admirable badge of courage, Rose found the painting on the P47's cowling far easier on the eye.

Then, feeling her eyes on him, Rose smiled apologetically at Molly's picture and looked away. *I wasn't looking, Moll, honest.* Besides, his attention should be on the sky around them, not ogling some painted nude.

From inside, the intrepid ground-attack pilot gave him a weary wave, and Rose caught sight of the scarlet staining the American's white scarf. *We need to look after him, seems like he's been in a hell of a scrap and looks just about done in, but where? Eindhoven, that's closest, long runways in case his brakes are kaput. We'll escort him there.*

'We'll escort this chap to Eindhoven, Two. He looks as if he's been in a bit of a scrap.'

'Received, Leader. You should see the other guy!' Micky quipped in response.

Rose smiled, cheeky bugger. But they were far from home, and as Molly was fond of quoting ad nauseam after reading Thackeray's *Pendennis*, 'there's many a slip 'twixt cup and lip.'

And so it turned out. They were 'buzzed' three times, once by a formation of twenty plus 'Razorback' P47s heading south-east to the Ardennes, once by a pair of 8th AF P51s, and then by a squadron of Spitfires which accompanied them for a short while before becoming bored and turning east for something more exciting to do.

That's it, Nigel, go and find something more exciting to do, Rose thought disparagingly, wondering if April Munday's nephew was amongst them. And *that made him think of her trim figure and the warmth of her smile ...*

Of the Luftwaffe there was little sign *(thank God!)*, only the faraway condensation trails of a Me162, high to the north, hurtling incredibly fast across the cobalt blue canvas, and once a pair of FW190s nosed towards them but turned tail as soon as Rose turned after them, leaving Micky to protect the battered Thunderbolt.

At Eindhoven they radioed well ahead, for like all military flyers, Rose had a great deal of anxiety flying around unfamiliar airfields when it came to anti-aircraft gunners, even friendly ones.

He had been shot at on more than one occasion by those supposed to be one's friends. It had not quite been a regular occurrence when he had been on night fighters, but it had happened often enough (one barrage coming close enough to make Chalky accidentally swallow the painfully sharp pieces of a Sherbert Lemon he had had in his mouth at the time, although he had not received a great deal of sympathy from Rose).

It had also happened when he had been on the Channel Front, and even when his own airfield's gunners had taken a pot-shot at his Hurricane P-Peter during the height of the Battle of Britain when Nazi bombers were raiding RAF Foxton. The offending ack-ack gunners had received a scalding, ear-popping diatribe from a very irate and exceptionally beautiful WAAF Flight Officer which left them abashed and remorseful.

Their officer later apologised in person to Rose and Molly, but she had been unforgiving, and given the poor man a lecture on aircraft identification.

Rose smiled at the memory, the sight of the shocked gunner's face making him want to laugh. What an extraordinary woman Molly is, he thought gloatingly (*and all mine!*).

He thought no more of it until a week later when an envelope arrived from the Air Ministry, forwarding a handwritten note from the CO of the damaged P47's pilot in which he thanked both Rose and Micky and heaped praise on their 'generosity of spirit and heroism'. There was also a smaller note from the pilot who had been evacuated from Eindhoven to Britain, and it read, 'Thanks, fellas. Look me up when you get back. I owe you both a juicy steak and a cold beer.'

Also inside the envelope were two medal boxes, each containing a US Air Medal, a golden star-shaped medal suspended from an orange-and-blue striped ribbon.

It was a lovely gesture from the Americans, and a gleeful Micky immediately sewed (slightly askew) the ribbon onto his uniform tunic. One more medal in a very unique row.

Watching the youngster's enthusiasm (and complete lack of skill with a needle and thread), Rose smiled. *I'm lucky to have him*. Micky was an exemplary flyer in addition to being an outstanding wingman, and, like Frankie, was able to protect Rose while also managing to shoot down the enemy, too.

Rose decided he would put the papers in for a bar to their DFC's. It was well deserved and well overdue for both of them.

Micky howled as he pricked his finger, and Rose shook his head, trying not to laugh as the boy stuck the injured finger in his mouth.

I'd better sew on the DFC bar rosette when it's approved, daren't let Micky do it or he'll do himself a mischief!

Chapter 18

At the beginning of the war, the RAF comprised both regular and volunteer reserve units. The regulars were of mainly middle-class origin, whereas in general the reservists came from wealthier, even aristocratic backgrounds.

The raging cauldron of war changed all that.

As the years of fighting whittled down their numbers, and replacements from Civvy Street were drafted in, the makeup of the units homogenised to be far more representative in terms of the mix of backgrounds.

With men hailing from a wide variation of backgrounds, Rose had a number of memorable characters on 63 Wing which were hard to forget.

His young band of Frenchmen were on the whole from middle-class backgrounds, friendly enough but deferential. Even though he spoke passable French, Rose found them polite but distant when he sat amongst them, save for one of Gabby's section commanders, a rather battered-looking man called Boucher in his mid-thirties and sporting a permanent sneer.

At first Rose thought it was an expression of scorn for his Wing

Leader, and felt himself bristling, but later discovered the expression was due to a facial injury suffered while a *gendarme* patrolling the docks in Marseilles.

The man enjoyed chatting with Rose about his experiences in wartime London, having chosen to accompany a friendly London Bobby on his beat. The policeman was glad for the company on his beat around the heavily bombed Pool of London whenever Boucher had leave, their measured steps along deserted wharves and towering warehouses, the faint fragrance of tea, spices and fruit and all matter of exotic and mundane goods mixing with that of the stagnant aroma of the Thames' murky water, all carried along by a salty breeze, the sighing wind accompanied by the rattle of equipment and lapping waves. For the lonely ex-*gendarme*, the London Docks must have been the closest thing he had of home.

Rose found the trove of tales of those walks fascinating—they were murky tales of Dockers, prostitutes, Fifth Columnists and Black Marketeers—even though it meant having to endure the choking fumes of the *Caporal* cigarette which seemed a permanent fixture of Boucher's face, dangling precariously from his lip. Boucher's stories reminded him of Maigret's adventure, *The Crime at Lock 14*.

Another Frenchman, 'Mignon' Aubert, was neither small nor sweet, as his nickname suggested. Rather he was tall and broad, low brows over dark eyes, a huge barrel of muscle. It seemed improbable that such a goliath would fit inside the cockpit of a Tempest, yet incredibly he did.

Aubert's reminded Rose of a history lesson in which the teacher had vividly described a bloody confrontation between the forces of Wessex under King Alfred the Great and Guthrum the Dane at Ethandun, shield walls clashing together brutally and warriors gouging away at each other, the clangour of metal as swinging axes and stabbing swords or spears crashed into shields and mail and flesh, the curses and shouts of men mixed with the cries of the dying; Rose thought that the great looming Aubert would not look out of place in such a rank of shields, clad in helmet and mail, a shield in one hand and huge war axe in the other, glowering and ferocious.

Yet when the Frenchman spoke, it was in measured and cultured tones and with great humour, courteous to Rose and disappearing to see his Dutch girlfriend whenever he could. Rose was glad to have such a man in his Wing.

And there was Flying Officer Alex de Rond, who was anything but. Rather than round he was painfully thin, his face narrow and gaunt, with eyes deep-set. Even when he sat amongst his countrymen he seemed alone, saying little, his lips seldom stretching into a smile.

One evening, late after dinner, Rose was relaxing in an almost empty bar, sitting alone with a cold cup of Camp coffee beside him and a letter from Stan Cynk in his hand.

The letter had been posted in the United States, where Stan was now a Military Attaché in the rank of *Pulkownik*, an Air Force Colonel, for the Polish government in exile. After a distinguished (but short-lived) RAF career in which his dear friend had earned himself a DSO, DFC and bar to add to his plethora of Polish decorations which included two Gold and two Silver Crosses of *Virtuti Militari* and four Crosses of Valour. Stan was now settled with his wife, a beautiful ex-WAAF, and their two children, in Washington, and the family had just been granted US citizenship.

Rose held up the letter and sniffed it, catching the bloody awful mixed odour of cologne and cheroots and smiling as he remembered the huge belly laugh of that giant of a man, his vitality and his kindness for his friends, the atrocious and discordant singing that deafened anyone unfortunate to be within a hundred yards of him, his passion for his homeland and his complete and utter hatred of the Nazis.

Looking up, he noticed that De Rond was hunched in one corner, reading a book.

Rose wanted to be alone, but something made him get to his feet and approach the man; he was after all their Wing Commander, and should get to know all of his men.

'*Monsieur Commandant*?' De Rond hastily got to his feet, almost tipping over his unopened can of beer and clasping the book protectively to his chest.

Rose gestured for him to sit. 'Flying Officer, might I join you?'

De Rond stood respectfully and nodded, eyes hooded. '*Mais oui*, Commandant, please?'

Once seated, they stared at each other for a moment, the Frenchman holding his book against his chest, one finger keeping his page. It was a copy of Dickens' *A Tale of Two Cities*.

Another of Molly's favourites, and one which he had enjoyed. '*It was the best of times, it was the worst of times*,' Rose quoted aloud.

The man nodded solemnly. 'Indeed so, sir. An excellent opening line. It ignites the interest and stirs the emotion.' He offered the book to Rose, who took it carefully, for it was obviously treasured, the corners of the cover and the pages within not dog-eared but much used.

On the front page was a note, written in dark blue ink, faded where a finger had traced lovingly over it a thousand times:

Je serai à toi jusqu'à ce que je cesse de l'être,
 Car je ne peux aimer personne d'autre que toi, mon
précieux cœur.

Votre Annette.

I will be yours until I cease to be, for I can love none other than you, my precious heart. Your Annette.

Rose closed the book. 'Annette?'

'My wife, Commandant. The name means one with grace, and so it was with her. She was the most graceful creature on God's beautiful earth. We lived in Paris, *rue de la Roquette,* above it *la boulangerie.* Annette would run down the stairs before dawn, and we would watch the first light on the *Seine,* with fresh *croissants et chocolat.*'

The gaunt face had softened, the words soft. 'I can never forget the sound of her laughter, the fragrance of flowers and chocolate, being with her was being in a true heaven on earth.' He lifted the book. 'This was her book, and she gave it to me. With my memories, it is all I have left of her.' De Rond's face was tight, a carefully adopted mask devoid of emotion.

Rose closed his eyes for a moment, feeling the pain of the man's loss. 'Was?' *Put your bloody foot in it again, you absolute ass!* He understood what De Rond must have felt for his wife, for it was only when he was with Molly that he felt true happiness and peace.

'There was an act of resistance, some senior Nazi functionary died. They collect the hostages to shoot.' The voice was quiet, bitter. 'It is customary for *les Boches.*' The mask had cracked and De Rond's face was heavy with misery. 'I find it hard to recall the sound of her voice. Is it not strange? What a pitiful man am I!'

Having made the *faux pas,* Rose did not know what to say, feeling the Frenchman's despair.

De Rond was silent for a moment, and then continued. 'They killed ninety-nine other innocents that day. *Cent âmes, pouf!*

A deep sigh, a bleak sound of hopelessness, the book lovingly held to his lips. 'She was a teacher, Commandant, good and wise and sweet.' His voice hitched on the last word and he fell silent, eyes closing and his head nodding.

So many stories of loss, so much cruelty over the years. Stan and Cowboy were just two amongst millions whose happiness had been stolen by the Nazis.

Merciful Lord, he thought, hand stealing up to rest on the pocket beneath his wings and ribbons, where he kept her photograph, *thank you for sparing me the ones I love. To lose them would surely drive me into madness. Thank you for your mercy. Such a loss is enough to drive one completely mad.*

The thought of a world without Molly brought tears to his eyes and he sat silent with the wretched young Frenchman, one hand gently grasping the other's shoulder to comfort him and to share the misery.

'I'm sorry.' Words of sympathy that could not heal, were of no help against the pain.

But now he understood De Rond's incapacity to smile and his quiet demeanour, why Gabby's men surrounded him protectively. *What was there that could heal such terrible pain that could shred a soul?*

In truth, nothing. When he was ready there might be the chance of love, but having lost the one to whom his heart belonged so cruelly, could a man ever be truly ready again? To truly love again? Rose thought not.

And amongst his Australian veterans, there were similarly note-worthy individuals.

One of these was Flight Lieutenant Alf 'Kipper' Maddox. A stocky barrel of a man, with the weather-beaten face and heavily muscled arms of a fisherman from the Gascoyne region of Western Australia. The man had a broad, sun-reddened and wrinkled face with a ready smile who had endeared himself to Rose with his openness, sheer aggression and enthusiastic (but often bizarre) suggestions on war fighting.

Kipper had flown Rockphoons (rocket-firing Typhoons) in the push to Falaise, and he had bombarded his then-CO with requests to modify the RP-3 unguided rockets with necklaces of empty beer bottles wound evenly around the shafts of four of his eight rockets using fine steel wire.

Doubtful but desperate for a bit of peace and quiet, his CO had finally relented, saying he would ask for advice from London, and nothing should be done until The Ministry had ruled.

Eager to try out his idea and secretly helped by his intrigued armourers to prepare the modified rockets, Kipper ignored the warnings he had been given by both the armaments and engineering officers. Kipper had been beside himself with glee, almost dancing a jig, desperate to try out his invention. He'd show the doubters how to increase the destructive power of the RP-3!

Later that same day, Kipper's squadron were detailed to attack a retreating column of motorised infantry heading south on the road to Potigny.

Begging to be allowed to attack first to maximise the destructive effect of his modified weapons, the Squadron Leader, ignorant of the secret modifications, allowed Kipper to approach the nose of the column from the south, coming in low, just above the trees and launching all of his rockets in one massive salvo as soon as he was within range.

Anticipating the usual trajectory followed by rippling explosions as the rockets sped off his Rockphoon's wings, Kipper was dismayed to see the unbalanced rockets wobble and spin almost as soon as they left the rails, the bottle necklaces rapidly unwinding, dragging their rockets off target and catapulting the weapons into various trajectories to either side of the road, all of them away from the astonished Germans.

So astonished were the enemy troops by the terrifying but harmless display that they were belated in their return fire, which gave Kipper the chance to escape.

Instead of the enemy being hit by high explosive bursts with expanding shells of tiny shards of broken glass, Kipper found himself on the receiving end of the bottles, shreds of wire catching and damaging but (thankfully) not winding around his wings or propeller.

He was hugely fortunate that his Tiffie's air intake did not draw in any of the bottles as they separated from the wires for that would have finished him, but a number of them did spin back and shatter against his aircraft's wings and fuselage, flashes of glittering smears of brown bright against his propeller and the resulting damage making the fighter bomber almost uncontrollable during the trip home.

Instead of receiving a pat on the back or a commendation for getting his damaged Typhoon back to base, the irrepressible Australian was given the choice of a posting on to Tempests or a court martial for endangering government property.

And so Kipper joined Rose's 63 Wing.

Kipper's current interest was in German Metropolitan flak towers. A friend of his serving as a rear-gunner in Bomber Command had spoken of the terrifying gauntlet of anti-aircraft fire over Hamburg and Berlin: 'A bloody firestorm with Lancs being shot down all over the friggin' shop'. Both cities heavily defended by dense flak which was further strengthened by protective AA blockhouse complexes built to titanic proportions.

The flak towers of Hamburg each comprised a twinned combi-nation of a G-Tower (gun tower) working alongside an L-Tower (fire-control tower).

The G-Towers were virtually impregnable chunky concrete monstrosities (capable of housing 10,000 people and 30,000 at a pinch during a raid) equipped with eight fearsome 128 mm guns, multiple 37 mm flak cannon and numerous 20 mm Flakvierling quadruple-barrel guns.

Each flak tower complex's L-Tower had a radar dish which could be drawn into a thick concrete shell and sheltered behind a steel dome when retracted and was in turn supplied with its own associ-ated batteries of 20 mm guns.

With Berlin being a touch too far, and knowing nearer Hamburg 'only' had two in comparison to Berlin's three tower complexes, Kipper had proposed a bomb-carrying sortie by the Wing to Hamburg. 'I'm not saying we should attack the gun tower, Skipper.' He'd grinned cheerfully. 'No, that would be daft!'

Rose thought the whole endeavour daft, insanely so.

Kipper continued with enthusiasm. 'No, what we do is creep up at low level and drop bombs into the radar tower while it's still raised, sir. Wreck the tower and wreck the defences! Bit like ol' Gibson's boys at the dams!' Gibson had lost a third of his attacking force and Rose rather fancied his casualties would be higher with such a hare-brained scheme.

Then to further sweeten the idea and encourage Rose, he said, 'You'd get the VC, sir, just like Gibson! And just imagine what a difference it would make to all the metal Jerry throws up at the bomber boys, Skipper!'

Hm, maybe, but it would be a posthumous gong…

Rose, who felt that the idea made him want to throw up, listened to the proposal quietly but at the end was merciless and told a crestfallen Kipper he thought it was the 'silliest thing I've ever heard', and he was advised to get the 'damned fool notion out of your bloody head this instant.'

Being aware of Kipper's previous unauthorised modifications to his RP-3 rockets, Rose reminded him that if he were to entertain the daft notion of having a bash on his own account without it being sanctioned by the RAF, and were the young ex-fisherman to actually survive such an act of idiocy, Rose promised Kipper sincerely that he would be court-martialled and cashiered for insubordination, but not before Rose had kicked his backside so hard that Kipper would be the first man to land on the moon.

Once the downcast Kipper had left his office, Rose turned to a grinning Sheep and shook his head in askance. 'Bloody Nora, I've heard it all now!'

'His heart's in the right place, the silly galah, and you can't blame a bloke for trying, eh, sir?' was Sheep's only response.

And the ebullient Kipper continued to cast the odd hopeful glances at Rose, to be answered with a baleful shake of the head.

Then there was Sheep's Senior Flight Commander, Flight Lieutenant Ben Duncan, an ex-lawyer from Brisbane, tall like his Squadron Leader but dark with dark brooding eyes and a petulant mouth, though he was anything but petulant. He was thoughtful of both his pilots and groundcrews, and was always with his men, either in the monastery's refectory or at the bar, where he drank very little but listened a lot.

It was not unusual for Rose to set foot on Volkel well before dawn to find Duncan already there with the ground crews laughing at a joke over a mug of compo, or learning about the Sabre (something of which Rose still knew little, despite Granny's despairing attempts to teach 44 Wing's pilots the basic of aircraft and engine maintenance).

At defaulters one evening, when considering an aircraftsman for being drunk, Duncan had spoken eloquently to an irritable and tired Rose about the man's exemplary duty and of the strains of a life in which a man must be torn from a young family (something his grouchy Wing Commander could identify with closely), and despite his urge to set an example Rose was surprised to find himself setting a punishment of one day on 'Jankers', two days stoppage of leave and straight afterwards issuing a week's leave pass.

Sheep had seen Rose's approving eyes on Duncan one evening, as the man spoke to one of his pilots for being unable to attack a barge on the Rhine during an armed reconnaissance. Instead of haranguing the man he had recognised the signs of a veteran who had reached the end of his personal limits, and instead of arranging courts martial or some other such inappropriate punishment, Duncan arranged for him to be sent back to Blighty for a rest.

Liking what he saw, Rose asked and Sheep explained that before the war Duncan had acted as the lawyer for cases of rural domestic violence where sanctuary and redress was rare for the women and their children in toxic and hopeless situations. Duncan had taken it upon himself to be their champion, as he was the champion of all those in his charge.

And Duncan must have been a contentious fighter in the courtroom, for he certainly was one in the air, with twelve kills marked on his Tempest D-Dagger and a well-earned DFC and bar on his chest for his courage.

Often when lonely and waking from a restless sleep, Rose would take Sugar into the air to watch another dawn above the clouds, and

Duncan would accompany him ('You'll need a wingman, sir, we're not in Kansas anymore!'), his Tempest close and reassuring in the lonely early morning sky, an unobtrusive and watchful companion with a firm mouth and warm, caring eyes.

Chapter 19

For the next few days, US Thunderbolts and RAF Typhoons flew thousands of sorties, pounding the enemy on the ground while Allied fighters provided a protective canopy against Luftwaffe intervention.

At twelve thousand feet they could see the uneven eastern edges of the Elsenborn Ridge, a raised grey outline, numerous thick plumes of smoke and crops of flak merging to form a sullen smear on the road south from Monschau and well east of the Baracken crossroads, heavy and angry and thickening the dirty haze which obscured the desperate battle on the ground.

Had they been nearer, they would have seen in the air above the battleground the constant sparkling rash of flak and the intermittent flash of light catching the surfaces of fighter bombers from IX Tactical Air Command and 2TAF as they dived and climbed, ravaging the packed mass of tanks, half-tracks and trucks of the Nazis in 1st SS Panzer Division, matched below by momentary eruptions of agonising brightness on the ground as vehicles blossomed into destruction, every now and then the shattered panzers being joined by the torn and burning wreckage of those of their aerial attackers brought down by the thick curtains of 20 mm flak and automatic fire.

Rose did not envy the ground-attack boys in their Thunderbolts and Typhoons as they gallantly braved the flak to reduce the numbers of 1st SS before the vehicle columns reached the men battling grimly on the front line, his own terrible experiences from well before the Invasion up until Falaise still scarring his mind and haunting his dreams, yet a part of him felt an irrational yearning to be amongst them and raining bloody horror and death onto Jerry.

I must be mad to even think it, but where we're going now is no less dangerous, for today 63 Wing's task was to suppress and diminish Luftwaffe fighter activity and protect the fighter bombers by strafing Dusseldorf airfield.

Protected by the city's flak belt, the airfield had 'only' seven light flak and two heavy flak positions, although each of these comprised at least one battery of guns. With main buildings arranged mainly along the southern edge of the airfield, Sheep would take his lads down for one pass in three formations of four line abreast along the southern half of the airfield, spaced apart by sixty seconds so as not to catch it from flak lagging behind preceding Tempest quartet in front.

Rose had asked to lead the third section, but Sheep was loath to lose his Wing Commander in the formation which would be last through the gauntlet of fire and at its most dangerous. Instead Rose and Micky found themselves as the element leader and wingman in Sheep's leading section.

As soon as he caught sight of the Rhine's dark squiggle and the twin patches of brooding red, brown and grey which were Dusseldorf and Duisburg to the north, Sheep ordered them into the section crooked line astern battle formation to confound the flak and tipped them down into a power dive to tree-top level. The Intelligence Officer at

Volkel had assured them of no power lines to entangle them, but still Rose searched anxiously for the tell-tale pylons.

With the distinctive isosceles triangle of runways visible in the light expanse of concrete, he corrected a couple of degrees to port away from Dusseldorf's city centre and line up with the southernmost boundary of the Luftwaffe airbase.

High above, twelve Tempests bearing the Cross of Lorraine and the Oriflamme weaved at fifteen thousand, a couple of miles to the west of the Rhine and just out of range of the concentrated flak belts of the two great German cities, Gabby's squadron of Frenchmen acting as cover and to provide early warning of approaching bandits.

Once Hobart were clear, Gabby would also lead his men down but instead of attacking the aerodrome his target was the railway marshalling yards a kilometre to the south-east of the great airfield in a single strafing pass, 63 Wing striking at the airfield and the transport hub in one (almost) fell swoop.

Safety off and gunsight on, eyes taking in the airfield with its four large dispersal areas and associated aircraft shelters and blast shelters, aircraft lined up in small clusters, flak and tracer already reaching out and the sun warm against his right cheek.

As the polluted waters of the Rhine flashed beneath them, they pulled up to fifty feet over a cycling couple racing one another on the path beside the western boundary fence, the tiny faces of a Wehrmacht squaddie and a slim redhead upturned and comical in their sudden terror as, distracted by the terrifying din of approaching Sabres, their bicycles wobbled then collided, pitching them into a jumbled heap of arms and legs and spinning tyres.

And now the airfield was laid out before them and somehow he had fallen a little behind and Rose pushed forward the throttle to catch up, brown smoke and glittering empty shell cases trailing back from Sheep and his wingman as they opened fire.

Rose saw a pair of parked trucks and touched the gun button for a moment, 20 mm rounds slashing across to miss one truck completely but thumping into the other, bowling it over and demolishing it into twisted metal, what looked like a sack of rags thrown from its cab.

Two large hangars to starboard, one smaller than the other, a tiny whatchamacallit, a Kettenrad motorbike/halftrack tractor hooked up to a Me262 jet parked beside the nearer hangar, men in black overalls scattering as the stream of explosive shells from Micky's R-Rooster slammed into them, tossing the Kettenrad upwards like a toy and blowing off the streamlined nose and canopy of the jet, the loss of its nose-wheel undercarriage tilting the wrecked fighter tiredly forward as Micky raised Rooster's nose to leap clear of the raised shark's fin tail and the hangars, Rooster's 20 mm shells hammered into the hangar's wall and across its roof, clouds of dust and fragments billowing and flying as some of the shells ricocheted crazily upwards, a bright lash of tracer too far behind and in any case far too high to connect with the raiders.

Micky whooped over the R/T with excitement, and Rose felt a humourless smile tighten across his cheeks, *Typical! I get a lousy truck but that cheeky little sod bags a blinking 262!*

Easing a little to port, pushing her down, Sheep's pair slipped away to one side, the distance between them widening as they spread apart to attack individual targets, a wall of flak bursting and lashing whips of glowing white, yellow and green tracer soaring over them and a frozen ball of fear low down in his gut, tightly sucking at his stomach, groin and buttocks, the turmoil above and the cushion of air below making Sugar porpoise erratically and his jaw clenched as he fought to keep her steady.

His hands were like vices on the control stick, Sugar bucking and bouncing in the fierce tumult, muscles straining to hold her steady, his eyes restive to guide her nose onto targets, the tinkle and bang of shrapnel inordinately loud against her lithe shape, louder even than the thump and crash of flak.

And there were more than enough targets to go around. Ahead of him he could see the dark shapes of three aircraft neatly lined up. He lifted her nose to drop a burst of cannon fire onto them, dipping her nose and then easing her closer to the ground again and following it up with a second short burst closer too, seeing the aircraft were a trio of Ju88s as Sugar's cannon shells ripped right through the nearest bomber's thin fuselage close to the tail to break her into two and rip off her undercarriage so that she tilted, then rocked heavily onto the concrete beneath. Rose slipped to port in case one of them had full tanks and exploded.

Of the other two bombers, he could not tell if Sugar's fire had done any damage although her cannon shells must have spilled across them.

Luckily none of the Junkers exploded, for he was too close for comfort and any slap of concussion might have driven him into the ground or thrown him up into the beautiful but deadly ceiling of flak bursts and colourful tracer.

Sugar was forcing herself through a hard storm of shrapnel from the exploding AA shells, and Rose gritted his teeth and squinting as her propeller caught against them, tiny sparks and smears of light like fairies dancing along the clear shining disc of her propeller, and the enduring clatter of the downpour of shrapnel against her airframe.

Rose saw that Micky was still flying along the tarmac apron,

Rooster's shells crashing against vehicles and parked aircraft and Rose turned Sugar's 20 mm onto the five hangars of the south-east corner of the enemy airfield. The airfield HQ and main administration buildings were situated there, and he slipped her over to starboard, as he tried to catch up with the youngster, tracer which was lagging behind the young Australian lashed out in front of Sugar's nose, though a little high.

It was a dangerous occupation flying behind an aircraft being fired upon, as the lagging aircraft was more likely to be hit by flak aimed at the leading aircraft.

An MG post and a 20 mm flak emplacement midway along the perimeter track between the two clusters of hangars, the latter's barrels pointed towards him but not firing (a stoppage?), stick over to port, and a nudge of rudder to correct and keep her up, level her out, centre her and flee towards the sanctuary of the eastern edge, grimacing as the MG loosed off another burst of fire, behind but not by much, *more throttle,* heart pounding fit to burst and forearms and shoulders and chest aching with strain and anxiety and effort.

Breathing hard through a mask feeling too tight and pushing against the bridge of his sweaty nose as a blob of oil flew back to smear momentarily across one of the windscreen's side panels.

Rose caught sight of a spinning disc ahead, a single engine fighter preparing for take-off at the pointed junction where the two longer runways intersected; he would need to adjust further to port to spray the enemy with fire but the tracer was chasing him too closely, and he cursed aloud, face aching from the tautness of his jaw, feeling the punch of several impacts into her fuselage and the thump of bullets against the armour plate at his back, but still her Sabre snarled sweetly and still she responded to his deftest touch, *good girl, time to get out of it ...*

The taxiing fighter, a grey speckled 190A, was between him and another flak position, shielding him from their fire and he pushed Sugar to full throttle, through the gate and into emergency boost, stick easing back to clear the boundary, the enemy unable to track his racing Tempest, the meteoric speed thrusting him into his seat and away from the danger.

A Tempest was pulling a thin streamer of smoke half a mile to port, more of his fighters were at various heights further away, and Micky's Tempest was a quarter of a mile ahead and so low some treetops were above him.

Rose slipped Sugar a little lower too, edging her to starboard to close up with his wingman.

Pull back throttle a little, but not too much because there'll be soldiers on the ground and all it takes is a single bullet, though at this speed with a bit of luck the chance of a hit has got to be infinitesimally small, but nonetheless ...

As if to make a mockery of his thoughts, the damaged Tempest to port wobbled and then reared up suddenly as a single line of white tracer connected with it, flipped inverted and dived into the ground, a bright flash of light and a raging globe of rising flame marking the sudden and terrible end of one of his men.

Rose felt the crush of pain squeeze his heart knowing that another of those who he had flown alongside was gone, his only marker not a headstone but a plume of thinning smoke, to mingle with the myriad columns curling into the haze from the burning airfield behind them.

But they were in the heart of danger and it could be their turn next ...

This area's going to be lousy with bloody power lines, he thought, though he couldn't see any pylons. 'All aircraft, beware of power lines. Hotspur Two, climb at full boost.'

They were over a mile away from the airfield now and would just have to brave the layered flak belt of this metropolitan region of Germany's Ruhr Valley, probably the diciest place to be over Germany, with Dusseldorf, Duisburg, Essen, Wuppertal and Solingen established so very close together.

'Received, Leader.' The boy's Tempest pulled up into a climb, the light catching her wings thrusting hard through the smoke and smog, his voice thin with anguish. 'Oh, merciful Lord! Did you see Bear go in?'

'Dear God, that was Bear?' Rose closed his eyes for a moment.

Big Bear McCullough, 5'2" and always smiling, hailing from New South Wales' Jervis Bay, with a battered-looking surfing board in one corner of his cubicle at the seminary, boasting he'd been taught to surf by Isma Amor (whoever that was) and his walls covered with photographs of girls.

Bear's life had been short, filled with much experience and fully lived, over too soon.

'Hobart Green, clear.' The leader of Sheep's third section, confirming that the last of his Tempests had cleared the field.

Gabby: 'Marengo, *oui*.'

Almost immediately, Frankie, '*Bandits! Plus de quarante!*'

For fuck's sake!

'In English!' Rose roared in exasperation.

'Forty plus bandits, Hotspur, *uh, pardon*, twelve o'clock, three miles east, low,' Frankie said contritely, but nothing from Amélie.

Sheep, urgently, 'Hobart, immediate regroup at ten thousand, one mile west of Dusseldorf.'

'Hotspur Leader to Wing, reform together at Hobart rendez-vous point.'

Rose pulled out of his climb, looking for the others, eyes searching as he guided Sugar around westwards after Rooster, jinking and changing height to confuse the radar-guided heavy flak batteries of the combined city defences, trying to calculate how many cannon shells he had remaining, and understanding however much it was, it was not enough.

Forty plus! His blood ran cold at the imbalance in numbers.

Come on, *come on,* 'Pull your ruddy finger out, 63!' Rose's voice was harsh in his concern that they might have less ammo than he would wish for, and he cursed softly. *Don't let your lads see you panicking when the odds are against you,* Granny had once told him, years earlier. *Be a man, grab your balls and hold on tight.*

The formation of bandits was one of those swarming, haphazard ones in which some of their number were always turning, fighters dipping and rising, climbing or diving, which Rose thought rather diverted their attention away from the surrounding sky as the jumbled, chaotic group of bandits tried to avoid one another while remaining together.

With the two squadrons hurriedly reformed (one eye anxiously watching the approaching bandits), Rose had nineteen Tempests from the original twenty-four available (with Bear lost, he had sent the Tempest with empty ammo trays and the two Tempests damaged during the attack home with a fourth as their escort).

In the meantime, the bandits were a lot closer and had settled into a far more stable formation.

'Hotspur Leader to 63, adopt twelve-eight battle formation.' Even though they were only nineteen in number, he knew they would understand.

Nineteen! Nineteen of us up against forty-plus of them! Dear God! He cringed again at the numbers, a stab of bowel-weakening fear, unexpected and shocking.

The men of his Wing were outnumbered by more than two-to-one, and he knew that with their superior speed the Tempests could turn away and avoid combat. But if his Wing were to turn tail and scarper, then these bandits might fall upon the ground-attack boys over the Ardennes. He could not allow that.

But having just lost one of his men during the attack, he quailed at the thought of surely losing more of them. But his duty was to the men on the ground who even now were fighting a desperate battle on frozen ground giving everything they had to stop the enemy armour.

He could almost hear Granny. *Grab your balls, sillyarse, and hold on tight.*

His squadrons were arrayed in battle formation, three sections of four in line abreast but stepped up in height horizontally from port to starboard, with two sections of three and four in a similar formation led by Sheep and Gabby respectively, the trailing seven a mile astern of Rose's leading twelve. *If the enemy split their formation into two, things will get worse pretty bloody quick,* he fretted, and began to pray for the enemy to stay together.

There was no more time to think as the two formations raced together at a combined speed of almost seven hundred miles an hour, the dots rapidly expanding into an alarmingly large cloud of enemy fighters, wings flashing as the enemy opened fire, and Rose hunched as he pressed his own gun button, a mere touch for they would pass one another in a fraction of a moment.

In a storm of sound and vibration the two formations interpenetrated, a shadow passing huge and dark across Sugar's canopy, a barb of terror making him duck involuntarily and clench his eyes shut, the snarl of the bandit's engine a spike of dulled sound, and then suddenly the bump and buffeting as the Tempests flew through into the chaos of the enemy's slipstream, and he pushed the throttles further forward, pulling Sugar up into a thirty degree climb.

The sections on either side broke into hard turns to port and starboard, and the enemy formation, scattering to pursue Rose's Tempests and forming easier profiles to target for the second flight of Tempests, were hit by the cannon fire from Gabby and Sheep's sections, livid white flame guttering from a Bf109, its nose lifting and the fighter falling onto its back on the way down.

As the burning fighter rolled inverted, it struck the tailplane of another and the second 109, minus its entire tail section, fell away into a slow spin and the enemy pilot managing to escape the cockpit of his doomed fighter.

A third fighter, a FW190A, was hit side-on by a broadside of eleven 20 mm cannon shells from the second group of Tempests, its fuel tanks exploding and it, too, slipped into a death-dive, shedding burning fragments and blobs of flaming petrol on its way earthwards.

The enemy were scattering, but they broke formation into turning circles which were wider than the far tighter turns of the two sections of Rose's group which had broken hard apart to either side after interpenetration, and now those Tempests were turning inside the turning circles of the bandits, spraying explosive shells in a spreading fan across the paths of the mixture of 109s and 190s, hits flaring across some of the shapes.

Half a dozen bandits were winged, and a small number of them, streaming thick smoke from their exhausts, peeled off to escape.

But one of them lost a wing where a shell had weakened the spar, a tank torn open and fuel spilling and catching alight and it began to whirl and tumble earthwards out of control like a giant St Catherine's wheel firework.

But it did not go all the way of the Tempests. Hit in the first confrontation, one limped away west trailing smoke but not for long as a pair of 190s fell upon it, and with a flurry of cannon and machine-gun fire shot it tumbling down, the pilot not managing to escape.

Another was turning hard with its wings almost perpendicular to the ground as three 190s whipped after it, ugly snouts spitting destruction, one of the enemy wobbling and then falling out of control as it stalled.

All of this was happening behind Rose as his four Tempests separated into the break, Rose and Micky to starboard and his second element to port.

Eyes skating from the all-around search for threats further away, he turned tightly back into the fight; pressed back into the seat, mask pushed a little to one side and digging into his lower eyelids, Rose saw that the two groups of aircraft had spread into a smear of individual (or not so individual) combats, fighter chasing fighter in the typical welter of combat growing smaller by the moment, the dogfights spreading apart, blurring with distance and fading away into the haze, his earphones alive with shouted interjections and expletives.

And danger close, closing fast, a loose group of 190As, not the longer-nosed more powerful 190Ds, around five hundred feet higher and noses pointing down at their Tempests.

'Hotspur Leader, four bandits, half a mile, one o'clock above, coming down.' Micky's hurried voice was almost gabbling to warn Rose.

Rose pulled his mask back into position, 'I have them, Two.'

'Christ! Jink, Hotspur! Bandit at your six o'clock!'

What the … ? Mind racing. *Can't break or else the 190s ahead will get me …*

Instincts taking over even as he belched out a cry of shock and sudden fear, pulling the stick hard over to starboard, kick rudder, minimal aileron roll and she was slipping and rolling to one side, *enough*, hold her, a burst of yellow-green tracer, bright and shocking and streaming above and to port, close enough to sear past him and light up Sugar's cockpit, close enough to hear the urgent streaming *zip-zip-zip* and enough to make Rose's bladder loosen.

Micky, breathing hard, 'You're clear, leader, he broke away when I gave him a burst!'

The 190s ahead peeled apart on either side of them, contrails pulling sharply from their wingtips as they began to execute early the incredibly sharp reversal the 190 was capable of, their shapes just beginning to lengthen as they risked Sugar's teeth.

The bandit was going too fast to follow with Sugar's cannon but he squeezed the button anyway for a moment and he thought he saw a flash on the pale belly as the 190 skimmed past close enough to touch; it was likely wishful thinking but still he felt the thrill.

Stick hard back, and she wallowed and skidded as momentum dragged at Sugar even as her nose lifted, the pressure on his chest making it hard to breathe.

Sugar was dominant in the climb against the 190A, and he knew the enemy must be falling back. Panting nervously, Rose eyed the mirror, but it was all clear with no immediate threats above or around, a guttering flame trailing a smear of dirty smoke behind him a mile away, no sign of the victor.

'Micky, they're turning early, they're going to box you in if you follow me, dive away!'

'OK, Leader.' The young voice was calm, not even out of breath.

That must be enough separation from Jerry, stick over and forwards, rudder to take her down in a wide sweeping spiral, nothing on his tail and Micky's Tempest a shape racing earthwards, two smaller shapes (*where was the third?*) nimbly flipping inverted and falling after Rooster like a pair of hawks.

Drop her nose further and tighten the turn, the harness biting into him and mask slipping again on his sweaty face as her corkscrew dive became steeper, the sunlight spinning around his cockpit and glinting metal catching his eye, the ground a faded watercolour laid out before him, a bandit heading straight down minus its canopy and pilot (Micky's doing? Did he get one of the early reversing enemy fighters?).

Another 190 turning towards him but still distant, light flashing from its canopy, about a mile and a half away; *too far and too slow to catch me …*

He had lost sight of Rooster, but the two diving 190s tailing his wingman were still only around a thousand feet beneath him, lines of smoke trailing back over their wings as they opened fire on Micky, *even though they must be out of range. You won't startle him into pulling out early, you bastards, he's a canny fighter and he'll use his speed to increase separation …*

Mirror, nothing …

Sugar's performance was better in the dive than her opponents, little need for deflection in an almost vertical dive from astern, and he thumbed a second's worth of 20 mm after them as he saw Rooster for a moment, wings tipping her into an erratic, undulating turn and she was pulling out of the dive, and Sugar's rounds would not catch the young Australian's Tempest.

A glance behind, *nothing.* Heart racing and the mad buzz of battle searing his nerves, no sign of the 190 which had momentarily caught the light. *Hopefully he's pissed off after someone else.*

A flash, and then two more, bright on the hazy silhouettes of the enemy fighters and the 190s twitched suddenly apart, exhaust smoke trails thickening as the bandits split formation, rolling away from one another, and he eased Sugar after the one which was sprinting after Rooster; his eyes slashed across the canopy and then into the mirror, grunting under the pressure of the dive and turn, feeling his chest being crushed and mouth open as he clawed after the 190 chasing Micky.

Sugar's superior speed thrust her after the 190 and he sighted, fired off a short burst, the shells ripping away to pass beneath the enemy's tailplane. *Damn it!*

Eyes in the mirror, *clear.*

The ground was far closer now, its colours sharper.

Too low, and the 190 rolled away and Rose corrected, caught the enemy fighter with a third burst, hits rippling bright across the bandit's starboard wing and its pilot jinked, right, left, right, too close to the ground to risk diving again lest he lose control and pile into the nearby ground; Rose tapped the rudder and aileron-rolled with the bandit, matching the enemy move for move, conscious of the ground and of the sky behind.

He was thinking furiously as he threw Sugar around after the 190, trying to remember how many seconds of ammunition he must have left. After the airfield it might not be enough.

A man jumping from the cab of a tractor in a ploughed field as the two fighters screamed past overhead, a wretchedly small herd of bony cattle scattering in slow motion.

Rose's fourth burst of 20 mm sprayed out in a swathe that enveloped the bandit, tearing into the fleeing 190, explosions flowing like a string of firecrackers from the *Balkenkreuz* forwards across the cockpit and starboard wing root and onto the cowling, and the enemy pilot was pulling his stricken fighter back up into the sky ...

The 190's shining propeller disc began to break up and stabbing white sheets of flame burst from beneath the shredded BMW radial piston engine, patchy wisps of smoke thickening until the 190 was half hidden beneath a thick shroud of grey-black smoke, the plume curling backwards, half the starboard wing blown off and twisting away by a slew of cannon shells, and the bandit began to fall, spinning about its axis and cloaked in swirling embers and thick smoke.

Cordite, smoke and burned oil sour in his mouth and nostrils.

Check mirror, *clear.*

The bandit was breaking up, transformed from a deadly fighter aircraft into three or four separate pieces of flaming wreckage spinning and rolling earthwards amidst a spreading shower of burning globs of fuel and fragments.

Rose's eyes flicked around the environs, checking the enemy sky, Rooster half a mile distant, turning in a wide circle with sunlight bright on its wings, watchful, further away the yellow speck of a parachute settling slowly on the ground, the fires of the vanquished bright spots amidst the drifting smears on the frozen ground.

Lord God, let Jerry not have decimated my lads ...

As every fighter pilot learns when flying into combat, one minute he might be in the midst of a whirling, wheeling mass of duelling fighters, the next alone in an empty sky.

Rose could still hear the muted shouts and cries in his earphones as the fighting continued, but individual pursuits had taken fighters in all directions and heights, expanding outwards across many of miles and now the sky was a smoke-blotted void, the aerial battle spread out across the emptiness and its protagonists hidden to Rose by haze and distance.

But only a fool would allow themselves to relax in this seemingly safe situation with the air battle in such close proximity to the fighter airfields of north-western Germany (indeed Rose fancied that he could still smell the stench of Dusseldorf airfield's swelling mantle of smoke following their attack in his nostrils), it was certain there would be enemy fighters rising from their airfields nearby to pursue the intruders of 63 Wing.

We've broken up a far larger enemy formation and given them a bloody nose, the lads have done me proud, and it's time to edge inconspicuously off the stage while the going's good and there's an interval.

Fighting individually or in pairs, his men must be watching their fuel gauges anxiously, would be dog-tired and dangerously low on ammunition. *Sheep's lads will be as short of 20 mm as I am, but at least Gabby's boys had not attacked the marshalling yards, and would have started the fight with a full load.*

No sign of Jerry, nor of his lads. The mayhem of his men fighting quieter in his earphones.

He eyed her smile longingly, 'Hotspur Leader to Wing, disengage and head for home, repeat, disengage!'

God only knows if they can hear me …

He wiped his forehead and sore cheeks with a soggy cuff, eyes searching for more of the enemy, but they were alone in the hostile sky, and he felt the adrenaline drain from him.

Low in ammunition and fuel, grateful for having survived the strafing of Dusseldorf fighter base and the subsequent dogfight, Rose led Micky back to Volkel.

Chapter 20

Beneath his flying overalls, Max's body was slick with sweat, his heart pumping fit to burst, '*Was für ein verdammtes Durcheinander!*' he cursed aloud, his mouth sour with bitterness and his heart sick with pain.

And it was true, it had been a bloody mess.

They had been scrambled too late to intercept the incoming *Ami* bomber raid; the only hope was that the target was deep inside Germany and that at full speed they might yet catch the mighty four engine bombers before they reached their target.

As they climbed furiously towards the distant white scratches, still nursing their delicate engines, for with low thrust it took forever to accelerate (if only the automatic acceleration device currently in development was available *now*), gradually building up speed until they were fast enough to close the range to the slower enemy bombers, Max's *schwarm* of four 262s had been bounced by a formation of Yankee fighters.

The four airfield protection FW190Ds had already broken off, falling behind Max's accelerating fighters, and the pair at six thousand feet over the airfield itself were too far away to help.

Having built up their speed in a dive, the plummeting USAAF Thunderbolts had seared through the 262 formation without warning, the preceding hailstorm of bullets from their M2 Brownings reaching out ruinously for the German aircraft.

Fortunately for Max (*Lucky Max* again, he thought bitterly, my friends die all around me but I just sail through), his 262, Red 6, had been leading the other three jets, a little ahead of the others in his eagerness to catch the enemy before they could drop their bombs, and whoever had been trying to down him had aimed poorly, for the single bullet hit (*thank God!*), had been unable to damage his *Schwalbe*. (If they had been cannon shells the outcome might have been very different indeed!)

He had somehow managed to escape the enemy's thrusting attack, but the same could not be said for his three companions.

Young Peterkin had been directly behind him when the .5 inch bullets came down and as the boy's warning cry ripped through his earphones, Max had thrown all caution to the wind and pushed forward the throttle, risking damage to the spinning blades or danger of the engine flameouts they all feared from the overly sensitive Jumos.

Looking back he saw the big, chunky P47s (six, seven?) blur past, saw Oberleutnant Kaminski's 262 already falling away, swathed within a blinding white sheet of flame coursing out backwards from wingtip to wingtip.

Saw that Kaminski's *rottenflieger*, Unteroffizier Krebs' 262 was a lopsided shape, diminishing, gyrating and tumbling in an uncontrollably twisting spin, shedding fragments and one wing torn off inboard of the port Jumo, disappearing into the cloud below and the airframe fragmenting.

Saw that there was no sign of either of their parachutes.

He felt the stab of pain and loss pierce through him, remembering the day they had entered Russia; Kaminski had shot down his first enemy plane, more by luck than chance, and had drunk so much captured vodka in celebration that he had been sick all over the Geschwaderkommodore's shiny boots.

The celebrations had faded away into the frozen horror of the brutal Russian winter, and now another of the remaining survivors was gone.

Heart thumping and eyes wide as he raced her away from the Americans, Max now saw that not all the Yankee fighters were unscathed as they blasted through the ruined formation of jets.

One Thunderbolt almost collided with Kaminski as the latter's blazing jet slowed and fell, the 262 now only visible as an unrecognisable ball of writhing flame, while the tail-end P47 began his pull-out early, hoping to catch Max's jet too, but colliding accidentally with Peter.

The big Curtiss Electric propeller's spinning disc caught Peter's tail fin, the tips of those four broad spinning blades ripping off the upper half of the jet's vertical stabiliser, the hated swastika on its tailplane shredded and the hard, sharp sidelong jolt of sudden torque from the big prop's revolutions pitching Peter's Me262 into a fast, flat, uncontrollable spin, the disintegrating jet fighter punching a ragged drawn-out hole through the clouds below, and he lost sight of it below.

Oh, Peterkin.

Had Peter been flying one of the jets which had one of those new ejector seats? No matter how hard he tried, Max couldn't remember. Any chance of survival seemed non-existent, the memory of that uncontrollable jet gyrating and shedding pieces.

Please God, let the boy live, let him get out. Take the jaded dogs like myself, but protect the young ones, the good ones. Please God …

The big USAAF fighter which had collided with Peter's 262 continued its way earthwards, falling inverted and its bent propeller blades windmilling.

All this was seen over his shoulder as he pushed down the nose on his 262 fighter, 'Red 6', seeking salvation in the mountainous cloud beneath him, forced to keep the dive angle less than the thirty degrees beyond which recovery would be hard if not impossible.

The control stick was already stiffer, her airframe shuddering as the speed built up, the Jumos drawing thick plumes of black smoke, listening with trepidation for any change in the cadence of their whine.

'Mein Gott! Dear God, why? Why Peterkin … ?' The words were ripped out of him, and he felt the deep welling of loss and unshed tears burning behind his eyes, even though death was chasing close behind him.

Many times, too many times, in Spain, Poland, France, North Africa and God alone knew where else, he had suffered the loss of friends and colleagues.

But young Peterkin had become more than a dear friend. Following the destruction of his neighbourhood and the loss of family in Berlin, Peter had been a welcome and regular visitor at Max's home in Bavaria.

In their visits to the family farm in the Bavarian Alps, his youngest sister Elise-Marie and Peter had grown close. Each time little Lissy spoke his name, the softness in her voice revealed to the world her feelings, and the way his eyes shone and he grinned like an idiot each time their eyes met exposed his.

Peter was an honourable young man, but Max still feared what might happen between the two youngsters (*if it hadn't already?*), but hoped that perhaps one day there might be peace and …

Max looked back, thrusting his heartache away, and saw that the remaining P47s had bottomed out of their dives and that three of them were now pulling up after Red 6, the urgency driving him to dive away.

Mourning would have wait for later, *if I survive* …

The *Amis* had already achieved the impossible; bouncing a jet formation without its FW190D escort and chopping down three out of four was a glorious victory, but their blood was up and they weren't ready to go home yet. Losing one of their own in the collision would only spur them on.

But already the Thunderbolts were falling behind, losing way with the added speed of their dive gone and struggling to build up speed again after pulling out of their descent.

Two of them, the ones closest to the P47 which had clipped Peter, had broken away on to different vectors and were no longer a threat, leaving the remaining three too far back, already out of range, the distance opening up as the cliff face of cloud rushed up to meet him.

Reassured by the closeness of salvation and knowing the trailing P47s were no longer an immediate risk, Max eased back on the control column into a gentler angle of dive, the rush of air screaming past his cockpit and the trembling of her airframe lessening (even though his did not), breathing deep to ease the emotions cascading through him, a moment to pat Red 6's throttle levers and mutter a prayer of thanks for having survived, despite the guilt he felt for those he had just lost.

Now, with Red 6 safely contained within the swirling sanctuary of thick cloud, deep enough not to show (hopefully) a trail visible from above or below and with a wary eye on the altimeter, a singular wave of anger overwhelmed the unutterable feeling of loss and the rending shame for having endured once more, his first instinct, overriding his normal sense, to turn her around and rip into the USAAF fighter flight which had bounced them, the pain in his heart now replaced by fury and grief.

He would extract revenge for the loss of his *kameraden*.

And so Max bought himself some distance first, in case the P47s were still after him, for to turn too soon would allow the enemy to cut inside his flat wide turn and blow his fighter apart; then he slowed just enough to ease Red 6 into a wide curve around to starboard, checking her controls, and she was flying smoothly now, the contented whine of her turbojets a smooth tremor in his hands, head turning to check for any immediate danger first.

Swing her through 270 degrees in a wide turning circle and pray that the forces did not rip the ammo belts as occasionally happened, straighten out her nose, increase the throttles and pull her up out of the cloud, eyes all around to hunt for the enemy.

There.

The sky was empty save for three dark heavy shapes at two o'clock, tiny outlines tightly bunched together, still in hot pursuit, hoping perhaps they might have damaged him? That they might yet catch him?

All to the good, he thought, smiling coldly to himself; bunching up improved his chances of his getting a hit.

Don't worry, ice and hate in his veins now and hot screaming rage in his brain, focussing his fury into a single thought, *patience, I'm coming . . .*

Turn into them, little time to aim, nose up fifteen degrees to allow for cannon shell drop and lead for deflection, judge the moment, just one chance, and . . . *fire!*

With a ridiculously high closing speed, Red 6's nose cannon hammered out a glowing swathe of fiery 30 mm explosive shells, aimed into the centre of the little formation while turning into them, hard pressure on both gun buttons, a two second burst, the bitterness scraping at his throat and lungs, howling out a challenge into his mask as her cannon smashed out retribution.

He was well within range of the enemy heavy machine guns, and they were already firing back at him as Red 6's storm of cannon shells passed through their formation, their bullets not coming near enough as they struggled to find the correct deflection and rate of drop to compensate for the stupendous closing speed.

A flash on the wingtip of one fighter and it rocked with the impact and immediately broke away; he grimaced behind his mask. *These P47s are tough, the bastards absorb a lot of punishment, just like those fucking Sturmoviks …*

As the thought passed through his mind, Red 6's cannon shells slashed across and against the second P47 in a scintillating rash of flashes, and then suddenly the enemy fighter was an expanding ball of searing plasma, blown into thousands of tiny flaming pieces, burning fuel and debris cascading earthwards as the Tail-end Charlie flicked up and away from the fireball.

Max's face was set in a grimace, eyes following the Tail-end Charlie as it zoomed up, unable to track if because of his speed, the muscles of his stomach still cramping.

'*Abschuss!*' he called softly, for he was alone.

He'll go up, steep, then invert and come back hard, hard around after me, try for a lucky hit in the handful of seconds in which he's close enough to hurt or kill me …

But Max had pushed her nose down again, their acceleration

clearing the P47 rapidly, his eyes on the banking plan form of the Thunderbolt racing dark against the grimy sky, too late to exact revenge on Max, the USAAF fighter becoming smaller and falling behind, pulling up and away, knowing there was no chance of catching the 262, no sign of the other one he had clipped with a shell.

If he had been in a 190D, he would not have thought twice about re-engaging the Amis, but there was no question of dogfighting with deadly fighters like those P47s in 'Red 6'.

To turn with them would be to sign one's own death warrant, for while being unbeatable in speed, she manoeuvred about as well as a full chamber pot.

The remaining P47s were lost somewhere behind now him even though he yearned desperately to repay blood with more blood, and he could not catch the bombers now; he would be able to intercept them only on their way back when they would have already bombed.

Rheine control, 'Rotschwein Control to all hawks, heavy local enemy fighter activity, land elsewhere.'

Rage blossoming afresh, any of his men who tried to return to Rheine were in great danger from lurking enemy fighters, and it would be madness to try and land. With the time required to decelerate a 262 to landing approach speed and lower the undercarriage, during which the airfield defence flight remained on the ground for fear of being overwhelmed by the enemy's sheer numbers, there would be no protective screen for the returning jets outside of the airfield's protective flak corridor.

Peter's broken jet in his mind's eye, treacherous tears fogging his vision and his chest burning with bottomless sorrow inside, Max made up his mind. He had lost Kaminski, Krebs and Peterkin (*God, it hurt just to think his name*), but he may yet save some of his men as they tried to get back to Rheine in battle-damaged fighters.

He would cover their return.

Swallowing the lump in his throat and his eyes skating from the sky to his instruments and back, Max turned Red 6 in a wide easy circle towards the south-west. They had been bounced by the Thunderbolts soon after take-off, so it would not take long to return to Rheine.

Rotschwein Control warned him of two enemy formations, one to the east and the other west of the airfield, circling close (but well out of range) of the 'safe approach corridors' formed by Rheine's massed flak. Once within the corridors the returning 262s, 109s and 190s would be relatively protected from attack by all but the bravest (or most foolhardy) of Allied pilots.

There was thick but broken cloud between six and ten thousand feet, and after a moment's thought, Max decided that he would circle around, ten miles south of Rheine, in a holding position, waiting for any of his boys should they try to brave the Allied gauntlet.

After ten minutes of popping in and out of cloud and trying to remain unnoticed by the enemy while keeping an eye on the fuel gauge, Max was frustrated by the inaction. He had a debt of blood to collect.

Perhaps he would have been better employed conducting a *frei jagd* mission against Allied fighters?

Just as he had decided to make a single pass at high speed through the two enemy fighter formations before escaping and landing elsewhere, the Rotschwein Controller's voice spoke hurriedly in his earphones. '*Rotschwein* to *Falkenführer*, wounded bird with one engine on final approach, ten miles east of base.'

Max scowled in thought; he would need to coordinate his attack with the damaged 262's landing approach. The other jet was close, only ten miles, so he would need to act quickly.

Opening the throttles, Max eased Red 6 up into the cloud and onto a heading north-westwards, then gently began banking her into a starboard turn after flying around six miles, hoping that the twin plumes of smoke from Red 6's Jumos were veiled in cloud, for he needed surprise.

As soon as he assessed he was in the right position, Max pushed down her nose, fingers caressing the trigger, eyes seeking his targets in the haze.

And his estimation was good, with experience and skills honed after many years of living by instinct and action.

The plain, patchwork landscape below was one he knew intimately, and he immediately picked out a small number of dots, dark against the cloud and turning across Red 6's nose. The western enemy fighter formation.

Keep her pointed towards that distant swarm, no time to waste, settle her nose and throttles kept forward, check trigger guard off, gentle on the trigger, the enemy increasing in size, and … fire!

Pull back by twenty degrees to allow for the ridiculous level of drop after firing, 'Red 6' pounding off a long two-second swathe of devastation, feeling her quivering and the recoil tipping her nose as the spreading cloud of shells smashed outwards; the range was closing and the enemy's first tiny cruciform shapes rapidly growing into six single engine monoplane fighters in mere seconds, trim fighters with slender nose unlike the more pugnacious Tempests or Typhoons. Sleeker than the USAAF's Thunderbolts, similar to the dreaded Mustangs.

RAF then? Fast and deadly, and more importantly, quite a lot of them.

Six RAF fighters, four in line abreast and a pair behind, elegant in shape, not sturdy like Typhoons or Tempests.

The flash of elliptical wings, *ach so*! Spitfires! Once, when a guest of Goering's at Carinhall, Max had somehow brought down five wildfowl with a single improbable shot, and now he hoped for the same incredible twist of luck.

Now the RAF fighters were spreading apart and turning harder as they caught sight of his dirty exhaust plumes, but too slowly, too late, Red 6 coming into them from their two o'clock, her nose flashing a glowing cloud of incendiary and explosive shells at them and their own guns unable to bear on this swooping nightmare suddenly unleashed on them, hoping to blast his way through them before they could organise themselves.

A last glance, starboard, up, port and back, all clear, no unexpected surprises lurking nearby.

The formation scattered in slow motion as he bore down on them, a second or two stretching into what seemed like minutes, screaming defiance into his mask, Red 6 flashing through the middle of them like an avenging Fury, the third in the enemy line climbing upwards into the storm of fire, four incandescent smeared flashes of star-bright white twinkling on the tailplane and another on the port wing of the sleek fighter, shuddering beneath the impacts, a large chunk of the rudder and an aileron and one wingtip completely blown off, all seen in an instant, and then the Spitfire had blurred away to one side, yawing away and shedding fragments, a smear of vivid flame half-seen at the root of one wing, seemingly close enough to make him twitch, and then he was through, all done in an instant, leaning forward like a motor cyclist as if she might go faster if he did so.

Had he knocked down the one that he hit? He wasn't sure he'd done enough to down it. Winged it, certainly.

Fuck it, why not? *'Abschuss!'* he cried out, the stink of cordite and sweat the bouquet of his victory.

Remembering those on the ground, he thought of the watching gunners below, and he uttered a rushed prayer that none of them was feeling particularly trigger happy today, but also knowing his racing Red 6 was an almost impossible target.

The Spitfires wouldn't follow him unless they were insane or suicidally brave, or perhaps both, because now the westernmost boundary of Rheine's flak corridor was flashing past beneath Red 6's wings, an indistinct stretch of uneven, unremarkable grey beneath him, the protective flak defences shielding him from pursuit, no time to look back, focussed now on the second formation of enemy fighters to the east, eyes searching and not seeing them.

Where are you?

Ahead a single small blot of smoke, lengthening into a faint trail, a whisker-thin scratch almost invisible against the pale grey daub of the landscape, a gleaming dot now visible at its head.

A wounded and vulnerable 262, the normal twin grey-black smoke trails cut down to one by battle damage.

If I can see you my friend, then so can they, damn them …

Max eased back a little on the throttles. It would be all too easy to overshoot Tommi at high speed. His eyes, anxious beneath his goggles, looked for the tell-tale sign that might betray the second formation of Allied fighters lurking somewhere east of Rheine.

His expert eyes were honed in the search by years of aerial hunting, and Max caught sight of them at last as a distant gleam of light splashing across Perspex revealed four more fighters in a loose line astern formation at low level around three miles south-east of Rheine, wheeling around now as the warning from the first group reached them; but knowing there were almost five hundred AA guns in Rheine's locale they would be wary of the eagerly waiting defences, and they wisely kept their distance.

Around five hundred feet below and a mile or so behind the damaged 262 and heading towards him were the darting shapes of a pair of Spitfires, classy elegance dressed in the drab earthy camouflage so typical of the RAF, wheeling around cleanly and closing fast behind the arrowhead of the damaged bird, still too far beyond the protective umbrella of Rheine's flak.

The Spitfires ahead and below would know he was approaching fast, but they continued in their dash to intercept the other 262 now doubtless at a dangerously slow speed as it reduced speed to land, its undercarriage extended, one of the fastest things in the sky now wallowing like a pig.

The helplessness which must have been crushing the damaged jet's pilot thoughts would have burgeoned into hope as he caught sight of Max's approach.

The Spitfires were closing the distance hungrily, but Max was closing with *them* even faster.

The enemy leader continued after the winged bird, but his wingman was dropping behind, the nose coming around towards Red 6 …

They must think they have a chance to get him before I'm near enough …

Nose down gently, hold speed, track well ahead of the Spitfire leader, the tingle of tension and fear now a rasp along his spine, one chance to do this right otherwise the boy below is dead … steady …

The damaged *kamerad* passed through Red 6's Revi gunsight,

and at that moment Max jerked back on the trigger, unleashing a torrent of explosive and incendiary ammunition across the path of the oncoming Spitfire leader just as its own cannon began to thump out, the explosive shells meant to smash apart the vulnerable Me262, but destined never to reach it.

Similarly, the Spitfire wingman's guns began to pound out at Red 6, but calculating deflection on such a fast-moving target was nigh on impossible and the stream of destruction was well off the mark, disappearing below and to one side.

He did not see the leading Spitfire pass through his deadly curtain of 30 mm, did not see the shells rend and tear into the delicate beauty of the RAF fighter, did not see the gout of flame as Red 6's incendiaries tore into and ignited the fuel in the Spitfire's fuel tanks and turned her into a blazing wreck, did not see the long stream of fire flowing from it nor the explosion which blew her apart.

He felt the pressure waves of the Spitfire's death slap up against Red 6's undersides, heard the sullen thump of the explosion, knew he had aimed well and hit hard, but did not see what was left as the remains scattered like hot embers across the field close to the easternmost edge of Rheine's approaches.

Even as his shells were ripping into the Spitfire, Max was already adjusting his aim to swing her fire across in front of the second British fighter.

But the wingman's instincts were good and his reflexes sharp and he was already clawing for height and crabbing to one side as he saw his leader's demise and knew his riposte had missed by a mile, desperately breaking away from the curtain of destructive fire crashed out from Red 6's Mk108 cannons, avoiding the murderous fusillade and turning hard as Max blasted past, the elliptical wings of his foe almost perpendicular with the ground as she reefed around, slicing the air, scraping it for precious height and room to manoeuvre.

In breaking away, the second Spitfire no longer presented a threat to the damaged 262; losing ground already and being unable to cut back around to chase after the jet in time, the damaged 262 now safely entering Rheine's deadly bastion and the sanctuary of the landing approach flak corridor, the injured *Leutnant* at her controls unable to believe his good fortune, but able to land her within minutes of having whispered his silent prayer of salvation.

A prayer of hope, a forlorn hope, hoping against all the odds but not really believing that he might live when he saw the end approaching fast in his six o'clock, feeling utterly helpless as the pair of Spitfires had curved around in pursuit and slipped in behind him.

But in turn, the surviving British fighter had now become a very real threat to Max, for with its superior turning performance he would be coming around after Red 6 awfully quickly, the RAF pilot turned from hunter to hunted and then back to being the hunter again.

He knew too that the other four Spitfires would be coming, and he edged forward the throttles all the way to race away from the danger, his neck twisting to check for danger from other quarters, and to keep an eye on the Spitfire wingman, but the RAF fighter's turn was not as clean and sharp as Max had feared, the turmoil of Red 6's slipstream and the shock loss of his leader causing the Spitfire's wingman to fall too far behind as Max's 262 streaked away and out of range of the Spitfire's guns.

As the enemy grew smaller in his mirror, Max allowed himself a breath; he had survived and succeeded in what he had set out to do.

'Rotschwein to Falkenfuhrer, wounded chick recovered safely, well done!'

'Thank you, Rotschwein, recovering elsewhere.'

'Understood, Falkenfuhrer. And congratulations on your two Spitfires! That was fine work!'

He tried to inject some warmth in his response, but his voice emerged flat. 'Thank you for your assistance, Rotschwein.' That made three kills with the P47 Thunderbolt he had shot down earlier.

He had taken three of the enemy in exchange for the three he had lost, but there was no triumph, no sense of victory, only a deep, underlying feeling of tiredness and loss, and now with the tension of immediate danger past, the memory of his men's falling fighters came back, broken and burning and out of control.

Max ran a finger around his shirt collar, loosening the sweat-sodden silk scarf, once again aware of the absence of his Knight's Cross, Oak Leaves, Swords and Diamonds.

I've shown my support enough for the General, he thought shakily. *I'll tell Spinne to get my baubles out and onto my uniform again. The men are proud of me, I should really wear them again, at least for the ones who follow me so faithfully even though they deserve far better.*

His loyal batman Spinne, his faithful companion from as far back as the invasion of Poland back in the glorious days of conquest in 1940, would be pleased and proud to see his Colonel dressed properly, his many decorations once again on show.

And *that* thought reminded him of young Peter, who had not worn his own decorations for weeks in solidarity with his Colonel's show of support for Galland.

The unbidden memory of Peter's face, shy and self-conscious as little Lissy clasped his hand, no longer a little girl but now a beautiful young woman, the sun bright overhead and the rugged, towering contours of the Bavarian Alps their background. The happiness on their faces heart-breaking in its clarity.

'*Oh, Peterkin* …' he whispered, suddenly drained and empty of hope, pain hollowing him from within and making him feel terribly, terribly old.

Chapter 21

He was just beneath the trees at the boundary of the vegetable garden staring up at the window of their bedroom, and Molly was standing there behind the tape-trellised glass, her beautiful expressive eyes looking into the sky, baby Millie in her arms.

His wife was clad in the pink Fair Isle cardigan with flowers and diamonds he had bought for her in Draffens of Dundee, her rich, thick midnight tresses tied back with a matching ribbon, and she was weeping, cheeks glistening from heavy tears and the tip of her nose tinged red with sorrow.

It's alright, Moll, he tried to shout, *I'm not dead, I'm fine!* But nothing came out no matter how hard he tried. He tried to raise his arms and wave to her, but found he could not move.

Her eyes slowly shifted down to stare directly at him, more tears cascading onto her cheeks, and he saw her lips move. *I love you, Harry my darling, and I miss you so very much.*

He stood there helplessly, feeling the pain of her distress tear deep inside him, willing himself to break the paralysis that assailed him, to take her and their infant daughter into his arms and reassure her that all would be well.

277

And Rose woke up.

He was curled up in his bed at the seminary, face against the ancient, stained wood, feeling breathless, with drool running down his cheek to soak the blanket and an anxious flutter in his heart.

Oh God! It had felt so real! He sat up and cupped his hands over his face, feeling the draught play icily over his sweat-soaked pyjamas.

But he was the lucky one. It was nothing to the temperatures the soldiers were facing in their fox-holes, and the cramp in his calf was nothing when compared to the pneumonia, trench foot and frostbite of the front line.

There was a slurred mumble from next door, replaced almost immediately by gentle snoring. Had he cried out in his sleep in an effort to make dream-Molly hear him?

Rose took the tattered photograph from his pocket and stared at it in the poor light; her smile was exquisite and her eyes bright with mischief, but he could not forget the pain on the face of the mourning girl in his dream.

He closed his eyes, but could not banish the image of the face he adored suffused with such misery. He opened them again and looked at his watch. *Bloody hell, 6.20 am on New Year's Day, 1945. Another New Year far away from Molly and my children, no New Year's Day morning kiss or a fumble under the sheets to welcome in the New Year.*

His eyes strayed to the shelf of books, but he wasn't really in the mood for reading. He scratched his cheek and feeling the roughness of the stubble he eyed the empty bucket used for hot water morosely.

The blasted oil furnace had blown up again so there had been no hot water for the evening shave.

If only we had something else to feed it apart from 150 Octane petrol.

He reached for the light switch, wincing as the light from the naked bulb overwhelmed him for a moment. Picking up his notebook and the tatty pencil, he settled back. *OK, let's write her a poem …*

> *I must leave now to go where I must be,*
> *But my heart remains behind.*
> *My nights and days shall be filled with dreams of you,*
> *For my love remains behind.*
> *The sun shall be cool against my cheek,*
> *For your warmth remains behind.*
> *I shall go far beyond and see so much,*
> *Yet all that I care for remains behind.*
> *There will be no peace nor contentment for me,*
> *For my happiness remains behind.*
> *There can only be empty loneliness,*
> *For my beloved remains behind.*

Dear God! Rose groaned and shook his head.

The bloody thing sounded so damned grim! Guaranteed to depress. Hardly an expression of love, more of a lamentation of gloom. It'll have my love weeping into her tea.

He crumpled the paper into a ball and flung it into a corner.

Best to have another bash. I need to do better … a lot better …

He picked up his pencil again, rolling it contemplatively between his finger and thumb as he thought. Something a little more buoyant? Let's try that again, erm …

> *How blessed I am,*
> *Days and nights, minutes and seconds, shared with you,*
> *How blessed I am,*

To be privy to your thoughts and feelings,
And feel the light of your glory,
How blessed I am,
To know the profound wisdom of your soul,
And be illuminated by the brilliance of you,
How blessed I am,
Of what we made with our love,
The gift of my precious, wonderful children,
How blessed I am in you,
Your love is in my before and in my now,
And all I could ever want and need in my tomorrow,
How blessed I am in the love I have for you.

He sat back, the end of the pencil gently clamped between his teeth, reading through it doubtfully. *Hmm, not a classic by any means … not all that great but not all that grim, either. It'll do, I think. Hope Moll'll like it …*

He knew she would. Each poem he wrote her (and some were pretty awful, he was honest enough to admit) was greeted by Molly (bless her) as if it were a long-lost work of literary art.

Putting down the notebook and scratching his armpit absently, he stared at the wall, all notion of going back to sleep banished.

OK, now what?

Sod this for a bowl of petunias (or is it a game of soldiers?), he thought, feeling deflated. *I'm going to take Sugar up and watch the first dawn of this New Year from far above the clouds, feel its warmth well before it reaches Volkel.*

Next best thing to being with Molly.

That little snide voice again, *who're you trying to kid? It's nowhere near as nice as being with Molly, not even close. On balance, though, dawn viewed from ten thousand feet is a great deal nicer than a hefty kick in the balls …*

Shut up, he told it firmly, *you're not making it any easier.*

He threw back the warm sanctuary of his blankets and reached for his clothes, checking he had the little pink teddy bear and the smooth pebble safely tucked away, and slipped her photograph into the same pocket before making his way down to the dark and cold refectory.

The cooks began making breakfast early for the dawn readiness boys, but the thought of fried food or the lumpy porridge at this time of the morning made him feel nauseous. *Time for a bit of sweet-talking …*

So, instead of the usual grilled, fried or boiled fare, Rose's early breakfast was a thick slice of fresh bread, generously spread with butter and topped with a smear of strawberry jam accompanied by a hot cup of milky Camp coffee. He had little appetite, but forced himself to eat all of it, thinking to spend the day in his operations caravan (*New Year's Day? Bah, humbug!*).

After the raucous party last night, many of his hungover pilots would probably feel the same way. Feeling Molly's absence keenly, a cheerless Rose had shared a couple of drinks with his boys after dinner, feigning good humour, smiling insincerely and laughing with little feeling before retiring early to avoid putting a dampener on the others' enjoyment.

So steeped was Rose in his loneliness, he had not thought that his own men must also be missing their own homes and loved ones, and for the Aussies it must be worse, for the ones they loved were so very much further away.

Sitting in his room alone, the raucous hubbub below muted, he thought of the lads he had lost who were not fated to see 1945.

In his misery he remembered Excalibur Squadron's own Australian boy, 'Fanny' Adams, bounced with 'Whip' Whipple by 190s over Eglise Saint-Martin.

Fanny had been so proud of the lovely fair-haired girl, Marjory, waiting for him 'back down under' in Perth, but he had been shot down and killed by Jerry, caught near the ground and too low to manoeuvre, his life instantly over and hers shattered forever.

Their son James, named after his father and never held by him, would only know of him through the reams of letters 'Fanny' had written to her, would have only a few effects of his father's, the logbook and a trio of cases containing Fanny's DFC, DFM and the bronze oak leaf of his Mention in Despatches, a legacy which proved that his father was not just the strong, thoughtful and gentle man that his mother would ever love and never forget, but that James senior had also been a hero.

Alone in his room that night, before the birth of the New Year, Rose had fallen asleep, the tears shed and his lost friends still heavy in his thoughts, his prayers for the elusive peace and the aching emptiness of her absence weighty on his heart.

Arriving at Volkel, Rose found Sugar waiting for him next to the readiness kites which were having the finishing touches in preparation for the coming dawn, her cooling engine ticking in the tapering-off drizzle, his telephone call from the seminary half an hour earlier time enough for the bleary Duty Officer in the Watch Office to get her readied.

Rose thought of taking off straight away, but then decided to wait another hour; it was perhaps a little too early to go. Dawn was still over an hour away, and besides, the crack of Coffman cartridges shattered the peace and more than a few sore heads as 122 Wing readied for a sweep into Germany at full strength.

With temperatures dropping sharply overnight, there had been a hard frost followed by a gentle drizzle, so soft there had been no insistent *tap-tap-tap* on the frosted window of his room. Wary of ice and not overly keen on taking off from a treacherous and slippery runway, Rose walked back to the Watch Office to order more grit to be laid on the runways and taxiways. He would take off when it was done.

It was bitterly cold and, fearing snow which was already falling heavily further east in the Ardennes, Rose left instruction for a plough and a bulldozer to be prepared in case Volkel received a share of it.

In the meantime he could cadge a cup of tea from the tired-eyed Duty Officer's flask, or even a delicious mug of Bovril Beef Tea when he had a check on the poor early-birds at Dispersals. The readiness boys should be arriving soon, with their bleary eyes and headaches from the drunken revelries of just a few hours earlier, and the timekeeper would have lit the stove with that awful damp wood, and stuck the pot on the primus to get it bubbling. There was something about the stink of that wood burning that cleared headaches magically, so the lads ought to be ready for the dawn sortie.

He shivered suddenly, felt the disquiet whisper through him but dismissed it, knowing it would fade as soon as Sugar was in the air. He was only mildly surprised to see that Ben Duncan, the ex-lawyer, was already there, wearing his flying kit.

As far as he could remember the man had been squawking out some song ('Vict'ry Polka?') with his men as Rose had gone to bed, bloody awful racket like a lot of cats yowling, but now here he was, freshly shaven and full of beans, bright eyes and a cheerful smile of greeting. 'Happy New Year, sir! Fancy a spin?' He gave a chuckle at

Rose's grunted attempt at a joke, 'Not in Kansas this year either, are we, eh, Ben?'

Extraordinary.

Again he felt the warm gratitude that the young Aussie Flight Commander would cut short his rest to ensure his Wing Commander would not fly alone in the predawn hours.

Jelly was off duty, bless him, so he was strapped in by a sour-faced Corporal with a hollow cough and a dripping nose, wrapped up as if he were on the Eastern Front (which in all likelihood was unlikely to be all that much colder than Volkel on 1 January 1945).

Cruising in a wide circle at twenty thousand feet, Sugar's Sabre set at just over 3,000 rpm in minimum boost and with a keen-eyed Australian Ace silently watching his tail, Rose enjoyed the first dawn of 1945. He tucked her photo under a strap of his chest harness so she could watch the dawn with him.

The ground was hidden by a dark blanket of cloud spread unevenly beneath them, the western sky showing a subdued flicker of stars, their icy splendour fading in the pale glow lightening to the east as the brilliance of the sun presaged its appearance, the swelling light making the eastern cloud horizon purple, the violet hues gently fleeing westwards and unhurriedly pursued by reds and pinks and yellows, the edge of cloud laced with the golden fire of the sun's corona.

Above them, the night crept away, easing from grey to blue and ever onwards to the pale blue of daylight surrounding the new sun, but deepening to cobalt above and lighter to the west, the last of the stars finally extinguished in the flooding light.

He thought of her as the bright rays of gold washed over Sugar's canopy and leading edges, making the upper edges of the clouds below blaze fire bright.

Molly would most likely be awake, nursing their infant daughter in the predawn hours, seated in that battered armchair and looking out through the window into the emptiness, stoic and alone with their child in the darkness, apprehensive of what news the new day might bring of her husband, and perhaps whispering a prayer.

How I wish I could have shared this ephemeral display of golds, silvers, pinks, violets and blues with you, my darling.

A New Year's wish then, heartfelt, *Lord God, grant my dearest ones and myself salvation so that I may be a true husband and a true father when this is finally over. Please let me live.*

For an instant Rose thought that he glimpsed a flash of gold, though it might have easily been the sun's rays catching the Perspex, but superstitious as he was, Rose preferred to believe that it might have been a positive sign.

Please God.

Next year, Moll, I promise, even if it means going AWOL.

They were heading back down when Duncan suddenly cried out, 'Two to Hotspur Leader, bandit, three o'clock below, one mile!'

Rose saw it too, the dark shape of a Ju188 just broaching the clouds, the sunlight glistening on its mottled emerald-green wings and the peculiar glasshouse cockpit, like some evil dragonfly. It could escape them if it dived back into cloud and there was no time to mess about.

'Lead the way sharpish, Ben, I'll cover you, quick! Before he dives back into cloud! Get him!' Duncan's fighter immediately winged over into a steep turn to port before levelling out and edging to starboard to cut off the enemy bomber's path, losing height and gaining speed as he took his Tempest after the Junkers.

Close behind, Rose pushed the throttle lever forward as he fell behind. *If there's one …*

He brushed his eyes lightly across the clouds and up into the sky, watchful for more of the enemy. The crew of fools in the Junkers had not seen the descending Tempests and suddenly Duncan was close enough and trails of brown smoke and glittering spent shells streamed back from D-Dagger's wings as Duncan loosed a blistering storm of cannon shells at the bandit below and ahead of him.

The crew of the Junkers were not fools; they had got lost and had simply mistaken the Tempests for the Focke-Wulfs of JG6 Horst Wessel which they had been tasked to guide in the strike on Volkel. Navigation specialists, they had somehow lost their charges in the darkness and cloud, and the *Staffeln* from JG6 missed Volkel entirely and instead attacked the new airfields of Heesch and Helmond, getting a drubbing with little to show for it.

The FW190s from JG6 were taking part in Operation *Bodenplatte,* a concerted attempt by the Luftwaffe to destroy the aerial superiority enjoyed by the Allies by a dawn blitz on RAF and USAAF fighter airfields in the Low Countries.

With the Battle of the Bulge in a phase of inertia, if all went to plan by the end of the day the Allied fighter force would be significantly weakened or even neutralised entirely and the Luftwaffe in the ascendant once more, bringing new energy to the stalled push.

Bodenplatte should have originally taken place on 16 December, in combination with the launch of the Panzer Army's ground attacks, and an attempt to carry out the operation was made but bad weather made coordination and navigation almost impossible, and the attempt abandoned.

Now at last with better weather they could go ahead with their massed low-level attack and crush the Allies once and for all. And if the Tommies and the Amis were nursing sore heads after celebrating the New Year, well, so much the better!

Pathfinder aircraft with specialist crews would lead the massed fighter formations, but in the predawn some lost touch.

The hapless Ju188 pilot had decided to pop up into clearer air in the hope of finding some of his lost brood, but instead found Rose and Duncan, and now sparks flared like dying stars on the fuselage and wings of the Junkers as Duncan closed the distance, firing short, well-aimed bursts, a gout of sudden flame, followed by the violent explosion of the starboard Jumo 211 engine and suddenly the wing broke in half, tipping the aircraft into a wobbling roll from starboard to port. The pilot, dazed and bleeding from wounds inflicted by shrapnel and shattered Plexiglas, fought desperately to correct his mortally wounded bird but he failed and the crippled pathfinder rolled over, nose dipping into a vertical dive, rudder detaching to flutter and follow after the doomed aircraft, and the trailing arc of spiralling black smoke remained behind after the wrecked bomber as it disappeared into cloud below, like a passing marker of its destruction.

'Good shooting, Ben! No doubt about that one! That's as confirmed as they come!'

'Easy-as-peasy, Leader!' The other pilot was quietly elated by the victory, a wonderful way for him to start the New Year. It was his thirteenth kill, lucky Duncan, unlucky thirteen for the pathfinder's aircrew.

Rose's eyes slipped ritually from the clouds to the sky and then into his mirror; nothing else showed, but his tingle was still there and that thought again, the itch of dread worrying away at his nerve endings, the hairs on his forearms stirring.

'Two, there might be more of them under cloud, could be part of an attack, let's get back to base. We might be needed.'

'Roger, Leader.' Rose could hear the tension in Duncan's voice. *He* felt it too.

As they dropped through the broken cloud, one eye watchful to hold a safe distance from Duncan, Rose keyed his microphone.

'Hotspur Leader to Marmite, any custom?' the trickle of trepidation was like cold water trickling down his spine, and fear stirred in his mind.

The controller sounded unsure. 'Hotspur Leader, reports of heavy enemy activity, returns are confused and unclear, standby.'

Heavy enemy activity? Confused and unclear?

'Received, Marmite.' Well, that was no help whatsoever, except it did confirm the presence of bandits. They emerged from cloud into the greyer world beneath, and the hairs on the back of his neck began to stand up as well.

What the … ?

Mirror? Clear.

Rose looked nervously across to D-Dagger to check that Duncan was on station, when, to his amazement, three Focke-Wulf 190Ds crossed from port to starboard across Sugar's nose, a quarter of a mile ahead and a hundred feet below, in a flight path around twenty degrees to starboard of the Tempests.

'Hotspur Leader, bandits, one o'clock and below!'

With the imminence of action the fear receded, 'I see them, Ben, battle spread.'

Nosing Sugar into a gentle, curving dive to starboard, Rose's eyes swept around quickly, checking towards the opposite direction at his five o'clock, but nothing showed; eyes swept carefully around again but only the trio of long-nosed 190Ds, continuing on their way as if they had not seen the Tempests, looking for all the world as if they were lost.

Mirror, clear.

'Received, Leader.' With Duncan slipping alongside, Rose touched rudder and eased into an aileron turn so that she slipped after the bandits from astern and a little below, quick glance over his shoulder, nothing behind or below. Now they were level and parallel to one another; it was possible for each of them to ensure Jerry did not try and creep up from behind and below them.

'Close up, Two.' He eased Sugar lower, so that the slipstream of the bandits disturbed the air above the Tempests, the bumping of the flow gentle.

Mirror, clear, all readings on the gauges normal, push forward throttle and the stick to rapidly close with the bandits and then back a smidgen, nose up just a pinch, to prevent from overshooting and give him longer to spray the 190 on the starboard side of the formation. 'Attacking!'

Inexplicably, the 190s continued on blithely as if unaware of the Tempests closing behind. Unbeknownst to Rose, the wingmen were inexperienced; the slightly more experienced leader was panicky in having separated from the larger formation of which they had been a part and was busy trying to find out where he was. Desperately looking for landmarks below, he left it too long to clear his tail in what had been an empty sky mere seconds before.

Mirror, clear.

It was an easy shot, minimal deflection, the evil hunched airframe sitting squarely in Sugar's sights, and Rose loosed off a long two-second burst, recoil slowing her as glittering lines that ate up the distance between them in an instant and smashed explosively into the bandit, a twinkling cluster of erratic flashes along her silhouette and puffs of smoke and dust-like fragments erupting from her, propeller churning fitfully to a stop, slowing drastically so that she seemed to grow in the sight and he hauled Sugar up and closed the throttle, feeling her wallow in the bandit's uneasy air.

Got you!

The deadly fighter ahead floundered beneath the battering, fragments of her wings and airframe torn off to flick back in her slipstream towards Sugar, and the long canopy slid back as the enemy pilot clambered out, took one look at Sugar's deadly shape and hurriedly threw himself into the ravening slipstream, his 190's speed bleeding off and her nose dropping as his spread-eagled shape passed beneath Sugar's port wing.

Thank God the Jerry hadn't hit Sugar! Neither would have enjoyed the experience.

Mirror, clear. A glance at her smile.

Only one left, the 190 wingman flying to port also falling away and out of control, the shape twisting and burning like a torch from Dagger's deadly 20 mm; his wingmen gone, the 190 leader at last responded to the danger, rolling inverted and into a dive straight down, pulling thick streamers of exhaust smoke behind him.

Bandits over Allied Lines at dawn? Was it an attack? Marmite had mentioned heavy air activity, there must be an aerial assault underway!

He felt a terrible fear for his men on this New Year's Day, the first day of the year for all, and likely the last day for many.

Duncan was watching the surviving 190D, tiny as it descended. Two victories already this day, and now he yearned for a third. 'Leader?'

The 190D was far faster than a 190A though not as fast as the Tempest in the dive, and the two of them could have run it to ground, but the pursuit would take up precious time, time they could ill-afford if there were more of the bastards over Volkel.

'Leave him be, Two, we need to get back home, sharpish.' The 190D had pulled out of his dive now and was fleeing eastwards, and the tingle between Rose's shoulder blades had turned into a full-blown feeling of imminent disaster.

Already he was turning her for Volkel.

'Marmite to Hotspur Leader, multiple low-level bandit formations reported over Allied Lines, please await instructions.'

Not bloody likely! thought Rose savagely. *Bollocks to that, I need to check all's well at Volkel.*

'Keep 'em peeled, Ben.' He regretted the words as soon as they were uttered. What else was Duncan going to do?

The young Australian ex-lawyer had spotted the enemy pathfinder first as it broke through the clouds and now they both knew that there must be a surprise offensive happening, one with heavy enemy aerial support this time.

The thought of a second wave of German infantry and armour pushing after the first was terrifying to Rose. *Dear God, can we hold?*

'Right-oh, Leader.' With two New Year's Day kills to bring his total score to fourteen, Duncan's voice was cheery.

Heavens! Was I ever like that? And then, *thank goodness he was with me! He did well. I'd best prepare the papers for a second bar to his DFC, he's more than earned it! Where do we find men such as these?*

'Ops to Hotspur Leader, overflight by a few bandits, readiness fighters airborne.' There was urgency in the voice, 'Please vector onto heading two-five zero. Confirm.'

'Received.' But what about Volkel? Even now his lads might be fighting for their lives, and so he continued on towards base. 'Please confirm?' Volkel was less than ten miles ahead, and there were no palls of smoke or distant explosions, no stain of ack-ack.

With 122 Wing away on their fighter sweep, was Volkel still snoozing peacefully?

He was turning Sugar hard south-west on to the heading given, pushing her down to slip just beneath the lowest clouds, levelling Sugar at just under three thousand feet, faithful Duncan dropping back into a covering position, and in between his watchful reprise from the surrounding sky, controls and mirror, he squinted ahead, and wondered for a stupid moment if the smear in the haze was oil vaguely tarnishing Sugar's windscreen or smoke rising far ahead.

Seconds later, Rose realised that the smear wasn't a blur of oil on her Perspex at all.

It was Eindhoven, and Eindhoven was burning, numerous columns of thick oily smoke, veiled within a heavy pall of drifting banks of smoke which were shrouding the airfield below, though not enough to hide the multiple fires burning amongst and around the sprawling 'A' of its three kilometre long runways, more fires were burning unchecked in the woods on the western boundary where the three large munitions and storage areas were.

Rows of Allied fighters, fighter bombers, bombers and transport aircraft had been turned into blackened and blazing wrecks he saw as they drew closer, thick billowing smoke and the flash of explosions on the ground making Rose wonder how anything could possibly survive the terrible onslaught.

But many had found cover, even if it were in trenches that were two or three feet deep with freezing water and ice. But any port in a storm will do when cannon shells are flying disturbingly close to one's tender body.

Scores of bandits were wheeling, diving, zooming, strafing and skimming over the airfield at low level, dark cruciforms ripping holes through the disturbed curtains of smoke, racing across the patchy grey and white expanse of the frosted ground, the sparse freckle of AA bursts mostly too high and too few, the criss-cross of the odd glowing necklace of tracer ineffectively lashing up into the sky and Rose's heart fell as he caught sight of the myriad specks scattered on the frozen ground which were the corpses of the fallen.

Dear God! It was a disaster! It was a scene of utter destruction below, and for a short moment Rose was unnerved by the awful immensity of it.

What can a pair of Tempests do against this? Surely no one would question two Tempests not engaging? It'd be suicide against dozens of enemy raiders.

There're too many! Run, said the voice, *run while you still can!*

And there was nothing more he wanted to do, but how then could he face the man staring accusingly from the mirror? How could he look Molly in the eye and not feel the shame of cowardice?

The haunting image once more, bloodied WAAFs in bullet-torn blue, lines and lines of bodies beneath dirty tarpaulins. The darkness of the blood on Janet's dead lips, the dullness in the beautiful eyes which had once brimmed with promise, vivacity and mischief.

And then the blooming of overwhelming fury deep inside, the anger which drives one to act without thought, the only consideration now to injure and kill, to destroy the perpetrators of this devastation.

A *Rotte* of four Bf109s, darts racing hard against the snowy ground they dashed over, sleek and wasp-like, almost delicate were it not for the weapons they carried, transiting out over the boundary and turning to starboard almost arrogantly, and Rose was seized by the furious madness at the sight of the 109s swaggering arrogantly into a climb upwards to swing around and dive into another strafing run.

The swarming bandits had formed a looped rail track pattern of diving in from a thousand feet down to zero to slice in from the west at low level, strafe the airfield, then zoom out eastwards before re-forming for another go.

Despite this, there were plenty of other bandits milling around aimlessly and cutting across from north to south and vice versa.

A 190A zipped in and flew carelessly across the noses of a trio of 190 'Dora-9s', and he imagined the curses from the longer-nosed D-9s as they had to take evasive action and pull up, one almost flying into the ground.

He was turning and climbing to just below the cloud base. 'Ben, line abreast, we'll join the pattern from westwards and give as many of Jerry as we can a squirt, get in amongst them, the bastards'll just get in each other's way.'

Rose was almost breathless with rage and he sucked in a lungful of oxygen. 'Fast in, fast out, one pass only. Use your speed from the dive to zoom up into cloud. If you can, pick off any that stray too far from the action, and once you run dry, get out of it. One pass chum and gone, no heroics, Ben, OK?'

Duncan's voice was tight with anger and hate. 'Understood, Leader.'

A pair of 109s had picked up their scent and they were curving around, soaring into a climb to take his pair of Tempests in the rear, but they were too far behind, and far too slow in the dive.

A lingering glance at her warm smile. *I love you with all my heart, Moll. I pray that I live beyond this.*

A last look to see there was no one close enough yet to cause them harm, the pair of 109s still too far back.

He craned his head around, the bones in his neck cracking, check radiator shutter in 'up', throttle and stick forward to throw Sugar into a steep dive to build up speed, gunsight ready, the Sabre snarling sweetly, heart filled with wrath and thumping so hard it hurt, a touch of rudder tab to automatically correct for that yaw to port, watch her trim as the tail always feels heavier in the dive.

I'm coming, you murderous fucking bastards!

There was no fear now, only the blinding rage and the knowledge that they had little chance of getting away, that they were a Forlorn Hope.

Last time I saw so many of Jerry in one place we were fighting over the sunlit fields of Britain. There're too many, we'll likely be dead in a minute or even less. 'Good luck, chum.' He panted as he was pushed back into his seat, eyes skimming the ground and the sky, the 109s no longer a threat.

He could hear the stiffness in the other's response. 'Be seeing you, sir. And mate? It's been an honour I reckon!'

Rose smiled mirthlessly at the easy familiarity of his dawn companion and exceptional fighter pilot, the swarm of German fighters levelling them to the basics of two comrades-in-arms shoulder-to-shoulder and facing impossible odds, equals who were going into the fight in the sure knowledge of their own mortality, a last farewell as they entered their arena.

Lord my God, grant us thy mercy this day …

Mirror? Clear.

No more time for fear or regret, only for killing.

A gap had formed between six Bf109Gs and a pair of FW190As, and he dropped Sugar and Dagger neatly in between, jinking apart, fast from the dive and beyond pursuit by the trailing 190s, seeing the distant twin streaky lines of a jet's exhausts approaching at low level from starboard, two miles back and at their five o'clock, and he wanted to warn Duncan but found he could not speak, the pressure on his chest fighting the words, his teeth locked painfully into a grimace, eyes tracking the sextet of 109s ahead.

With any luck, at the speed he was doing, the oncoming jet pilot would not be able to tell them apart from the swarming Jerries until it was too late.

He looked to his wing, but Duncan had disappeared, and there was nothing behind him for half a mile. *Dear God, have they got Ben already?*

No time to worry about his companion, Eindhoven expanding in his windscreen ahead, and he dropped her nose a touch so that he could fire up into the enemy bellies and not furrow the Allied airfield with his 20 mm, could feel the ravening red beast within screaming at him to fire his guns, concentrated on breathing steadily and inhaling the stink of burning aircraft, gun smoke and fuel, hoping that ammunition 'cooking off' beneath would not inadvertently bring him down.

Bring back the throttles a hint so he would not overshoot, and the brightness of pure joy glowed within him as he loosed off a short burst at the 109 on the far right of the formation, seeing the rounds spark bright across its empennage and tearing away its aerial mast even as he was swinging Sugar's nose to the next in line, the fighters surging through the smeared and dirty air, oil flying back to spatter against a canopy already streaked with smoke stains.

Mirror? Clear.

Beneath them a line of Typhoons strafed and torn apart, the fallen bodies of their ground crews strewn around them, their clothing smeared red, his mind still filled in the midst of this desperation by the memories of those lines of dead girls in RAF blue lying on the concrete at RAF Foxton, Moll's WAAFs, dead these last four long years but still very much alive in her thoughts and dreams. Known and unforgotten.

Leaning forward as much as he could by his harness, which wasn't a lot, Rose bellowed his ferocious challenge as Sugar's explosive shells ripped across the second 109, one wingtip and aileron torn off it, debris streaming back towards him even as he slipped Sugar further to port, a burst of searing white-hot flame rippling from it like a thin banner of light and scorching along the starboard side of the bandit, and it tipped forwards, falling, its propeller wind-milling helplessly with shattered blades. It was out of the fight. This close to the ground it would be unable to recover and its pilot was a dead man.

Fearful of the explosion, Rose banked hard to starboard, steep as he dared, eyes cast back for a second to check on the 190s, but they had turned to attack Eindhoven's northern boundary and instead Rose's breath caught as he saw death racing towards him from out of the smoke-dulled west.

The Me262 was far closer now, its nose cannon sparkling, fiery balls rushing towards him in a deadly stream, a flock of glowing orange-yellow harbingers of death thrusting towards him on smoking trails. Rose's sudden turn had saved him as the 262's cannon shells passed to one side, and the enemy jet was pulling after him.

Time seemed to slow as certain death loomed, the cannon fire closing the distance with Sugar at a leisurely pace and his arms and legs were moving like lightning, experience and skill guiding his movement instinctively into avoiding action, Sugar climbing fifty feet as he turned and side-slipping Sugar further to starboard, knowing instinctively that he had evaded the jet's destructive snarl and pushing Sugar down again as the boiling and tumultuous air pushed up at her ...

The enemy shells were too low, passing beneath Sugar and to port as he jinked up and further to starboard, leap-frogging the stream of glowing cannon shells which streamed past to explode far ahead.

Christ! So close he could hear the hiss of the enemy's 30 mm fusillade, and now the enemy fighter's profile lengthened and lifted as jet pilot eased the pale grey twin-jet into a climb.

Impulsively Rose eased back the throttle and aileron, rolling her back to port, and Sugar wallowed but obediently eased over towards the left and he pulled up her nose, deftly loosing off a long burst of her cannon in a single flowing motion as the fleeting shadow passed over him.

He had a momentary sight of the jet's profile passing through his gunsight, oil-streaked and stained, a graceful arrowhead into which his explosive rounds crashed. If it blew up it would have taken him with it, so close was he to the jet fighter.

The jet was slightly to his starboard as it howled over him, but not far enough to avoid the torrent of Sugar's burning wrath as 20 mm cannon shells fired point-blank; they hammered into and sheered ruin into the port Jumo 004 engine, tearing the sophisticated but delicate axial-flow turbojet into torn and twisted metal.

One engine wrecked, the 262's port wing dropped as she veered further to port, a sheet of flame stretching back and already rolling before slamming into the gnarled and blackened wreckage of a once-graceful Spitfire burning on an ashen hard standing, fresh fire blooming bright amongst the flames.

The twin-jet's slipstream shrieked past, a thin howl of sound and a blast of heat, but not hot enough to blacken her windscreen, thrashing Sugar downwards and he hauled back on the stick to keep her from crashing, a cry of fear as he fought to hold her wings steady and nose up, a grey-dappled 190D with a bright yellow cowling and rudder slipping past, the helmeted head of its pilot staring disbelievingly at Sugar, but the Luftwaffe fighter was too fast and too close and unable to turn into Sugar.

Instinctively he fired a quick burst but it missed, slashing away off into the distance.

Other enemy fighters, blurry shadows in the dark, drifting smoke, the bright heart of some ack-ack ahead, no danger to him, as some valiant or foolish gunner braved the storm of shot and shell to heave up his defiance, a flare of light and its accompanying dull *crump!* as something crashed and exploded to starboard, near the perimeter.

The 262's expanding globe of flame, vivid and awful, flicked harshly at a 109G which flew too close, making it wobble and almost augur in but somehow staying airborne, shedding fragments of itself as the expanding sphere of concussion, fire and smoking metal shards slapped and tore at it.

He saw the 262's end but could not celebrate the lucky and unexpected kill delivered by good fortune, experience and instinct.

Mirror, a dark shape filling it.

And Rose was kicking her to starboard and pulling back hard, the Tempest jerking and terror blooming sharp within him, a grunt of fear escaping as a glowing line of cannon shells battered past to the left of Sugar, seemingly close enough to touch yet not a round came close enough to even kiss his Tempest.

Lady Luck still with him in this maelstrom of fire and death.

The smoke-blemished sky filled his windscreen as Sugar tore upwards over Eindhoven's eastern boundary, the stench of the 262's smoke rending painfully at his throat as he pushed the throttles 'through the gate', almost standing Sugar on her tail (or so it seemed at an angle of fifty degrees) as she rocketed skywards at full throttle and in fine pitch, his body squashed back by the intense centrifugal forces of the climb, the bandit in his mirror gone, unable to match the sudden manoeuvre, and with greying vision squinting to look down at her picture, the serenity of her smile soothing; but still his nerves were screaming and his heart aching with the effort, his muscles feeling as if they might tear with the strain.

Grey cloud was rushing to meet him and suddenly he was within it, hardly believing he had survived the chaotic melee over Eindhoven, the comfort of its blanketing protection palpable, and he eased her out of the screaming, shuddering climb and into level flight, emerging into a void between cloud layers, thankfully empty, and he croaked, 'Ben?'

He swallowed dryly two or three times, dry lips and a dryer tongue, his throat cracked and sore and he tried again more correctly. 'Hotspur Leader to Two, come in.'

No response, and he fought to quell the burgeoning sorrow. *Please God, grant your blessing of salvation onto that good and faithful man who would not let me go alone, please.*

He had done his best, killed the enemy and destroyed two, perhaps three of the attacking fighters, including a 262. With the 190D earlier, he might have downed four in total!

No one could turn to him and say that he had not earned his keep today, yet the shame flowed like ice through him. Hundreds of men like him were dead or dying below, and Sugar's ammunition trays were not yet empty. How could he return to Volkel while Eindhoven burned and Sugar was still armed?

He did not want to go, baulked at the very idea. The fire of anger was spent, leaving the elation of success and the relief of having survived even if it was dulled by the thought of going back into the danger, and he pushed her reluctantly back down into cloud. With empty ammo trays and low fuel a man can fight no more, and there can be no disgrace in that. He would have to empty them into Jerry.

He went back because duty and honour demanded it of him, knowing Molly deserved a man with strength and character, not a cringing, snivelling coward who ran from the sound of guns.

He could not see that he had done more than enough, had fought and won and survived through luck and skill in a dawn battleground dominated by sophisticated German machines of war. Rose understood how he could easily have died moments ago, but his damnable sense of duty required that he fight until he could fight no more or was dead, and so duty led him back to the enemy and to danger.

What good are a few shells in your panniers when there're literally hundreds of Jerry milling around down there?

D'you want to win yourself a VC, you raving lunatic? Your family need you, not a medal to remind them what a brave boy you were!

Ignoring the voice of reason because men like him were still dying below, he adjusted his harness, feeling the palpitations of his heart beneath his fingers and wondered how much more of this he could manage, then touched her picture with a lingering, trembling finger and felt for the little teddy bear and the pebble.

He took a shuddering deep breath as his eyes scanned the controls; then he half-rolled Sugar to slice down through the cloud again.

For what we are about to receive ...

Chapter 22

Emerging into the grimy, smoke-thickened air, Rose found he had popped out of cloud three miles west of Eindhoven, and the air above it was still dense with smoke.

Billowing masses of smoke, a wall of smoke, merging messily with the cloud base and bringing it lower, Eindhoven itself an expanse of fires and wreckage, the occasional flash of an explosion as fire caught hold of yet more fuel or explosive ordnance.

In the surrounding fields yet more fires burned beneath oily black columns, signifying that the raiders had not escaped unscathed, but also that some defenders might have got airborne and been shot down by the overwhelming wave of enemy aircraft.

Please God, let one of those not be dear noble Duncan, he prayed fervently.

The bandits above it were now far fewer in number as fuel and ammo ran low amongst the attackers, and even those stragglers now broke off and headed eastwards, but the raid had inflicted severe damage to the airfield, and to Rose the destruction wrought looked even worse than that which had rendered RAF Foxton unserviceable on that awful day when Nazi shrapnel had driven itself cruelly into Molly's back and almost killed her.

Bastards! He could feel the anger rousing again, wondering how many had just died, his eyes sweeping the sky for threats and targets. Tears were forming and, pulling up his goggles for a moment, Rose brushed roughly with his gloves to clear them.

Still descending he pushed forward the throttle again to pursue and attack those departing bandits, but he stiffened as he saw four more 190s lancing in from the north.

As he began to turn to cut them off before they reached Eindhoven, now almost hidden beneath an enveloping bank of smoke, Rose realised that they weren't bandits at all, but were Eindhoven's early morning weather recce flight just returning, and they were also turning in vengeful pursuit of the fleeing raiders, even though the damage was done.

The four Typhoons in hot pursuit would catch fifteen 190s as the enemy fled, and two of their pilots would each bag a pair of bandits near Helmond, finally recovering at miraculously untouched Volkel with Eindhoven unserviceable and its two Wings of Canadian Typhoons and Polish Spitfires smashed.

Rose spotted a pair of Spitfires some miles south-east, also chasing after the enemy, but there were no other bandits close now. Nonetheless, with the enemy fleeing he might yet catch one, and Jerry might choose to mount a follow-up lightning raid, so he set course after the raiders, knowing that with Sugar's superior performance he would just catch them, just before the quartet of Typhoons, despite the Tiffie's head start.

Maintaining his watchful surveillance of the sky, Rose was alarmed to see straight twin trails emerge from the cloud some miles behind the four Typhoons, and he pulled Sugar into a climbing turn to port, anxiously scanning the cloud for any more, but the enemy jet raider was alone.

Alone he might be, but the shape, another 262 from KG51, was on its egress eastwards and home.

As Rose opened up the throttle to try and catch it, the German pilot caught sight of the climbing Tempest and grimaced.

Having already done much damage to petrol tanks and parked fighters in a couple of searing passes over *Gilze-Rijen* airfield, and now low on ammunition and fuel, the veteran *Stabsfeldwebel* from KG51 knew there was no future in dogfighting a Tempest and that the Typhoons ahead would now have been warned of his approach.

Frustrated by the lost opportunity to add a Typhoon to his score for the day, the 262 pilot turned away and climbed back into cloud, taking heart in the pall of smoke over Eindhoven.

Rose breathed out a sigh of relief. God only knew how much 20 mm he had left. Jerry had gone and Rose was still on the field of battle. He had done his bit.

Dawn seemed so far away now on this morning of death and destruction, and Rose turned Sugar's nose for Volkel again.

It had been a disaster, and now he would need to get word back to Molly that he was alright before the alarming news of the dawn attack reached her.

Twenty-seven airfields had been attacked with varying degrees of success by more than a thousand FW190s, Ta152s, Me262s and Bf109s, resulting in the overall loss of around five hundred Allied aircraft at the cost of roughly three hundred Axis fighters lost to Allied fighters and the combined ack-ack of both sides.

Rose was thankful to see that Volkel Airfield looked untouched, in contrast to the burning ruins of Eindhoven and breathed a sigh of relief to see Duncan's battle-stained Tempest safely parked at Dispersals.

The young ex-lawyer had managed to down a Bf109 over Eindhoven to make his score for the day three, and now he trotted across to Rose, a huge smile and tears of relief in his eyes. 'Oh, thank God! Thank God! I thought you were a goner, sir! There were so many of the bastards, and I got six of them on my arse and I couldn't follow you in! Had to jink like crazy to get away, still can't believe I escaped! I tried to stay with you, but they drove me off! God, am I glad to see you!'

The normally quiet and measured young man was almost bouncing on his feet in exhilaration as adrenaline and delight in Rose's survival surged powerfully through him. 'The boss would've knocked my ruddy block off if you hadn't got back, sir!'

You led them off me, Ben, you brave boy. I was able to get a few licks in because you drew them off my tail. If you hadn't, Sugar would be burning amongst all the other wrecked aircraft on Eindhoven's concrete. I owe you my life. But his throat was tight and he couldn't say a word, instead managing to force a fixed smile onto his taut face.

Duncan turned to a group of pilots. 'The CO attacked about a thousand Jerry all on his lonesome over Eindhoven. He's a bloody Leonidas!'

He grinned at Rose, his stained face animated by the danger they had shared and by their survival. 'Or a bloody lunatic! I saw you get at least two 109s and a 262 over Eindhoven, sir, and with that 190 earlier, that's four kills all told! Fucking amazing! Never seen anything like it!'

Kipper was awestruck, his eyes wide. 'You're a mad fucker, sir!'

Jelly was elated, and Rose thought for a moment that his fitter was going to dance a jig on Sugar's wing. 'Four kills? Four? Stone the flamin' crows! I'll get the paint pot out, shall I, sir?'

Exhausted and emotional, Rose had been unable to do more than grunt a monosyllabic reply and try to smile as Jelly took his mask and helmet, tutting and solicitously wiping Rose's greasy face with a dirty rag.

If he had had the energy, Rose would have laughed as the oily cloth dabbed gently at his cheeks. *Crikey! I'm going to look a right picture!*

His body felt stiff with tension and exertion and he felt drained and flat, and Jelly helped him gently down back onto terra firma to lean against Sugar's side until the trembling in his arms and legs settled, while his excited pilots gathered around him, Molly's picture gripped in one hand, the other placed over the pocket containing the pink teddy bear and the polished pebble.

Sweet Lord, thank you for the mercy of my salvation … he could feel his eyes burning and swallowed, *Stone the crows! I think I'm going to cry …*

Sheep and Gabby bounced up in a jeep looking grim, the shock of the enemy attack still evident in the expressions, but taking one look at Rose's pale, oily face and strained smile, they unceremoniously bundled him into the back of the jeep and drove him back to the peace of his Ops caravan to recover with the rejuvenating comforts of a hot, sweet mug of compo half-filled with something fiery from a bottle Sheep had taken from the battledress pocket. 'This'll put hair on your arse, sir!', before covering him with a smelly blanket to still the trembling and the chattering of his teeth. At last, as he slept, his squadron commanders slipped out.

83 Group was hardest hit by *Bodenplatte*, and it was the AOC, Harry Broadhurst (a lucky survivor of the horrendous assault on the airfield housing his HQ), while mourning the loss of so many of his men and so much of his force, who rearranged 83's Order of Battle with his survivors and reserves from Blighty.

His intermediate operations while the losses were made good were assumed primarily by the remaining serviceable airfields which had escaped damage, to maintain the aerial status quo, with Volkel's 122 Wing in the vanguard of the continued Allied aerial offensive, and Rose's 63 Wing flying defensive patrols for the next few weeks.

As a result, with few attacks from a mortally injured Luftwaffe, 63 Wing were spared the acute losses suffered by 122 Wing as the latter took the fight to the enemy over the next fortnight and beyond, while the Allies scrambled to make good the losses by dipping into the ample reserves of men and machines available to them.

It had been a victory of sorts for the Luftwaffe, achieving complete tactical surprise and severe damage, but it was a hollow triumph which came at an unacceptable cost to the Luftwaffe and Germany. Too many irreplaceable and experienced veterans, including almost sixty experienced fighter leaders had been lost killed or injured, and too many aircraft destroyed.

A despairing *General der Jagdflieger* Adolf Galland, mourning the loss of so many of his precious flyers including many old friends, would later lament, 'The Luftwaffe received its death blow at the Ardennes offensive. In unfamiliar conditions and with insufficient training and combat experience, our numerical strength had no effect.' He added sorrowfully, 'In this forced action, we sacrificed our last substance.'

An already faded Luftwaffe would be unable to mount an effective daytime defence of Germany following the mortal blow it received in *Bodenplatte,* leaving only the shrunken and under-resourced night fighter arm to continue to mount a formidable resistance.

On the ground, the Germans had been halted and the bulge in the Allied Lines began to slowly shrink as the Allied response pushed them back, Axis forces gradually withdrawing in an orderly manner.

The Bulge would continue to contract over the next month or so until the Germans had been repulsed to the lines from where they had started on 16 December 1944, marking the failure of the offensive, and the irreplaceable loss of men and materiel that would be sorely missed in the final defence of the Fatherland.

Both sides had suffered great losses, and while the Germans had pushed back the start date of the Allied offensive to take Germany, it was a terrible defeat.

Germany had lost too much of its future in the Battle of the Bulge and in *Bodenplatte*; Adolf Hitler's Luftwaffe fighter force had been broken, and it would never recover.

Chapter 23—Scarborough

With poor conditions over RAF Leeming and low on fuel, Rose was forced to land at RAF East Moor, a RAF Bomber Command airfield of 6 Group (RCAF).

With Sugar tucked away safely inside a cavernous hangar beside one of the hulking Handley Page Halifax III's of 415 Squadron RCAF, and armed with his travel permit and coupons, Rose was dropped off by a little Canadian WAAF at York railway station.

The poor girl drove superbly but was quiet and pale, close to tears throughout the little journey, her lower lip swollen from where she had bitten it.

Knowing that the bomber boys were suffering heavily over Germany, and supposing the girl's beau was a recent casualty, Rose said nothing, and was ashamed by his silence and inability to offer gentle words of comfort.

He remembered the rents and holes on the side of the Halifax.

With a Lancaster's bomb load capacity being more than twice that of a Halifax, two splendid bomber crews risked their lives flying Halifaxes where one could do the same in a Lanc. But in war, the lives of fighting men are counters to be sacrificed for the greater good.

An almost inaudible sob from the girl behind the steering wheel. Another casualty. Just one more, one of untold many.

Just one of those things.

Light glistened softly on the wetness of her cheeks, deepest sorrow radiating from her, chest heaving and a sniffle, suppressed.

And I just sit here like a stone, can't find any words to ease her suffering. This bloody war has hardened me, made me a heartless swine.

When … no, *if*, the time came, who will comfort Molly? Superstitiously he laid a palm over the pocket containing the bear and the pebble.

Should I offer her my hanky? If I pat her shoulder and murmur, 'chin up, girl', will she think me an cold and pompous fool? Of course she will. I can do nothing to soothe her pain. Rose remained silent, his jubilation to be back diminished a little by being unable to ease a despairing girl's grief.

And after five years of war, five years of broken dreams, bitter tears and empty prospects, what words were there that could heal this heartbroken girl?

The disconsolate girl's grief made him feel a sense of guilt for the bounding happiness he felt at the coming weekend with Molly, but he could not lessen it.

Despite her anguish, Rose's heart soared. *Two days! Two whole days with Molly!*

York Station's Rail Transport Officer, a harried and haggard Major who looked as if he had recently pulled out all of his own hair, was delighted to see him and immediately detailed Rose to accompany a detachment of twelve young WAAFs on their way to Scarborough for a course.

There were the usual delays, with only essential maintenance work being carried out in wartime and a deterioration in the hard-working rolling stock, as was apparent in the weary tiredness of their carriage when the train finally arrived.

While tedious, the trip was not as rowdy as expected. The youngsters in his charge were chatty and excited about their new posting, respectful but clearly awed of Rose. In the purgatory of war, at the age of twenty-four he was 'the old man'.

Not only was their appointed rail guardian a very highly decorated Wing Commander, but he was also *the* famous 'Typhoon Rose, Ace Scourge of the Nazi Raiders', a name penned by the papers.

His peers and friends ribbed him mercilessly over it but Molly was delighted by it.

While her father (the kindly but distant Air Marshal of which he was still more than a little scared) kept their medals in his safe at home, beneath Rose and Molly's marital bed was a troika of brimming hatboxes, one containing all of her newspaper clippings detailing his exploits (much to his embarrassment and secret pleasure), and the other two all of his letters and poems to her.

The trip along LNER's York to Scarborough line was picturesque, and Rose and 'his' girls marvelled at the raw and icy beauty of the landscape.

Ushering the girls out and stepping down onto the platform, Rose looked around. With the keen eyesight of a fighter pilot and the second sense that helps all those seeking the ones they love in a crowd, he caught sight of her.

Molly was already looking straight at him, a smile on her lips, and his breath caught with excitement and he waved enthusiastically before realising it wasn't what was expected of senior RAF officers sporting three rings.

She had seen him as soon as he opened the door to let out his temporary command onto the platform in a chattering horde. There was that familiar tightening and wave of warmth and joy as she saw him, that peculiar prickling in her eyes as her husband, the efficient RAF officer, caught sight of her and turned back into the eager but bashful young man she had met in the darkened inn's garden so long ago.

In the first moment they met after time apart, Rose would discover an instant of shyness and wonder that their reunion was a reality, followed by a wave of pure delight which flooded through his body and across his face, easing the stiffness from it and smoothing the veteran's lines.

She began to walk across towards him through the milling crowd as another WAAF, a Section Officer, introduced herself to Rose, holding out her hand and he took it.

'Wing Commander Rose? Section Officer Dana Andrews, I'm here to pick up the girls. Hope they behaved themselves?' She leaned closer, still holding his hand. 'I must say it's a pleasure to meet you. I've read all about you in the papers. Might I … ?'

'I'm sure that the Wing Commander is thrilled to hear it, Section Officer.' The coolness of Molly's calm contralto seemed to cut through the sound of people, baggage, and the clatter of the quiescent loco-motive. 'And now if you'll excuse us, I'm keen to make the most of my husband's leave.'

Andrews reddened, nodding as she stepped back flustered, then surprised recognition and respect in her face as she came face-to-face with one of the WAAF's most decorated heroines, celebrated in the papers and interviewed by the BBC for her exploits and bravery. 'Of course, Squadron Officer, ma'am, do forgive me. Thank you, Wing Commander, sir, for looking after the girls.'

He smiled. 'Don't mention it, Section Officer, it was an absolute pleasure. They're a good bunch, take good care of them, will you?' But his eyes were on his wife alone as Andrews hurriedly withdrew beneath Molly's flinty gaze.

Molly took his hand, the fingertips of her other hand coming to rest gently against his stubbly cheek, her voice softer now. 'Wing Commander Rose, *sir*.'

'Molly, my love.' He drew her hand to his lips and kissed her fingertips, relishing the impossible reality of her nearness.

Molly saw his happiness and the desperate hunger in his eyes and felt as if she would cry. 'I see that the RAF has resorted to rewarding their best fighter leaders for their gallantry with more than just rank and medals. WAAF harems for their best, is it? What was that? Twenty young girls to sit on your knee and beguile away the trip? Forty?'

He grinned uneasily at her playful words, feeling the hot flush at his collar. 'Hardly, my dearest, there were only twelve of them, and they were very well behaved.'

She cocked an eyebrow in amusement. 'Hmm! I'll bet! And how well behaved was their Wing Commander? And that cheeky little Section Officer seemed a bit keen … ?'

He pulled her towards him, revelling in the incredible sensation in the way they fit perfectly together, the embrace bringing the soft curves of her body delightfully against his, albeit fully clad and her gas mask case getting in the way. 'Enough of your nonsensical babble, wench! Give me a kiss, will you?'

She put a finger to his lips. 'Very masterful, dear, a good effort, perhaps a five out of ten? Quite a nice try. But what's the special word?'

Rose rolled his eyes, frowning. 'Bloody hell!'

Molly smiled prettily and shook her head. 'No, Harry dear, it's not that, and that's two words, not one. There's quite the difference between one and two, you know. You're getting colder.' She cocked her head to one side speculatively, eyeing him with a sparkle in her eyes. 'Where was it you said you went to school, dear?'

He felt like sighing with contentment, but instead scowled in a way in which he hoped looked quite intimidating, but his ever-hopeful puckered lips rather ruined the overall effect of his scowl, and he tried to resist an overwhelming and urgent desire to grasp the pert swell of her glorious buttocks. 'Please? Please might I have a ruddy kiss?'

The finger stroked his lower lip. 'Since you asked so nicely …' She licked her lips and pressed them softly against his, mouth opening and the tip of her tongue pushing through to lick gently against his incisors, the fragrance of her skin and scent intoxicating, and he closed his eyes with pleasure, and this time he *did* sigh. Bliss.

She pulled back slightly. 'And pray tell, Mr Wing Commander, sir, how's my dear little friend?' Despite where they were, Molly surreptitiously reached down to push between the buttons of his greatcoat with one gloved hand and squeezed his crotch playfully, exclaiming, 'Goodness me! How lovely! Not so little after all!'

'Cripes! You're a bit fresh, Mrs Rose!' It felt wonderful and more of the same would be most welcome, but he shifted uncomfortably, the enforced celibacy of the last few months and now her exciting and delicious closeness triggering a physical reaction not acceptable in genteel company. 'He's looking forward to seeing you, very much so, Moll, but please don't squeeze him again otherwise it might be all over, in every sense!'

'You're my husband, *Mr* Rose, and I've got marital rights over your bits, so I'll do as I like!' She pouted, kissed him lightly again and defiantly gave his pride and joy another mischievous squeeze, but somehow, he managed to control himself, though it was a very close-run thing.

'Good grief, woman,' he scolded, looking around them in case someone had seen, 'will you never listen to me?'

She smiled wolfishly. 'Never!'

'God save us all. Love, honour and obey, madam, remember?' he grumbled, voice and face stern, lifting his hand to indicate his wedding ring. But he was still wearing his gloves, and he lowered it, feeling foolish.

'Not likely! I didn't mean any it, just said the words to keep you happy and get your ring on my finger!' She laughed and kissed him again, lingering delightfully, to the good-natured and loud appreciation and encouragement of a group of tanned Matelots climbing aboard the train, their Petty Officer shouting them into silence with a grin on his face.

Embarrassed with the good-natured banter and their attention, Rose found to his horror that a flush was spreading up his neck and onto his cheeks.

He gave a feeble wave to the Navy, but Molly grabbed the strap of his gasmask container and pulled him along after her to further cheers. 'Come along, Wing Commander, and don't tarry! We've only got a couple of days and I've got plans for you!'

With a start he awoke and stared at the whiteness and the ornate ceiling which rose above him for a moment, confused and wondering where he was, and why the years-darkened ceiling and the dusty bulb of his cubicle at the monastery was missing. And then the memory of their arrival at the hotel rushed in and he smiled.

A weekend with Molly!

Stiffly, he sat up and saw Molly sitting beside the window, the light of the sky draining as dusk harkened its way to them. She looked up from the book she had been reading and smiled the smile that continued to enchant him.

'Harry, you're awake!'

He realised he was still wearing his greatcoat and was grinning foolishly at her. 'Oh, Moll! I didn't fall asleep on you, did I?' The words were slurred as he tried to moisten his sticky mouth.

She crossed the room to perch on the edge of the bed, a hand settling lightly on one foot. She must have taken his socks and shoes off, he thought blearily.

'There was I, the eager wife ready to welcome her hero home with a great deal of zeal …' she teased, eyes twinkling mischievously, 'but as soon as he sat down, he was out like a light! I had to put him to bed, poor lamb, but I left the greatcoat on as I didn't want to disturb you.' She leaned forwards to kiss him gently, just the hint of her tongue. 'You must have been exhausted! Train journeys with a gaggle of teenage WAAFs must be such hard work!'

But Molly did not tell him how his face had remained taut, the lines not softening, nor how light he had seemed as she settled him on the bed, nor the single word, a name, whispered in his sleep, 'Jacques?'

Molly had wept silently as he slept, wondering at the merciless strains placed on her husband, and how it must damage and torment him, torturing the decent and honourable boy she had married, battering heartlessly at his sensitivity and kindness.

As always, she thought only of him, overlooking her own daily torment as her husband flew against a harsh enemy who sought only to strike him from the sky with the best equipment man could create.

Molly thought herself just one of the many who suffered and survived and wondered hour by hour if their loved ones were still alive, wondering if the dreaded telegram was already on its way, trying to pass through each day while tormented by the ignorance of distance. And now she felt like weeping again at the way in which the tightness had disappeared from his face, and at the sheer pleasure in his eyes as he looked at her.

Oh Lor'! He scrambled to her. 'Oh Moll!' Aware of how stupid he sounded, he said, 'I'm sorry, my darling!' *God how inadequate! Alone at last with his wife after weeks of separation and he'd fallen asleep! Idiot!*

She kissed him again, and then her fingers crept up to his groin, unbuttoning his trousers and reaching inside to grasp him deliciously. 'Hmm! something's full of beans!' Molly eased him out and kissed the tip before looking up to smile at him beguilingly. 'Best get these trousers off, Harry. We don't want to make a mess, do we?'

Their first night with one another again had been one of intense passion and release interspersed with periods of rest and deep sleep. Molly had been ready and willing each time he awoke, and she held him afterwards in the tender sanctuary of her embrace as sleep would reclaim him again.

They awoke together and he anxiously asked yet again of his children, unwilling to say how much he missed them or share his fears they might forget him and (God forbid) that he might never see them again.

She assured him softly once more that all was well at home, that his children loved him and missed him, and that he need not worry for they would be waiting for his return; she reaffirmed her love for him at length, aware of the importance of that confirmation and reassurance, knowing the joy her words brought.

Breakfast was a shared pleasure, although he did not share her pleasure for marmalade. Molly adored the monstrous stuff, slapping it thick onto her toast, and because the abomination seemed to glisten maliciously at him, he looked away from it, preferring to shovel scrambled reconstituted dried egg onto his toast, generous salt and pepper on the egg and delicious Marmite (yummy!) helping to blunt the slightly unpleasant after-taste of the powdered egg.

She was perfect in almost every way, but there was this one flaw, her love for marmalade! It was strangely comforting to know that even an exceptional individual like Molly had a fault. It showed that she was only human, after all.

Rose, remembering the delicious memories of the night and not yet sated, wanted to return to their room for a morning in bed with his wife but Molly was firm, stern even.

'I've missed you so much, Harry, and the last time I was in Scarborough I was ten, so I want to see the sights with the man that I love.'

She pinched his cheek gently. 'But as he's indisposed, I'll take you instead!' She laughed at his expression.

It was raining, but not hard, so they borrowed an umbrella from Reception, and promised to be back in time for tea. The elderly woman behind the desk needlessly warned them not to stroll on the sands or the cliffs, that they were closed off because of the mines and because a woman, Mary Wardell, had been shot dead by mistake as she wandered on the South Bay sands by a wary and overly diligent sentry back in 1940.

But Molly and Rose had no intention of getting sand between their toes or clambering over coils of barbed wire, pillboxes and other barricades. (*The sooner we're back, the sooner I can get this gorgeous creature back into bed …*)

'I'm afraid The Arcadia and the North Bay mini railway are closed for the duration as well, dear.'

He felt his mood drop. *No ride on the mini railway? What a swizz!* Gloom settled over Rose, although any Jerry raider looking for something to strafe would have had a field day. It would be easy to confuse the mini stream trains with those of the main line.

'But the cinemas are open,' the woman continued, lighting a cigarette, her forehead puckering. 'I think the Odeon's showing *Double Indemnity*. Don't you think that Fred MacMurray's simple dreamy?'

No, thought Rose sourly, *I bloody don't.*

Molly grinned at Rose's face. 'Oh yes. Very manly,' she agreed and gave him a wink.

The old dear was still burbling, 'Oh, and dusk is around four pm, dinner for seven, so don't go too far, but at least the Blackout isn't in effect anymore! Alright, dearie?'

As Molly unfurled the umbrella on the street outside, she gave him a wink. 'I'm going to walk you all over the place, darling, and I'll likely wear you out. So after we've had our tea, I'll tuck you in so you can have a little rest in bed before dinner tonight.'

Despite his grumpiness at being in the rain and the disappointment of no train ride, Rose perked up. 'I might be scared on my own, Moll. Might you join me?'

Her eyes were on him, amusement sparkling in them, and he added hurriedly, 'It's winter and my feet get a bit cold, too.'

She sniffed and rolled the umbrella, forcing him to take avoiding action lest she took an eye out with one of its ribs. 'I might, we'll see, it all depends.'

'On what?' he asked suspiciously.

'On how much I enjoy traipsing around today in the rain with you. If I enjoy myself, it might make me amenable.'

Crikey! Molly was very much an outdoors type, and she had walked him half to death across different scenic parts of Britain, though it had been a pleasure to share the beauty of the British countryside with a person who knew so much about the areas they visited.

Besides, all that wandering kept her fit, and she was as lithe as the day he met her, even after giving birth to their two beautiful children.

Not for the first time, Rose wondered why on earth such a sophisticated, elegant and intelligent woman had settled for someone like him, not that he was complaining, of course.

Thank you, merciful God, for your boundless kindness.

True to her word, Molly spent the morning walking everywhere it was possible to walk (*thank God he'd brought his walking stick, though to be honest he really didn't need it!*), as close to the sea front and Esplanade as it was possible to get, and then on into the town, although as a garrison and training town the place was packed with members of all three services, many of whom wore a wide variety of shoulder flashes including Australia, New Zealand, Canada, Rhodesia, South Africa, India, France, Poland and Czechoslovakia.

Ack-ack positions in Albert Park prevented them from walking through it, but they managed to admire the headland and the ruins of Scarborough Castle from Queen's Parade, the twelfth-century stronghold shelled (along with residences, shops, and music halls) by two Imperial German Navy battleships just before Christmas 1914.

They had thought to have lunch in the Grand Hotel, but like the majority of the hotels in Scarborough, it had been taken over by the armed forces and the place was full, as were all the other hotel restaurants on the seafront. A Lieutenant Commander with one leg, grim-faced and alone in the sleeting rain, told them of a British restaurant in the town offering three courses for just 9d each, but they deciding against tramping back around the streets in search of its smoky, crowded and cramped dining room.

Instead, Molly and Rose settled on a lunch of fish and chips. Rose was doubtful with the poorer quality of the oil available to the chippies in wartime Britain, but as it turned out, his reservations were not justified, and the fish and chips were crunchy on the outside and deliciously soft on the inside.

They sat in an empty tourist shelter facing out towards the North Bay, the rain pelting down now and the fragrance of the sea and their lunch in his nostrils, looking into the veil of haze with Molly next to him, and Rose wondered how life could be more perfect than this.

Finishing first, Molly sighed contentedly, and reached over to steal one of his chips. He gave her a mock-indignant look and she stuck out her tongue at him, a tiny smear of Daddies sauce on the cupid's bow of her lip. She reached for another and he brought the crinkled nest of chips closer to her, slowing his pace so that she might share more with him.

'God, but I love you, Moll,' he said under his breath to himself.

She smiled and leaned into his shoulder. 'What was that, you foolish boy?'

'Nothing,' he told her curtly. 'I was just thinking to myself.'

'Strange. It sounded awfully like you saying that you love me.'

He stared into the seething deluge. 'You're mistaken, madam, I don't.'

'Fibber! I know you do because you gave me your heart, and I've got it pickling nicely in a little jar at home!' Teasingly, she added, 'It was a marmalade jar before!'

Molly grasped his chin and turned his face so that she could kiss him. 'And I love you, so very much that I want to scream because I can't tell you how much.'

He felt the stupid grin settle on his face and knew that a little of her ketchup was on his lip, and he could feel the shameful warmth behind his eyes. *Dear God, I'm going to blub in a moment!*

Just then there was a flurry of activity in the pouring rain and two drenched figures all but threw themselves into the shelter.

'Oh, I say! I'm awfully sorry, but would you mind terribly if we share this shelter, it's absolutely pouring down!'

'We' were a youngster with the single whisker of a Pilot Officer on the shoulders of his sodden greatcoat, and an even younger looking pale-faced girl who looked as if she might cry.

Well yes, Rose was about to say, *I do bloody mind! I want to be alone with my wife, so piss off, will you? Find your own bloody shelter!*

But instead Molly answered quickly for them both. 'Not at all, please do take a seat, there's plenty of room for everyone.' Her smile was bright and welcoming, and it was true, there was comfortable seating room for ten or twelve people. Rose stared at her sourly, but she ignored his truculent behaviour and continued to smile serenely at the youngsters.

'Gosh! Thanks ever so much!' The boy waited until his companion sat before sitting himself, Rose noted approvingly. His hair was plastered to his skull because the girl was wearing his cap, and now the lad shook out his handkerchief and passed it to the girl. 'We're on our honeymoon, you see. Maisie and I have been looking forward to being together for ages, but now we're here at last, the weather's been shocking!'

Molly nodded sympathetically, but Rose just grunted, still feeling churlish for the intrusion on their comfortable solitude. He had hoped to share a kiss and a cuddle after their chips, but now ...

The boy looked with adoring eyes at his wife. 'Maisie's been very patient with me. She didn't have to wait, but she did. She wanted to get married last summer, but I wanted to finish my tour, first.' He looked at his wife. 'In case ... you know.'

'Because I love you.' The girl whispered the words shyly, but Rose and Molly heard them despite the noise of the rain, and Rose felt his wife gently take his hand.

Dear Heavens, this stripling has just completed a tour of operations! Didn't look like he shaved yet, the poor mite, but he's a veteran!

His voice was still gruff. 'What were you flying?'

The boy replied with pride, 'Bombers, Avro Lancasters.'

Molly's younger brother Edward was a bomber pilot, now a Wing Commander with two DSOs, two DFCs and a Mention in Despatches, and he heard her murmur something as her fingers tightened in his.

They both knew the calibre of those who flew in the hostile darkness to brave vicious defences. She had seen the damage it did to young men first-hand, seen the strain and the relief when Edward was finally rested from command of a Lancaster squadron the previous summer. One of the lucky few who had survived flying into the dangerous skies of occupied Europe for years on end.

Rose also had personal experience of the crews of RAF Bomber Command and shook his head in admiration, for he considered them the bravest of the brave. Flying for hours to get to their targets in the freezing cold and pitch black, in kites that were nowhere as swift or manoeuvrable as dear Sugar, with heavy flak and swarms of night fighters waiting for them, the crews of those bombers were truly made of stern stuff.

And this lad with his hairless chin and eager eyes had somehow managed to survive Germany's extensive and organised defences in that winter of 1944, one of the deadliest for the men of Bomber Command.

Rose looked closer and noticed the slight tremor in the boy's left hand, discerned the fine lines at his eyes and the corners of his mouth, the thoughtful eyes, and was ashamed of his surliness.

The girl was shaking too, but from the cold. He could see she was shy of them, but suddenly she chirped out proudly, 'Paul's got the Distinguished Flying Cross!' She seemed shocked by her outburst and lapsed into silence again, her eyes huge in the murk but her pride palpable.

'Now there, Maisie.' The boy gave a lopsided grin, but his eyes were shy. 'She thinks I'm some sort of hero! They give it to anybody these days!'

Rose knew better. 'She's right to think you a hero and she's every right to be proud of you. A tour on Lancs and a DFC to boot! Well, when this rain eases a bit, young man, I'm going to stand you and,

er, Maisie a drink. The biggest ruddy drink I can find for a real hero.'
Gently Molly squeezed his hand.

The boy flushed with pleasure, glad his wife had heard the praise, and then his eyes flicked to Rose's shoulders, and he almost leaped to attention in fright as he recognised Wing Commanders' rank tabs, but his wife was hugging him as if her life depended on it, and he stayed put.

But his face searched Rose's, and the latter irritably realised that he must look a fool with the smear of ketchup on his face and he impatiently wiped his lips.

The boy's voice was tentative. 'I say sir, aren't you—?'

'No, I'm not,' Rose interrupted, 'I'm no one special.'

Molly's voice was soft. 'Yes, you are, Harry, you're very special.' She raised her voice over the seething rain. 'And yes, you're right, he is too.'

The boy was awestruck, eyes wide as dinner plates. 'Oh my word! Maisie! It's Typhoon Rose!'

He felt Molly straighten beside him with pride, and he cringed, feeling a bit of a phoney.

Dear God, here we go …

Wet and miserable, Maisie looked at him, trying to look interested but she was clearly unimpressed by what she saw. 'Who?'

Beside him, Molly giggled, and Rose began to laugh.

She snuggled closer to him, the gas heater against the wall hissing softly, the room dim and warm in its orange light.

'Strike a light an' stone the bleedin' crows, missus! Maisie! Maisie! Look! It's Typhoon Rose! Oo-er!' she said in a hushed voice filled with awe, and tittered. For some unfathomable reason most of Molly's impersonations were with a cockney accent, regardless of the background or accent of the person she was imitating.

Rose tutted and kissed her forehead, his voice brusque. 'For Christ's sake, Moll! Will you stop going on about that?'

She hugged him tight. 'D'you remember how flustered you were the first time we met, Harry?'

I still feel like that when I see you, he thought, arms tightening around her, *you amazing, lovely woman. How do I survive our long separations?*

'I was smitten, and I really wanted you to like me.' His voice was gruff, 'I'd never met a girl like you before.' He kissed her again. 'Never have since.' He thrust aside the guilty memories of Charlie. 'You're amazing, Moll. Can't understand why you married me.'

'Neither can I!' She giggled again, pleased with her witticism, and ignoring his baleful look.

Rose touched her hair, the strands like delicate thread beneath his fingertips, enjoying the way the light caught her hair and her skin, radiant like burnished gold.

It was dim, but wherever she was, Molly seemed to light up everything.

They had enjoyed passionate intimacy already, once after tea and then again after dinner, and now he found that he was aroused again. She felt the eager pressure against the inside of her thigh and she stroked his cheek. 'Goodness, Wing Commander, but you're insatiable!' She raised herself to kiss his lips, the lightest touch, soft as a feather. 'I love you, Harry Rose, always have, and always will.'

He gazed into her eyes, enjoying her beauty. 'For which I shall be forever grateful, and which I reciprocate completely. I would share each moment of my life with you and it would still not be enough. I adore you, Moll.'

Molly's lips smiled softly, her eyes shining. 'Oh, Harry.'

His hands encircled her waist as she raised herself, sliding one slim leg over to clamber astride his thighs, reaching down to guide him, and he reached for her breasts with pleasure as she eased herself onto him, his eyes eager to hold on to the enchanting vision of her as they began to move together, revelling in the exquisite feeling of her body and his senses overwhelmed, her thick midnight tresses a curtain casting her beauty into shadow as she leaned forward to place her lips against his.

Rose pulled her down into his embrace, her breath hot and fragrant on his face, her breasts heavy and nipples hard against him, his hands sliding to grasp her securely, thrusting rhythmically into the gloriously yielding tightness as she gasped, and his breath hitched in the sheer wonder of her, his thoughts lost in the warm depth of her gaze.

The act was a gentle one quickened by desire, relaxed and filled with an intimate tenderness in which they were consumed, her lips soft and light against his face, Rose thrusting sinuously into the overflowing heat as she moaned, enthralled in one another and the caresses and sweetness of their union.

Time flowed as they moved together and was lost until at last she gasped in his arms and buried her face into his neck, body jerking against him and hands gripping his shoulders hard, her muffled cries loud against one ear and he allowed himself the blessed release, the recurring waves of consuming pleasure rippling and radiating from his groin out through his body and mind as she clutched at him tightly.

They lay entwined together for a long time, half asleep and fulfilled in the enchantment of their embrace.

In the contentment of his stupor as he drifted into sleep, Rose offered up an earnest prayer: *Please, Lord, let me live ...*

Chapter 24

Tamping tobacco into his battered pipe, Max leaned against the wooden fence comfortably, sighing with contentment as he put a match to the bowl of his pipe.

Looking out across the pasture as he puffed the pipe alight, he reflected that for the first time in many months he felt at peace and hopeful for Germany's future.

The wedding had been the best experience he had had for some time, or at least since the adjutant had received the phone call from the military hospital just west of Bersenbruck, telling of a miracle Max could not have thought possible.

With his broken 262 spinning down and out of control into the cloud the day their formation was bounced by the P47s, young Peter Stark could feel his consciousness slipping as the severe forces strained him against his harness, forcing him so hard to one side so that breathing was almost impossible and he felt his ribs might break when suddenly the destructive forces of the gyrating spin had torn his doomed jet fighter to pieces.

Thrown abruptly from the disintegrating aircraft into a screaming whirlwind, the dazed youngster just about managed to get his fall stabilised and his parachute deployed before passing out, and being unable to control his landing, broke his right ankle and his left wrist. With dented ribs and two fractures, Peter would be out of the fight for months, and Max quickly phoned a friend in OKL to get Peterkin a medical discharge.

With a bit of luck, this meant that when the Allies were victorious, they would leave him be, a veteran discharged because he was no longer (nor likely to be) combat effective. Peterkin would be angry and upset, but what happened now did not matter, he was thinking of the boy's future. A future with his precious Lissy.

Not expecting to survive the final brutal weeks or months of the war, Max would safeguard the futures of two of the people he cared for most in the world, and with his father a prisoner of the Americans, the future of the family's dairy farm west of Rosenheim in the rolling foothills of the Alps would be secure.

As soon as he was able, Max commandeered a Me110 and flown Peter down to the Luftwaffe's main airfield at Munich, cloud-hopping all the way, for the *Zerstorer* was not an aircraft he would duel in with enemy fighters. The boy's face was a grimace of pain when helped from the gunner's position of the heavy fighter, but the grimace turned into a joyous shining smile as soon as he saw Lissy, while his sister's eyes were filled with such delight that Max could have wept.

Reassured that he might not be making a big mistake after all when he saw them together again, Max had been glad that he had given the little box to Peterkin on arriving at Fliegerhorst München-Schleissheim.

Clutching the box gratefully, Peterkin had looked north, remembering the previous year's summer stroll with Lissy on the grounds of Oberschleissheim's historic castle, with Max walking a discreet distance behind (After all, little sisters had to be chaperoned by their older, perhaps overly protective brothers, didn't they?). During the stroll, Peter had asked Lissy then if she would marry him, but the girl had hesitated.

Dearest Lissy had been thinking of the farm, not of herself, and how her mother still needed her. With a husband captured and one son missing in Russia, the other fighting in the Luftwaffe, *Mutti* could not look after the family business alone, and Lissy was her support.

Seeing her hesitation Peter had said no more, instead commenting on the loveliness of a collage display of yellow alpine anemones, cobalt blue Bavarian gentians and delicate pink alpine roses, bending forward to sniff them so that Lissy could not see the flush of his embarrassment, his heart aching at what he perceived as a refusal.

With a bit more sense he might have questioned her indecision and discovered the dilemma Lissy faced over her future and that of the farm, but he did not question her, trying to save face rather than push for clarification. With time he would learn that talking surely beats a wounded silence.

Some distance behind but listening with a brother's sharpened ears, Max had sighed in exasperation, and resisted the urge to run up and kick Peter's silly arse into the flowers. He himself had learned and suffered the cost of wounded pride.

The little box contained a diamond engagement ring Max bought at *Boucheron's* in Paris's *Place Vendôme* after the fall of France in 1940. It had been meant for Isolda Eisner, once a classmate, now a teacher at the local school, and Max's first true love.

Enthralled by the excitement and danger of aerial combat, first in Spain and then in the Low Countries, and caught up in a world of revelries hosted by party officials and meaningless relationships with UFA movie starlets, Max was immersed in enjoying himself as one of the Luftwaffe's most renowned, and he forgot about the girl waiting for him.

Tired of waiting for an inconsiderate and selfish youngster, Isolda married a kind and considerate one instead.

Returning home in June 1940 with a Knight's Cross at his neck, a glittering diamond engagement ring in his pocket, with a bottle of champagne in one hand and carrying a box containing a Nina Ricci dress in the other, Max was shocked to see *his* Isolda arm in arm with a handsome young *Panzertruppen Leutnant,* the black wound badge, Iron Cross First and Second Class on her husband's chest proof of his service during *Blitzkrieg*.

For once, Max was the vanquished.

Max saw Isolda's happiness, but not the wistful regret in her eyes when she saw him. Knowing she was content and cared for, with a punctured ego and his heart unfulfilled, Max returned to his life as a feted hero of the *Reich*.

Lucky Max, celebrated air ace and hero of the Third Reich, lucky in war but unlucky in love.

Isolda's husband was thoughtful, loving and generous, and she blessed him with a beautiful daughter. He was also a brave and honourable man, and won himself glory in North Africa, a Knight's Cross and a Gold Wound Badge at Mersa El Brega, in addition to a headstone in the battle for some anonymous fly-speck in the Egyptian desert 106 kilometres west of Alexandria, called El Alamein.

Learning of her husband's death as he huddled over a flickering stove deep in Russia's winter, and wanting to write to her but thinking Isolda would rebuff him as an opportunist, Max did not try to contact her.

He later understood that comforting words to a heart sorely bereft would have been kind and bolstered Isolda's flagging spirit. But when

Max realised it would have been compassionate to have written to her, it was too late.

Ego, hubris and pride. The enemies of conciliation and happiness.

Seeing the happiness on her face as Peterkin struggled painfully onto one knee, Max felt that he had both gained and lost in that instant. He would keep a dear friend and gain a brother-in-law but he had lost an engagement ring he had kept for over four years. Feeling strangely dispirited, Max dismissed the feeling and made his way to the church to make the final arrangements with Father Karl.

That evening they came together in *Polterabend*, the traditional breaking of china and porcelain into tiny pieces, the tinier the pieces, the luckier the union would be, all glass safely hidden away to protect against the misfortune associate with breaking it.

Cleaning up afterwards was the job of the happy couple as the first act of their blessed alliance, the first of many.

Lissy was radiant in the sunlight outside the church the following day, a beautiful bride shining bright and glowing with happiness, clad in the customary black dress and voluminous white veil, white shoes and bouquet of Bavarian winter blooms tied together with white ribbon.

Max walked Lissy up the aisle to Father Karl and her bridegroom Peter, blissfully happy and splendid in Luftwaffe blue, resplendent with a chestful of medals, the Knight's Cross with Oak Leaves, German Cross in Gold, both Iron Crosses First and Second Class, Honour Roll Clasp, the Silver War Cross and the East Medal. A true German hero.

The church had been packed with their friends and neighbours despite the short notice, and Max noticed amongst them the slender figure of Isolda, golden hair loose on her shoulders, big blue eyes and her gentle smile, looking so very vulnerable in a simple blue dress.

Now, as he leaned against the fence, puffing cheerfully on his pipe, he remembered the beauty of the day, and was glad for God's mercy in Peterkin's salvation and for bringing this day that ousted the shadows from Lissy's eyes. He thought of the fright on Peter's face when asked by Father Karl for the ring before a grinning Max handed it to him, and he chuckled.

She shifted beside him, long legged and willowy, golden hair piled high with a clip. 'What's so funny?'

He turned to look at Isolda, surprised that he could have forgotten how beautiful she was in the intervening years of war; unlike the painted mannequins of the UFA, her skin and eyes were clear, her cheeks glowing. 'A little thing, Peterkin had forgotten about the ring, but he needn't have worried, poor lad.'

'They look a lovely couple, I'm glad for them. God grant them every happiness.' She sounded wistful and he wondered if it was for her husband or for what they might have had together. She reached up and removed the clip from her hair so that it cascaded onto her shoulders. He wanted to reach out and touch it but stayed his hand, and knowing he was staring, he looked away.

Say it. 'Izzy, I'm sorry.'

'Sorry for what?' She sounded surprised.

'For not writing when ...'

She looked away then, her eyes distant and the wind caught in her hair so that its wisps glowed like a halo around her head in the afternoon light.

'It wouldn't have helped if you had, Max. Richard was a good, gentle man, brave as a lion, and losing him almost killed me. Nobody expects to be widow when you're young, even during wartime.' She sighed, adding bitterly, 'Although God knows there are enough widows younger than me in Germany these days.'

Although they were alone, Max reflexively looked over his shoulder. 'Careful what you say, Izzy. It isn't safe.'

Isolda shrugged indifferently, eyes unreadable. 'Don't worry, Max, I know I can speak my mind, I know I'm safe with you. Besides, Emmeline needs me so I'm very careful what I say in public.'

She smiled at him again, and dazzled, he tried not to stare at her in case she thought he was some sort of pervert, stupidly feeling like a clumsy fifteen-year-old schoolboy again, not a highly decorated and lauded *Oberst*. He wondered how on earth he had been arrogant enough to let a lovely girl like Isolda go.

What an idiot I've been!

She was amused. 'Have I got a cowpat on my face, Max?'

He flushed in embarrassment, awkwardly looking down at his pipe then back at her. 'Sorry, Izzy, was I staring?'

'Just a little bit.' She smiled wryly at him. 'You used to look at me like that before, once upon a time. As if I were something wonderful.'

'That's because you were.' He mentally kicked himself and hurriedly added, 'And still are.'

Impulsively, Max reached out and gently took her hand, half expecting her to pull away and slap his face, but she didn't and the touch was so familiar that memories flooded through him, the years in between suddenly blown away like dust. Strangely, he felt moisture in his eyes, 'Izzy. I've been a fool. I should have returned earlier and asked for your hand, after Spain, I mean. Can you forgive me?' He felt an overwhelming urge to weep for the squandered years, but sternly controlled himself. *Don't.*

She turned her face so it was hidden by her hair, her voice a whisper, forcing him to lean closer. 'I waited a long time for you to come back, Max. It hurt me when you didn't. It hurt me a lot.'

He cringed at the gentle remonstration, blinked his eyes to clear them. 'Forgive me? Please?'

She turned back, her eyes wet. 'I forgave you a long time ago, Max. God tells us to forgive, and it must be more so for the ones we love.'

The ones we love? His heart soared but he kept his voice even. 'Might you grant me a chance to make amends? Please Izzy? May I call on you?'

She didn't answer him, but neither did she pull her hand away, instead asking, 'Do you still whistle your magic to the cows, Max?'

He was surprised. 'You remember that?'

'Of course I do! They used to come running when you began to whistle. I used to tease you that it wouldn't work on me.'

He grinned, enjoying the feel of her hand in his. 'It doesn't work on them anymore, either.' He took a deep breath and whistled, a long, ululating sound.

None of the cows scattered across the field reacted, although one did twitch up a tail to release a thick jet of steaming urine onto the grass.

Inwardly, he grimaced. *Oh dear, not very romantic ...*

She smiled her gentle smile, beautiful eyes mesmerising, and gently squeezed his hand. 'Come for dinner tomorrow with little Emmeline and myself? We can talk about the way things once were?'

He felt an overwhelming wave of emotion, but kept his voice calm. 'Sounds lovely, Izzy.' Then, humbly, 'Thank you.'

He looked back towards the house. 'May I offer you my arm, Izzy? They must have finished off with the *Spitzwecken* caper, though how they found a three-metre-long cake at this stage of the war confounds me! Shall we go back?'

'Only if you promise me the first dance!'

'An easy demand to satisfy. And if anyone else dare ask you to dance thereafter, it'll be a matter to be determined with duelling pistols!'

She giggled and slipped her arm through his, her light touch and scent heady.

And suddenly, having resigned himself to dying for Germany before the end of all of this madness, Max had an overwhelming reason to live.

Chapter 25

With the *Jagdwaffe* mortally injured by *Bodenplatte*, enemy air activity diminished but fighter cover was still a necessity for Allied ground-attack aircraft, for the enemy continued to mount an aerial defence, mainly with 262s and Dora-9s whenever possible, but with greatly reduced numbers and far patchier than before.

Rose had seen from a distance the incredible acceleration of a Me163 *Komet* as it speared through the sky like something from one of Sheep's science fiction comics (with his Aussie friend's frustrated profanities turning the air blue in Rose's earphones as his Sheep pushed his Tempest through the gate at emergency boost yet still unable to catch the tiny arrowhead climbing impossibly fast).

Rose scoured intelligence reports in the evenings after dinner for more such unpleasant surprises, aware that the Germans were devising new weapons.

But with the terrible losses of so many fighters and pilots on New Year's Day, and with much of Germany's industrial infrastructure destroyed, fuel shortages, inexperienced aircrews and the effects of sabotage in their factories, the Luftwaffe were effectively a spent force.

Nonetheless he learned as much as he could about new jets such as the Bachem Ba349 and the He162, or the peculiar Do335 with its distinctive push-pull arrangement, and also learned the terrifying development of ground-to-air anti-aircraft missiles.

But while a part of him wondered about the possible threats they may face, the Allies still had to worry about the current threats by the Me262s.

At sunrise and sunset one would often streak along at low level and at almost 600 mph in a reconnaissance sortie and to occasionally drop a bomb or two, while sometimes a larger formation would *blitz* Allied positions.

Waiting on the runway and all set to go, the readiness pair had in the past often been too slow in catching a marauding jet, there being too little time to intercept them, but luck played a part and even the AA Bofors boys at Volkel had had their fair share.

Usually unable to track the fast-moving 262s in their gunsights, one had chosen to bomb at just the wrong moment as gunners practising on the eastern perimeter had been facing the right direction and were perfectly aligned with its strike run approach. A handful of 40 mm shells were all it took to blow the 262 and its luckless pilot apart.

The popular Richard Brooker (better known as Peter Brooker) took over 122 Wing in January, and together with 2TAF's senior fighter controller at Kenway, Wing Commander John Lapsley, new tactics were devised to try and kill the intruding jets.

In future, two pairs of fighters (the first as the anti-jet countermeasure pair and the second pair the fighters for Volkel's aerial defence) would be at immediate readiness with their pilots already strapped in their cockpits.

As soon as a jet was picked up on radar, Kenway would issue an immediate scramble alert for the anti-jet Tempest pair.

The Tempest pair would not try and intercept the interloper, but rather, would make straight for Rheine, arriving less than ten minutes after their scramble take-off and patrolling at height over the approach path to the German airbase, ready for the 262 intruder's return, while it was vulnerable, slow and with its undercarriage down, unable to manoeuvre.

The results were dramatic, enough to keep Max up at night until he and his veterans conceived a countermeasure to respond to the Lapsley-Brooker Move (aka the 'Rat Scramble'). Although it was 122 Wing's thing, Brooker spoke to Rose and generously invited 63's leaders to take part.

Having shot down a 262 over Eindhoven on New Year's Day already, Rose had achieved his jet kill, and not really liking the idea of being strapped into Sugar at readiness for hours on end and then stooging around over Rheine, he left the glory to his eager squadron commanders, both of whom managed to kill a 262 on their sorties.

For Sheep, it was his second jet kill, his first victory scored on 11 December when they had bounced the 262 formation close to Rheine, and now he joined the (very, very) small group of elite Allied fighter pilots who had achieved two jet kills.

Max's response required 262s to return to Rheine at full throttle and very low level, to merge into the ground until the very last minute so patrolling Tempests had little or no time to get into position, by which time the bandits were in Rheine's heavily defended approach path, a path five miles long and on either side of which were sited more than 150 *Flakvierling* quadruple 20 mm which would create such a thick defensive umbrella of protection that it accounted for seven Tempests which strayed into it in the first week. Once safe in the flak lane, the jets could be slowed and wheels lowered for landing.

With these sudden losses, Allied pilots were ordered to stay well clear of Rheine's defensive envelope, and things returned to the way they had been before.

Rose suggested to HQ 2TAF that two radar sets be placed close to the frontline, in the lowlands to the north and south of a line drawn between Volkel and Rheine, in the hope that the incoming jets might be detected earlier.

Unfortunately Rose's bright idea meant the system operators and equipment would be vulnerable to enemy attack, and so the precious sets remained where they were.

Since the late summer of 1944, the Allies in the West had been campaigning against the defensive fortifications known as the *Westwall* (but better known to the British as the Siegfried Line), extending along the western German border from the Netherlands as far south as Switzerland.

In 1939, the lyricist Captain Jimmy Kennedy had written 'We're Going to Hang out the Washing on the Siegfried Line', and it had become an extremely popular song, often added to and even parodied by the enemy. But to hang out the Allied washing, first the *Westwall* would have to be taken.

Between August 1944 and March 1945 (interrupted temporarily by the Battle of the Bulge) the Allies conducted a series of short offensives against the Siegfried Line, sequential operations gradually hammering down the German ramparts in the early months of 1945.

The capture of Remagen's *Ludendorff* Bridge relatively intact allowed 9th US Armoured Division to battle across and generate the all-important Bridgehead to the eastern banks of the Rhine.

For ten days after its capture, the Germans threw everything they could at destroying the bridge, including Arado jet bombers, V2s and combat frogmen, but each time they failed.

Sheep was flying high cover (mainly due to the fact that although they had been recognised as 'friendlies' and the black and white ID stripes on the undersides were clearly visible from below, the twitchy gunners continued to fire on them sporadically) on one of the days the jets came. Warned of the approach by Kenway, Sheep immediately turned his two sections after the six Arados when a 'bastard great horde' of 262s and Ta152s burst out of cloud.

With 40 mm streaming up from below and bandits falling on them from above, Sheep was forced to do the only thing he could do, give up the stern chase on the Arados and scatter. He kept his finger on the gun button as he turned into the swarm, hoping to hit *something* and in return got a cannon shell through one wing which passed straight through without exploding. In the chaos he managed to score a slew of hits on a 262 and a Ta152, though he lost sight of the bandits.

There had been so many of them that the bandits were getting in each other's way as they tried to shoot at the startled Tempests, although Micky later confessed to Rose that he had been so busy trying to get out of the way of the descending Jerry fighter juggernaut that he hadn't fired a single shot and could not believe that he hadn't actually collided with one of the enemy.

The boy was still shaking as Rose handed him a beer.

Fortunately, the bridge was still there as the last of the enemy streaked away back into cloud, as were all of Sheep's Tempests.

In the ten days before the weakened bridge finally failed, the Allies had built a Pontoon, Steel Treadway and Bailey bridges, getting six divisions across before the Allied break out.

Rose, his men and their machines were worn out as the pace of operations increased with the start of the campaign to take western Germany, the airfield crowded with Tempests, Typhoons and Spitfires, and such was the chaos, both on the ground at Volkel and in the air above it, that Rose half joked with Brooker that they should change the name of the airfield from Volkel to Bedlam.

How there were no collisions when taxiing or when flying in the circuit was a mystery (and as Sheep marvelled, 'a ruddy miracle').

During this time, Rose's 63 Wing formed a part of the air defence shield and continued to provide fighter cover for the ground-attack boys, but with the German skies belonging to the Allies and Luftwaffe airbases daily bombed or strafed and Luftwaffe sorties dwindling, there was negligible resistance.

More often than not Rose's pilots were reduced to the role of passive observers as the Tiffies blasted the enemy ground forces, usually with little or no flak. Familiar with the ground-attack experience, Rose would watch (while keeping one eye in the mirror) as the cab ranks of Typhoons would peel off one by one to bombard the battered Nazi defences again and again, remembering his own forays into the heart of the flak.

Rose's Tempests were also involved in providing fighter cover for Operation Varsity, the largest paratroop drop in a day in one place, with thousands of aircraft and more than a thousand gliders used to deliver the British 6th Airborne Division and US 17th Airborne Division into ten landing zones, seven for the 6th and three for the 17th.

The operation, while hugely successful, was a nightmare for those involved.

Not present at Arnhem, Rose was awed by the sight, clouds of parachutes dropping earthwards amidst a veritable cauldron of flak of all calibres, aircraft exploding even as paratroopers streamed out of them, burning and exploding aircraft falling in flames, cutting their way through parachutes in some cases or collapsing them and setting the canopies of others alight, white parachutes, dark smears of smoke and bright flames.

A Stirling Tug reared up as it was hit, losing airspeed as the first of its crew bailed out, the glider pilot having the presence of mind to release the cable and brave the turmoil as its tug fell out of control, other gliders disintegrating as their precious cargo scattered like swirling chaff behind them and still more crumpling into high ground or ripping through power lines in flashes of shockingly bright bluish white light.

Ranks of Rockphoons danced their deadly dance with the flak positions below, the familiar tilt over into a dive, the smoke trails of rockets lancing out at the guns as the Typhoon pulled up and out, fists involuntarily clenching as the flak took off a Tiffie's wing and it scraped a searing bubble of bright flame across the ground.

It was a glorious yet terrible sight as fire and smoke and blood rent the air over Wesel and Hamminkeln.

With the Bridgehead secured and now protected with a barricade zone of captured land and thousands of protective paratroopers, the Germans were forced to frantically divert troops into attacking the interlopers, taking pressure off the Bridgehead itself.

Spreading out across the enemy homeland, Allied forces pushed eastwards into the industrial heartland as great pincers closing from the north and south. The remnants of the German Army, sapped by the loss of the strategic reserves in the Battle of the Bulge, fought fiercely but to no avail.

The advances across Germany were rapid, but here and there the fight was harder, areas of intense resistance, such as in Leipzig where the AA defences were used to deadly effect against the men of the US 2nd Infantry Division before the flak guns were finally overcome.

With the war clearly and irretrievably lost, the enemy leaders allowed the continuing death of their people and the destruction of their land, culture and history by refusing to capitulate, and it seemed that some of the enemy were even entertaining the belief that the Allies might unite with what was left of the German armed forces to confront the looming Soviet juggernaut as it rolled ever closer to Berlin.

It was an insane and irrational belief, for with a long and detailed history of innumerable and unbelievable horrors perpetrated by an inhuman regime, only total and unconditional surrender would do.

In his book, *Das Dritte Reich*, Arthur Moeller van den Bruck first coined the expression, '*Tausendjähriges Reich*', and taking rather a shine to the phrase, Hitler and the Nazis took it for their own.

This vaunted 'Thousand-Year Reich' lasted all of twelve years, and in those dozen years the Nazis managed to slaughter and brutalise many millions, taking genocide to an industrial scale, and in so doing, doomed Germany to the consequential bloody horrors to come.

Chapter 26

Gabby pushed his plate away. 'Your English digestion is a mystery.' He poked the greasy chunk of meat with disgust. 'It must be why you all wear the same sickly expression and are so feeble.' A flick of his eyes to Rose. *'Pardon, Commandant.'*

'Piss off, you cheeky beggar, I'm no Pommie bastard.' Sheep grunted in outrage through his mouthful, jaws working manfully and a quick nod of apology to his Wing Commander. 'Sorry, sir.' Not sounding in the least apologetic.

'Hmm.' Rose grunted in reply, fearful that if he opened his mouth the tough meat might escape. The kitchen staff had managed to appropriate a batch of *Wehrmacht* tinned meat rations, and the gristly thing in his mouth was resisting his molars staunchly; he gave up the fight, swallowing the rubbery lump with a grimace, *uck*. 'What do you mean, Gabby?'

Oh Lor', it felt as if the bloody thing had lodged in his throat. Rose took a sip of tea (*hot and sweet—mmm!*).

Gabby sniffed. 'You English appear permanently ailing and bilious. This I know for I have seen it, and so I eat little of your grey, vulgar fare.'

The knob of meat was pressing against his windpipe. *Get down you*

347

beast. Swallowing vainly, he took another sip to push the damned thing down. 'Gabby, you've been in Blighty eating the food for years, you must have eaten something you liked, surely?' He thought wistfully of Molly's exquisite cooking and swallowed again.

'Like? Nothing. The English food is dry and drab. What else can the people be who consume it? Dry and drab. Like the dried turd of the camel.' He speared a wretched looking piece of the meat. 'The diet *Francais* is eminently more refined than this putrid waste.'

Rose felt he should make a stand, saying mildly, 'This is Jerry rations, Gabby, not English at all.'

'Pah! English, German, it matters not. It is not French!' Gabby had mopped up the sauce and vegetables with a hunk of bread, but the remaining pieces of his processed meat were huddled together protectively on one side of the plate. The piece on the end of the prongs of his fork joined them, and Gabby finished the last of his bread with the smear of sauce which had been beneath the chunk of meat.

Dear Lord, give me strength. Rose looked at his plate of *Rindfleisch* stew and wondered if his teeth and jaws might survive the encounter. He rather doubted it. It looked nice and was quite tasty, but chewing the bloody stuff was quite another matter …

'More refined?' he asked. Another sip as the lump lodged further down, and he wondered if he should ask one of his friends to give him a back-slap or two to dislodge the wretched thing.

Chewing vigorously Sheep shook his head mournfully. 'God save us. Now you're for it, sir. If you want to save yourself a bit of earache, I'd stick a bit of bread in your ears.'

Gabby purloined a crust of bread from Sheep's plate. '*Regardez,* sir, for you this is bread, but you are one whose palate is destroyed by the fare *Anglais;* however, for one such as I it is little better than dirty cardboard. The bread *Francais*, she is beautiful and flavoursome, you understand, *non*? *Et fromage Francais! Mon Dieu!* But how I desire the real cheese! *Fromage Anglais?* Pah! It is like the wax! Like the dirty earwax of an unwashed old man! *Uck! Pthoo!* I feel to vomit!'

Rose, rather partial to a piece of Wensleydale or Stilton, was taken aback and blinked at the Frenchman's ferocity. He'd always found French cheese rather tasty (if a touch whiffy). 'I say, Gabby, old chap, steady on! That's hardly fair!' He glanced across to Sheep.

The Australian seemed to be winning the struggle with the chewy meat. 'I'm an Aussie, so don't look at me for support, sir. Personally, I like a couple of slices of Kraft processed cheddar on my crackers, takes me back.' He swallowed mightily, swallowed again, then reached out, the knob of flesh defeated and ignominiously routed. 'Might I have my grub back, Gabs? Don't want you hogging it all, do we?' Sheep took the crust of bread from Gabby's fingers and popped it into his mouth, smirking at Rose as his chewing resumed.

'And the English *oignons*! *Zut!* So sharp and strong! So acidic! Filled with the poison! English poison!' Gabby's eyes rolled in emphasis, and Rose resisted the urge to laugh at the theatrics.

Still grinning, Sheep screeched in a high falsetto, '*Oh, merde! L'oignon toxique!*'

Gabby scowled darkly, casting the Australian a look of irritation, but continued his diatribe, warming to his theme. '*Mais oui! L'oignon toxique Anglais!* The killer of the sophisticated palate! Unlike the *oignon Francais!*' He closed his eyes in raptured imagination. 'Ah! Gentle and flavoursome, whimsical upon the lips, gentle and sweet like those of a woman!'

Sheep grimaced, making a face. 'Cripes, Gabs, you must have been sleeping with a right rough Sheila if she tasted of onions down below!'

The young Frenchman bristled. '*Putain de merde!* The soft lips of the mouth they are I speak of, *Toi stupide gros cochon*, not those of the *vagin!*'

Sheep tutted, winking at Rose. 'Coo! Fancy having a pash with an onion-breathed Sheila! You got some strange tastes, Gabs!' He smiled and gave Gabby a knowing look then winked at Rose. 'Perhaps Gab's *Mademoiselles* chew onions so they won't be able to taste his kisser when he slobbers at them!'

Chapter 27

The order had been unambiguous. Rose was to report immediately to his AOC at Eindhoven, and he was to bring both of his squadron commanders and Flying Officer Francois 'Frankie' Marais with him 'at his earliest convenience' (i.e. yesterday or the day before).

Frankie looked nervous, clutching Amélie tighter against his chest. 'I am in trouble, *Mon Commandant?*' Gabby sighed and Sheep grinned. Amélie had not been included in the summons, but she was with them nonetheless, and she stared at Rose accusingly.

Rose smiled reassuringly. 'I don't believe so, Frankie. I'm in as much of the dark as you are as to why we're here.' He looked at Amélie. *Look! I don't know, OK?*

Her eyes seemed to glitter. *Honestly, I really don't!*

They were shown into Air Vice Marshal Harry Broadhurst's outer office at Eindhoven and the AOC was standing at the door to his office, a thunderous expression on his face.

Uh-oh …

'Rose. Gentlemen. We'll speak in a moment.' He looked at Frankie, and Rose thought he saw compassion flicker. 'Frankie. Will you go in? There's a surprise for you in my office.' Broadie looked with disapproval at the doll stuffed into the young Frenchman's tunic. 'And I see you've brought, er, Amélie with you. Wonderful.' The last word sounded as if it was anything but.

'*Oui*, sir,' squeaked Frankie anxiously. Dear Frankie, brave as a lion, accomplished fighter pilot and first-rate wingman, but terrified witless of his AOC.

Broadhurst nodded grudgingly at them as he ushered Frankie into his office before closing the door, remaining in the outer office with them and sticking out his hand. As his sleeve rode up, Rose caught sight of a large purple bruise on his AOC's forearm, a legacy of the crash landing of his commandeered Storch at Evere just a few days earlier.

Thank God the old boy survived landing and then falling through the hangar roof, he thought. The 'old boy', who happened to be thirty-eight years old, gestured for them to take a seat.

Rose thought he heard a sharp cry (or was it a sob?) from behind the closed door but couldn't be sure.

'Sit down, gentlemen, do.' The great man rumbled, 'Once my aide is free we'll have a cup. Monty sent me a batch of top-notch Jerry coffee, none of that ersatz rubbish Jerry pour down their necks, but the real stuff.' Again the sound of something falling behind the AOC's office door, then silence, broken by the sound of hushed, tearful voices and weeping from within.

Concerned, Rose and Gabby were on their feet but Broadhurst waved them back. 'Don't worry, gentlemen, your young man is perfectly alright in there. I had some unexpected visitors this evening. I believe even De Gaulle was involved in getting them to me.'

He leaned forwards, addressing Rose. 'I had a word with the SOE people, just as you asked. And lo and behold! They found her! Starved and ragged and living in the forest with a bunch of cut-throat Maquis types, but alive and well.'

Rose felt a warm wave of relief and gladness as Gabby rose to his feet again. 'Found her? Who is it you speak of, sir?' A long look at the closed door. 'Her?' He gasped. '*Mais non*! Not … ?'

Sheep whistled in surprise. 'Hogan's ghost!'

Broadhurst's face crinkled into a smile. 'Yes indeed! They found Frankie's sister! Turns out Jerry were taking her back to barracks after killing her parents, and the blasted swine didn't treat her gently, either, the poor lamb, and her just a kid! You can imagine what would have happened back at the barracks.' His lips thinned with anger, and Rose thought of his own Amelie and thanked God she was at home safe.

Broadhurst's voice was gruff. 'Anyway, the convoy was ambushed and the resistance types rescued young Amélie. She couldn't go back, because it wasn't safe, couldn't leave word, and she's been involved with the Maquis since. Jerry had killed Amélie's parents in front of her, and not knowing where Frankie was or even if he was still alive, she stayed with the only people she had left.'

He sighed. 'Very brave young girl, by all accounts. Took part in ambushes and potted a few Jerry herself. One of the SOE liaison types had been parachuted in just before D-Day to work with the Maquis, and she remembered seeing a young girl who matched the details in your request for information. So she went back out there especially to look for her after we liberated France. Luckily, our agent found Amélie again, and the Air Ministry got in touch with the French Government and somehow De Gaulle heard of it, you know how the press is always looking for a story and they asked De Gaulle about it, and before you could say "blow me down with a feather", the girl and our agent were here on my ruddy doorstep without so much as a by your leave.'

Broadhurst looked keenly at Rose. 'Amélie's been through enough and lost too much already, poor girl. Young Frankie's the only one she's got left. I can't send him back with you, Rose. I'm sorry, Gabby, but I need to send him home. De Gaulle's making him an ADC to his DG's Chief of Staff. It'll give the youngsters a chance to comfort each other, God willing. I'm placing him on indefinite leave immediately, and he'll accompany our girl and Amélie back to Paris tonight.' He smiled, 'And Rose? I'm pleased to confirm your recommendation for the bar to Micky Lynch's and Frankie's DFCs have been approved. I've given our girl the letter of Frankie's award. Your other recommendations were also approved today. Should get the official confirmation in the next few days.'

He sat back and the seat creaked beneath him in protest. 'Gentlemen, I've a couple of things to add.'

It was quiet behind the door now, and Broadhurst stood suddenly, his knees popping. 'Right, they've had my office long enough and I've got a bloody war to fight, time to chuck 'em out.' But despite his grumbled words, he knocked gently on the door.

The door was opened by a diminutive WAAF, fair curls beneath her cap, an impish face and a wide smile for the AOC, the ribbons of the MBE, '39-'43 Star (with the oak leaf of a Mention in Despatches) and the Croix de Guerre avec palme on her chest.

So this is what an SOE agent looks like, thought Rose admiringly. Operating beneath the nose of the Nazis, the threat of betrayal, capture and brutal torture a very real threat every minute they were 'in the field'.

'I'm obliged, sir, for the kind use of your office, and for your hospitality. I'd like to return to Paris with Amélie and Francois straight away, if that's alright?'

Broadhurst nodded. 'Of course, Flight Officer. I've prepared travel documents for my officer and I believe he'll be joining the General's staff in Paris? Good. Thank you for finding Amélie, you've done us all a very great service. Take good care of him for me, will you?'

She nodded firmly and took his hand. 'I will, sir.'

'And you won't forget to give him the envelope?'

'As soon as we're on our way, sir, I promise.'

Behind her Frankie led his sister out, his eyes glistening with emotion. She was small and painfully thin. A pale, tear-stained face and large dark eyes, the resemblance to her brother clear.

Frankie looked dazed, emotions warring on his face. He had one arm around her shoulders and she gripped his waist tightly with both arms, the doll clutched in one hand.

The doll's eyes gazed emptily at Rose and he felt a peculiar regret that he might never see it again, his fingers resting against the teddy bear and pebble in his pocket.

So long, Amélie. Look after him.

'*Mon Commandant! C'est Amélie!*' Frankie's face was suffused with incredulity and joy when he saw them, and Rose was astonished by the huge difference in his faithful wingman.

The girl did not spare them a glance, her eyes fixed on the only person in the room who meant everything to her, a soft smile on her thin face and tears still trickling down her cheeks.

Rose squeezed the boy's shoulder. 'I'm so very glad for you, Frankie. I owe you my life, thank you. For flying with me and for looking after me. Time for you to look after Amélie, now. Send your details on to me when you get a chance, will you?' His throat felt ridiculously tight, *pull yourself together, man*! Distrusting his voice, he nodded with gratitude at the WAAF.

Sheep's voice was gruff, and he ruffled Frankie's hair. 'Look me up after this little lot is over, OK cobber?' He turned to the girl in blue, smiled charmingly and looked as if he were about to say something but felt the gimlet eye of his AOC pierce him and he closed his mouth again.

The girl smiled and gave Sheep a playful wink. 'Next time, Squadron Leader, eh?'

Gabby clicked his heels. *'Bonjour Amélie, un plaisir de vous rencontrer. Au revoir, François, mon brave.'* He said nothing more but instead reached out to put his arms around the pair of youngsters and he hugged them tightly for a long moment, and Frankie let out a sob, quickly extinguished.

Rose found that his eyes were smarting as Harry Broadhurst noisily cleared his throat. 'Gentleman, shall we?'

Rose led his men into Broadhurst's office, and once they were seated, the AOC leaned forwards, palms flat on the blotter on his desk. 'We'll cut to the chase, shall we? Tell me, what do you know of *Mistel?*'

They had all read the intelligence reports. In their continuing efforts to develop new and more dangerous weapons, the Germans had developed a bomb delivery system comprising a small, manned fighter detachably secured by supports to a larger unmanned aircraft filled with explosives. The Luftwaffe had accomplished varying degrees of success in attacks on both the eastern and western fronts with these weapons.

'A 190 piggybacked to a Junkers 88, sir.'

'That's right. Jerry's been strapping 190s or 109s to a bomb-filled unmanned 88, the fighter flies it to the target before separating and dropping the bomber. The unit that operates them, KG 200, has pretty much ceased to exist. The thing is, one of our agents in Germany sent back an urgent message. It seems that there's an operation involving *Mistels* to attack Paris, destroy the Eiffel Tower, the Champs Elysees and the Provisional Government of the Republic.'

Gabby's face was pale. 'When will it be, sir?'

'We don't know, Gabby,' Broadhurst responded grimly. 'The agent just mentioned the attack was meant to be soon. Jerry's using a new combination, a He162 jet fighter cobbled to an unmanned 262.'

Gabby groaned. '*Zut!* If they get into the air, we cannot chase them!'

Broadhurst's face was bleak. 'Quite so.' Then with a shrug, he said, 'but the He162 can't carry the 262 bomb on its own, not powerful enough with just the one, so it needs the 262's engines to help, and the *Mistel* will be slow while the Jumo's are spool up. Damned thing's likely to be bloody heavy too, which will be a pain for the Hun piggybacking. You'll have a window, Lord knows for how long, soon after I's taken off to catch it and bring it down.'

'But why do it now, sir?' growled Sheep. 'What good can it possibly do them at this stage of the war?'

'Perhaps they think that if they can kill De Gaulle the Allies will discuss terms? Perhaps they think we'll respond the same and if we do the German people will rise up *en masse*? Or maybe *Der Fuhrer* wants us to react a hundredfold and destroy what's left of the Fatherland? They aren't fighting to the last man, woman and child as he told them to, so perhaps he wants us to make it happen?'

Their AOC rubbed his face wearily. 'Who knows what goes through their twisted minds? All I do know is that he should surrender straight away, if only to save his people, but the criminal fool won't countenance it.' His eyes were drawn unwillingly to the envelope on his desk containing the latest casualty reports and Broadhurst hauled them away, back to his aghast officers.

Those evil fools in Berlin would rather see their own people blown apart by us than surrender and save them, and all the while we're fighting and haemorrhaging good men when we needn't …

Rose spoke quietly. 'How can we help, sir?'

'We make sure the buggers don't get into the air, of course! We don't know where they are, not exactly, Rose, but apparently the aircraft are going to be taking off from an autobahn near Bielefeld, they're being hidden somewhere in the Teutoburg Forest.'

Despite himself, Rose felt a shiver tremble through him at mention of the Teutoburg Forest, where in 9AD all-conquering Rome had lost three of its powerful legions. The disaster in the low forested hills to Arminius's alliance of tribes had ended all Emperor Augustus's ambitions of conquering Germania.

Was that why the Germans were using the forest now to assemble the attacking force, some kind of symbolism, perhaps?

'So that's where we hit 'em, sir?'

Broadhurst nodded. 'As we're speaking, the SAS have parachuted men into the forest. They're going to go hunting tonight, to try and blow up those jets in the darkness, but if they can't manage to get all of them, and if they survive the night, they'll mark the location of any surviving *Mistel* aircraft with red smoke at dawn. I want your lads up and over the forest by the time dawn breaks, Rose, and set up a rota for flights to be relieved. A Wing of Tiffies will be on readiness with bombs and rockets, and you'll be able to call on them to blow the site to Kingdom Come.'

'What if there's no smoke, sir?'

Broadhurst grimaced. 'If there's no smoke, the SAS will all be either dead or captured, God forbid, and we'll have to assume they didn't get all of them and you're to maintain a continuous aerial watch. Gabby's lads will maintain constant cover in case one or more of the *Mistels* manage to get off. If they manage to evade you, Gabby, Sheep's lads will maintain a defensive picket line just across the border. Eighth AF will be conducting fighter sweeps so what's left of the Luftwaffe will be keeping its head down, and there'll be additional fighter patrols nearer Paris.'

'My senior Intelligence Officer is waiting to see you with all the details you need. Any questions? No? Then gentlemen, I wish you Godspeed and good hunting.'

Chapter 28

In the grey light of predawn, the forest was a deep grey, not enough light to show the green of the trees, and there was no sign of red smoke.

No red smoke whatsoever, but still they knew exactly where to go, for there was a thick pall of heavy oily smoke rising sluggishly above a stretch of burning forest, where the flickering flames brought colour to a patch of its surrounding trees, visible even as the eight Tempests picked their way around the northern border of the Ruhr's flak belt, Dortmund to the south and Munster north of them, dark patches in the patchwork of grey below.

A distant rash of heavy AA bursts speckling the lightening sky as a diehard showed his defiance before being cuffed by his NCO for calling unnecessary attention.

But the Tempests were not interested; they had bigger fish to fry.

Rose had eyes only for the flames burning bright in the heart of the forest, a conflagration from fuel and explosive.

The men of the SAS had succeeded in finding the *Mistels*!

Parachuted in and surrounded by the enemy, at least one of the teams had found their prey and done serious damage to the hidden enemy while also providing 63 Wing with a guiding beacon.

In his earphones he heard Gabby's urgent request for the Tiffies to be scrambled. There would be enough light soon for them to lay down a carpet of destruction.

Were the ghosts of Varus and his men still haunting that low ridge of hills, gloating in the destruction wrought on the descendants of the tribes which had slaughtered his men on that awful autumn day of bloodletting and horror? Despite the warmth of Sugar's cockpit, Rose shivered.

'Hotspur Leader! *Regardez vers le sud!* Look south, five miles, two o'clock above!' The urgent shout was Alex de Rond, his new wingman following Frankie's sudden departure.

Sure enough, a trio of slow moving orange lights, unlike the few faded stars sprinkled in the westwards well of night. *Lord God above! Had three of the enemy launched?* Then childishly, *they're early!*

Of course they would have launched as soon as they could, knowing that the operation had been discovered.

De Rond's Tempest, P-Pimpernel had broken formation and was already belting at full throttle after the lights, knowing that a second's hesitation might cost the lives of hundreds of his countryfolk and the loss of irreplaceable history.

Kick rudder and stick back hard against his right thigh, and Rose was hauling her around desperately in pursuit, breathing hard and heart thumping madly as he thumped the throttle lever forwards, three lights!

Was it three composite pairs or just one? *Merciful God, if those were the Mistels, how would they catch them?*

'Marengo Leader, detach one pair to maintain patrol over target and stop any more taking off, Hotspur Section with me!'

His only hope was that the damned composite configuration of He162 and 262 was slower than its individual parts, unwieldy, and that the Jumo engines of the 262 bomb would take as long as a normal 262 to get the turbojets spooled up.

If I'm wrong, our goose is well and truly cooked. He looked at her picture. *I hope I'm right, please God.*

Gabby, '*Mon Dieu! Marengo trois et quatre, Restez ici et abattez tous les autres qui pourraient décoller!*' Leaving Marengo Three and Four to patrol above the forest and shoot down any other *Mistels* attempting to take off, Gabby turned with his wingman after the fleeing German composite bomber.

Rose's six Tempests were stretched out into a straggling line as the sun's first rays burnished their sides bronze and gold, all semblance of formation lost, thundering frantically after the enemy.

De Rond was pulling his fighter into a climb, surging ahead as he pushed her throttle through the gate, and the bright orange dots remained together in an oddly triangular fashion, the fuselages and surfaces of the two aircraft clearer now as the Tempests grew closer.

The bastards had only managed to successfully launch a single *Mistel!* It might mean that there were still others on the round, but Rose doubted it. Jerry would have launched all their aircraft in a single wave to ensure some would break through. All or nothing.

The feeling of relief was instantly quenched, for a single *Mistel* could still manage a catastrophic amount of damage in the heart of Paris; just one to create hundreds of orphans and destroy centuries of history and culture.

It seemed that the enemy pilot must still be in one of the most dangerous phases of his sortie for the *Mistel* was not surging away as expected, and now De Rond was tipping his Tempest's nose down and descending hard after the enemy at full throttle, desperate to catch up with the composite bomber, short banners of grey smoke streaming back over the wings as she spat out a couple of short bursts of cannon fire, the rounds falling agonisingly short and De Rond's Tempest losing vital headway as recoil snatched her back.

Rose was about to warn De Rond of the danger of getting too close (the memory of watching Jacko successfully nurse home a badly damaged fighter after pursuing a V1 closer than he ought to have when he blew it up), but then stopped.

De Rond knew what was stake and did not need to be told to be careful, for to show hesitancy now might be just enough to allow the enemy to succeed in destroying a piece of the city that his lost love had adored.

There was too much at stake for caution.

De Rond's Tempest was closing with the *Mistel,* the smoke from the jet engines thicker now as the composite bomber began to surge upwards, and Rose despaired even as there was a shout over the R/T. 'Bandits, bandits, two pairs, line astern, eleven o'clock high, two miles!'

Rose cringed. *Merciful God, where had they come from?*

De Rond's fighter was trailing a thread of smoke and losing ground now, Pimpernel's Sabre strained beyond limits, and it would only be seconds before it might seize, tendrils of smoke streaming back once more from Pimpernel's wings, and shell cases cascading as he opened fire again, a long, despairing burst.

He could see the bandits and knew he could not catch the composite bomber, and he hauled Sugar around in a tight turn, gasping as the pressure against his chest worsened, the harness digging painfully into his shoulders and petrified that Sugar's Sabre would cut out as he jerked her around, panting, 'Hotspur three with me, Marengo section continue pursuit.' If De Rond managed to damage Jerry at least, the others might still get it.

Two glistered shapes closing fast, another pair trailing by a mile, shapes not coming in directly at him as they bored in to their port, trying to stop De Rond's attempts to down the composite bomber; Rose eased Sugar to starboard to allow for deflection and lead the foremost enemy fighter, an FW190 he could see now as the distance diminished shockingly fast, the brightness of the rising sun stabbing painfully at his squinting eyes.

Rose squeezed the button and she trembled, trails of cannon shells reaching out and the image of the enemy fighter shimmered, a single flash on her empennage and a second on her tailplane, and then she had passed beyond Sugar's nose.

He was trying to drop her nose now to flail at the enemy wingman, looming fast, a yellow and olive-green blur less than a hundred and fifty yards as he pressed out a swathe of 20 mm, the hurried burst of cannon shells coiling away uselessly beneath the enemy fighter (*Damn it! Missed!*), as it too vanished beneath Sugar's nose.

They would go after De Rond and he dismissed them for the moment, for the rest of Marengo would have to deal now with the first 190 pair.

Rose felt the anguish of despair, knowing he could not turn after them, he had to continue east for the trailing second pair were closing fast, and these ones had their noses unerringly centred on him.

With what was left of his flight raggedly spread out and still in pursuit of the *Mistel*, Hotspur Three would likely get a decent shot at the bandits, approaching from their port forward quarter, but Rose would be there at the centre of their attention, and he was about to fire another burst to distract and discourage the approaching Dora-9s when there was a intensely bright flash of light from behind, bathing the sky and forest below eerily in a flash of brilliance.

What ... ?

And then the expanding blast wave of the exploding *Mistel* clawed at Sugar, tossing her upwards and onto her side and he gripped her, conscious of a dark shape (one of the enemy fighters from the second formation?) horrifyingly close, banking to his starboard side as Sugar lurched beneath the buffeting pressures of the blast-waves, first from the composite bomber violently blowing apart as De Rond's shells set off the huge bomb, then its weaker reflected wave of pressure rebounding from the ground, the sound of the explosion like a sullen rumble of thunder, felt and heard over the sound of Sugar's Sabre.

Feeling her about to yaw and fearful of a stall, with a little rudder Rose let her slip to one side before he levelled her wings and eased back on the throttle, neck twisting this way and that as he sought to make sense of what was happening around him.

Behind him there was a massive cloud of smoke hanging heavy in the air, all that now remained of the composite bomber, a multitude of pieces of debris and glowing embers streaming brightly earthwards dragging tendrils of smoke down after them.

Two 190Ds were fleeing in the distance, one burning and dragging grey smoke after it, Gabby and his number two in hot pursuit, another a thousand feet higher and banking shakily around towards Sugar, the fourth about a mile and a half away, sweeping upwards in a gentle turn to starboard.

Of Hotspur Three there was no sign.

Close to the ground, a burning torch tumbling beneath an expanding column of oily black smoke, Pimpernel's wreckage, a coffin for De Rond's earthly remains.

Somehow, as the 190s had charged at them, De Rond had hit

something vital in the composite bomber causing their mutual destruction, and in so doing, saved his wife's beloved city from one last Nazi horror.

There was no parachute, and Rose knew that the lonely Frenchman was at last reunited with his beloved once more.

He felt angry tears but knew this was no time for sorrow, there were still two more of the enemy to fight, no friendlies close enough to help, and he had to hit them while they were still separate. His men over the forest may come to help but they needed to remain on guard, and so he keyed his microphone. 'Marengo three and four, hold position, look out for bandits.' There may be more 190s coming …

Jerry must not be allowed to launch a second *Mistel*, even though it left Rose facing two bandits with dogfighting characteristics similar to Sugar.

Marengo Three: '*Oui,* received, Hotspur Leader.'

He pulled the stick back and to one side, pitching her up into a climb to starboard, closing with the nearer bandit, and the enemy tightened his own turn, seeing that Rose would have him in Sugar's sights before he could bring his 190's guns to bear.

The range closed in a flash and the bandit was still turning at an angle of fifteen degrees to Sugar's line of flight, still diving and now about three hundred feet in front of him.

Rose fired off a quick burst, allowing around half a ring of deflection in his gunsight, and he was rewarded with the flash of strikes along the starboard side of the bandit's fuselage and a single flash of flame, rolling Sugar smoothly to one side at the same time to allow for clearance.

The bandit returned fire, rippling flashes more hopeful than aimed, but it was still turning and not lined up properly and its return fire hosed away below and to starboard of Sugar.

The 190D's performance was better in the climb but worse than Sugar in the dive otherwise they were reasonably evenly matched, but with the second 190D barrelling in, Rose could not pursue the one he had just wounded. There was a danger that the pilot in the bandit he had just winged might yet twist his bird into a sharp aileron climbing turn to get onto *his* tail, that dangerous party trick the FW190 possessed due to its high rate of roll and aileron responsiveness, but with another FW190D attacking, Rose dared not reverse after the first to give chase.

Instead he quickly eased Sugar to port with stick and rudder, in towards the oncoming threat, centring the fast-approaching shape in the gunsight to minimise his profile to the German pilot, and ripped off a second's burst of cannon, and to his surprise saw the 190 aileron roll to starboard, his 20 mm streaming uselessly through the space where the bandit had once been. The bandit had gambled that performing a sharp aileron reversal he would be able to perch himself close behind Rose as Sugar thundered past.

Rose's response was automatic, years of experience taking over. With Jerry reversing into a clockwise turn to straighten, he would begin to level out in anticipation of Sugar continuing in a straight line for some distance to open up their separation before turning back to re-enter the fight. This would allow Jerry to come out of the turn close behind Sugar at Rose's six o'clock.

However, Rose now wrenched Sugar hard over into a turn to starboard, feeling the greying at the peripheries of his vision and the pressure forcing the air out of him, the situation not helped as a blob of oil flew back from seepage to smear messily across his windscreen.

In the corner of his eye he caught sight of the first 190D, still heading down, and was surprised to see that its canopy cover had been released and the enemy pilot had already climbed out, the dun-yellow of his deployed parachute stark above the rich sunlit green of the forest below.

Oh dear Merciful Lord, thank you! he thought gratefully; at least that was one less to worry about and this thing was just between Sugar and the second 190D now.

In the turn the Tempest and the 190D were very similar, but the former had the edge overall, the poor quality of the German aviation fuel a significant hindrance.

The second bandit, surprised by Rose's anticipatory break to starboard had decided instinctively to turn after him, but Rose was already so far around the perimeter of his turn that his slight superiority in speed with full revolutions and boost allowed him to close the gap rapidly.

Below them the first 190D hit the ground in a bright flash, a billowing globe of fire and smoke marking Rose's victory.

But Rose was not watching, he was fighting, for as soon as he had closed enough with the second 190D to try a shot, the enemy pilot closed his throttle, the reduction in velocity allowing him a sharp turn and causing Rose to shoot past.

Immediately, despite knowing that Rose could out-dive him, the enemy pilot pushed his fighter into a dive away, but Rose corrected quickly enough to come down after him so that the German pulled his 190 back into a climb, using his initial superiority in the climb to pull away before turning back into the turning circle before Rose could draw a bead on him.

Three more times Rose closed the distance inside the arena of their shared personal turning circle, an arena marked recurrently by the sharp lines of condensation from their wingtip contrails, and each time, knowing there was no sanctuary in a climb or a dive, the German pilot would slip back into their battle circle to begin the whole thing again.

Behind the controls, both men were straining, feeling the forces draining them, their muscles and frames aching, lungs burning and eyes stinging, sweat-soaked and sucking at the oxygen masks pressing painfully onto their faces, bodies weakening with strain and fatigue.

It had turned into a grim contest of stamina. Each time the 190 pilot anticipated his overshoot to turn back into the circle but each time his burst of fire skidded away out of their turn, the German fighting to hold his fighter out of the incipient stall and unable to allow for correct deflection, and there was little risk to Rose and his superbly performing Sugar.

Despite the pressure and the wicked thumping of his heart there was no fear or anxiety, just the exhilarating madness of battle whistling through him.

And then there was the blur of more aircraft above the turn and Rose's hurried glance showed that the Tempests of Gabby and his wingman had returned and were above his solitary battle with the German pilot.

Knowing that there was no future in the continuing turn, fuel running low and more RAF fighters above, the 190D *Langnase* pilot waited for Rose to close again, closed throttle and turned away, then pushed his fighter into another dive at full throttle, unable to climb with the two Tempests waiting for such a move.

Quick as a flash Rose half-rolled after him, cutting the enemy's lead quickly, closing rapidly from almost directly astern, and he opened fire with minimal deflection, reducing throttle to hold Sugar in position behind the long-nosed bandit.

As Sugar's cannon spat, the 190D started to jink desperately, the enemy pilot kicking rudder to port, starboard and back again, moving the stick back and forth and side to side as he desperately tried to evade Rose's short bursts, while behind him Rose fought to hold Sugar steady in the turmoil of the 190's slipstream.

A plethora of flashes on the starboard wing, another just behind the cockpit, blowing off the aerial and shattering the long teardrop canopy so that fragments of metal and Perspex billowed back in the enemy slipstream, shorter-lived flickers as Sugar's propeller smashed some of them into oblivion.

The 190D suddenly hauled back the stick and the fighter jerked upwards back into level flight, Rose bringing up her nose quickly to spray the bandit, but then he stayed his thumb, for the enemy pilot had released his harness and was stepping from the cockpit as the starboard wing began to dip.

The enemy's cockpit armour had protected him from the 20 mm impacts which had smashed his wing and torn off his aerial, but Rose could see blood on the man's tunic, probably from the shattering of his canopy.

The German looked across to Rose as he slipped Sugar to one side to allow clearance between them, and their eyes met for a moment, the German raising a hand briefly in salute before stepping from the wing, a piece of the wing's surface following him a second later.

As the German's parachute streamed open, the stricken 190D, flown so well by a man who had achieved *Experten* status years earlier, slipped inverted and fell to earth, a thin trail of grey smoke forming a dispersing arc behind.

It was Rose's final victory of the war.

In the distance, bright flashes in the forest and RP-9 trails showed that the Typhoon Wing on standby had arrived and had begun to lay down rockets where the two remaining Tempests of Marengo flight had seen a flash of metal, the autobahn alongside the area bearing scorched lines where jets had landed, and where one had taken off on its failed mission.

Twice the rockets set off a massive explosion which blew trees and soil high into the air as the remaining (but abandoned, unbeknownst to them) *Mistels* were destroyed. There was no flak but one of the Typhoons set off an explosion from a hidden *Mistel* and was clawed from the sky by the violence of the blast, auguring into the forest, the final Allied casualty of a plan designed to kill hundreds and deny culture and history to future generations.

With a large section of the forest burning and covered by an expanding cloud of heavy grey-black smoke as the final rockets were laid down, Rose led the five remaining Tempests of his flight back to Volkel, leaving the haunted forest to welcome its newcomers.

He thought again of De Rond, whose desperate single-mindedness and sacrifice had destroyed the one *Mistel* successfully launched, and remembered lines from Annette De Rond's favourite book, *A Tale of Two Cities*.

It is a far, far better thing that I do, than I have ever done; it is a far, far better rest that I go to than I have ever known.

Lines such as these should be written for De Rond, and he promised himself that he would ensure the lonely Frenchman's ultimate sacrifice would be known, feeling the heaviness of his wingman's loss, and sorrow filling his eyes.

Rose looked at her picture, his companion in so many sorties yet her smile had not faded and still enchanting, and he reached out to touch the photograph.

Still here, my love.

Pulling up his goggles, Rose cuffed the tears away, and offered up thanks for their success.

Lord my God, thank you for our success and for my life, and for allowing me to keep your precious gift of it this day when I might so easily not have. Thank you.

Pulling down his goggles, Max watched the departing Tempests snarl into the distance where the forest was burning, the flames livid, and gave thanks the RAF pilots had chosen not to machine gun him as he descended.

So many of his friends had died in that manner, but he had not shared their fate, and once again, he had survived.

Lucky Max.

Once his luck had seemed like a curse as his *kamerad* were killed in action one by one, leaving him alone time after time, but now he was grateful for that luck, for there was much to live for; he closed his eyes for a moment, recalling Izzy's beautiful smile, her eyes heavy with happiness and those thick tresses glowing pure gold against the pillow in the early morning light.

He felt the pieces of Perspex in his cheek gingerly, the once-warm rivulets of blood now cold on his face, and offered a silent prayer for his salvation when, with a well-flown Tempest on his tail and two more waiting to jump him, he had believed himself dead.

Danke, allmächtiger Gott, für mein Heil, gib mir das Leben, damit ich mich meiner Liebe erfreuen kann.

Words whispered with the joy of salvation, heartfelt gratitude and hope for what might be, *Thank you, Almighty God, for my salvation, give me life so that I can enjoy my love.*

* * *

63 Wing's reward for their contribution to the success over the Teutoburg Forest was to be its immediate disbandment.

Broadhurst flew to Volkel from Eindhoven in his own personal Spitfire a couple of hours after their return to base.

Clad in his characteristic spotless white 'Prestige' flying suit, shoulder flaps heavy with rank braid, the AOC shut himself in with Rose and his two squadron commanders in 63's Operations caravan.

'It was already on the cards, I'm afraid,' he explained apologetically. 'De Gaulle wants his men back. He says they've done enough over the last few years, and as veterans flying one of the best fighters we have, he wants them to be the core of France's post-war fighter force, and Winnie's agreed. I'm sorry Gabby, but you and your lads are to re-muster at *Saint-Dizier* airbase. There are USAAF units there at the moment, but they're to vacate the airfield in the next week or so. You will retain your Tempests for the time being, but they're to keep their RAF markings.'

Gabby's eyes were dark with fatigue and emotion. '*Oui, monsieur.*'

The AOC turned to Sheep. 'Australia House are keen to get your boys back, too, Sheep. They want you and your lads involved in the coming Invasion of Japan. You're to form and command a RAAF fighter wing in preparation for Ops in the east.'

'Tempests, sir?'

'Spitfires.'

Sheep looked as if he had lost a shilling but found sixpence. 'Wing Commander, eh?'

'General De Gaulle will be meeting with Winnie in London next week, Rose, and there will be a French medal presentation for you and your men in Downing Street. I submitted a list of recommendations, as I mentioned last night, and I'm pleased to say they have been approved in full.'

Broadie's face crinkled into his pugnacious smile. 'Harry, you're to receive a second bar to your DSO and another Mention in Despatches for a job well done. There's a DSO for each of you as well, Gabby, Sheep, very well deserved, I must say, you both worked quite splendidly together and I'll be very sorry to bid you farewell.' He sniffed, 'Though a little bird advises me there's a silver lining, and it's rather likely that I shan't be losing any more biscuits.'

He gave Rose's stunned deputies a hard stare.

Rose could sense the discomfort of his friends as they tried not to squirm, and he tried not to smile.

The AOC let them stew for a long minute, then pulled a piece of paper from his pocket and waved it at them. 'And another thing, Queen Wilhelmina of the Netherlands was intrigued to hear about my composite Australian and Free French fighter wing, and she's awarded you each The Bronze Lion. I'm sure someone from the Dutch government will be in touch to make the necessary arrangements to pin the medals onto your manly chests.'

He shook his head apologetically. 'I'm just sorry that you won't be here for the final curtain,' the AOC muttered heavily. 'You've all earned the right to see Berlin.'

I'm not sorry, Rose thought fervently, trying to look disappointed. *You're more than welcome to it. I'd much rather be with Moll and my babies.*

Rose's men were crowding the entrance to the caravan, and now Broadhurst turned his face to them, raising his voice to a quiet bellow and almost deafening Rose. 'Chaps, thank you for being a part of 2TAF. I'm grateful for your courage and your sacrifices, it's been an absolute pleasure and I'm very proud to have commanded you.'

Not half as proud as me, thought Rose.

Broadhurst turned to them and held out his hand. 'Gentlemen. It's time for me to have a natter and a cuppa with your fine lads. But in the meantime, I wish you all the very, very best. I'm very proud in what you've achieved.'

Chapter 29

He was still in bed when Molly returned from her shower, hair wrapped in a towel, and she eyed him suspiciously. 'You've had your wicked way with me once already, *Wing Commander*, and in case you're wondering, the bathroom's free.'

He nodded cheerfully but stayed where he was. 'Yes, dear, I know.'

'Hmm.' She dried her hair vigorously for a moment then peered at him from beneath the towel. 'Well? What are you waiting for? I'm sure they didn't give you extended leave just so that you could lay around in bed all day long.'

He sighed with contentment. 'Only if you're in it with me, my love.'

She smirked at him. 'You might have noticed that I'm not in it, you beastly man, and what with you being an air ace and all, perhaps I ought to be, but there's no chance of me getting back in it because I've a busy morning. And then there's the drive this evening.'

'But I'm a hero!' he protested, holding out a hand to draw her towards him.

She flicked at his hand with her towel. 'The only hero here is me for sharing your bed, you dreadful creature! I'm sure my thighs are six inches further apart than they were on our wedding night. It's a wonder I can walk at all in the mornings! So get that manly bottom of yours out of my bed and get washed this instant!'

He didn't move. 'I think I'll watch you get dressed first, get an eyeful of gorgeousness. Didn't get much to leer at in Holland.'

'Heavens! Haven't you seen enough yet, you monster?' She looked down at her bathrobe. 'I'm not even naked!'

'I've not seen nearly enough yet!' He thought for a moment. 'Although I have to say, one of my Aussie lads did let off a couple of rounds from his pistol in the bathroom, and the French lad who was in the tub at the time jumped out and chased him around the seminary in the altogether. Would have knocked young Micky's block off with the scrubbing brush if we hadn't intervened!' He shuddered. 'Bloody awful sight, believe me, gave me nightmares for weeks! I'd much rather ogle at you in your birthday suit in the early morning light, nothing lovelier, I can tell you! I'm not moving 'til I've had my fill!'

Molly wagged a finger sternly. 'My mother use to warn me about men like you.' Then her face lit up with a beautiful smile. 'Thank God I found you!'

Just then Daffy bounded into their bedroom and jumped onto the covers, barking joyously and slobbering at him (as she had done every morning since his return).

'*Urgh!* Down, Daffs, get down!' he complained, trying to push the excited dog off, and reaching for the covers to wipe his face dry.

'Harry Rose! Don't be so filthy! Don't you dare wipe your face with the covers!'

He dropped the covers. 'Filthy? Me? How dare you, madam! It's this bloody horrible brute, slobbering and belching and farting all over the place like there's no tomorrow!'

Molly tried not to laugh at his wretched expression. 'Nonsense, you silly man, she's not filthy, she's a sweetheart!'

Rose's face was wet and sticky. '*Yeeuch-pooh!* Give me something to wipe my face, will you, Moll?'

She arched an eyebrow severely. 'What's the special word?'

He adopted a stern expression. 'Now! Give me something to wipe my face with now!' He stared at her imperiously.

Molly stared right back, saying nothing while Daffy applied a second layer of slobber over the first, and knowing he could not win, he yielded reluctantly. 'Alright, alright! Get off me you bloody horrid thing! Please, Molly, please give me something to wipe my face! *Please!*'

Molly looked down her nose at him, a single word, 'No.' Unable to maintain her stern expression, she grinned impudently at him.

He gaped at her stupidly. 'No?'

God, but she was beautiful! And it's me she shares her bed with, he exulted. 'What d'you mean, no?' He returned her grin grudgingly.

'It's time you got yourself into that bathtub, you dirty, randy brute. So go and wash your face while you're there!' She opened her bathrobe cheekily to reveal a lovely breast before drawing it over herself again, her cockney accent again. 'If you behave yourself and do as I say, ducks, I might just choose to share my bed with you tonight as well!'

'Crikey, miss, it's a deal!' Jumping out of their bed, Rose pecked her quickly on the lips (*mmm, lovely!*), gave her bottom a squeeze before snatching up his bathrobe and scuttling from the room, Daffy in hot (and deafening) pursuit.

With their children (and that bloody awful dog) being watched by

Molly's mother Deborah and her old *ayah*, Noreen, Rose and Molly set out for the Gable, a towering summit in the Lake District.

It took them just over an hour, with the pace relaxed, the fragrances of the blooming countryside soothing, and saying little as they enjoyed the shared pleasure of being together again.

For the first time in years, Rose felt a tranquillity in his soul, an unfamiliar stillness in which the remorseless whisper of disquiet and apprehension which had been an almost constant companion of his for so very long was now hushed, replaced by a feeling of muted joy and contentment that threatened to bubble over without warning at random times of the day.

His heart was at peace and still slightly disbelieving that against all the odds he had survived, and lulled by Molly's soft voice and calm driving (how different from the break-neck racing in that little red sports car!), Rose was half asleep by the time they reached the Borrowdale Hotel, the calm beauty of the Lake District lovely in the afternoon.

Molly parked up their Vauxhall saloon by the side of the hotel, snuggled cosily at the base of Shepherds Crag in Borrowdale valley and looking out across Derwentwater; the Gable huge to the south-west, darkly foreboding against the bright sky, its lesser companion the Green Gable impressive in its own right.

Looking up at the summits, he found his eyes drawn beyond them, searching the sky for enemy fighters which now would never come.

The owners of the hotel, Mabel and Elsie, were old friends of Molly's and they welcomed the couple with open arms before sitting them down to a late lunch.

Mabel switched on the wireless, and they listened in silence to the Prime Minister's three o'clock address to the nation. It was a statesman's speech in which he thanked the people for their courage and their endurance, and reminded them that the enemy to the east had not yet been defeated.

Parting company with his first Wing was a bittersweet experience for Rose. They had survived the last campaigns of the war in Europe together, and now they were going their separate ways.

Their last time together was at the presentation in which De Gaulle had pinned both the *Croix de Guerre* and the *Legion de Honneur* onto each of their chests. Frankie had joined them, in the uniform of the Free French Air Force, like Gabby and his other Frenchman, looking unfamiliar in his contentment and without Amélie tucked inside his tunic. He smiled and kissed Rose on both cheeks and gave him a fleeting hug. '*Merci, mon commandant.* I never forget.'

Gabby had wept and clung to Rose, and told him when he returned to France to look for a little village in *Aix-en-Provence*, where there would always be a place for him should he seek 'sophistication, intellect and true culture'.

Micky had wrung his hand and whispered fiercely. 'Come and meet my folks in Riverina, sir? I want them to meet a hero.' And he had replied that Micky's parents had no need for another hero when they had one already in their son, one in which they should be rightfully proud.

Sheep's normal smile was dimmed as he said goodbye, solemnly intoning as he crushed Rose's hand that, 'You might be a Pom, sir, but you're a Bloody Fine Bastard.'

Ben Duncan had grinned. 'If you ever find yourself in gaol, sir, give me a call, eh?'

Kipper had given him a bear hug that made him wonder if any

of his ribs were broken, despite being denied the chance to attack a flak tower, and laughed. 'You're a mad fucker, sir!'

De Rond's *Legion de Honneur, Medaille Militaire, Croix de Guerre avec etoile et palme,* along with his DFC and Annette's copy of *A Tale of Two Cities* would go on permanent display at the new French Air Force Academy in honour of his sacrifice for his country.

Broadhurst had already provided Rose an assurance that he would not be required to serve against the Japanese, and tapping his nose, 'Broadie' hinted strongly that a post-war regular commission in the RAF was in the offing.

His face had crinkled into a smile. 'For you, Harry, the war is over.'

In the meantime, Rose was to enjoy a long leave at home with his wife and family.

As the last of the light leaked away from the sky and day transitioned to night, a number of beacons were lit on the scarp, fires to celebrate the end of the darkness that had fallen across Europe, sparks in the night to herald a time of peace after so much suffering.

It was a time to celebrate a new dawn, but as he watched the crowds adding to the fire, dancing and singing and laughing, he thought of all those he had known not fortunate enough to survive to see the flames and smell the woodsmoke.

Rose thought he saw Jimmy Rawnsley, who along with 'Cat's Eyes' Cunningham had forged night fighter legend and doctrine, amongst those around the fire but it was only for a moment, and he could not be sure. He did not seek Jimmy out, for tonight was for celebrating a rosy future with their loved ones, not the past.

That idealistic boy alighting from the train at RAF Foxton all those years ago had been forged into a witness and participant in the cruelty and brutality of war, an innocent who had seen the wholesale loss of dreams and humanity, the loss of friends and strangers alike. He had been forged into the man of today through immense strain and heavy responsibility.

Rose had survived so much, faced the enemy square on and done his duty, but the feeling of guilt would always be there, for others had not. He felt the total peace that Molly brought him, but a part of him could not forget the dead, so many dead, and he felt undeserving.

How can one speak of that special feeling which grows between comrades as they face death again and again, often with only one another in support? How can one share what it is that exists between those who would willingly give their own lives for their friends?

And which words can truly describe the utter feeling of failure and loss when members of that special group are lost? Only those who face the enemy to fight and sometimes die together can know the sentiment, surely as deep in its own way as true love, feeling each death like a part of themselves.

Names and faces might fade over the subsequent decades, and the survivors would revere each day of life for the gift it was, but the scars and pain and guilt for having survived would remain.

Overcome by the conflicting tumult of joy and sorrow, still disbelieving that he had a future to look forward to when before it was all one could do to hope for tomorrow, Rose began to weep quietly.

Molly, clinging to him and blissfully grateful for his survival, felt his emotion, and knowing her dream of a future against all the odds with the man she loved was at last a reality, hugged him tighter to comfort him even as her own tears of compassion and gratitude fell.

Together they wept for all they had gained and all they had lost.

They had dared to love at the worst of times, in time of war, and with peace in Europe they would have a future to build together, a future in which their love would have the chance to flourish and endure.

Thank you, merciful Lord, for the chance to know tomorrow.

The world had been set alight, but now it was all over.

Epilogue 1—April 1982, Bavaria

Peter Winter eased his Porsche 911 from the autobahn and onto the slip road leading to the viewing area that looked over the landscape he had known intimately since childhood. His companion leaned forward and *oohed* in appreciation.

In the foreground, gently rolling lush green hills and ranges of verdant forest, merging into the foothills of a background of mountains, the alpine peaks white-tipped and magnificent, their broad bases covered by rock and forest, dulled into light and dark grey by distance and haze.

Truly it was a glorious view, but one he had known all his life.

Over there, the ragged copse of trees a quarter of a mile away where Uncle Peter (after whom he had been named) had built his nephew and namesake a hide; just barely visible amongst the westernmost range of forest was the roof of the old barn where the boy had become a man with Brunhilde, and in the near distance his family's home, half hidden amongst the trees.

Peter himself was rather enjoying the view he had of the slim, long-haired girl now staring in wonder at the scene from the passenger seat. 'Well, Suzi, how do you like Bavaria?'

She turned to face him, delicate features and large eyes, her face lit up with delight. 'Oh, Peter! It's beautiful!' She opened the car door and bounded across to the guard rail, breathing in deeply and gazing onto the gentle hills.

In the distance, just audible, the thin ululations of someone whistling, eerily rising, falling then rising again.

'Peter! Look!' He joined her by the rail, saw the tall, familiar figure standing beside a distant fence, and smiled affectionately.

'Look at what, *liebling*?' he asked.

She was jumping up and down with excitement. 'That man! Look!' She turned to face him. 'That man! He was whistling, and look! The cows are coming!'

Certainly the herd of cattle, dotted haphazardly across the expanse of grass, began to make their way slowly towards the lonely figure to clump together beside him.

Peter laughed, saw her expression and leaned forward to kiss her gently on the lips. 'Oh, I'm not laughing at you, Suzi. That's my Vati, doing his party trick. He used to say that if he whistled *Mutti* would come, but I've never seen it.'

Surprise showed on Suzi's lovely face. '*That's* the General?'

His father noticed them and waved, Suzi waving back with both hands, still jumping.

Peter raised a hand in response to his father and nodded. 'Believe it or not. Ace of the wartime Luftwaffe, post-war *Generalleutnant*, and now a dairy farmer like generations before him.' And the idea appealed, after a life of excitement, wouldn't the serenity in these low, forested hills make it the perfect place to retire?

From amongst the trees a woman had appeared, walking gracefully towards the old General. 'Oh! And there's *Mutti*!' He took her hand and led her back to the car. 'Come on, let's go and meet them so I can show you off!'

As the Porsche merged back onto the autobahn, she said shyly, 'They must be very proud of you, Peti?'

Having served tours in JG71 '*Richthofen*' flying Phantom F4s and the F104 Starfighter (the latter also known as the 'Widow-maker' to its pilots because almost a third of the nine hundred F104s in West Germany's Luftwaffe would be lost in accidents over the course of its service), Peter had received an early promotion to *Oberstleutanant*, the *Bundesverdienstkreuz* and been appointed to the command one of the Luftwaffe's new Panavia Tornado squadrons.

His father was a hero, receiving literally every military decoration of the wartime Luftwaffe, but the old man was far prouder of his son's achievements in peacetime than of his own in time of war.

Peter slowed the car and turned left into the Estate's entrance, stopping beside his parents' Mercedes Estate and turning the engine off.

'Oh they are, sweetest Suzi, and they'll be even prouder when they see what a beauty I've brought home with me!'

Epilogue 2—April 1982, London

Jimmy nudged me. 'Go on then, you daft beggar, don't dawdle, give them the message and ask 'em if they'd like some more tea. Offer them biscuits, too. Sir Daniel loves a custard cream dipped in his tea.'

'Them' were a couple of the members at the Armed Forces Club we worked at, a pair of old codgers; they must have been in their fifties, at least. Bloody ancient.

I looked through the door that led into the main room, partly cleared of members now that the great slab-sided aircraft carrier had departed Portsmouth harbour, her imposing bulk just a grey shape now, dulled by funnel smoke and haze. It had been an impressive sight, but my interest was solely in the hope that the girl who had been flashing her boobs at the sailors earlier might appear again and give us a second look.

We had been watching the steel grey behemoth's departure in Jimmy's office, though I dare not call him Jimmy to his face. To me, he was Mr Baxter (bow, scrape, yes sir, no sir, three bags full, sir, Mr Baxter, sir).

I hesitated and he nudged me again. 'Well? What are you waiting for?' He chortled. 'The next bus?'

'He's a bit strange, Mr Baxter, and he's always asking for a fag. I think he's a bit touched! Can't you do it?' I pleaded.

In truth, I was a little scared of the retired Air Chief Marshal. Jimmy said Sir Daniel had ejected from a jet plane twenty years earlier, and I reckon the old bastard must have hit his head on the window on the way out.

I lowered my voice and leaned forward diffidently. 'He called me a "daft bag of drawers" the other day, just because I didn't have any cigarettes on me!'

Jimmy sniggered and looked away. 'You soft lad.'

The other one, Air Chief Marshal Sir Harry Rose, seemed alright. He might look a bit stern but he had kind eyes. I had once noticed him transferring a creased and faded photograph, a tatty little pink stuffed toy and a little shiny rock from one pocket to another. I didn't think he was potty, not like Scary Sir Dan, just a little peculiar.

Worse, they had crazy names. Scary was called 'Granny' by the kind one, while Sir Harry was in turn called 'Flash' by Scary.

Flash. Why was he called that? I always felt uneasy at being in the same room as the kind one when it was quiet, in case he was a flasher. He seemed OK, quite a nice bloke, really, friendly and kind, but appearances can be deceptive, can't they?

I mean, who wants to have their eyeballs bruised by having to look at an old geezer flashing and flapping his prehistoric meat and two veg in the wind?

Not me, pal.

Pair of old weirdos. Goodness only knows how we won the war.

But then, old people are all a bit strange, aren't they? My Dad just turned fifty-six and thinks The Jam are 'noisy buggers'. See? Crazy.

Jimmy passed me a cigarette from the pack he kept in his pocket (even though he didn't smoke). 'You daft lug. Here, lad, give him one of those, that'll keep him happy, and be properly respectful, he's earned it.'

Jimmy looked fondly at one of the photographs mounted on his wall. I think it was the one with the crowd of men standing in front of some old aeroplane with a propeller, not a saucy little jet like those Harriers on the carrier, just some old piece of crap in camouflage with a heavy nose. Probably flew like a drowsy pig.

'More than earned it.' Jimmy was still gazing at the picture, whispering, as if to himself, 'They both have.'

Feeling like a gladiator entering the arena, I approached the pair of fossils, but they were talking and I stopped to one side, not wanting to disturb them (or wanting to get Jimmy's boot up my arse for having done so).

Sir Harry's voice was gentle. 'Another war, a different place, but the same old story, eh, Granny?'

Scary's eyes, incredibly, glittered with wetness. 'Sending more youngsters to bleed and die. They send our future, the ones we should keep safe, Flash. It's the old boys wot make the mistakes and the young wot pay. They should send all the silly old bastards like us who've already lived too long.'

Sir Harry snorted a laugh. 'Speak for yourself! I intend to live to be a hundred!'

Well that's not long, then, I thought sourly.

On the telly, the distant carrier was just a ghostly, faded shape, blending into the washed-out grey of the sea and sky.

I'm usually pretty polite and patient with the aged, but I wanted to get off on time because I was meeting Tracey at the local Odeon later. (My enthusiasm was less to do with whatever we were supposed to be watching but rather more to do with the fact that she was a phenomenal kisser when the lights dimmed, and even better, her hands wandered.)

Scary noticed me and blinked, his melancholy magically transitioning to cheer. 'Tiddly!' crowed the old fart happily. He might act like a nutcase, but the old bastard's eyes were shrewd and intelligent. No vacancy there, sharp as a bloody knife.

I tried not to scream, 'It's Tony, sir.' My voice sounded truculent. *Jimmy would beat the crap out of me if he'd heard me.*

He grinned, like an aged schoolboy. 'What is it, my dear old sticky knickers?'

He looked at me keenly, and I felt as if I were on parade, and tried not to twitch. *Sticky knickers?* I worked to keep my voice even. 'I'm sorry to bother you, er, Sir Daniel, but I have a message for you and Sir Harry.'

Sir Harry grinned sympathetically at my discomfort.

On the screen, even the outline of the big boxy grey carrier had disappeared into the sea haze.

'Go on then, son, can't read your mind and I can feel petrification setting in, so, spit it out will you, laddie?' Scary sniffed, and the old sod must have mislaid his false teeth again because his broad smile was gap-toothed.

Scary Sir Daniel looked me up and down, and I felt my knees tremble involuntarily as he intoned, 'Got a fag, have you?'

Fumbling the cigarette Jimmy had given me earlier from my pocket, I passed it across to him (or rather, had it snatched from my hand). 'Ta very much, pants old bag!' crowed the demented fossil.

Pants old bag? They were still looking at me expectantly, and I gave them my best ingratiating smile.

'Er, gentlemen? Lady Belle and Lady Molly have asked me to remind you that they'll be here for lunch in around an hour, sir. In the meantime, while you wait, would you care for some more tea?' The words came out as a nervous rush and I clamped my mouth shut.

Lady Belle and Lady Molly. I'd seen their ladies before, and for a pair of old girls, they were pretty hot stuff.

Sir Harry nodded gently. 'That would be very welcome, Tony, thank you.'

Scary Sir Dan rammed the cigarette so hard into the gap between his teeth I thought he might accidentally swallow the bloody thing, but no such luck, and it hung disconsolately off his lower lip as if asking to be saved.

'Pints of tea, good fart,' he slobbered around the miserable-looking and unfortunate cigarette, 'and hot buttered toast, toast slathered with butter, lots of crunchy toast dripping in hot butter! And plenty of it!' he cackled.

'Granny,' Sir Harry remonstrated, glancing at me almost apologetically. 'We're having lunch with the ladies in an hour, so perhaps we should just have some tea?'

Scary ignored him, warming to his theme. 'And biscuits, my dear old fartypants! More fags and lots of biscuits! Piles of biscuits! Mountains of biscuits!'

The old Admiral in the corner sniffed loudly and Sir Harry shook his head and sighed, but Scary Sir Dan fixed me with a demented stare.

I caught a mischievous twinkle sparkle in his eye, and then he winked.

The daft old bugger was teasing me!

Acknowledgements

My thanks to Kate Lyall Grant, Eve Lynch, Imogen Buchanan, Becky Slorach and Sharon Rutland at Lume Books for making this book possible, and to my very dear friends, Ray Fitzhugh, April Munday, Heather Barr, and of course the wonderful Russell and Angel Gallon, for their love, friendship and support.

9 781839 015656